Rogue Plunder

Christopher
Morin

CHRISTOPHER W. MORIN

Rogue Plunder
Copyright © 2019 Christopher W. Morin

ISBN: 978-1-63381-182-9

Designed and produced by:
Maine Authors Publishing
12 High Street, Thomaston, Maine
www.maineauthorspublishing.com

Printed in the United States of America

To all the avid readers who seek out historical fiction when perusing the bookstore shelves, and especially to all those who support local Maine authors, I hope that you enjoy this imaginative tale.

TABLE OF CONTENTS

CHAPTER 1

The New World: 1716

T he warm summer breeze circulating over the rocky shoreline of the mainland twisted, turned, and washed over a nearby island nestled under a blanket of sparkling stars and a brilliant full moon. The undulating waters offshore moved in mesmerizing unison until they reached the shallows of the island and lapped against the coarse sand of the beach. It was nearing midnight, and there was an eerie tranquility in the air. Save the wind and the soft *whoosh* of the tide, there was no other sound to be netted by human ears. Even the usually chatty whippoorwills were silent. It was as if the world was in a deep slumber and even Nature itself was reluctant to wake it.

Atop the island's highest point was a spacious clearing that offered marvelous views of the mainland, the vast expanses of the ocean, and a neighboring islet a short distance across a narrow channel to the east. At the top of this towering hill, among the tall swaying grass, two mischievous lovers frolicked in the moonlight, challenging the serenity of their surroundings with moans of sexual bliss.

Positioned between two rusty lanterns, a lovely nubile woman with long, raven-black hair spilling down her back sat astride a tall and wiry young man—neither wearing a stitch of clothing. The two were joined—both emotionally and physically—as they reached the apex of their lovemaking. The woman's groans of ecstasy intensified with each downward thrust upon her lover's hardened masculinity. She enjoyed being aggressive and rough during such intimate acts. She liked controlling and dictating the tempo. She was not one to want a soft or timid touch from a man when engaged in carnal activities, and was not afraid to voice her thoughts—critical or otherwise—when unfulfilled for any reason.

The woman drove herself down deeper and harder at an accelerated pace, constantly searching and maneuvering for the ideal position that would unlock the definitive orgasm she craved. Boldly, she pulled the man into a sitting position, wrapping her legs ever tighter around his waist. Without restraint, she smothered his mouth, chin, and cheeks with deep, wet, impassioned kisses. In turn, the man wrapped his arms around her upper torso with near asphyxiating ferocity. The harder he squeezed, the faster she ground her lower half into his. Seconds later, the woman arched her back, breaking free from the man's grasp. She let loose a powerful cry of pleasure, signaling her partner that he had thoroughly satisfied her. Now it was his turn to experience the ultimate sensation of intimacy.

In one swift and unified movement, the two changed positions. The woman, now on her back atop a tattered patchwork quilt, yielded control to the man. Her knees slowly fell apart in anticipation of the final erogenous act. Without hesitation, the man fell upon her with thrusts of unbridled passion. His muscles tensed as the momentum built. His whole body became taut with each plunge as the moment of climax neared. He clutched the woman's ample breasts as if further inciting her to scream out with desire. Finally, after one decisive moan of delight escaped her lips, the man could hold back no longer. He closed his eyes and tilted his head back as his rigid member blasted forth a torrent of fluid ecstasy. He then emitted his own groan of relief and rolled onto his back next to his lover. They kissed for a moment, then looked up at the sea of twinkling stars above them. They were both breathing heavily as the cool ocean breeze danced over their bodies. After a moment of quiet contentment, the woman spoke.

"Thy sorcerer's wand was quite powerful this night," she said playfully, adding, "Methinks I might start referring to thee as 'Merlin' from this day forth."

The man chuckled at the compliment and stood up to stretch. He reached high into the air as if he might pluck one of the stars out of the sky. Close by lay a pair of worn, tan breeches and a long white linen shirt with a low neckline. He slowly got dressed. The stripling, aged twenty, had straight brown hair that was near shoulder-length in the back. His face was ruddy and boyish-looking with hardly a trace of whiskers. He was tall and lean, standing at six feet and two inches. Though he didn't appear very muscular, his body had known hard work his entire life and was capable of prolonged periods of heavy lifting or laboring behind the plow. He collected his black leather boots, his black cocked hat, and a brown leather satchel, setting them all together next to one of the glowing lanterns. He then sat down beside his lover, who was now temptingly lying on her side wearing an impish grin, her head propped up by her arm and wrist. She seemed quite content in the warm air and showed no interest in retrieving her dress. For the moment, and much to the young man's satisfaction, she preferred to remain mischievously exposed.

"What would thy mother think if she bore witness to her only daughter's nocturnal adventures...or was privy to the salacious words that just slipped off her tongue?" asked the man with a twist of sarcasm in his voice.

"I should think she would admonish me in a most disagreeable fashion. Her Puritan blood would boil, and she would denounce my character in such manner that all who heard her fiery invective would immediately call for my burning at the stake," replied the woman nonchalantly.

"I should think thou art most correct. I'm mildly vexed, however. How doth thou remain in such good stead with thy mother? And also with the Almighty, my dear Miss Elizabeth Eustis?" the man asked with playfully bated breath.

"That, William Estes, is my secret. And as thou art quite aware, Mother does not approve of many of my bad habits...at least the ones she knows about."

"I'm smitten with thee. I daresay I love thee," William said with confidence and without hesitation—a strong hint of yearning in his voice.

"I'm smitten, too," Elizabeth replied without making eye contact.

She rose seductively to her feet as if putting on a little performance for her audience of one, who never took his eyes off her stunningly disrobed form. She teasingly turned her back to him and mimicked his earlier actions by reaching up to the stars with a long and soothing stretch. William gazed at her hourglass shape glistening with perspiration that trickled down her back and bare behind. The young man had never known a woman to possess such beauty, and often found himself childishly befuddled in her presence. He lusted after her constantly, and her image was never far from his thoughts, even during the most grueling hours of his daily routine. And even though they shared intimate knowledge of each other, and though he hid it well, William was still never completely at ease or in total control around the lovely young siren who had him completely under her spell.

Elizabeth stood five feet eight inches tall. Her eyes were brown and her black hair draped halfway down her back. She had long, slender legs and a voluptuous body with copiously rounded breasts and a pleasingly shaped bottom. She took a few steps away from William before bending over to recover her dress, which lay messily on the ground. The faded blue cotton garment was hardly a prime example of appropriate Puritan women's clothing, and it enraged Elizabeth's mother whenever it was within her sight. The skirt was heavily frayed at the hem and only covered the legs just past the knees. The bodice was tight and too form-fitting to the prudish eye, and the neckline sagged low and was much too revealing. Elizabeth's mother referred to the dress as unfit for even a French whore. Nevertheless, the young woman slipped into the contentious attire without a care in the world.

"We should make our way home," said William. "The night is waning, and I fear our absence may be discovered if we tarry much longer."

"Thy father sleeps like the dead and has no mind to challenge thine actions—thou knows this to be true," replied Elizabeth.

"It is not my father that concerns me, it is thy mother."

"Mother is of no concern. I shall outmaneuver her every query and every action should a confrontation arise...which it will not."

"I am in awe of thy confidence and shall take thee at thy word, my darling. However, I must press thee to make haste. We must return without delay."

Suddenly, a thunderous boom ripped through the air, causing William and Elizabeth to jolt with surprise. They looked upward but saw nothing but the starry sky.

"I was not expecting a storm," said Elizabeth as she extended her right hand with the palm up as if waiting for a raindrop or two to fall upon it.

"All the more reason we need to make haste. I do not wish to crawl into bed wet as a fish."

Another sharp report rang out, followed by another and another in quick succession.

"What is that, Will? Surely it is not thunder," said Elizabeth.

Will's eyes were drawn down from the sky and became focused on the sea. In an instant, his heart began to race as two mighty warships sailed into view just offshore of the smaller islet to the east.

The hill, with the bright moonlight above, provided the perfect vantage point to observe the action developing across the channel. Will instinctively dropped down and lay flat on his stomach as if he feared being spotted. Elizabeth followed suit, scuttling up close to him. They stared in silent amazement as the origin of the thunderous sounds now became obvious—it was naval cannon fire.

"Elizabeth, retrieve my spyglass from the satchel," said Will, his eyes locked on the sea battle unfolding before him. "And hide the light from the lanterns...quickly."

She reached for the satchel and pulled out the small handheld telescope, promptly passing it over. Then she gathered up both lanterns, moving them out of the open to where the light could not be seen from a distance.

"Who are they!" Elizabeth asked, crouching again close to Will. "Are they English ships? French?"

Will extended the spyglass lens and focused on the vessels. The smaller of the two was dangerously close to the islet's shoreline, while the larger remained within firing distance but further out in deeper water. With the wind now permanently spilled from their sails, the ships lined up precariously broadside to one another with the larger one conspicuously on fire. Both men-of-war were square-rigged, and both had three masts, but they were most assuredly in different classes, from what Will could establish. He scanned the masts and what little he could see of the stern of the larger ship for any signs of a standard or vessel identification marker. He saw nothing, and soon his attention was drawn back to the vicious discharge of gunfire.

"I see no flag of allegiance on either vessel," was his answer to Elizabeth's question. "The larger appears to be a frigate of sorts, while the smaller...hard to determine...a galley perhaps?"

Cannons from both warships continued to spit fire and lead at one another with murderous ferocity and desperation. The smaller vessel was outgunned but appeared to have the upper hand as the larger was swiftly becoming enveloped in flames and had acquired a perceptible list on its larboard side. The decks of both ships were abuzz with frenzied activity amid shouts and screams that Will strained to hear in order to determine their origin. He soon had his answer.

"Lay me alongside at pistol shot! Straight at them, Mr. Holloway!" boomed a voice in English from the burning frigate. A moment later, the order was responded to with, "Helm don't answer, sir! Rudder's shot away! We're dead in the water!"

Then suddenly, through his spyglass, Will saw a cannonball from the galley strike the frigate's mainmast. Within seconds, the towering structure, its sails rapidly incinerating in a blistering wall of fire, crashed into the mizzen, then toppled over into the water, instantly killing a number of sailors as it folded over. The frigate was now mortally wounded and completely unable to maneuver under its own power. The vessel's list increased substantially and the top deck became entirely enshrouded in flames. Its cannon went silent, and all that could be seen through the smoke and the shouts of "Abandon ship!" was a trickle of officers and crew who had somehow managed to scurry into a longboat in an attempt to escape from the blazing pyre around them. Will and Elizabeth watched in horror as the men desperately tried to lower the boat and escape from the burning frigate. But before their boat touched water, a massive explosion tore apart what was left of the dying warship. The blast sent a fiery hailstorm of splintered wood, twisted metal, and human carnage into the air in all directions.

"Lord in heaven, have mercy," whispered a stunned Will.

What was left of the frigate sank rapidly under the waves, leaving nothing but a mass of burning debris on top of the water. There were no signs of survivors—wounded or otherwise—bobbing in the cold sea below. When a heavy thud echoed through the channel, Will's attention was instantly drawn back to the galley. He swept the spyglass in the direction of the smaller ship and noticed a drastic change in its disposition.

"She's run aground," he said.

"Let me see," Elizabeth replied, grasping at the spyglass.

Will relinquished the instrument but kept his gaze firmly on the motionless galley, which had now acquired its own considerable list and was conveniently illuminated by the burning wreckage of the frigate.

"I see not a single soul on deck," said Elizabeth. "It has the haunting appearance of a ghost ship," she added with a shudder. Then she gasped as tiny sparks of pistol fire flashed through the open gun ports below deck.

Numerous shots rang out, and then all was quiet again. Several minutes went by with neither Will nor Elizabeth letting a single word escape their lips. They looked on in stunned silence, each desiring the view through the spyglass, and neither wanting to share it.

Gradually, the gentle rolling of the tide quenched the burning flotsam, leaving only the moon and the stars to illuminate the shadowy vessel. Will wrested the spyglass away from Elizabeth for good, and directed his attention to the water directly around the ship's hull.

"I know well the shallows she now rests in. She's not going anywhere, even when the tide reaches its zenith. She's forever aground on the rocks below her keel," said Will.

"What of her crew? Doth thou presume there are injured sailors in need of help below her decks? What should we do?" asked Elizabeth.

"There is not a single seaman, able-bodied or otherwise, astir. I dread the thought of the carnage undoubtedly strewn on and below her decks. There's a wickedness in the air—I can feel it—as if witches and demons are about at this unholy hour. We should flee this spot at once. Let us return to the refuge of our homes and await the morning light. There is little we can do in the darkness, and we're ill-prepared to assist any person in need or combat any deviant who means to do us harm."

"I heartily agree. I'm frightened and wish to return home without delay," said Elizabeth, hastily folding the quilt and picking up a lantern.

"Let us make our exit then," said Will after donning his boots and hat before snatching up the second lantern.

They scurried down the hill through the darkness as quickly as the dim lantern light would allow. They rushed into the heavily wooded interior and kept to the central trail that would bring them through the dense growth with as little difficulty as possible. It was about a mile to their homes on the western side of the island, and Will confidently led the way with his left arm extended, his hand holding the lantern up high like a beacon. His right hand clutched Elizabeth's as he guided her along.

Soon they emerged from the woods and crossed through tall grassy meadows and past rows of neatly planted crops. Somewhat out of breath, and still shaken at what they had witnessed, they rushed right past the Estes cottage, hurrying along a new trail until they eventually arrived at the Eustis house. The residence was nothing more than an unassuming log cabin made of earth and wood. It was completely dark inside except for a few glowing embers in the fireplace. There was no sign of life up and about, and Elizabeth felt reassured that her mother was soundly dozing and hadn't noticed her absence when she'd snuck away hours earlier.

"Mother's asleep. If she knew I was out with thee, she would be standing in the door, hellfire blazing, Bible in one hand and leather strap in t'other."

"Thou mustn't breathe one word of what we have seen this evening," said Will. "Rise at first light tomorrow. After thy morning meal, tell thy mother that thou must assist me down by the shore. Inform her that my nets and lines need repair and that I cannot go out to fish without thy help in mending them. I will meet thee by my boat. We'll row over to Belle Island and investigate the wreck. Hopefully we'll discover its origins and intentions."

"What about thy father?"

"He has become more feeble in the mind. He won't question my peculiar early-morning absence. I'll set him some tasks that will keep him occupied throughout the morning. If I don't return at the regular time, he'll simply assume I was delayed fishing...if he is even capable of assuming things anymore," said Will sadly.

"Rest well, Will. Until the morrow." Elizabeth blew out the candle in her lantern and then kissed him on the cheek. She crept into the cabin and closed the door quietly so as not to cause any commotion that would wake her snoring mother.

Will hesitated a moment and then made the short trek back to his own homestead. He entered his house—which was similar to the Eustis cabin in virtually every detail—with less concern and discretion. His father was sound asleep. Will took off his hat and boots and put away his lantern and satchel. He made no attempt to be quiet as he knew with certainty that a lightning bolt from the heavens above could strike the roof, split it in two, and not wake his father, Mr. Cyrus Estes.

Will tended the fire and then crawled into the narrow bed opposite his father's. He pulled the covers over his head and hearkened to the silence around him, which was challenged only by the tiny crackle of the slow-burning firewood. He closed his eyes and listened intently before allowing himself to relax enough to fall asleep. He practiced this ritual every night, eavesdropping for abnormal sounds that might signal an approaching threat. The Estes and Eustis families lived in a dangerous place during a very precarious time. Menace abounded in all forms and from all directions. Will knew it was unwise for him to ever let his guard down in the face of hostile man, beast, or weather. All three were capable of causing instant death and destroying what little life he had created for himself and the precious few around him.

A short time later, Will could fight his exhaustion no more. He dozed off into a deep slumber that his tired body desperately needed to revive and recover for the upcoming morning's activities. All was quiet and content for the moment. His last conscious thought revolved around what he had seen earlier. He feared what he might discover across the channel and, more importantly, he feared *whom* he might discover.

CHAPTER 2

The Repulse *and the* Firefly

Will's eyes snapped open at dawn. He had been dreaming, but try as he might, he couldn't recollect what he had been dreaming about. Dread of the unknown festered in the pit of his stomach like a piece of rancid fish. The youthful courage and eagerness to investigate and explore the remains of the naval battle had unexpectedly waned. The idea of deliberately *avoiding* the unknown mysteries and hazards that lay on the shores of neighboring Belle Island flashed through his mind as he forced his thoughts onto his chores and daily duties—most specifically, fishing. However, as he dressed he realized he couldn't ignore it. He thought of Elizabeth and what she had said. What if there *were* Englishmen alive and in need of help? He couldn't just turn his back on their suffering and let them perish. It was decided then and there: He would go...and bravely confront whatever unknowns awaited him.

But one thing had to come first. He turned to his father still lying in bed. He looked down upon Cyrus with feelings of ambiguity and remorse. The man was but a shell of his former self. He was fifty-eight years old and rapidly approaching the end of his natural life. He was lean, and still had a strong back that could handle arduous work, but his mind had failed, the result of a blow to the head from a fall down a slippery slope near the shore years back. Will remembered the incident and how his father had nearly died after several days unconscious. He remembered how he and his dear mother, Mildred, had dragged his father's lifeless body up to the cabin and tended his bloodied, bruised, and swollen head. Neither thought he would live, but eventually the outer wounds healed and he regained consciousness. But the man that awoke was not the same man Will and Mildred had known before. Cyrus spoke not a word and was unable to do any task on his own. He lay in bed for weeks needing constant tending and nurturing like a newborn babe.

"The toil was too much for Mother," Will whispered now. "She could not handle the additional burden heaped upon her. And I... well, I was forced to become a man much sooner than intended."

Will's thoughts wandered back to his mother, who became ill and perished that harsh winter after his father's injury. He was only fifteen when she departed. That was five years ago, yet the enduring pain of losing one's mother made it seem like yesterday. Will's head drooped as he remembered his lost parent and the joy she had brought him when he was a young boy.

Cyrus stirred. Slowly, he opened his eyes and beamed a childish smile through several long and scruffy layers of his hoary beard. He sat up and looked at Will then down at his crotch. Knowing what had to be done—as they went through this exercise virtually every morning—Will brought a bucket and water to clean up his father, who had urinated all over himself in his sleep.

Once Cyrus had been washed and dressed, Will fed him what little food was available and then led him outside into the foggy morning. They stopped at the nearby field where Will had tried unsuccessfully to grow potatoes after failing miserably with corn. The soil was thin, sandy, and acidic. It was difficult to grow anything, but Will persevered. He had brought along a basket and started to pick small stones and undesirable weeds from the tilled soil. With careful and painstaking detail, Will demonstrated exactly what he wanted his father to do. After several minutes, he finally received the affirmative grunt from Cyrus that indicated he understood the task put to him. Will relinquished the basket and watched as his father mimicked his earlier actions, albeit at a much slower pace.

Satisfied that he could now leave his father unattended for

several hours, Will collected his satchel, his gunpowder and shot, and his musket and started toward the southeast end of the island where his boat was, and where, he hoped, Elizabeth was now waiting for him. As he walked away through the thick fog, he glanced back at Cyrus, who was on his hands and knees mindlessly scratching at the unforgiving soil. His heart ached and he wondered how a gentleman of such wisdom, character, vision, strength, and leadership could have been so easily reduced to such a sad state of frailty and dependence on others.

The fog hindered his progress to the southeast shore. He wondered if Elizabeth was ahead of or behind him, and if her mother had caused her any early-morning unpleasantness or delay. Making his way through the woods in the center of the island, he found the trail that would lead him down to the small stretch of beach where his boat was. Soon he could clearly hear the high-pitched sounds of seagulls wailing at each other in flight, which sharply contrasted with the slow rolling sound of the tide sloshing against the shore. The unmistakable smell of the clean, salty air filled his nostrils just before he emerged from the woods, slid down a narrow path, and stamped his boot prints into the soft beach sand.

He unslung his musket and satchel and propped them against a tree that had blown down onto the beach after a storm. Will often used it to sit on and clean fish or mend his nets. A short distance away was his longboat, upside down and partially leaning against a jumble of rocks jutting out of the sand. The craft was covered with long grass, tree branches, and leaves to make it look like a natural part of the land if spotted from the water. Will considered this a necessary precaution.

After brushing off all the debris, Will righted the boat with a great heave that exposed his oars and all his fishing nets and gear beneath. The boat could seat eight grown men comfortably, was equipped with a rudder and a tiller, and could be fitted with a mast and sail when needed. Will got behind the boat and with a mighty push, slid it down to the water's edge before loading up the oars, his musket and satchel, and his fishing gear, not knowing if there would be sufficient time or opportunity to fish later in the day.

With everything in place and the boat ready to launch, he sat down on the narrow transom, crossed his arms, and looked to the end of the trail where the forest met the beach. No more than a minute passed before a familiar figure emerged from behind a pine tree. There had been no detectable sound of movement through the brush, which prompted Will to wonder if Elizabeth had been there the whole time—watching him.

"Come hither and be seen," Will said, his arms still crossed and his rear still seated.

From behind the tree, Elizabeth playfully bounded onto the sand wearing the same dress from the night before. However, this time her feet were not bare, as was so often the case, but secured inside a pair of shoes.

"Hath thou been here long?" asked Will.

"I have. I arrived before thee," she replied with a smirk.

"Why did thou remain hidden? Thou could have helped with—"

"I needed to disrobe from those ghastly Puritan garments my mother imprisons me in and dress in more suitable attire for our forthcoming exploration."

"Where *are* thy ghastly garments—as thou so colorfully term them?" Will asked, climbing out of the boat for a proper greeting.

"Hidden in the woods. I shall retrieve and enrobe myself in them upon our return and before we venture home. I do not like their restrictive qualities," replied Elizabeth as she drew in close to Will, seductively placed his hands on her breasts, and gently pulled his lips to hers in a long, enticing kiss that wiped all other thoughts from his mind.

"Shall we get under way?" asked Elizabeth the second their embrace ended.

"Yes, we mustn't waste any more time."

"Good; let's be off."

Elizabeth climbed into the boat and promptly sat down in the bow. She smiled at Will, who buried his shoulder in the stern and pushed for all he was worth until the longboat slid off the sand and was afloat. Will climbed aboard and placed the oars in the oarlocks before sitting down on the thwart amidships with his back to Elizabeth. But before he began to row, he retrieved the spyglass from the satchel and pointed it in the direction of Belle Island. The fog was still thick and partially hid the smaller islet to the east with irritating defiance.

"This is not going to be easy," Will said as he tried to pierce the veil of murkiness with his lens and find the exact spot where he believed the wreck was located. He grew frustrated as he swept the glass back and forth with no result. He knew every topographical feature of Belle Island. He had sailed around it countless times and had fished off its shoreline with great success. He prided himself on being able to navigate its waters and the waters of the great bay itself without fear of ever getting lost. However, he quickly realized that his navigational prowess was completely dependent on one factor: clear visibility. The fog confused him and threatened to force him in the wrong direction. Finally, impatience and stubbornness overcame him. He slid the spyglass back into his satchel, took up the oars, and rowed away from the beach and into the morning mist toward the place where he calculated the wrecked vessel lay aground.

Intermittent layers of ghostly fog enveloped them, at times becoming so thick that Will could barely make out Elizabeth's figure when he looked over his shoulder toward the bow between the dip and pull of each oar stroke. They both felt the moisture on their faces and heard nothing but unsettling silence, save the tiny splash of the oars' blades slicing into the water.

Elizabeth broke the tension and nervously asked, "How much further doth thou reckon?"

"We cannot be far now. Judging by the time spent rowing, we must be—"

Suddenly, the boat collided with something in the water, and Elizabeth cried out in surprise before Will could finish his sentence. She looked over the side and watched a small wooden cask float by. Will shipped the oars to stop the small craft's forward motion. The fog started to thin, revealing a tangled mass of floating debris drifting around them. Fragments of charred wood in all shapes and sizes made up the bulk of the jumbled detritus, but interspersed among it, Will and Elizabeth spotted tattered sail canvas, shattered rigging, floating boxes and barrels, shredded blood-stained clothing, and what even appeared to be mutilated body parts.

"God in heaven!" gasped Elizabeth as her hands cupped her mouth in shock at the gruesome sight.

They sat for a moment in stunned silence before Will spoke up.

"This must be from that exploded ship."

Just then Will spied what appeared to be a flag floating nearby. He scooped it up with an oar and dropped the saturated ensign into the longboat. Grabbing it with both hands, he opened it as far as he could. The flag had a white field emblazoned with the red cross of Saint George and the Union Jack placed in the canton. The unmistakable English symbols left no doubt in Will's mind: It was a ship of the Royal Navy he and Elizabeth had seen burning hours earlier. Upon closer inspection, Will saw the name HMS *Firefly* sewn into the lower corner of the flag in small red stitching. He showed it to Elizabeth, who now had a worried expression chiseled on her face.

When the boat started to gently bob up and down in the water, indicating to Will that they were close to shore, he stood up and Elizabeth turned around.

"There!" Will shouted, pointing enthusiastically. A short distance away, off the bow of the longboat, a dark shape began to appear from the rapidly thinning curtain of fog. Will took up the oars and rowed straight for it. Elizabeth sat and watched in bewilderment as the specter of the derelict galley slowly emerged.

The longboat cut through the water and wreckage until it reached the stern of the ship. Elizabeth looked up and read, "*Repulse*...another English ship?"

"English man-of-war," said Will as he noted the many cannon muzzles jutting out from open gun ports.

"Was not the origin of the voices we heard from the opposing ship, English?" Elizabeth asked.

"Yes. The frigate that burned and exploded was most assuredly another English man-of-war. This flag proves it. I would stake my very life on it," said Will.

"Why would two English warships be fighting one another?"

"I cannot be certain. Perhaps French privateers stole this ship...or Spanish slavers? Perhaps she was being hunted by the Royal Navy. We won't know for sure until we board her."

Elizabeth gave Will a look of foreboding, then reluctantly returned her attention to the *Repulse*.

Will rowed around the larboard side of the vessel scanning for any signs of human activity. He saw nothing and concluded that the ship must be deserted.

"Not a sound. Quiet as the grave," he murmured.

"I fear that's all she is now—a grave," Elizabeth responded.

The *Repulse* was heavily damaged. Enemy cannon shot had torn through her upper deck and penetrated parts of her hull. Her sails had been reduced to tatters swaying uselessly in the breeze, and her rudder was cracked and twisted beyond any reasonable hope of repair. She still exhibited a conspicuous list but hardly moved with the motion of the tide. Will soon discovered the source of this oddity: The *Repulse* had impaled itself on a stretch of partially submerged rocks that extended from the shallow ocean floor to the shoreline of Belle Island. Initially, she had slid over the jagged mass, but as the water rapidly shallowed, the rocks had torn into her forward hold like a spear thrust upward into the belly of a hunted beast. The bow section of the ship's hull sat noticeably below the waterline, and there were holes in it that would inevitably widen in the course of time, thus dooming what remained of the upper decks still above water.

Will rowed completely around the stricken vessel, searching for a suitable place of embarkation. Finally, he spotted tangled rigging draped over the starboard side roughly amidships. That would be his point of entry. He wanted to board the *Repulse* and try to unlock whatever secrets she might harbor concerning her identity and last official undertaking. But another seemingly more pressing and greedy thought elbowed its way into his head—salvage. There was still no indication of survivors or injured sailors anywhere, and Will suddenly became more focused on any potential goods that might be stored belowdecks.

"Elizabeth, I will put thee ashore. I intend to board her and have no wish to expose thee to the blood spilled belowdecks. Wait for me. Perhaps she holds goods that we can recover and use to improve both our families' tenuous existence."

With that said, Will rowed toward Belle Island. He followed the shoreline a short distance until he found a suitable area of soft gravel and sand on which to beach the longboat. Elizabeth jumped out into the shallow water and scampered ashore, while Will remained in the boat and checked his musket. Elizabeth removed her shoes and started walking down the shore. Her attention drifted toward the open ocean. She gazed off toward the horizon, which was gradually emerging from the dissipating fog. She took another step and abruptly toppled over onto the sand. When she saw what she had tripped on, she shrieked.

"Will!"

Will jerked around, and seeing Elizabeth's frightened posture, he leapt out of the longboat and quickly dragged the bow onto the beach. He grabbed his musket, slung the satchel over his shoulder, and raced over to her. What he then witnessed sent an icy chill and a twinge of fear shooting through his gut.

At his feet lay the bloodied and bloated corpse of a slain seaman covered with buzzing flies. He was white as a nobleman's powdered wig and tangled in a web of seaweed. The sight of the solitary dead sailor was gruesome enough, but as Will surveyed the beach, he saw more bodies that had also washed ashore. He took Elizabeth by the hand as they meandered through the labyrinth of deceased mariners. Elizabeth, her free hand pressed against her cheek, stared in shock and horror at the grisly sight. Will held her hand tight and mindlessly led her forward. He was so distracted he was unable to realize that the carnage around them was exactly what he had been trying to prevent her from seeing.

As they passed each body, Will jabbed at it with the barrel of the musket. It was his crude way of confirming that they were, in fact, dead. When they reached the end of the line, they had counted sixteen bodies. Some were burned, some had wood or metal shards peppered into their torsos, while others were missing arms, legs, and in one case, a head. Will noticed that some were wearing naval uniforms while most appeared to be ordinary Englishmen in common sailors' garb. The sight and smell of the rotting corpses soon became too much for Elizabeth. She tugged hard at Will's hand and pointed her body in the direction of the longboat.

"Let us go back," she implored. "Let us leave this dreadful place and return home. I fear what more we'll find if we remain here or venture forth. I don't wish to explore any further. No one could still be alive and needing our help...we'd hear their screams. Let the sea swallow up the remains of the carnage that man hath wrought and give us safe and speedy passage home."

"We should tend to the deceased," Will said solemnly. "They are our countrymen and deserve a decent burial."

"We were not born in England," retorted Elizabeth. "We're colonials with allegiance to *this* soil, which is far from England. Much good *England* has ever done for us," she added in a querulous and insolent tone.

"Nevertheless, it is the decent Christian thing to do."

"How doth thou intend to dig graves for sixteen souls without a pick or shovel?"

Will thought for a moment and came up with a solution.

"We shall honor naval tradition and bury them at sea. I will fill their pockets and boots with pebbles and wrap each sailor in the ensign we found. I will then row out far enough, unwrap the flag, and commit them to the deep. I will repeat the act until all are properly laid to rest. The pebbles will ensure that their mortal remains sink to the bottom. Wilt thou help me...my love?"

Elizabeth crossed her arms and looked away in defiance. Will watched as she strolled back toward the longboat, eventually stopping and sitting down on the sand, her eyes fixed on her home island across the channel. Will sighed and walked up to her. They had played this game before, and he knew exactly what was going to happen next. Elizabeth would remain peevishly silent and ignore him until she got what she wanted, which in this case was simply to leave immediately. Not wanting to incur the wrath of his lover, yet also determined to do what he felt was right, Will said in compromising fashion, "I will take no longer than is absolutely necessary. When the job is complete, we'll be off. In the meantime, I shall build thee a fire."

"And catch a fish with thy bare hands to cook for me as well, I suppose," she answered crossly, still not looking at him, a tear rolling down her left cheek.

Will sighed again and went off to collect wood and kindling. He made a foundation for the fire with large dead branches that he then covered with twisted knots of dried grass and twigs. He freed the piece of flint from the jaws of the musket's hammer, reached into his satchel, and pulled out his fire striker. He fiercely struck the two elements together to generate sparks which, after multiple attempts, ignited the small nest of grass and twigs. A single wisp of smoke wafted upwards, and Will leaned over to gently blow on the fragile little ember. Gradually, the smoke increased as the glowing cinder came to life. Within seconds, small flames erupted and began consuming the kindling. Will fed the fire with larger pieces of wood until he was confident it would burn steadily. With no word or hint of appreciation from Elizabeth, Will got up and set about his unpleasant task.

One by one, he prepared the bodies and rowed them out to deep water. When ready, he recited the Lord's Prayer then gently rolled the corpse out of the flag and into the sea. He then rowed back to shore and repeated the process. After committing the fifth body to the briny depths, Will decided upon a new course of action that he hoped would improve Elizabeth's frame of mind and bring them both some measure of hope. He maneuvered the longboat through the floating debris and began scooping up anything that appeared salvageable or useful, particularly sealed wooden boxes. One of the first items he recovered was the wooden cask that had struck the small craft. Following that, he recovered a large sea chest that was bobbing in the shallows. Lastly, he pulled a sail, a heavy hawser, and some rigging out of the water and onto the boat. Back on shore, he dragged everything up next to the fire where Elizabeth remained unmoved, her back still turned. This was the critical point in Will's plan.

"We should get this chest open. There might be useful items therein. That cask is full of liquid, and there's a spigot at the base. Perhaps there's suitable drinking water to be had. Maybe thou should give closer inspection? I must finish my task before I can assist thee," said Will.

Elizabeth didn't stir until Will was back on the water. He repeated his burial duties directly followed by more salvage. Each time he set foot back on shore with additional goods, Elizabeth became more responsive. He watched her closely as he prepared the final body for its journey into the sea. She was moving with renewed vigor and using every means at her disposal to break into the newly acquired cargo. When the final body was laid to rest, and when there was no material left afloat worth salvaging, Will returned to the beach, where, to his surprise and relief, she happily spoke first.

"Look, Will! Lord be praised! Sweet nectar from the heavens," she said as she opened the cask's spigot and collected an amber liquid in her cupped hands. She brought them to her mouth, swallowed every drop, and beamed a great smile. Will looked closely at the cask and discovered one word etched into the wood—RUM. "And look in this chest," she added excitedly. Will noticed that she had apparently been able to smash the rusty lock off with a large stone to gain entry. Inside was a bottle of red wine and two glasses, a small sack of tea, one of sugar lumps, one of salt, corked glass bottles and jugs of treacle and other unknown liquids, scrolls of blank paper, quill pens, a glass jar of ink, a bundle of candles tied with twine, several pewter plates, knives, and spoons, a small pestle and mortar, a book on human anatomy, and a medical kit—all relatively dry and undamaged by the salt water.

Excited about the alcohol and foodstuffs, Elizabeth hurriedly opened the sacks and tasted the salt and sugar. She grabbed the glasses and poured herself and Will more rum, smiling again as she brought the intoxicating brew to her lips. Will sipped his, coughed a bit, and then focused his attention on the anatomy book and medical kit, which he found to be the most fascinating contents of the chest. He opened the kit and found several surgical instruments of varying types. There were long-handled, slender knives with smooth and precise edges, and stubby little saws with jagged teeth. There were scissors, probes, needles, thread, and all manner of pincers, tweezers, tongs, and forceps, all of differing shapes and sizes. There were also small glass jars containing various roots and herbs, all sealed with corks.

After examining the surgical tools, Will picked up the book and started to peruse the English text. After reading a bit, his attention was drawn to the many vivid drawings and their descriptions. Elizabeth, showing some faint interest, looked over his shoulder at the graphic images depicting internal human anatomy—but immediately turned away in disgust and poured herself more rum. She welcomed the libation and drank with no inhibitions. It, along with the other finds, had fulfilled Will's hope. The salvaged goods had kept Elizabeth happily distracted and had greatly improved her foul bent of mind.

The two spent the next hour sifting through the remaining wooden boxes brought ashore. They found nothing of extraordinary or particularly useful significance save some clothing, a little gunpowder, a carpenter's mallet, and an abundance of wooden pegs. Shiny trinkets of trumpery briefly enchanted Elizabeth, but were widely ignored by Will. When everything had finally been revealed and collected, it was all placed in a large pile. What was saturated with seawater was left to dry in the summer sun.

The day was moving along more quickly now it seemed, and Will took an hour to row out along the shore to catch some food with his cast net. He was rewarded with a few small codfish. He brought the catch ashore, cleaned and filleted it, then skewered the fish with sharp sticks to cook over the fire. When it was ready, he and Elizabeth sat together and ate their meal, imbibing more rum. She had resumed speaking to him, and was now acting normally. Together they stared out at the *Repulse*, each wondering what the other was thinking. Finally, Elizabeth cleared her throat.

"If that destroyed ship...the one that exploded...the...ahh... the *Firefly*...could cast into the ocean the small, scattered bounty we've amassed today, imagine what's on board *that* ship...intact and untouched by the sea," she said, pointing to the *Repulse*.

"Yes, she could possess a most desirable and plentiful cargo. There could be crop seeds, food, tools, lumber, guns, clothing, and any number of other useful manufactured goods and raw materials," replied Will. "We could use the goods to rebuild our homes and restore our crop fields. Perhaps this is the very start of reinvigorating our island community," he added with renewed enthusiasm.

"Reinvigorating our island community? Sometimes I truly wonder if thou art stark raving mad," fired back Elizabeth. "Our island community—Storm Island—is but a slowly sinking lifeboat, a pitiful refuge from the native savages that run rampant and have laid waste to the mainland for years now. Falmouth Neck is nothing but a ravaged, barren land, uninhabitable from what mine eyes have seen and from what horrible stories fall off thy tongue. What hast thou truly discovered during thy scavenging journeys to the Neck, Will? What lies beyond the burned-out homes, sunken fishing boats, scorched fields, and the overgrown savage-infested woods? Nothing, Will...nothing but death a thousand times over and there's nothing that thyself, Massachusetts Bay, or even the Queen of England can do about it!"

Will put his hands on his hips and lowered his head. There were many things he wanted to say, but he couldn't find the words. He didn't have a chance, at any rate. Elizabeth wasn't through.

"What future do we have, Will? Thy father is an invalid and thy mother is dead. My mother is a devout Puritan who cares for nothing save what comes from the Bible or from her own teachings and toil. Her fanaticism has blinded her to the realities of our meager existence. God has done little to save or protect us no matter how many times a day she calls to Him in prayer...and He did nothing to save my murdered father."

"God will provide and *I* will provide," Will vowed. "We will persevere and prevail, as God is my witness. And one day the Neck will flourish again, as will Storm Island and this one, too...Belle Island," he said. Then he added, "Honor thy mother and thy father."

"I will do no such thing, William Estes. Those are *thy* wishes and *thy* dreams. They are not mine. Falmouth Neck is dead, reclaimed by the savages, assisted by their filthy cohorts, the French. It will be only a matter of time before they reclaim Storm Island, too. They will slaughter us and destroy every trace of civilization...and even if they don't, thou hath hunted virtually every creature that walks, crawls, or flies on Storm—and on this pathetic little rock as well. We are slowly starving. Nothing grows in this accursed soil. We've tried everything from corn to squash to lowly potatoes, and nothing thrives. Thou always argue that the sea provides. That I cannot dispute. Thou art a great fisherman, but the winters are long, cold, and dangerous. The sea does not yield its bounty as readily in the winter months as it does in the summer. And what of the storms? I fear that if the Indians or the French don't wipe us out, surely a massive gale will sweep us off these islands for eternity."

"My eyes have seen traces of revived life during my journeys to the Neck, Elizabeth. Traces of fire and civilization...I've seen it!"

"Savages, Will. Thou hath seen what the Indians hath done, nothing more. The village is gone...forever. Our families were fortunate to flee and find sanctuary here during those turbulent and destructive years, but our time is over. This colony is dead and so are we if we remain here much longer."

"What would thou have me do then, Elizabeth? I love thee. I want to marry thee and raise our children here. I know we can survive, and I know we can flourish if we just persevere and allow enough time for our English brethren to return."

Paying no mind to Will's comments about love and marriage, Elizabeth simply said, "Thou knoweth what I want. I desire to leave this place for good. We should pack up all our possessions and sail south until we reach Massachusetts Bay and civilization."

"In the longboat? Four of us plus supplies? We'd never survive the journey. We'd starve, die of thirst, capsize, or get smashed against the rocks with the first gale that blew. If not that, then we'd be tracked and hunted by the savages, who would swarm us by the hundreds the moment we went on land. We'd be no safer from them in the boat because they would come for us on the water in their birch bark canoes. We are sheltered right here...and that is where I intend to stay."

Elizabeth looked at Will coldly and said, "What makes thou think there would be four of us in the longboat?"

Confused, Will had no reply. He turned away from Elizabeth and began loading the goods onto the longboat. She again angrily sat down next to the dying fire and stared off into the distance at the *Repulse*. The day was waning fast, and it was taking Will longer to accomplish his work than he expected. When the boat was finally loaded, he walked over to Elizabeth and said sternly, "We need to return home now. It's too late to explore that galley. The tide has risen too high to search her lower decks without fear of her capsizing." He added after a short pause, "I've left Father alone for much too long, and I fear for his safety. Thy mother is undoubtedly worried about thee, as well, and we should put her mind at ease. I will return here on the morrow, alone, and search the ship. Whatever I find of use I will retrieve and divide up equally with thee and thy mother. Thou may take everything we found today except the book and the surgical kit. I want those for myself."

With that, Will walked to the longboat and pushed it into the water just enough to get in but not float away. Elizabeth sat with her back to him and did not move.

"Elizabeth!" he shouted. "We must leave. There is nothing else to be done here. If thou love me, please obey me now. I promise we will discuss thy grievances at a later time. Please come now," he said, adding "my dear," in hopes it would soften her heart and entice her to heed his request.

Elizabeth hesitated but slowly got to her feet. With a harsh look on her face and a deliberately slow gait, she returned to the boat and got in. She glared at Will as if she wanted him to know that he was not in charge of her and that her actions were a result of *her* resolve and not his. Satisfied for the moment, Will clutched an oar and began to shove off. As the blade dug into the sand and water, a strange sound caught their attention.

"What was that?" asked a visibly startled Elizabeth under the guise of anger.

Will stood perfectly still and listened. A moment passed before the unusual sound came again—with greater intensity.

"What *is* that?" Elizabeth asked a second time. "It sounds like a howling apparition or a demon."

Will picked up his musket, poured powder, shot, and wadding into the barrel, then tamped it down hard with the ramrod.

"What art thou doing? Let's be off immediately!" said Elizabeth. "Put that down and row us home."

Will ignored her and climbed out of the boat. He remembered the missing flint used to start the fire earlier and promptly secured it back into the hammer's jaws before bringing the mechanism to half cock. He added powder to the flash pan and closed the frizzen. He then moved up the beach and into the woods in the direction of the unsettling noise.

"Damnation, Will!" Elizabeth exclaimed, hopping out of the boat and charging after him. She clutched his arm firmly, half enraged and half terrified as they cautiously ventured into the woods. Will feared they might be walking into a trap set by the Abenakis, who had partnered with the French and laid waste to English settlements all up and down the coast during years of unrelenting and brutal warfare. He hadn't seen them on Belle Island before, and he hoped he wasn't about to come face to face with them now.

"Will, take me away from this place at once," Elizabeth pleaded.

Another wailing noise echoed through the trees. Will brought the musket hammer to full cock when he noticed blood on the ground. To him, the noise sounded like a wounded animal, and he was determined to find out exactly what it was. They followed the blood that trailed a bit further into the woods until they came upon a small clearing. What they saw next took their breath away and sent a fresh wave a fear sweeping over them. Elizabeth screamed and recoiled in alarm as Will instinctively raised the musket and prepared to shoot. But before he could pull the trigger, he paused, gathered his senses, and looked good and hard at what was making the peculiar sound. He lowered his gun and said, "My God, Elizabeth...I think he's still alive!"

CHAPTER 3

The Soul from the Sea

T he day had been full of unexpected twists and surprises, but what now lay before the startled young couple was the most astonishing yet. Amid all their petty belligerence toward one other, their fascination with the mysterious galley, their greedy preoccupation with the salvaged goods, and Will's time-consuming insistence on laying the dead to rest at sea, they had forgotten the real reason for their day's exploration—to help any survivors in need.

On the ground at their feet lay an injured sailor. He was prone with his arms and legs splayed out. His face was clean-shaven and youthful, but also bloodied and weathered. His blond hair was long and tied back, and he cried out in prolonged, painful moans that were almost inhuman. He wore white breeches and tall black boots. His shirt was white and bloodstained, and over it was an unbuttoned red coat that convinced Will he was a soldier of sorts. His eyes were closed and he didn't respond to any of the verbal requests Will put to him. He simply continued to moan and wail in pain.

The two dropped to their knees on opposite sides of the man. Elizabeth used her sleeve to wipe away some of the blood on his face while Will slid his hands up and down his torso in search of wounds. He unbuttoned the man's shirt, opened it widely along with the coat, and found what he was looking for. Burgundy-colored globs of clotted blood thickly coated the man's lower left abdomen. Using his index finger as a probe, Will discovered a hole the size of an acorn slowly oozing blood. Instinctively, he surmised a musket ball had struck the man in battle, with the whereabouts of the soft lead as yet unknown. He reached underneath and concluded the ball was still lodged in the man's gut, as he found no corresponding wound on his lower backside. An impulsive and somewhat desperate thought entered his mind.

"Elizabeth, run back to the beach and fetch the physician's book and kit...bring them to me posthaste."

Elizabeth went stiff and turned a stunned and alarmed stare toward Will. He looked at her intently and said, "Go now!" After a brief hesitation, Elizabeth rose to her feet and dashed off.

Three seconds later, the man's body jerked and went limp. His eyes flicked open, then closed again as his head slowly rolled to the side. Will pressed his ear against the man's chest, listening for a heartbeat, then put his cheek near the man's mouth in search of breath. He was temporarily relieved after detecting faint indications of both.

"He's lost his ability to sense and perceive...for the moment," Will said when Elizabeth returned, book and kit in hand. "I shall take advantage of his wound-induced sleep and attempt to remedy his affliction."

He opened the book and hurriedly thumbed to a page he had viewed earlier that was filled with drawings of internal human anatomy. After finding the one particular illustration he deemed most useful, he turned his attention to the surgical kit. From it he withdrew a probe and forceps.

"Thou art not a physician, Will. And this is not a giant fish simply needing to be cleaned, salted, and dried," implored Elizabeth. "Thou hath no knowledge of medicine beyond that of thy fanciful healing inclinations derived from my mother's books. How can thou possibly help this man recover from such a grievous wound? He will most certainly expire in the attempt."

"What would thou have me do? He needs help and we're the only ones here. Long ago, my father told me about musket wounds and the damage they cause. If the shot remains in the body, it continues to wreak havoc unless extracted from the affected innards.

It *must* be removed before the wound suppurates. Then and only then can the stricken begin to heal. I must find the ball first," Will said, gently probing deep into the wound.

"I could understand if it were an injured arm or leg, but—"

"Swab away the blood," Will interrupted. "Use thy sleeve or thy bare hands if necessary. I can't see—"

Just then the tip of the metal probe struck something hard. Will gently prodded and poked until he was able to determine the shape of the solid mass—round. Unable to see the lead shot through the bloody mesh of damaged tissue, Will kept the probe in contact with the target as he reentered the cavity with the forceps. The flow of blood increased with each tiny adjustment of his surgical instruments, and he knew he had to work fast lest his patient bleed to death.

"I think I got it," Will said. With a hard squeeze and quick jerk, the bloody forceps were carefully wrenched free from the wound. Clamped between the pincers was a crimson-covered lead ball slightly flattened on one side. Mesmerized, Will held it up in the light and examined it as if he had made a major discovery.

"Will...the bleeding!" exclaimed Elizabeth, her hands coated in bright-red blood and her dress sleeves similarly stained.

"Needle and thread," he replied after dropping the forceps. Elizabeth retrieved both from the kit and handed them to Will, who promptly set about preparing for the final stage of his first operation. After threading the needle and tying off the end, he began to sew up the wound. Soon the grisly job was complete and the deadly flow of blood arrested.

"In God's hands now," he said.

"What is thy next course of action?" asked Elizabeth after they had paused a moment to ponder what had just happened.

"I do not think it is prudent to inform thy mother of these recent happenings—the sea battle, the dead sailors, the salvaged goods, or this wounded man. Something deep in my bones tells me her knowing would be burdensome for us both."

"I am not in disagreement with thy sentiments, Will, but how can we keep such a large secret from either my mother or thy father?"

"My father's mind is but an empty shell...robbed of independent thought or action. He is of no concern in such matters. Thy mother's immersion in her devout religious beliefs and undertakings, as well as her authoritative manner, makes her meddlesome and unpredictable. She's also ignorant to our daily struggles of survival, thinking only of the grand church she hopes to see constructed on Storm and the words of the Bible. Her practical schoolings have become more infrequent and less useful...and often drowned in a deluge of religious insinuations. I fear Winnie's mind is becoming unsound, as well."

Will stopped short of expressing his true thoughts concerning Elizabeth's mother. In truth, he deeply felt that Winnie Eustis had gone quite mad and was suffering from a brain malady for which there was no cure—not even from God himself. The strain from years of isolation, harsh living, and constant fear of Indian attack had undoubtedly taken its toll on her. Even her rigorous Puritan faith in God could not shield her from the unforgiving physical and mental torment of such a grueling existence.

"For now, we'll return to Storm. We will provide care and shelter for this man at Fort Hope," declared Will. "We'll store the salvaged goods with the other provisions kept there. Perhaps when this man recovers, he can provide us with some answers to the many questions we have...perhaps even share news of his travels and what is occurring in distant lands as well as on the waters surrounding our home. Help me get him to the boat."

Will slung his musket over his shoulder, then reached under the man's arms and clasped his hands around his chest. As he lifted, Elizabeth strained to pick up his legs. They clumsily lumbered back onto the beach, where Elizabeth's strength and desire to help swiftly vanished. She suddenly dropped the man's legs, causing Will to lose his balance and tumble backwards onto the sand. As he looked up, he couldn't tell by Elizabeth's expression whether she was filled with anger or despair. He chose not to scold her, as she was most assuredly under enormous strain, with the impact of the morbid sights she had witnessed throughout the day now bearing down on her in full force.

Will loaded the sailor into the boat and turned to Elizabeth, who was soaking her bloodstained hands and sleeves in the ocean. He, too, waded into the cold water and tried to wash away as much blood as he could. It was then that the full magnitude of what had happened hit him. His body began to shiver, and he was certain it wasn't the chilly water causing it. He scrambled quickly into the boat with one thought in his head.

"The time to leave is now. Let us finally be off, Elizabeth," he said, oar in hand.

Elizabeth climbed aboard, taking her place at the bow, and Will shoved off. He strained at the oars because the longboat sat lower in the water with the added weight. The sun was setting as the boat slowly pulled away from Belle Island. Will watched as the *Repulse* got smaller and smaller with each stroke. Neither he nor Elizabeth said anything as they crossed the channel, but by the time they arrived back at Storm's beach, Will had devised a plan. Elizabeth jumped out of the boat as soon as the bow plowed into the sand.

"Thou should make thy way home on foot," Will said. "I will row over to Fort Hope, unload the goods, and provide for our injured guest."

Elizabeth, seemingly oblivious to the words spilling from Will's mouth, simply walked up the beach toward the trail leading into the woods. Will watched as she reached a certain point and began disrobing. Her nude form, partially obscured by the trees and brush, sent an arousing pulse rushing through his body. Despite all he had seen and all he had done throughout this horrifying day, nothing released more raw emotional energy in his body and soul more than the sight of his lover in her natural state. The effect was both spellbinding and strangely unexplainable.

Will finally snapped out of his little trance as Elizabeth reemerged fully clothed in traditional Puritan dress. Her attire now consisted of a white shift, a tight, dark-blue long-sleeved waistcoat, a petticoat of similar color, and a long white apron draped down the front. Her hair was no longer loose, but tightly trapped under a white coif. The only parts of her body now visible were her hands and face. In one hand she carried the bloodstained dress.

"Take this with thee to the fort," she said, tossing the garment into the boat. "There's still some lye soap there to scrub out the stains."

Will nodded and said, "Rush home and placate thy mother now—and see to my father, if thou please. I will return as soon as possible. I pray this man does not expire before we reach the shelter of Hope. I will come for thee when everything is in order."

Elizabeth nodded in turn and then departed into the woods.

Will hesitated a moment and stood at the bow of the boat like a statue, staring at the trail and half expecting Elizabeth to reappear bristling with reassuring sentiments and a warm physical touch that would put his mind and body at ease. It soon became apparent that that was not going to happen. Will turned to the injured sailor, who was still unconscious, and watched as his chest slowly rose and fell with each shallow breath he took. Confident it was still possible to help the man recover, Will shoved off and began rowing toward the northwest side of Storm Island, where Fort Hope was located.

The ocean was calm, and Will tossed out a few hooks and lines in hopes of catching a codfish or two before the sun fully set and darkness was upon him. He watched the fiery orb slowly dip below the horizon to the west. The white clouds in the sky slowly became decorated in glorious hues of red, orange, and yellow. *The Lord wields a magnificent paintbrush, and all the sky and heaven above is his canvas*, Will thought. A smile crept across his face as he wondered if God was rewarding him with such a splendid sunset for the service he had rendered earlier to the deceased sailors. His smile widened seconds later as a fish hit his first line.

The forest trail seemed gloomy and uninviting whenever Elizabeth walked it alone. The thick canopy above blocked out most of the sun—even on clear days—and the mossy-scented air seemed filled with black clouds of blood-sucking mosquitoes and other unwelcome insects. Elizabeth hurried along, hampered by her dress, which had to be picked up so she would not trip and fall.

She meandered through the woods silently and cautiously, looking out in all directions. While in the thicket, she always felt as if a thousand devilish eyes were observing her every move. In her imagination, she conjured up terrors of unnatural creatures such as ghosts, witches, or hobgoblins emerging from the shadows and whisking her away to the darkest regions of the unknown, never to see the light of day again. Her fears, though fanciful, were not totally unfounded, as the threat of Indian attack was always present. Grim reminders of the vicious Indian wars that had ravaged the nearby mainland—particularly Falmouth Neck—were never far from her thoughts. And though she hadn't actually seen an Abenaki Indian since she was a little girl, she knew they were present in increasing numbers along the coast, and nearly invisible when on the warpath. The very thought of falling prey to a savage ambush was more than she could bear. Her step hastened.

Finally, she was out of the woods and moving through the grassy fields that led home. As evening began to fall, she hurried past the darkened Estes cabin and sensed no real comfort until the first whiff of smoke from her mother's cooking fire grazed her nostrils. Soon the light inside the Eustis cabin became visible, putting her partially at ease. As she approached her home, she sighed heavily and wondered what form of harsh reception she would have to endure from her mother the second she appeared.

She pushed the door open, and through the dim candlelight the first sight that caught her eye was old Cyrus sitting at the table with a bowl of soup. He looked up but said nothing and slowly spooned more of the warm broth into his mouth. Looming over the black cooking kettle in front of the fireplace was a seething Winnie Eustis. Her arms were crossed and her face was carved with a wicked and indignant scowl. Her clothing matched her daughter's almost exactly, and her predominantly gray hair was done up in a tight bun beneath her white, close-crimped coif. A long wooden spoon jutted from her right hand, appearing more like a sorceress's wand than a simple cooking implement.

Winnie often struck an intimidating and sinister-looking pose. To Elizabeth, she more resembled an evil witch standing over a fiery cauldron of vile, bubbly brew instead of a woman of God devoted to Puritan values of life and worship. There were times when Elizabeth wondered if there was actually a difference between the two—especially where her mother was concerned.

"Doth thou live to burden me with unending worry?" asked Winnie. "I expected thy return at a much earlier time of day. Where hath thine idle hands and empty head been selfishly lingering this day...which is now wasted?"

Elizabeth shut the door hard behind her. She again looked at Cyrus, who continued to show no interest in anything except the soup in front of him.

"Thou will answer now, or no supper shall pass thy lips," commanded Winnie.

"I was with Will—"

"Cleary," Winnie angrily interrupted.

Cyrus perked up upon hearing his son's name, then focused again on his soup.

"He needed help mending his nets. The task was a daunting one, as many are worn and frayed beyond usefulness."

"And this common chore required a full day's effort from both of thee?"

"It was necessary...yes."

"I hear no truth in that," Winnie said. "Surely the two of thee were off lazing about in solitude, engaging in some form of God-less sin."

"No, we were not," Elizabeth replied tersely, adding after a few seconds of thought, "We were improving our collective means and ensuring that food continues to be harvested from the sea and brought to our tables."

"Thou art overflowing with lies, of this I am certain. Thou goest off with William, against the Lord's wishes, and fail to accomplish even one chore I task thee with. How many candles or bars of lye soap did thou make today? How many garments did thou mend? How many baskets did thou weave? How much food and firewood did thou gather? How many fish did thou clean and smoke? And how much time did thou take to read God's scripture from the Bible today? The answer is most assuredly *none*...am I wrong?"

Oddly, the now silent Elizabeth was caught off guard by her mother's harsh line of questioning and couldn't find the proper reply to stifle her tirade. Normally, the clever lass was adept at entangling her mother's truthful accusations in a flawlessly spun web of imaginative lies and deceptions, thereby rendering Winnie's denunciations harmless, and providing herself with a temporary reprieve; only this time, her mind wandered, and the mendacity did not flow freely from her lips. The sheer magnitude of what she had witnessed earlier still weighed heavily in her thoughts and affected her ability to outmaneuver her mother with her customary ease. She decided to shift the focus off of herself.

"Why is Mr. Estes here and not at his own table?" Elizabeth asked.

"Ha! Perhaps I should ask *thee* that question? I found him wandering about aimlessly. William—same as thee—was nowhere to be found. With inspiration from the Lord, I took it upon myself to offer some food, sanctuary, and temporary companionship to this enfeebled soul who was so callously neglected today."

Elizabeth sat down at the table across from Cyrus, which allowed her to avert her eyes away from her mother's cold, hardened gaze. As her eyes slowly met Cyrus's, they managed a feeble smile at each other and nothing more. Elizabeth knew that any words of greeting would be countered with an awkward gesture or some incomprehensible gibberish. She pitied the man's sad state, but also had little use for or interest in him.

"Lies, insolence, and immoral behavior are all thou ever bestow upon me," fumed Winnie as she turned to the fire and began stirring the soup in the kettle. "And now thou sit there like a queen and expect me to provide thy supper like a common servant or slave. I'll have none of it...and thou shalt have no supper! Take Mr. Estes home and return forthwith. Perhaps the walk and an empty stomach will help restore thy senses and God's teachings. Thou art wicked, Elizabeth...and only jointly can we cast out the demons that have poisoned thy soul. We shall pray together until dawn if necessary. I will reclaim my daughter from the jaws of Satan!"

Unable to listen any further, Elizabeth shot up from the

table and slapped the soup bowl away from Cyrus, who recoiled in fright. The wooden bowl flew across the room and hit Winnie in the back. The old woman spun around in a rage and charged at her daughter with the wooden spoon raised high. But before she could strike, Elizabeth landed a hard slap across her mother's cheek that sent her reeling back several steps. Cyrus stood up and covered his face like a child trying to hide from a monster. Elizabeth rushed at Winnie, who was off balance and crumpled onto the floor, her right arm raised and shielding her face in anticipation of another blow.

"Thou shalt not accuse me!" bellowed Elizabeth. "I will not be ordered about or condemned by thee any further this evening, nor will I listen to thy hollow, maddening, judgments. I am of sound mind, which is more than can be said of either Mr. Estes or thee. I will do as I please and return when I wish," she said, and then dashed for the door.

Tears streaming down her face, Winnie managed to express a final thought before her daughter could run out.

"Remember what I told thee happened years ago in Salem! Remember that I was there during the accusations, and the trials. Remember what can happen to innocent girls who ignore the word of God and are seduced by the Devil. Rid thyself of thine evil before it is too late!" she exclaimed, getting to her feet and reaching for her Bible.

Elizabeth paused a moment as her mother's threatening words sank in. She looked at Winnie, then back at Cyrus before rushing out the door and slamming it hard behind her. Without pause, compunction, or even a candle to guide her, she darted off into the final fleeting moments of dusk.

Fort Hope stood atop a small cliff in a clearing amid dense trees overlooking the northwest sea approaches to Storm Island. It was a palisaded log fort, rectangular in shape and fortified with two roofed blockhouses, one on the northwest corner facing the sea, and one on the southeast corner facing the woods. Ladders in each blockhouse granted access to the interior second level and to the high wooden ledge that ran along the inside perimeter. The ledge allowed defenders of the fort to look over the wall and rain fire upon any band of attackers. It was also high enough off the ground so that it couldn't be reached without the aid of a ladder or a secured rope of sorts. The main entrance consisted of two large, hinged doors that swung open inward and were secured with a heavy wooden crossbar.

The blockhouses themselves were built with observation windows and small firing ports to accommodate defenders armed with muskets and assorted small arms. They were also equipped to house a total of four cannons, but none were ever installed. Toward the rear of the open fort was a crude barracks that could comfortably shelter a limited number of occupants. Though structurally sound, and conceived by individuals determined to protect and defend what they felt was rightfully theirs—to the death, if necessary—Fort Hope was small, poorly stocked, and incapable of fending off an attack by any organized force. In fact, a barrage from the sea from just one contemporary warship could easily reduce it to nothing but a pile of burning cinders. Nevertheless, the fort was completely suited for fulfilling the task for which it was specifically designed—protection from threatening Indians.

At the moment, Indian attack was the furthest thing from the mind of William Estes as he lumbered up the one tiny path that led from the rocky shoreline to the fort. In one hand was a glowing lantern while the other cradled a sack of goods. The unforgiving little trail was winding, steep, and littered with annoying obstructions that hindered the movement of any traveler upon it. Sweat poured down both his brow and his aching back with each labored step. When he reached the doors and entered the fort, he buckled from sheer exhaustion. He had made many grueling trips up and down the challenging little trail, arms loaded with the salvaged goods—not to mention the wounded sailor. Fortunately, this was his last trip.

After a few minutes of rest stretched flat on his back, Will recovered enough strength to get back on his feet and stagger over to the barracks. It was dark now, and he placed the lantern on the wooden table that stood not far from the makeshift feather-stuffed mattress in the corner. It was on this worn and improvised piece of furniture where he and Elizabeth had had many sexual encounters, and where now rested the still-unconscious sailor. Upon close examination, Will again confirmed that he was still alive. His chest still rose and fell and his heart was still beating.

Will turned his attention elsewhere. The barracks was constructed with a crude fireplace and chimney for cooking, so he built a fire to prepare the fish he had caught and cleaned earlier. He was very hungry and lingered about impatiently, waiting for the cod to roast over the open flames. While he waited, he studied the stacked-up barrels, boxes, and chests of goods in the corner. He had managed to haul all the salvaged material inside and add it to the inventory of useful assets already there. He desperately wanted to examine each and every item harvested from the sea, but it was late, he was too tired, and food and drink was all he craved. He took a seat on a squatty little stool in front of the fire.

It grew very quiet. Will closed his eyes and listened intently to the sound of the crackling flames that licked at the spluttering fish on the spit. The noise was curiously soothing and began to lull him toward a deep slumber. Just as sleep was about to overcome him, his ears caught the sound of a gentle rustling outside. Instantly, his eyes snapped open and he stood up. He reached for his musket and readied it to fire. With a start, he remembered he hadn't secured the doors to the main entrance of the fort. A chill went down his spine. The sound of movement grew more pronounced, and he concluded that the source was not some wayward animal skulking about. The windowless barracks offered no comfort, as no advance warning could be had without opening the door. Will had just reached for the latch when he heard one of the main entrance's doors being swung open. Summoning all the courage he could muster—as he was sure he was about to do battle with an Indian raiding party taking advantage of his carelessness—Will flung open the barracks door and pointed his musket directly at the first shadowy hint of movement.

"Show thyself!" he ordered.

"Fear not," came the reply, "it is only I."

Will lowered his gun and retrieved the lantern. Its weak radiance pushed aside enough of the inky nighttime to reveal the intruder. Sitting on the ground in a defensive posture was Elizabeth. Before Will could say anything or help her to her feet, she sprang up and scurried through the barracks door. Will walked over to the main entrance and secured the doors with the crossbar before returning to the barracks. He shut the door behind him and placed the lantern back on the table. Elizabeth fidgeted in front of the fire, and Will could easily sense that she was upset.

"Why art thou still clad in that blood-soaked shirt and breeches? Where is my dress? Has it been cleaned? I won't stand to be clothed *this* way another moment," Elizabeth said as she ripped the coif from her head and started to undo her petticoat.

"Thy dress is right here. I have not cleaned it yet; there hasn't been time. I was not expecting thee—"

"She struck me," blurted Elizabeth as she reached for a plate and a knife. "Nay, she *beat* me and shouted horrible things. She would not allow me a bite of supper. I feared for what she might do next, so I left."

In her agitated state, Elizabeth removed the fish from the spit and onto her plate. She slammed the plate down on the table, sat, and stabbed at the fish with her knife, placing a bite on her tongue only after it had properly cooled. Suddenly, she shot up again after spying the rum cask Will had brought in earlier. She found two wooden cups and promptly filled them with the luscious alcohol before returning to the table. Will sat down next to her and cut a few portions of fish for himself. They ate and drank in silence until Will's curiosity got the better of him.

"Didst thou spy my father? Is he safe? Has he been looked after? I must get home. He's been alone for too—"

"He is with my mother," Elizabeth grumpily retorted. "She was kind enough to provide for *his* well-being with food and companionship, which is far more than she could spare her only daughter this evening. Fetch me a basin and fill it with water so that I may cleanse this rotten clothing of ours."

After taking his last bite of fish, Will got up and retrieved the wooden washtub hanging from a long peg on the wall, and placed it on the floor near the fire. With the largest bucket he could find in one hand and the lantern in the other, he made his way outside the fort and down the trail to the shore, where he scooped up enough seawater to fill the bucket. He made several laborious trips back and forth until the tub was filled to Elizabeth's satisfaction. When the water had warmed, Elizabeth rolled up her sleeves and began to attack her bloody dress with a heavy wooden washing beetle and a bar of lye soap.

"Give me thy shirt, and fetch some buckets of fresh water if it is available in sufficient quantities," Elizabeth ordered as she beat and scrubbed.

"I'll check the rain barrel, but I fear there's not much there," Will replied as he stripped off his shirt and handed it to Elizabeth.

To Will's surprised, the rain barrel outside the barracks was nearly half full. He hadn't checked it in days, and fortunately the hot weather hadn't dried it up completely. He scooped up three buckets' worth and brought them inside by the fire.

"How is our guest?" Elizabeth asked.

"He lives...for now," Will answered, adding, "but he remains unresponsive and unable to wake."

"How can we care for him? What happens if he dies?"

"I'll bury him if he passes before dawn. I've gotten a little water down his throat. I think it important to do everything in our power to preserve his life. Something inside me desperately yearns to hear about this man's travels and the reason God brought him to us," Will said.

"Thou sound like my mother," sighed Elizabeth. "Why must all life and the events that comprise it be part of 'God's' plan? Don't mere mortals make their own destinies?"

Will had no response and simply sat back down at the table.

Elizabeth finished her laundry and hung her dress and Will's shirt by the fire to dry. She walked over to the sailor and lit a fresh candle so she could see his visage more clearly. She dabbed a cloth in a bucket of fresh water and proceeded to clean his face, which was still heavily soiled with dirt and dried blood. The more she cleaned, the more distinct and striking his facial features became. What followed next was a curious sensation that, under the circumstances, surprised even her—attraction, then arousal. This feeling prompted her to casually remove his coat and shirt, which she placed in the washbasin to soak. She then took her wet cloth and wiped away any blots of blood on his torso, specifically around his wound. When she was finished, she ran her hand across his bare chest and then coyly turned around to see if Will was watching her.

His back was turned as he tended the fire and disposed of the remains from their dinner. He unpacked some fresh candles from the salvaged goods to replace the ones lit earlier, which were rapidly dimming into messy pools of tallow. Upon replacing the lantern candles, he was pleasantly surprised to discover that they were made from beeswax—a luxury substance not readily available and utilized only by the very rich. Intrigued, his thoughts wandered back to the *Repulse*.

Some time passed as both Will and Elizabeth busily occupied themselves and silently contemplated what might come next. Elizabeth finished laundering the sailor's coat and shirt and hung them up to dry by the fire. She hauled the washbasin outside and dumped out the dirty water. Upon returning, she refilled it from the buckets of clean, warm freshwater and what remained of the lye soap. Will stopped fiddling with the fire and stared at her, wondering what she was up to.

"Take off thy boots and breeches and step into the tub. The time has come to rid ourselves of the foul odors and filth clinging to our bodies," said Elizabeth.

"*Our* bodies?" asked Will.

"Yes...our bodies," Elizabeth said softly as she began slowly peeling away the layers of her clothing.

Will responded in kind until both of them stood completely naked.

They stepped into the washbasin and tightly embraced with warm caresses and passion-fueled kisses. Occasionally, Elizabeth reached down and scooped up water to teasingly splash on both of them. They took turns seductively applying the soap to one another, then rinsing it off. Their playful lustiness intensified until Will couldn't contain his fiery desires any further, so he picked Elizabeth up and carried her wet, sultry form over to the table. She reclined onto her back as Will blanketed her body with slow, lecherous kisses that left no part of her anatomy untouched. He worked his way up and smothered her neck and bare breasts with his mouth and tongue before settling on her lips. Elizabeth let out a short moan as her legs fell apart and the two lovers became one. Will plowed forth with a surge of sexually charged thrusts that swept Elizabeth up in a whirlwind of physical pleasure he was certain she had never felt before. The moans intensified into erotic screams that stimulated their lust into deeper, harder, and faster acts of sexual play.

They exchanged positions several times, attempting to capture and magnify every sensation of arousal they could discover. On the precipice of attaining the apex of carnal ecstasy, Will's rapid penetration grew stronger and deeper while Elizabeth's moans grew louder. Finally, the raw sexual energy couldn't be contained any longer. It burst free with untethered potency, producing hitherto unmatched and seemingly unending feelings of pleasure. They slid off the table and onto the floor, where they happily leaned against each other, breathing heavily and completely at ease.

Elizabeth reached for a nearby bearskin blanket and wrapped herself up. After a moment passed, she looked directly into Will's eyes and said, "Let us stay here tonight. I wish to go with thee tomorrow. We can strike out at dawn. I want to help thee explore the wreck, unlock whatever secrets it holds, and share in whatever bounty it possesses. I'm not afraid anymore, and I cannot bear Mother much longer. She poisons my very essence with her cruel and deliberate attacks."

Will hesitated, and before any discouraging words could escape his lips, Elizabeth spoke again with added determination.

"Thou did not witness the hurt and shame she heaped upon my soul a few hours ago. She beat my body and hurled unspeakable threats at me. I fear what she will do without sufficient amounts of time to soothe the demons within, time she will undoubtedly use to pacify herself through prayer and Bible reflection. Stay here with me tonight...take me with thee tomorrow."

Will was finding her resolve and her pleadings more and more difficult to combat. As he locked eyes with her, she leaned in and engaged him with a long, slow kiss. As they kissed, Will felt his hand taken by hers and drawn higher and higher between her thighs until it could travel no further. The teasing continued until Elizabeth was satisfied through Will's facial expressions and bodily responses that she had gotten what she wanted. At that moment, the sexual play abruptly ended. With a smile and a silly little wink, she stood up, wrapped herself tight in the blanket, and lay down close to the dying fire, where she happily and almost instantly fell asleep.

Will wanted to make love to Elizabeth over and over again before the early hours of dawn were upon them, but seeing her tightly bound in the blanket and motionless by the fire, he knew that she was in no mood for further intimacy. He stood up, put his breeches back on, and forced his mind to focus on more pressing matters. Thoughts of the *Repulse* and the injured sailor dominated his attention, but amid scattered and scathing thoughts of Winnie, and the story Elizabeth had imparted earlier, he was oblivious and unobservant to the fact that she did not have one visible mark on her face or body.

I need to explore that wreck as soon as the tides allow, he thought. *If I can get belowdecks and into her main hold, I can uncover and hopefully retrieve whatever precious cargo she possesses that's still intact. Time is of the essence. The longer she sits aground with a damaged hull, the more susceptible she is to the wind and tide. It's only a matter of time before she breaks apart. One good storm will seal her fate...that's for certain.*

It was getting late, fatigue was setting in, and it was becoming apparent that neither he nor Elizabeth would be venturing home tonight. Will blew out all the candles, including the ones in the lanterns. The room was now shrouded in darkness except for the bit of light and the eerie shadows cast by the slowly dying fire.

Will yawned and looked down at his lover curled up by the fire. He knelt beside her, preparing to join her in peaceful slumber, when a muffled sound caught his ears. He stood up and gazed across the dimly lit room. Another barely audible sound came from the corner where the injured sailor lay.

"Elizabeth...bestir thyself," Will said gently, shaking her shoulder.

"Hmm...what?" she groggily replied, her eyes flickering open.

A louder and more distinct groan pierced the darkness, and Elizabeth bolted upright and wrapped the blanket ever tighter around her.

Will cautiously stepped toward the man, who lay mostly hidden in the shadows. As he got closer, he could barely make out parts of his legs and waist, but his upper torso, particularly his face, was totally obscured.

"Light the lantern and bring it here," Will said as he crouched beside the man and tried to make out his face in the darkness.

Elizabeth used a hot cinder from the fire to relight the lantern, passed it to Will, and knelt beside him. He shined the light on the man's face.

"Christ!" shouted a horrified Will as his eyes locked on the cold and unforgiving eyeballs buried deep in the callous face now staring directly at him.

Before Will could utter another word or move a single muscle, the man's right hand sprang up and clutched his throat in a powerful grip that threatened to choke the life out of him. Simultaneously, the man's left hand appeared and swiftly stuck the tip of a blade under his chin. Will froze in terror while Elizabeth shrieked and toppled backward onto her rear. The man's eyes bored into Will's, and through gritted teeth he managed to struggle out three raspy and foreboding words.

"Friend or foe?"

CHAPTER 4

Friend or Foe

T he surprising force choking the air out of Will's windpipe—and the life out of his body—intensified with a sharp inward press of the sailor's fingers. Will went limp and very nearly lost consciousness. But before the fatal amount of pressure could be applied, or the knife driven up into his chin, the stranger shuddered and his grip weakened. The blade slipped away from his left hand, and his right hand slid down and dropped away. Will wrenched himself clear of the man's hands, coughed and gasped several times, and choked out the word, "Friend."

Will toppled backwards onto his side near Elizabeth, who promptly pulled him further away to safety. The man turned his head and glared at them. He began to thrash about in an effort to get to his feet and finish the lethal task he'd started. But his wounded body was sapped of the energy and strength needed to rise up and pose a legitimate threat. He tried to swing his legs out and sit up while grasping in vain for the fallen knife. The most he could muster was to clutch his injured side and let out a sharp cry of pain, followed by several labored gasps for breath.

Stunned and terrified, Will and Elizabeth dared not move for fear of unleashing whatever lethal fury the wounded and agitated stranger might yet be capable of. Slowly, he raised a ragged finger and pointed it directly at them. Then, with a bone-chilling scowl and a croaky voice that made Will recollect every demonic sound he had ever imagined in his early childhood, the man ominously warned, "Stay away from that ship...she's the Devil's Chariot...touch not a rope swinging from her deck or face eternal damnation."

His arm dropped, his head went limp, and his eyes rolled back under bruised-looking eyelids. After a moment's pause, Will got to his feet and cautiously walked toward the individual who had just threatened them. He snatched up the knife and pointed it at the man. Hoping he was dead, and even entertaining thoughts of plunging the knife into his chest if he wasn't, Will reluctantly checked for a heartbeat and any slight breath escaping his mouth. To his dismay, he discovered both.

"Is he dead?" Elizabeth asked with trepidation as she slowly got off the floor, still wrapped up tight in her blanket.

"Nay," answered Will, adding, "he lives...for the moment."

Gradually regaining his composure, Will was able to temporarily drive the fear from his mind and body. Anger toward the man who had just tried to kill him now fueled his actions. In a frantic state, Will scavenged around the barracks' supplies until he found some rope. Quickly and thoroughly, he bound the man's hands and feet together, rendering him immobile and unable to stand or attack again. When satisfied that the immediate threat had been removed, he turned to Elizabeth, who was reaching for her clothing.

"What art thou doing?" Will asked.

"Surely thou doth not plan to remain here with this madman?" Elizabeth said, hurriedly dressing in her despised Puritan apparel.

"Hath thou forgotten about thy mother's foul temperament and abuse of earlier this evening? Would it be wise to simply wander back and seek refuge in her unmannerly nest? Was it not thee that firmly declared thou wanted to stay here tonight?"

Elizabeth, her back to Will, offered no reply. Her only noticeable reaction was a slight dip of the head followed by a pause in securing her petticoat. She pondered what she had told Will upon her arrival at the fort, and what had actually happened during the confrontation with her mother. After considering both, she finally spoke.

"What are we to do, Will?" she asked somberly. "I'm frightened of what this undesirable character from the sea will do to us if we stay here and he is able to free himself while we slumber. Furthermore, I know the harsh welcome that will be thrust upon my head by the thick end of mother's ferule should she lay eyes upon me before dawn."

Will located his musket and took it in hand. He checked it over carefully to ensure it was loaded and ready to fire.

"We'll stay here together until the morrow," said Will. "I will remain awake and alert, standing guard whilst thou sleep. If any danger is brought upon thee by our troublesome guest, I will waste not an instant in putting a ball through his head. Thou hath nothing to fear. I will protect thee now and forever. That is my eternal pledge."

"But what are we to do with this man if he recovers from his injury and awakens permanently? He's obviously dangerous and unpredictable."

"I think it wise to continue to care for him. We knoweth not what his purpose for being here is, nor his true intentions. He's hurt, sickly, and confused. His earlier attack on me could have been brought on by a clouded mind and the trauma of the sea battle we witnessed earlier. I want to question him and learn his story before I condemn him to death. The sputtering about the ship...to stay away from it...I want to know what that means and why. We need knowledge of the outside world and its current happenings. I say again, this man could hold information key to our very survival."

"Thou art mad, Will," replied Elizabeth indignantly. "He attempted to kill thee, foiled only by his weakened state, the result of his wound. Do away with him. I fear nothing good can result from this plan of thine."

Will put down the musket and crossed his arms as he stood and stared at Elizabeth in silence. It was his way of telling her he would not be swayed from his approach to the problem at hand. She understood but remained indignant.

"And how doth thou expect to keep thy father and my mother unaware of this man's existence? Surely my mother will have a negative opinion on the matter upon discovering his presence."

"We'll keep him here, of course. My father is of no concern. Thy mother never ventures here unless accompanied by one of us. She fears this place and the painful memories retained within its walls. Thou certainly should understand—"

"I understand," Elizabeth interjected. "Do not dredge up the past. I am in no mood to revisit that wickedness. The very thought of it causes me to shudder and only increases my desire to leave here at once."

She made an impulsive move toward the door, but just as she was about to push her way through, a stream of bloodcurdling shrieks and high-pitched cries chillingly echoed through the night air. She froze in place, gradually turning toward Will with a look of terror etched on her face.

"The spirits of the dead are lively tonight," whispered Elizabeth. "I fear a haunting has befallen this wretched place."

Gingerly, she backed away from the door and drew closer to the fire. She recovered the bearskin blanket and wrapped it around her body and over her head so that only her face was visible. She then huddled on the floor close to the dying flames.

Will picked up the musket and sat down near Elizabeth in a protective posture. He was not one to challenge a person's views or beliefs concerning the spirit realm—he had been besieged with tales of ghosts, witches, and otherworldly specters since birth—but he was sure Elizabeth's initial observation and statement was incorrect. In fact, he would almost have preferred that she *was* correct compared to the alternative.

"I can't establish if those shrieks originated from the sea or not," whispered Will. "I hope they're not on shore."

"Who?" whispered back Elizabeth.

"The savages. Those are Abenaki war cries...I'm sure of that."

"My God," said Elizabeth. "Doth thou think they are becoming emboldened enough to strike out from the Neck? Is our presence here known? Doth thou think they intend to wipe us off this island once and for all?"

"One cannot be certain of their intentions. Father always told me that the savages believed Storm and Belle were cursed and thus would not step foot on either. He also used to say that great numbers of their dead were buried here, and that they would stay away out of respect for their fallen...or possibly to avoid unpleasant encounters with restless spirits."

The haunting legends of Indian dead reigning over the accursed island soils were interesting and intriguing, but also simple and convenient bedtime stories explaining why the native Abenaki were never seen on Storm or Belle. Fascinating and scary as the tales were—often told at night by the fire when Will was a child—the experienced young seafarer relied on a more practical and logical reason to account for the lack of native presence on the islands. During his years of fishing the waters around the two home isles, Will had discovered strong and hazardous currents that swirled about the shorelines and were hard to navigate without experience and a sturdy boat equipped with a hoisted sail. In time, Will had learned the best places to launch and beach the longboat to avoid the worst of the unpredictable surges. A strong back at the oars would also defeat them, but he often wondered if the Abenaki, in their smaller, more primitive dugout canoes, knew that the chances of capsizing and drowning were far greater than reaching the shore safely after a long paddle from the mainland... hence they never tried to breach the islands' natural protective barrier. Elizabeth had her own theory.

"Mother always told me that God protected us and that this island was a sanctuary that shielded all from the savagery of the natives—as long as we had faith."

"I have faith," said Will. "As God is my witness, I will protect everything I cherish until my dying breath—both of our families, our homes, and our future."

As the last two words escaped Will's lips, he glanced at the bound sailor and instinctively cocked the hammer back on the musket. Elizabeth let out a great yawn and laid her head down in Will's lap. Seconds later, fatigue overcame her fears and she was asleep. Will leaned back against the wall and got as comfortable as the situation would allow. Try as he would, despite everything that had happened, he could not clear his thoughts of the mysterious ship aground off Belle Island. One last muffled shriek from far away in the distance barely reached his ears but instantly got his attention. He gripped the musket tight.

The darkness of the night was soon cast away by the warm rays of the rising sun. Light crept through the chinks of the barracks walls and shone upon Will's face. His eyes flickered open. As soon as he realized where he was, he looked at his bound prisoner and silently cursed the fact that he had allowed himself to fall asleep. The man's chest moved up and down ever so slightly, and Will could hear the breath being drawn in and exhaled from his open mouth. His eyes were shut, but he was still very much alive.

"Elizabeth," said Will softly. "Elizabeth, wake up."

Still weary, she groaned, then slowly came back to life with a gentle roll and a long stretch. Will felt paralyzed from the waist down, as both legs were asleep—the result of Elizabeth's having used them as a pillow.

"Help me to my feet," he said.

They rose up together with Will using Elizabeth as a crutch. He stomped around a bit until the tingling sensation returned to his legs and the paralysis subsided. Still groggy, they cautiously stepped over to check on their mysterious guest.

"The knots are still taut. He looks as if he didn't struggle at all last night," said Will. "Get him some water...I'll ease it down so he doesn't choke."

Elizabeth fetched a dipper from the rain barrel. Will propped the man up while Elizabeth trickled the water down his throat.

"We'll have to leave him here for now. I'll keep him bound and secure the door from the outside."

Gathering up their possessions, they quietly exited the barracks. Will searched the ground until his eyes discovered a wedged-shaped piece of wood near a pile of old logs. He jammed the wedge into the earth under the barracks door to prevent it from opening. He hoped it would be sufficient should the man escape his ropes and be strong enough to attempt to leave.

After sipping a bit of water, Elizabeth let out a cough or two and Will instantly detected the rum on her breath. Apparently, she had gotten into it again during the night while he slept. He said nothing, but slung his musket and satchel and led the way out of the fort.

"Where art thou going?" Elizabeth inquired the second she realized they were not heading down to the shore where the long-boat was beached.

"I think it best that I conduct thee home. I must check on Father, and thou must placate thy mother. I suggest thou remain out of sight and busy thyself with useful and purposeful tasks—tasks that will put thee back in good stead with the Lord in thy mother's eyes."

Elizabeth shot Will a surprised and exasperated glance when she realized she would not be getting what she wanted—to go with him back to the *Repulse*. She was further incensed knowing that her tempestuous acts of sexual persuasion the previous night had not produced, let alone *guaranteed*, the results she desired and had become accustomed to easily obtaining. Angered, but able to control her emotions, she decided against lashing out and took a more sensible approach.

"I do not wish to return home or engage in any activity on behalf of my mother," said Elizabeth firmly. "I cannot take another beating. Let me help thee further thy salvage endeavors. Thou need—"

"Nay, out of the question. Thou cannot avoid thy mother indefinitely. Thou must make amends. It is the only way to restore balance and not raise suspicions that will only further confound an already difficult situation. Let me establish a firmer hold on the thorny matter at hand before we are forced to deal with meddlesome involvement from thy mother. Thou knowest nothing gainful could come from that. I am thinking of the greater good and protection of us all. I know not what treasures or horrors could be released from that ship, and I've only narrowly escaped the menace of that sailor. I prefer to keep both a secret until any potential threat is decreed null. I will not put thee in danger, which is why thou must remain at home—and keep far from the fort. Do I have thy pledge on that?"

Her ire, temporarily restrained by a thin layer of reason, made her sigh mightily and walk a few steps ahead of Will. When Elizabeth turned to face him, they both stopped.

"Agreed. I will obey thy wishes," she said. "Mother likes to pray at this early hour of the morning before commencing her daily chores. She often journeys to a spot down by the water's edge not far from our cabin. Methinks her conversation with the Lord will be long of breath this morning. Chances are good we will not cross paths immediately."

Will nodded, and they resumed walking.

The trail leading from Fort Hope to the Eustis home wound downward along gently sloping ground that hugged the western shoreline. The path offered spectacular views of the ocean and the mainland—particularly the sacked settlement of Falmouth Neck. Parts of the trail provided excellent vantage points from which Will routinely looked out for ships, guarded against potential threats, and generally searched for any signs of activity on the Neck. It was a clear morning, and as the two made their way, Will gazed out over the water and began calculating time and distance back to the *Repulse* so he could catch the tide at its lowest point of the day. Satisfied after a moment's thought on the matter, his attention shifted sharply to the sound of a muffled voice approaching them. Both he and Elizabeth stood stock-still as they strained to determine the source of the spoken words.

"That's mother!" said Elizabeth, and without a second's hesitation, she dashed into the woods and out of sight.

And before Will could even react, the unmistakable and irascible image of Winnie Eustis traipsing toward him filled his entire field of vision. She spotted him immediately, and her incomprehensible mutterings soon transformed and exploded into a loud verbal tirade that was clearly and indisputably directed at him.

"William Estes!" she boomed. "Where is my daughter?"

Temporarily at a loss for words, Will debated whether a cordial greeting was in order first before blurting out a response to Winnie's demanding inquiry. His reticence was not appreciated, and the old woman came after him again.

"Where is she? It is time for both of thee to face God and repent for thy sins. She has the Devil in her, and I will cast him out with all the power of the Lord's teachings at my disposal. And *thee*...thou art not the God-fearing influence she needs. Thou art full of sin and wicked thoughts of lust when in her company. Thou hath spiritually and physically driven the innocence and purity from her body...nay, from her very soul. Eons ago, back in Salem, the church, the community elders, and even thy closest Puritan neighbor would not have tolerated such comportment and would have commenced the most stringent of actions to purge thee of such immoral wickedness. Admit thy sins, William, or fear the example of God's justice as meted out upon the witches of Salem in the year of our Lord 1692. Let the happenings of that time forever be stitched upon the fabric of thy soul!"

Will moved not a muscle and kept unflinching eye contact with Winnie during her assassination of his character in the eyes of God. As she fell silent and relaxed her posture, Will tempered his stance, put down the musket, and crossed his arms to show that he would not be bullied by an elderly woman whom he truly felt had gone mad.

"I know not of Elizabeth's whereabouts, Mrs. Eustis," said Will. "I last saw her yesterday when she assisted me in mending my nets. They are a fright to behold and needed much attention if their usefulness in capturing fish is to continue."

"Lies—nothing but untruths from both of thee! She's at the fort, is she not? She is hiding from me in that accursed shelter... and thou were there with her last night weren't thee? Thou surely were not tending to the needs of thy father. It was I who was burdened with those duties. I fed and sheltered Cyrus when his wanderings brought his growling innards to my door...and when I escorted him home and put him to bed, thou were nowhere to be found. Why was that, William? Were thou off committing debaucheries with my daughter?"

"I would never engage in sinful activities with Elizabeth—not out of wedlock. It was late when our work was complete, and Elizabeth insisted she did not require me to escort her home. Upon her departure, I deemed it necessary to journey to Fort Hope to retrieve fresh powder and flint for my musket. After being delayed there longer than I had hoped, I found myself too weary to venture home. I slumped down on a pile of hay in the barracks and did not awaken until this morning's first light. I assure thee, Elizabeth was not by my side. I sense she has run terribly afoul of thee."

"I confronted her in a most irritable but justified manner last evening. She became annoyed and absconded from our home. She has undoubtedly fled to the other side of the island and slept on the beach again, of this I am now certain," Winnie said. "I am without question that she now hides in the woods, gleefully neglecting her chores. And William, thy selfishness and irresponsibility toward thy father astound me. Thou constantly puts thine own wants before those of others, especially thine enfeebled father. Shame, William, shame on thee and the malevolent forces that compel thee to neglect the needs of others. Thou art perilously close to losing God's favor for all eternity if thou doth not change thy ways."

Will lowered his head as thoughts of his father in a helpless state entered his mind. At times he *was* neglectful and did put his own desires and duties above all else, but he couldn't help but believe all his actions were for the ultimate benefit of the two families' survival. Nevertheless, Winnie's tongue-lashing continued.

"It is time for thee to accept God's vision for this community to thrive. Thou must pick up the Bible more than the musket or the hook and line. Thou must return to my classroom and resume thy lessons that once so easily captivated thee. Thy thirst for knowledge was unquenchable...thine *and* Elizabeth's. What happened? What happened to my two precious students whom I taught to read and write? What happened to that desire to learn about the world God made for us? I always envisioned thee returning to Massachusetts Bay and furthering thine education by trumpeting God's word at Harvard. And what of God's teachings? Of late thou hath become as neglectful of my preachings as thou hath of my lessons. When art thou going to devote thyself fully to God and endeavor to build the grand church we so desperately need here?"

Winnie then began to gesture wildly and quote random Bible verses that seemed to make no sense and only emphasized her lunacy. At this point in her lecture, Will went against his true feelings and decided to employ a different strategy in order to halt the old woman's blathering.

"Thou speak the truth, Mrs. Eustis, and thy words shall be heeded with the utmost attention," Will interjected. "We are truly blessed by the Lord to have such wisdom and leadership bestowed upon us from thy teachings. I shall endeavor to improve my wicked ways by following thy good example. In time, together we will restore the virtue that Elizabeth has lost, and convert her into the very model of an ideal Puritan woman. I shall be an archetypal example for her to follow, and one day, we will all attend services in the newly erected church that will reign supreme on this island—an island that will flourish with a healthy Puritan community."

Will's words, as empty as they were, positively impressed Winnie and even generated a smile on her typically dour face. He had set the hook and was now poised to pull in his catch.

"I thank thee, Mrs. Eustis, for thine inspiring words. With help from God, I am sure to see the light. As a token of my appreciation for thy divine wisdom, I shall bring thee more fresh fish than ever before. The sea will provide a bounty unlike anything feasted on in the past. It is my gift to thee. In return, I must ask a small favor. Would thou be so kind as to see to the needs of my father whilst I am at sea today? He is easily occupied for hours with menial tasks, and it would be of tremendous benefit to know he is in thine—and God's—care this day. Also, fear not concerning Elizabeth and her whereabouts. She is no doubt safe and I will find her, impart thy wisdom upon her, and return her home unharmed and wiser. I pray thou will show kindness and leniency toward her...as God would."

Winnie sighed loudly, and a grim look crept across her face, but she nodded affirmatively.

"I will travel to thy cabin and look after Cyrus. Perhaps he can assist me with collecting firewood. Godspeed, William. May thy day on the water be a bountiful one...and I pray thou art a man of thy word."

Winnie turned and started back down the trail away from

Will. After a few steps, she turned once more and said, "Beware, William Estes. The Devil is in that daughter of mine...beware...or suffer the same fate as she." With that, the old woman resumed her trek and was soon out of sight.

Will let out a breath of relief and shook his head before glancing off in the direction of Elizabeth's retreat a few minutes earlier. He picked up his musket and began to dwell on the conversation that had just transpired. He wondered if he had said and done the right thing. He was not skilled in the fine arts of deception, and was a firm believer in honesty, which he felt built integrity; but lately he had found himself seduced more and more by lies. He wondered if the Devil *was* influencing his judgment.

"Thou may safely reveal thyself. She has departed toward home," Will said, talking to the air. A rustling sound preceded the reappearance of Elizabeth.

"I assume thou were privy to that entire conversation?" Will asked.

"Yes, I heard."

"I have no doubt thy mother will forgive thee. I suggest we go back together. No harm will come to thee in my presence. Together we can placate thy mother until the anger toward thee is fully driven from her," reasoned Will.

"Perhaps," Elizabeth replied sullenly in a preoccupied tone of voice. She looked off at the ocean for several minutes before Will decided to get moving.

"Let's be off, then. The morning is waning and time is precious," he said.

They continued down the trail until the Eustis cabin came into sight. Still a short distance away, Elizabeth stopped in her tracks. She tugged Will's arm, halting his advance and pulling him back in line with her. They surveyed the cabin's exterior, looking for signs of activity—looking for Winnie.

"I see no smoke wafting from the chimney," said Will, "nor do I smell any food cooking. I would surmise she has gone straight to my cabin, to my father."

He and Elizabeth entered the cabin and confirmed it was empty. Elizabeth walked over to the fireplace and used her fingers to scrape soup residue from the cooking kettle still suspended over a now dead fire.

"I must get about my business," said Will. "Please thy mother, Elizabeth. Be useful this day. Make her proud of the work thou will accomplish, and all will be set right again. Have no fear. She will not hurt thee, I promise that."

"I will take thy word and heed thy advice," replied a disinterested Elizabeth, her back again turned to Will.

"Good, I will summon thee at a later time once I have the answers I desire. Simply concentrate on keeping thy mother happy, and go about daily routines as if nothing out of the ordinary has occurred these past few days. And stay away from the fort. That, of course, requires no explanation. Remember, I love thee…my dearest. And I will make our lives more fruitful…as God is my judge," he said with enthusiasm and a broad smile.

Elizabeth slowly turned around. She looked at him with her head tilted and her face devoid of expression. Her eyes wandered and didn't meet his. Will's smile slowly faded with her lack of response or any measure of gratitude acknowledging his declaration of love and assurance of their future happiness.

"Indeed," was Elizabeth's sole reply after an awkward pause. Her eyes finally fell into line with Will's, but her face remained oddly devoid of warmth and feeling. At best, she appeared aloof.

Not understanding what her vague, one-word reply meant, Will decided it was best not to let another syllable slip from his tongue. He tipped his hat in a gentlemanly manner, then turned and left without uttering a sound. As he walked away, he felt strange. He wondered why he had felt compelled to tip his hat; moreover, he wondered why a woman he loved so much—a woman he had known all his life, had intimate knowledge of, and wanted to marry—could make him feel so denigrated and insecure with so few words or actions. There was a mystery about Elizabeth, a murky, nameless quality that Will was reluctant—and sometimes afraid—to explore.

Upon reaching his own home, Will did indeed find Winnie looking after Cyrus. Smoke was drifting out of the chimney, and Will
could detect the faint aroma of cooking in the air. Cyrus was busy
collecting dead tree limbs and ample-sized sticks from the ground
while Winnie sat on a stump mending a pair of breeches. Will
approached his father and saw that he was smiling and appeared
in good spirits while performing his humble task. He spoke a few
encouraging words to the old man, which were acknowledged
with a happy grunt that put Will at ease. Turning his attention
to Winnie, he found her to be a bit more lucid and made sure to
sing her praises with several grateful and flattering comments
that always included complimenting the Lord. He told Winnie that
he had spoken with Elizabeth and that she was safe and sound.
He lied and said that she was sorry for being difficult and was
going to work extra hard during the day to make amends. Winnie
seemed satisfied and showed no further ill feelings toward her
daughter that would suggest she might employ physical violence
against her.

After taking time to eat, Will gathered up his satchel and
musket and headed back up the trail to Fort Hope. Passing by the
Eustis cabin, he paused, wanting to see Elizabeth again. He wanted
to talk with her and know that she was all right. He almost found
himself going to the door, but he didn't. Somehow he felt another
conversation would be disastrous—even with comforting news
concerning Winnie's improved frame of mind. So he did what he
considered best and continued on toward the fort.

The return up the trail seemed eerily different this time.
As Will walked along, he constantly stopped and turned around.
He felt as though he was being followed and his every movement observed. The sounds of the rolling ocean lapping against
the shore, the smell of the salty wind gusting through the woods,
and even the melodies of the birds singing and tweeting around in
the treetops all seemed normal, yet Will felt strangely uneasy. His
pace quickened and his head swiveled left and right. His thoughts
returned to the mysterious shrieks that had assaulted his ears
the night before. Visions of marauding Abenaki natives on the
warpath filled his head again as he pondered the likelihood of a

daytime ambush. He knew there was virtually no way to defend himself against superior numbers and understood that any native incursion on Storm meant only one thing for the tiny settlement: total obliteration. His pace accelerated to a vigorous trot.

Panting and almost completely out of breath, Will arrived back at the gates of Hope. His mind still awash with a sense of dread, he pushed open the doors and raised his musket before slowly approaching the barracks. When he drew close enough, he could see that the wedge had not been disturbed. He dislodged it and yanked the door open. As the sunlight beamed in, he pointed his weapon in the direction of the mattress. His heart pounded wildly and the surge of adrenaline nearly caused him to inadvertently pull the trigger. To his relief, the injured sailor was still bound in the same position, and looked as if he had barely moved at all. He was still unconscious but alive. Will forced a little water down his throat and checked to see if he was still properly restrained. Satisfied that the man was still unable to move upon awakening, Will swiftly exited and jammed the wedge back under the door.

Before leaving the fort, he entered the front blockhouse and retrieved a short mast and a furled sail. He secured the gate and carefully lugged the heavy load down to the shore where the longboat waited. The mast was erected and secured in place at the center of the boat, and the shabby sail was unfurled.

"Tide should be near the right level," he said as he looked toward the sun, boarded the boat, and shoved off. He hoisted the sail and manned the tiller, setting course for the wrecked *Repulse*. The wind was strong and propelled the vessel along much faster than if he had been forced to row. Will felt more at ease now. He always felt safe on the water and was excited to finally get on board the mystery ship that had consumed much of his recent contemplations.

Luck is with me today, he thought.

Back on shore, atop the cliff and lurking just behind the tree line, a pair of probing eyes watched the longboat sail out of sight. With silent precision, a shadowy figure moved away from the cliff's edge and stealthily approached Fort Hope's main gate. Upon entrance, and after quick examination of the two blockhouses, the barracks became the point of interest. Step by step, the figure crept closer to the building until the door wedge was within reach and carefully removed. With chary manipulation of the latch, the door gently swung open.

Inside, the furtive individual, fully draped under a long and thick black bear's pelt, skulked around the stacks of salvaged goods until the bound sailor became the center of all attention. The open door allowed plenty of sunlight to pour inside the gloomy space, allowing the mysterious figure to kneel down and properly view the bound enigma who still lay unconscious. A hand emerged from the thick pelt, reached out, and touched the man's face and then his bare chest all the way down to his abdominal wound. The hand was then joined by another that reached up and pulled back the hood from the individual's head, bringing light to the face. The heavy pelt then fell completely to the floor, thus revealing the identity of the visitor.

"Who art thou?" whispered a soft and distinctly feminine voice. "What secrets doth thou possess hidden in thy beating heart and buried away in the depths of thy soul? Tell me," demanded the voice of the one person previously warned to stay away from the unknown dangers tied up inside the barracks at Fort Hope—it was the voice of defiance.

Receiving no answer and realizing the state of the injured sailor had not changed since she'd last seen him, Elizabeth rose to her feet and began stripping off her Puritan habiliments. A moment later, she stood entirely naked before the man. For several minutes, she stared and posed as if she expected him to miraculously come to life, if only to expound upon her beauty, which, in her eyes, he surely would be captivated by. Her wish left unfulfilled, she reached for her common dress, hung up and now dry from the previous night's washing. She slipped it on.

The fireplace still had some hot embers buried under leaden

ash, and with the addition of some kindling, Elizabeth nurtured a new blaze to life. She relit the lantern as well and hung it over the sailor. She went out to the rain barrel and filled buckets with fresh water that she brought back inside to heat in the kettle over the fire should she desire another warm bath. Under her animal skin disguise was a bag she had brought along. It was filled with clothes that needed stitching and several books that belonged to Winnie.

At first she busied herself with some light mending and preparations for candle making, but her mind soon drifted with thoughts of a less constructive and more salacious nature. To distract herself, she wandered around the small courtyard, meandering in and out of the blockhouses in search of anything that caught her fancy. Inevitably, she found herself right back in the barracks, where she helped herself to liberal amounts of rum, stopping only when she felt a bit lightheaded. Next, her interests turned to the stockpile of salvaged goods, which she perused over and over until her fascination with the mostly worthless trinkets wore off. Ignoring the more useful consumables such as the treacle, tea, salt, and sugar, she poured herself another drink and sat down at the table with several books retrieved from her bag. One book in particular always held her attention, and it was the one she prized the most. It was thick and well worn. Most of the pages were frayed and several were loose. The cover showed so much wear that the title was completely illegible. None of that mattered to Elizabeth, however. She opened it up and marveled at every page.

It was an art book comprised of colorful and creative renderings of European aristocratic lifestyles, elegant fashions, pageantry, and excess that emphasized the power of wealth and nobility. Captured in vivid paintings, many notable monarchs were featured in this book dressed lavishly in frilly garments and fine silk robes that were accessorized with sparkling jewelry crafted from a dizzying array of precious gems set in princely amounts of gold and silver. There were pages illustrating extravagant banquets held in grand halls with a sea of guests seated at colossal oak tables heaped with platters of roasted meats, trays of golden, freshly baked breads, bowls of colorful fruit in ample varieties, goblets of fine wines and ales, and lusciously decorated desserts featuring an endless selection of towering cakes, dark puddings, and plump pies. Many other settings were depicted, as well, all of them showcasing beauty, extravagance, and an opulent way of life most could only dream of.

Elizabeth obsessed over each page and was keenly familiar with every image and every detail. She imagined what royalty felt like and fantasized of a life of unmatched abundance and boundless leisure. She savored the idea of the power of governance that came with the entitlement of nobility. She often lost herself for hours in this book, praising the kind of life it portrayed while silently cursing her own.

Eventually, her attention was drawn back to the sailor. The more she watched him, the more her fear subsided and was gradually replaced with a burgeoning sense of desire. She couldn't help but find him intriguing and attractive. Her exposure to the male sex had been extremely restricted in her adolescence, and virtually nonexistent in her young womanhood. Men were largely a mystery to her. As her mind and body developed and matured, questions driven by unusual and intense feelings abounded, but Elizabeth found precious few answers even when she occasionally dared to ask her mother about the mostly taboo subject of men. What she *did* discover had come exclusively from Will and no others—the unfortunate result of an isolated existence. Now she found herself with a unique opportunity, and she was determined not to waste it.

It started innocently in the guise of simple aid—washing his face and chest with a soft cloth saturated with soap and warm water. She curiously placed one ear over his heart and listened to it beat. She wiped away all remaining traces of blood, soil, and perspiration around his wound. The area near the stitches was still badly discolored and swollen, but in Elizabeth's estimation, it had slightly improved since the last time she'd seen it. She touched it gently, making small circles with her fingers around the wound. The sensation of touching another man's skin sent a pleasurable tingling down her fingers, and she slowly enlarged the imaginary circles she was drawing. Soon it was not just her fingers, but her entire hand that stroked the sailor's bare chest and face.

Suddenly, a surge of energy and courage ripped through her body, igniting a flame of erotic desire unlike anything she had ever experienced. It swept over her like a rogue wave tremor. The fleshly stimulation, entangled with her fear of the man and the dangers of the unknown, intoxicated Elizabeth with raw emotion, physical yearning, and a recklessness she found irresistible. The rum she had imbibed earlier had most certainly lowered her inhibitions, but she was blissfully unaware of its full effects. She longed to untie the ropes...or, at the very least, loosen them. This would surely escalate her fears and heighten the sensations of pleasure and excitement even more.

Acting on sheer impulse, but finding the ropes too difficult to loosen, she shifted her trembling hands to the man's breeches. She unbuttoned them with no thought or regard for decency, and with one mighty tug, the breeches were pulled down to his knees. Elizabeth cupped her hands over her mouth as her heart pounded wildly and her eyes grew to the size of hen's eggs. The warm, moistening lust between her legs signaled an urgency and desire she had not felt since the very first time she had lain with Will.

She could control herself no longer. It began slowly, almost timidly at first, but the pure sensuality of the situation overcame all inhibitions. She rubbed, kneaded, fondled, and groped, wishing the sailor's slumbering member would miraculously awaken and service her in the fashion her fiery loins desired. She climbed atop him, but dismounted when she realized the thick ropes binding his hands and feet together impaired her ability to straddle him properly.

Frustrated but undeterred, she hurriedly hunted for a blade that would slash through ropes and allow her the sexual pleasure she so desperately craved. It was not to be, however. Her frenzied search was fruitless, and her need was all-consuming. She rushed back to the man and resumed her aggressive fondling. The excitement built to new heights and Elizabeth cried out in pleasure, finally triggering a climax by her own hand.

She collapsed onto the floor and lay motionless with a thousand thoughts racing through her mind like the blood thumping through her heart. The moment of bliss passed, and her gasps of satisfaction were soon replaced with normal breaths. She got to her feet. Upon looking at the lifeless sailor again, she no longer felt consumed with feelings of lust. In fact, a sense of modesty intruded, and she promptly secured his breeches around his waist and buckled his belt. She wiped his cheeks with the damp cloth and placed a small kiss on his forehead.

Calmer now, she returned to the table, where she rediscovered her book. Getting lost in its colorful pages, Elizabeth let time slip by. Neglecting her more pressing responsibilities, she exerted herself only when she needed to pour more rum into her cup. Her thoughts did wander concerning Will's adventures of the day. She briefly pondered where he was and what he might be discovering—as well as how, when, and where she could properly reunite with him to allay all suspicion and cast herself in the best possible light.

"He can be such a fool...like all men are, I suppose," she muttered, turning a page. "Filled with irrational notions of family, common toil, and the pursuit of simple happiness. What does he really know? I shall enjoy reaping the rewards of his labors concerning that ship...that beautiful ship."

"Stay...away...from that ship."

Elizabeth recoiled in horror at the chilling words from behind her. Instantly, she wheeled around and met two sinister, glaring eyes staring back at her.

The raspy voice continued, "Avoid that vessel at all peril, or prepare to yield thy soul to the blazes of the infernal regions...for all eternity."

Struck dumb with terror, Elizabeth could only sit and tremble at the ominous sight in the corner. The injured sailor was awake!

CHAPTER 5

Boarding the Repulse

Will sidled the longboat up against the starboard side of the *Repulse.* The tide was low, and the gently rolling sea was pleasantly calm. He tied up the craft and reached for the tangled rigging hanging over the side that would provide the easiest access aboard. But before he started his climb up, his eyes were drawn back down into the water. They settled on a dark object, partially submerged and undulating with the tide. He fished it out of the sea with an oar and sloshed it down over the gunwale of the longboat. At first he thought it was a waterlogged blanket or a dark coat, but upon further inspection, it proved to be neither.

"That's a flag," he muttered.

He held up the sodden black standard, looking for signs indicating country of origin or military significance. What he discovered was much more astonishing. In one corner was a white, laughing human skull missing several teeth. Beneath it were two crossed cutlasses, each dripping with bright-red blood. These images and what they undoubtedly represented was both chilling and intimidating, even to Will, who had seen them in picture books.

Pirates! he thought. He looked back up at the *Repulse* and wondered if he was truly about to board a pirate ship. Where exactly was its port of origin? Was it indeed a stolen English vessel? Had it been fleeing from and unwillingly forced to engage the now sunken *Firefly*? And what was it protecting that had compelled its captain to risk everything in battle with a larger and more heavily gunned man-of-war? A dozen other questions entered Will's head before his mind settled on the realization that there could be something of tremendous value still on board—and as long as the ship was firmly aground and still intact, he had a good chance of recovering whatever lay hidden in its main hold. It was time to get some answers.

Will slung his musket and satchel, then climbed up the rigging and set foot on the upper deck. He had to balance himself with each step due to the list of the ship. He moved cautiously aft, taking in everything he could lay eyes on. He wondered if the ship had been razeed during an earlier time, as the top deck was devoid of a forecastle, a stern castle, a pilot's cabin, and other more subtle features commonly associated with such sailing vessels.

The deck was in shambles, strewn with shattered rigging, charred and mangled wood fragments of all sizes, warped shards of metal, and broken glass. There were also various weapons— mostly swords, daggers, and pistols—scattered about. Several of the deck guns were damaged and lay askew, the barrels blown clear off their carriages and trunnions. Will also spied several mounted swivel guns that appeared undamaged, but heavily used. Despite all the debris he had been expecting to discover, there was one thing oddly absent—bodies. Not a one...and scarcely a drop of blood or other indication of human remains...anywhere.

He warily continued aft, abruptly stopping amidships to look down through the massive wooden-grated hatch that covered the huge opening to the main hold. The wood was damaged, which allowed a better view inside. Will peered down into the hold, cursing both the angle of the sun and the ship's list, which hindered his ability to penetrate the darkness and see what lay deep down at the bottom. After a few moments of intense scrutiny, coupled with the *ker-plop!* of a cannonball fragment he dropped down below, Will realized the hold was flooded to a fairly high level, even at a time when the tide was near its lowest. Whatever foodstuffs or goods rested at the bottom—wrecked, ruined, or otherwise— were safely concealed for the time being.

Though frustrated and a bit disheartened, his attention was soon drawn to an odd sight. He walked over to the base of the mainmast. Stuck peculiarly in the ship's foremost spar, at about eye level, were two wooden arrows. The arrowheads were fashioned from flint, and the shafts were fletched with eagle feathers. Will looked down, and at his feet was what appeared to be a strip of torn leather leggings caught on a protruding iron hook. He plucked it free and closely examined the piece of material along with one of the arrows. Both were undeniable evidence of recent Abenaki encroachments. The arrows were almost identical to some Will had seen embedded in the skeletal remains of numerous bodies still littering the overgrown fields of Falmouth Neck.

A bolt of fear ripped up and down his spine. He now held in his hand indisputable proof that native savages had been aboard and were possibly still lurking in the area. He wondered how many and just how brazen they were...and, more importantly, had they managed to defeat the currents ringing the islands and successfully come ashore in strength? His thoughts went back to the shrieks heard the previous night. Had they snuck aboard in the darkness? What did the arrows mean? Were they a message...a warning of sorts?

He made his way to the quarterdeck with his musket at the ready should any form of danger decide to reveal itself. He entered the ship and meandered through twisted piles of battle-damaged refuse to find the Great Cabin. He felt that would be the best place to find answers.

Upon locating the captain's quarters, Will entered through the remains of a doorway that looked as if it had been struck heavily by cannon fire. To the rear of the cabin were shattered windows and gaping holes in the stern that had been shot away. Will imagined a few well-aimed cannon blasts were responsible for the damage. On the floor was a morass of detritus—pewter plates and cups, navigational brass dividers, a scale and troy weights, sheet music, a mangled violin and bow, brass candelabra, books and maps, empty bottles of varying shapes and sizes, quill pens, a blanket, two damaged pistols, and an array of other sundries, most of which had been destroyed in the battle or robbed of their usefulness through exposure to the elements. There was even some rotting meat in the corner covered with flies and emitting a foul stench.

Will searched for the ship's log and manifest. He examined several paper scrolls and parchments but found little of any significance. He also became keenly aware that there was nothing of meaningful value lying about in the cabin—no gold or silver, no princely garments, precious gems, or treasured consumables like tobacco, rum, salt, sugar, or exotic spices. If anything, the Great Cabin generated more questions than it answered. Will began to understand that if the *Repulse* was in fact a pirate ship, presumably of Royal Navy origin, and stolen, then perhaps it had been to the captain and crew's advantage to destroy all the routine nautical records to help prevent incrimination if captured.

Will exited the quarters and worked his way further below-decks. He stepped down into the poorly lit lower deck and found himself in knee-deep water. He slogged around carefully amid the flotsam, making his way toward the submerged hatch that led to the main hold. He was pleased to discover that the wooden grates that covered it had been dislodged, leaving a big opening that he could easily fit large objects through—including himself. A radical idea came to mind, and he returned to the Great Cabin and removed his satchel, hat, and boots. He propped his musket in a corner and returned to the lower deck.

At the edge of the hatch, he took a number of deep breaths and plunged into the cold, murky water. Almost instantly, his body went numb as he recklessly dove into the hold. He swam down for what felt like an eternity despite the vessel's reasonably shallow draft. He quickly reached the bottom and began mindlessly groping for anything that felt like a box, sack, chest, cask, or barrel. At first there was nothing save what he perceived was the ship's inner hull; then his hands slid over a hard and jagged mass that jutted upwards. He had discovered the rock formation on the ocean floor that had impaled the *Repulse* during battle. He swam away from it and toward the stern, thinking that the impact and the list of the vessel could have shifted the hold's contents down and aft, away from the bow.

As the frigid seawater numbed and gnawed at his bones and the absence of air began to impact his brain and lungs, Will surged forward with one last mighty push. And just when the physical stresses on his body began to threaten his life, he finally put his hands on several large boxlike objects that felt like cargo chests. His right hand then brushed against a small, round, and weighty object resting on the bottom. He was barely able to scoop it up with his numb fingers, but he managed to tuck it into a pocket of his breeches.

Courage would have propelled him to investigate further, but his time was up. His body needed air or he would surely drown, forever entombed in a watery grave. He sprang upwards and swam hard through the blackness until his hands hit wood. Frantically, he felt about for the opening to the hold. Disoriented by the darkness and sapped of strength by the cold water, panic set in and he nearly lost consciousness. His body began to sink back into the frigid and foreboding depths, but just as his eyes began to close for good, a glimmer of light came into focus. With his last bit of strength, Will kicked and lunged for it until his head punched through the surface. With a mighty gasp and several choking coughs, he regained enough energy to pull himself out of the hold and back into the knee-deep water of the lower deck. As he looked about, he saw a ray of sunlight shining through a damaged section of the hull and illuminating the opening of the hold just enough to light his way out. However, what he saw next was unnerving.

Now present on the lower deck and bobbing horizontally in the shallow water were three bodies. Bloated and white as ghosts, the corpses had presumably been freed from the depths of the hold during Will's explorations, or perhaps they had simply gone unnoticed prior to his plunge. Regardless, he was in no shape to investigate further.

He sat on the edge of the hatch coughing and shivering, not yet fully realizing how fortunate he was to be alive. Though out of immediate danger, he still needed to get topside before the icy water drained all the vitality from his body. He pulled himself up and staggered back to the Great Cabin, where he retrieved his belongings before collapsing in the sunniest spot he could find on the quarterdeck. He lay there still shivering, with his eyes closed, and took a moment to praise the Lord for blessing him with such a warm day.

Will soaked up the sun. It both dried and reenergized him, driving the watery chill from his body and soul. He dozed off several times under the warm blanket of sunlight. When his strength returned, all thoughts of pursuing further scavenging quickly abandoned him when he saw that the ocean had churned to life. Choppy whitecaps, whipped up by the wind, danced on the surface of the water as the tide began to rise. Will could feel the *Repulse* beginning to rock ever so gently with the intensifying sea, and decided it was not safe to remain aboard much longer. He couldn't risk an injury from a freak accident alone aboard an unstable ship. Besides, he needed to devise a proper plan to recover whatever useful or valuable loot lay hidden in the depths of the *Repulse*'s hold. It was also getting late, and he knew he could not go another day without filling his boat with fish. The mysteries of the *Repulse* would have to go unsolved a bit longer.

Taking a few moments to search the top deck for useful supplies or precious foodstuffs, Will eventually gave up after finding nothing worthwhile. He climbed down into the longboat and hoisted his sail. He set a course for his favorite fishing grounds and prepared his hooks and lines for a bountiful haul. He watched the *Repulse* slip from view as he sailed away, thinking about how he could recover whatever treasures lay hidden in its gloomy, flooded innards. Ironically, it was not treasure or material wealth that filled his thoughts—he had no use for money, or anything to purchase with it—but raw materials and food that could improve and prolong life on Storm Island. His ideas of riches came in the form of forged metal tools, rope, lumber, wooden pegs, iron spikes, nails, cloth, window glass, tar, and resin. However, he was most distraught at the lack of food aboard the ship, particularly seeds. He had hoped to find seeds with which to plant fresh crops and grow new life into Storm.

Some of the materials he dreamed about could easily be scavenged from *Repulse*'s decks at a later time, but others he feared would rot or rust away, trapped in a watery tomb forever. It was at this point that Will's frustration clouded his thoughts. He had to adjust his heading several times after straying off his initial course—the result of a distracted mind. As the boat rocked and swayed in the choppy sea, Will had to sit and stand several times to steady the small vessel and adjust the sail accordingly. As he did this, he became acutely aware of the weight in his pocket. He had completely forgotten about the small item he had hastily snaffled while submerged in the hold. He reached into his pocket and carefully brought its contents to light.

He sat there in awe as the object caught and reflected the sunlight. He had never held anything like it in his life, and knew nothing about its origins, but he was certain of one thing: In his hand was a gold coin. He studied the specie carefully, flipping it over repeatedly. One side was dominated by what looked to be a crown over an ornate shield, which Will took to be a symbol of royalty. On the edge was the name *Philip V.* The other side of the coin had a large cross on it that Will immediately associated with religion...plus one very interesting marking—a date.

"1714," he muttered.

After a moment of thought, he decided that the coin was probably of Spanish origin. He began to reminisce about earlier years when his father was of sound mind and would tell him stories of the warring nations of Europe, about how the English, French, Spanish, and Dutch sought to control the world through colonization and exploitation of conquered territories wealth. Cyrus had told him about gold and silver, and how the whole world longed for it. He'd shown him pictures of mighty Spanish galleons and spoken of the vast amounts of riches they hauled back to Spain from the seemingly endless tropical locales scattered throughout the New World. Will felt sure that a tiny fragment of those riches now rested in his hand. Try as he might, though, he could not come up with the word his father had used so many times to describe coinage of this nature. Finally, he remembered and said it aloud.

"Doubloon."

In that moment, Will's thoughts shifted in a more radical and far less practical direction. It was as if he had been infected by a potent and all-consuming disease—greed—and all he could think about was gold and how much of it might be within his grasp. He jerked the tiller and nearly brought his small vessel about...back in the direction of the *Repulse*. But fortunately, he regained his senses and sailed onward to his prime fishing spot.

"I cannot *eat* or *drink* gold, nor am I inclined to try. I must fill my belly before I fill my pockets," he said as he furled the sail and cast his first line into the water. "Patience," he mumbled. "Nothing good can come of this unique gift from God without proper reflection and preparation. I must be cautious and mindful...or risk losing everything." Such were his thoughts.

Dusk was soon upon the land and sea as the drowning sun plunged deeper into the western horizon. His boat filled with a healthy catch of cod, Will sailed back to Storm Island, where he promptly beached, took down the mast, and unloaded his fish on the southeast shore. He hurried along with his tasks, as he wanted to be home before dark. He was also anxious to find out what had developed over the course of the day while he was away. After securing his gear and overturning the boat, which he again hid under sand, dry leaves, and tree branches, he gathered the fish in his most durable net and swung the heavy load over his shoulder.

Will struggled along through the woods, his catch weighing down one shoulder and his musket and satchel the other. He made it home without incident, but he was tired and very hungry. Once through the door, he was shocked to find the cabin empty, with a cold fireplace and an empty cooking kettle. He dropped his load, stepped back outside, and looked around.

"Father," he called out repeatedly, searching the crop field and then wandering down near the shore. Returning to the cabin, it struck him that perhaps Winnie was making good on her earlier promise and tending to his father's needs in the comfort of her own home. The thought put Will somewhat at ease. He gathered up the fish, his musket and satchel again, and headed for the Eustis cabin. He hoped Elizabeth was there and that she had been successful in appeasing her mother and resolving their quarrelsome differences amicably.

He was happy to see light in the cabin and smoke billowing from the chimney upon arrival. He called out, and a few seconds later Winnie opened the door and ushered him inside. Sitting by the fire was Cyrus. He perked up and beamed a great smile at the sight of his son.

"Greetings, Mrs. Eustis," said Will. "I have brought thee bountiful rewards from my labors at sea this day. Please help thyself to as many fish as you desire. I shall take no offense if thou wish to procure them all. It was my intention to bless the Eustis home and all its Godly worth fully and abundantly."

"Be praised, William Estes! What a generous catch the Lord has bestowed upon thee today. I shall get to work posthaste. Thy arrival is timely, as I have just finished the current Bible lesson and am ready to start anew. I thought I would revisit the Old Testament and read from the Book of Genesis. Thy father has been entranced with God's words these past few hours, and I suspect thou shalt be as well. Be seated and we shall begin," said Winnie firmly.

"Perhaps it would be better if we tended to the catch before sharing the next verses of Holy Scripture. We do not wish to have the Lord's bounty spoil and therefore be wasted, do we?"

"Oh, of course not," Winnie replied agreeably as she went about lighting several crude wooden wall sconces to add light to the chore ahead of them. "Let us all get to work, then. I shall prepare a fire outside adequate to smoke such a large amount of cod."

With that, she exited the cabin leaving Will and Cyrus the unpleasant task of cleaning the fish. Will procured knives, and, as always, with patience and precision, he demonstrated for Cyrus exactly what needed to be done. The old man silently watched and then mimicked Will's actions with astonishing accuracy. They set to work cleaning the fish by separating the guts from the meat. As they labored through the catch, Winnie occasionally returned inside and disposed of the heaps of repugnant guts collected in wooden buckets. She then took the fresh fillets of meat and racked them close to the low-burning fire she'd prepared. Soon the air was filled with the scent of savory smoked cod.

An hour passed before the task was complete. It was dark now, and thoughts of Elizabeth suddenly entered Will's head as he and Cyrus washed up in a bucket of fresh water warmed by the fire. Winnie came back inside.

"Is Elizabeth somewhere dallying about?" asked Will. "Perhaps unsuccessfully struggling with a task thou hast given her this evening? Perhaps a chore that has taken her down to the shoreline and put her behind her time?"

"Thou hath not seen or had any contact with her since we last spoke?" Winnie replied, stopping in place and glaring at Will.

"Nay," Will lied, realizing that Elizabeth had obviously not gone home and reconciled with her mother. God only knew where she was and what she was doing. Terrible thoughts soon seeped into Will's head.

"William Estes, I demand thou take leave immediately and find my wayward daughter! Thou shalt bring her wicked soul back to me before the dawn! I sense the defiant witchery budding within her. The Devil will not make her an unwitting appendage of his ungodly being...to carry out his mischievous wishes and unholy deeds. She is channeling evil and performing black magic in her hours of solitude. Why else would she eschew my company for such prolonged periods of time? Witchcraft...it is the only thing that can describe her unpredictable behavior of late. I shall cast out her demons once and for all, or else she will suffer the same fate of those accused in Salem years ago! And thee, William...thou hast been seduced by her evil tendencies and desires. Though not completely under the Devil's control, thou too must be purged of wickedness before it takes permanent root in thy very soul."

Will stood silent as he locked eyes with Winnie, a bemused look on his face that contradicted the crazed expression on hers. Just then, Cyrus let out a few muffled grunts, which Will knew were an indication of hunger; however, no other sound was uttered or heard save the crackle of the fire under the cooking kettle. It was at this exact moment when young William Estes began to grasp the depth of Winnie Eustis's descent into madness. Again she spoke menacingly of darker times, of years past in that tortured Massachusetts town. Like other scary bedtime tales imparted to him as a child, Will was all too familiar with the happenings in Salem during the year 1692.

Salem had been mentioned on those occasions when Will's childish restlessness prevented him from falling asleep at night. Both his parents and Elizabeth's had witnessed and lived through the Salem witch trials. They had known those initially accused—Sarah Good, Sarah Osborne, and Tituba, the slave of Samuel Parris, the father of one of the afflicted children. The Estes and Eustis families had managed to avoid prosecution, tolerate the constant fear generated by the community, live through the harsh imprisonments, and accept the eventual hangings of those condemned by the court. Overall, it had led them to embrace a more stringent Puritan faith and way of life. In later years, the Salem stories became a useful warning for children prone to wandering off in the woods or skipping out of church meetings. The lesson taught was that evil lurked in the forest and that nobody was safe from the dangers of the Devil and his minions—especially those who did not take God's teachings to heart as laid out in strict Puritan doctrine.

As Will grew older, he adopted a more empirical and less religious view toward life's dangers. He gave more credence to hazards he could address and combat directly such as threats from the natives, food and water shortages, and the unpredictable weather, all of which he deemed more pertinent than the sorcery of witches, ancient Indian curses, or the lack of strict Puritan faith...which he had abandoned long ago. But facing him now was a threat of a different nature, one that embraced the supernatural and all it embodied. Rather than strike at it directly with logic and reason, Will sought a different approach.

"I will find Elizabeth and return her safely," he declared. "However, I cannot guarantee how soon. Whatever malady she suffers, I know it can be better treated with patience and tolerance than with harsh words and harsher actions. I believe we can all benefit from a thorough lesson from the Bible, which I'm positive will purge all sin from our collective souls. I challenge thee to prepare and administer that lesson, Mrs. Eustis. For the time being, please continue thy splendid care of my father, and I will help right all that is wrong. The power of the Lord swells within me. Of this I am sure. I must bid thee farewell...for now. I know not when I will return."

Will slung his satchel and musket and calmly headed for the door, uncertain of the effect his words had had on the disgruntled woman standing before him. He paused and waited for a reaction. Cyrus grunted again and motioned toward the cooking kettle.

"My father is hungry, Mrs. Eustis. Would thou mind serving him some fish?" Will asked politely. "Also, I meant what I said to thee earlier this day. Remember those words. They ring true."

Winnie slowly turned her gaze from Will to Cyrus. Gradually, she came out of her trance and began to set the table. Taking that as an indication of good faith, Will snatched up a lighted candle and opened the door. Just as he started to leave, Winnie spoke again.

"Be wary of inciting God's wrath with empty promises and unfulfilled tasks, William Estes. The Lord has no patience for liars and deceivers. I will pray for thee...I will pray for my daughter... but expect no quarter if thou incurs the Lord's fury with deception and impure actions in accord with the Devil's influence. God's justice is swift—and so is mine."

With those words hanging in the air, Winnie turned away and picked up her Bible—much to Cyrus's dismay. Will frowned and was off, closing the door behind him. He could hear his father whimper and knew the poor old man would have to suffer through another round of preaching before any food was placed in front of him. It pained Will's heart, but he had questions that needed prompt answers.

"If the Devil is at work on Storm Island, it is Winnie Eustis who is under his unsavory spell. Mad...that woman is surely mad," Will muttered as he wrapped up two fillets from the smoking racks in a hand cloth and stuffed the small bundle in his satchel.

The pitiful little candle lit the way through the darkness to the one place where Will knew he was sure to find Elizabeth. His mind raced with a thousand thoughts and emotions concerning his lover and the current state of the injured sailor. Why had she deliberately disobeyed him? What was she doing back at the fort? Had the sailor awakened and managed to free himself? Had Elizabeth fallen victim to rapacious savages or perhaps the sailor himself? What if she *wasn't* there? Then what? And what if he was heading straight into mortal danger himself? The questions mounted, and his step hastened.

CHAPTER 6

Introductions

The absence of moonlight severely hindered Will's progress to Fort Hope. He stumbled and staggered along the trail in the dim candlelight like a drunken man who had lost his way. Irritated but determined, he eventually reached the outskirts of the fort's grounds near the end of the footpath. He could smell smoke in the air. He made his way up to the main gate and saw that the doors were secured. Faint firelight from the courtyard cast a glow above the palisaded wall, making Will's heart pound with nervous anticipation. He snuffed out the candle and put it in the satchel. He then readied his musket and gently pushed on the doors hoping they weren't secured from the inside. Luck was with him, and he was able to peek in.

At the center of the courtyard, a small fire was burning. Next to it sat a solitary figure, slumped over and fully swathed in a bearskin blanket. Unsure of what to expect—for this might *not* be Elizabeth—Will slid around the partially unsecured door, stepped into the open, and trained his musket on the figure.

"Reveal thyself or risk a ball in thy brain," he threatened.

"Will," was the reply.

Then the blanket seemed to stand up on its own, resembling the animal from whence it came. Will took three steps forward as two human hands emerged from beneath the fur and threw the blanket onto the ground. He uncocked the hammer and lowered his gun.

"Why art thou here?" demanded Will, glaring at a very disheveled Elizabeth. "I instructed thee to stay away. Why hath thou so patently disobeyed my wishes and thoughts for thy safety? And what of thine issue with thy mother? How does avoiding her remedy any of that?"

"I was afraid," she said simply. "I could not summon the necessary courage to confront her...try as I might. I was also unsure of thine own wisdom and counsel on the matter, to be honest. I thought it best to seek refuge here, in relative safety and solitude, until such time as we might face her together."

"Did thou at least busy thyself with purposeful tasks that would help ingratiate thyself to her?"

Will let out a sigh as Elizabeth stood there with no response. He gazed about in dismay and saw no indication of industrious toil. As he drew closer to her, the scent of rum became obvious.

"I have seen and spoken with thy mother before coming here. She is quite off her head...and demanding thine. I thought the situation was healing nicely until I inquired about thine absence, with thoughts that thou had made amends earlier. Now she is so enraged that her lunacy has driven her to fits, invoking ideas of witchcraft and demonic influence. I don't dare let thee encounter her alone now."

"Then perhaps thou hath seen the light, Will," said Elizabeth more boldly. "My mother's fiery invective is not confined solely to spouting lengthy Bible verses and cursing sins and sinners. She is capable of inflicting physical harm beyond what is acceptable in God's eyes. I have fallen victim to her abuse, and shall not endure it any further. Thou must understand that, Will."

"We shall proceed cautiously. No harm will come to thee, as I have promised before. Now what is the condition of—"

A shrill cry pierced the walls of the barracks, causing both Will and Elizabeth to stiffen with fear. They looked at each and then at the barracks.

"Water...please...dear lass," said the voice inside.

"He's awake, and thou have been in his company!" said a shocked Will. "Thou did not release him from his bondage... did thee?"

"No!" exclaimed Elizabeth as she rushed forward into Will's arms. "I looked in on him earlier to gauge his recovery...I thought it the moral action to take. He awakened from his injury-induced slumber and spouted nonsensical musings, his mind undoubtedly still weakened by his wound. I became frightened and withdrew down to the shore. I didn't know what to do. I prayed for thy swift return and eventually sought refuge here in the courtyard once the sun went down. The thought of returning home to mother...I...I...couldn't."

"Thou should have heeded my words," scolded Will. "Now, matters are worse...on all accounts."

Elizabeth's head drooped like that of a chastised child when Will released her from their embrace. He sighed heavily and again readied his musket.

"Reach into my satchel and retrieve the candle therein. Use the fire to light the wick," Will said. Elizabeth promptly did as she was told. "Stay behind me. I want no surprises."

They walked over to the barracks. With one swift motion, the door was opened and Will rushed in, the musket barrel pointed toward the stricken sailor. Elizabeth was close behind holding the candle up high.

"Some water please. That is all I require. Please, show some mercy...if thou art English, have pity on a fellow countryman," said a voice obscured in the shadows.

"Light the lamps and build a fire," Will said to Elizabeth. "Inside my satchel is some smoked cod. It shall be our dinner...go and do as I say."

Will kept his gun trained on the shadow lying before him. Slowly the darkness in the room was swept aside, and the form of the captive sailor was brought into full view.

"Englishman?" asked the sailor as his eyes slid up the barrel of the musket and locked onto Will's.

"Of English descent, yes," Will responded gruffly, his gun not moving an inch off target.

"I have no intention of harming thee," said the sailor. "Please remove these ropes...allow me some water and the opportunity to relieve myself before I become inexcusably soiled—which I assure thee will make all our lives extremely unpleasant in these cramped quarters."

"Thine intentions are questionable at best, sir," Will replied, adding, "I seem to remember receiving a much different impression when thy hand and blade were at my throat."

"A regrettable first greeting...and one I wish to take back. But clearly, I was not of sound mind or body, and my violent undertakings mirrored those of a wounded animal in strange surroundings—acting only on an instinct for self-preservation. That is not who or what I am. My mind is sound, and I assure thee I have no malicious intent. Surely thou can understand my earlier unbalanced behavior, considering what I have been through?"

"Perhaps," said Will after a pause. "But my decision remains firm. Thy ropes shall not be removed."

"Could I at least persuade thee to lower thy weapon? A simple child could see that I am of no threat presently."

"As thou wish," said Will as he lowered the musket and stood it against the wall. He glanced over at Elizabeth, who pretended to be occupied with the fire and the food preparations. He noticed her slight trembling and the way she nervously looked over her shoulder in his direction. He could sense her fear and wondered if she could detect his.

"Good. I believe proper introductions are in order, my young friend," said the man. "I am Leftenant Philip Dunsbury of His Majesty's Royal Marines. I was in command of a detachment of twenty marines assigned duty aboard the Royal Navy frigate HMS *Firefly*."

"*His* Majesty? Does not a queen sit upon the English throne?" asked Will.

"Nay, Queen Anne met her demise two years ago. His Majesty King George the First now reigns over Great Britain," answered Dunsbury.

"Great Britain?" asked Will quizzically as he sat down.

"Yes...England has united with Scotland. The union of the two formed the Kingdom of Great Britain."

Will and Elizabeth turned to look at one another with puzzled expressions. Dunsbury noted their apparent lack of knowledge of the happenings in the world and decided to pose some inquiries of his own.

"Who are thee? How long hath thou been here...and where exactly *is* here?"

"My name is William Estes, and this is Elizabeth Eustis," Will said, pointing to Elizabeth, who in turn timidly nodded in acknowledgment. "This is Storm Island in the Province of Maine, governed by the Province of Massachusetts Bay. To our west on the mainland once stood the fishing village of Falmouth...the immediate area was often referred to as 'the Neck' due to its unique topography. The French and the Indians destroyed the village as far back as 1676."

"How did thou come to inhabit this island?"

"Our families were originally from Salem, Massachusetts... Puritans...who escaped from the Church of England's Catholic infestation, which many felt still dominated the 'incomplete' Protestant reforms. My parents were wed in 1677 and left Salem a year later to help resettle and rebuild this area. Elizabeth's parents were also part of that plan, bringing a more religious point of view. Both our fathers helped erect Fort Loyal for defense on the shores of the Neck. My father was a fisherman and Elizabeth's was a carpenter. The new settlement flourished until 1690, when another French and Indian attack destroyed the fort and decimated the area yet again. Our families fled back to Salem aboard a fishing vessel before the savages could get to them. Determined to return and prosper in this land he so passionately loved, my father and my mother returned in 1698 with a band of former settlers to build Fort New Casco and lay the foundation for a more secure and prosperous village...one that would rise from the ashes of the former. I was but a baby at the time."

Dunsbury suddenly coughed and writhed in pain, and Will motioned to Elizabeth. She stepped forward and gave him water, which he gulped down as fast as she could pour it. He thanked her and gestured for Will to continue.

"Things did not go well from the start, and our families suffered for many years. Eventually, information reached us from Boston that another war was afoot. The year was 1703 and I was age six. I remember my father reading the news of Queen Anne and her new territorial war...one that would once again force conflict with the French and Indians encroaching on our lands. As battles raged across Europe, so did the fighting here in the colonies. Falmouth was again ravaged and the whole area beset with death and ruination. Once again, my father cleverly engineered a timely escape, and my family and several others fled across the bay to this island. After unspeakable pain and hardship, we carved out a meager existence and survived. By God's grace, the savages left us alone, but sickness and lack of food did not. Today, only a tiny remnant of the Estes and Eustis families remain."

"And this place?" asked Dunsbury as he looked up and around. "Is this thy home?"

"No. This is Fort Hope. It was the first structure built upon arrival in 1703. Everything brought over from Falmouth was originally stored here. It was built for shelter and protection from the savages and the scourge of the Frenchmen in alliance with them. Fortunately for us, it has never been put to the test."

"Thou hath been here on this island, isolated and alone, since arrival all those years ago?"

"Yes," Will answered vaguely. "We have limited means and have lived under constant threat. I have not seen a ship pass through these waters in years...that is, until the other night, of course."

Dunsbury cried out again in pain and strained to reach for his side but could not place his bound hands near his wound. His agonized face, pale and pouring sweat, turned to Will with a final plea for mercy.

"My friend, show some clemency for a suffering man who has endured more pain and torment than any earthly being could imagine. Undo these ropes and allow me the opportunity to ease the stabbing pangs coursing through my belly. I beg thee, sir. I will not attempt any harm upon either of thee. Thou art Christians. As God is my witness, thou shalt not be in any danger from my weakened hand...please."

Will hesitated and looked back at Elizabeth, who had stopped what she was doing and was worriedly staring at the men. Filled with trepidation, Will reached for the very blade Dunsbury had threatened to drive up into his throat earlier. He could hear Elizabeth draw a sharp breath as he picked up the knife and slowly began to slice through the ropes. Once the final strand was broken, Dunsbury's arms and legs stretched out and immediately relaxed. He moaned in relief as Will stepped back toward the wall, putting himself within easy reach of the musket.

"Didst thou bind my injury?" Dunsbury asked after getting his first real look at Will's stitching.

"Yes. A ball was lodged in the wound. I was able to extract it and knit up thy flesh."

"Thanks are in order...I owe thee an extreme debt of gratitude. Thou hath saved my life, and I am grateful for thy kindness," said Dunsbury. "I must go outside and—"

The stricken marine tried to stand but couldn't. He collapsed on the floor gasping for breath. Elizabeth stepped forward to help, but Will halted her with a raised hand.

"My legs...numb...I cannot..."

Will cautiously helped Dunsbury to his feet using his left arm and the left side of his body for support. In his right hand he retained the knife but kept it out of sight and at the ready. Dunsbury moaned again. He was clearly in considerable pain and in a very weakened state, as evidenced by his near total dependency on Will to keep him on his feet. The two struggled outside into the darkness, where Will helped the lieutenant relieve himself before staggering back inside.

"Most kind," said Dunsbury as he collapsed once more on the mattress. "I must rest a bit," he murmured, closing his eyes and again losing consciousness.

Will sat down at the table making sure his back was not turned to the now sleeping Royal Marine. Elizabeth set two plates of smoked cod and two glasses of rum on the table and sat across from him.

"Why did thou reveal so much to him about us? That could be dangerous," Elizabeth warned. "And why hath thou not restrained him again?"

"He's of little threat. I believe he is who he says he is, and I intend to find out much more about him and the circumstances of his being here. The more trust we offer, the more he'll return. He may be the very key we need to unlock whatever riches lay buried inside that ship out there. And he may be the key to other important information as well," Will said between bites of fish.

"What did thou discover out there today? Did thou recover anything more of value?" Elizabeth asked eagerly.

"I boarded her and ventured belowdecks," Will replied. "Her main hold is severely flooded and shrouded in darkness. I found no manifest or record indicating what she was hauling or her reason for setting sail. In fact, she might not be a vessel of the Royal Navy...or any other navy. She could, in fact, be a merchant vessel previously in the hands of privateers—or even pirates."

Elizabeth's eyes widened at the prospect of a fat merchant vessel laden with rich cargo, aground and just sitting there for the taking. She pressed Will further.

"Surely thou must have found something to supplement and better our existence...food, supplies...something of value?"

Will took another bite of fish. He chewed slowly and glanced away from Elizabeth, who immediately sensed something was amiss.

"What is it? What did thou discover?"

"I found one item of interest resting on the bottom of that watery hold."

Will reached into his pocket and gently placed the golden doubloon on the table. It shimmered in the dim light, and Elizabeth gasped with excitement. She reached over and picked up the coin, examining it closely.

"There could be a substantial fortune in treasure resting in the hold of that stricken ship," theorized Will. "I was unable to determine it for certain, but that coin is encouraging evidence. If the *Repulse* was indeed a vessel commandeered by pirates, only the good Lord knows how much wealth it holds."

"We must go back without delay and find out!" said Elizabeth. "We must salvage whatever we can before it is permanently reclaimed by the sea."

"We cannot be unprepared in this endeavor, Elizabeth. We must proceed cautiously with plan and purpose; otherwise, we risk losing everything. We must gather more information from the leftenant here. We must discover what he knows and how that can be used to our mutual advantage. We must placate thy mother and anticipate any potential resistance she may generate upon learning of this situation. Finally, we must devise a proper and useful recovery plan. Procuring that single coin nearly killed me today."

"I understand," said Elizabeth. She put her hand on Will's cheek and said, "I am so relieved thou were not taken from me today. I do not know what I would do without thee. We will plan accordingly."

Will looked intently at the sleeping Dunsbury and said, "I want to understand what he meant when he warned me to stay away from that ship. He called her the 'Devil's Chariot,' remember? He knows something...and I want to know it, too."

"He sleeps now. It could be dawn before he awakens. What are we going to do?"

"We shall remain here and watch over him until morning... as before. My father is presently in thy mother's care. I told her I would bring thee back to her with the expectation that no harm would come to thee. A holy and lengthy lecture is in store for us upon our return, and we cannot avoid her forever. I will be with thee...I will protect thee."

"What about him...Leftenant Dunsbury?" asked Elizabeth.

"We shall see if his condition changes before morning. Perhaps a constructive conversation can be had before we are forced to return home. He is still very weak and poses little threat; however, I will truss him up again if he gives any indication to the contrary. With a vigilant eye and a hardened fist, I will insure thy safety. For now, let us secure this place from any outside threat and prepare for whatever tomorrow brings."

Together, they set about gathering extra firewood, securing the gate, bringing in water, and doing other tasks needed to pass a comfortable night in the barracks. Elizabeth did some mending by the fire while Will studied the doubloon in detail at the table. As the fullness of night enveloped the land, the silence lulled Elizabeth to sleep by the slowly dying fire. His mind heavy with thought, Will's fatigue gradually overwhelmed his ability to remain awake. He held up the doubloon one last time and yawned before deciding to restrain Dunsbury again. He could not risk the consequences of falling asleep and leaving Elizabeth unprotected. He put the doubloon back down on the table in full view and reached for the rope.

"By the looks of that coin thou possess, she's still afloat. Pity thou boarded her. Now thou also will suffer the same infernal fate as her accursed crew."

Will spun around to find Dunsbury fully awake and staring right at him. Using what little strength he had, the injured lieutenant sat up with great difficulty and rested his back against the wall. Will grabbed the musket.

"Thou doth not need that, boy," said Dunsbury with a sigh. "I told thee I have no intention of inflicting harm upon anyone... especially one who has saved my life. I doubt I could injure a mosquito in my present physical state."

Will sat down at the table. He turned his stool toward Dunsbury, keeping the musket in hand and ready.

"If it's the *Repulse* thou speak of, she's aground," Will replied.

"She's the Devil's ship, bringing death and misery to all who dare cross her wake."

"What doth thou know about that vessel and her secrets? And what of thyself? What is thy story, and how did thee truly come to be *here*...in such a faraway and uncivilized part of the world?"

"Thou wish to hear the horrors of my journey, the terrors of my duties and my past? Thou desire to unleash the demons lurking aboard that unsavory craft? Thou request to hear my story as if I were Odysseus or some other hero of the like?"

"I do not *wish* it, I *demand* it," said Will, his thumb caressing the musket's hammer.

"Thou sound like an educated young man, William Estes," observed Dunsbury. "Perhaps even just a few lessons short of a gentleman. Do not think me a fool. Thou might regret it."

"I do not intend to offer offense or belittle thy past exploits, sir, but considering that thy life would have ended prematurely if not for me, I believe I am entitled to an explanation of sorts," declared Will.

"Very well, I will indulge thy curious nature. Might I trouble thee for some more water and a bite of food before I begin?"

Will retrieved a cup of water and what was left of the smoked cod. He offered it to Dunsbury, who happily devoured both in the blink of an eye.

"On January first in the year 1713, the Queen ordered a small flotilla of Royal Navy ships, including HMS *Firefly*, across the ocean to patrol the coastal waters from French Acadia to Spanish Florida. Our mission was to disrupt, plunder, or destroy enemy shipping that threatened our colonies. We were also assigned to protect British merchant vessels in need upon initial encounter. Well, the tiny fleet was plagued with problems from the day we left port in southern England. Several vessels leaked from improperly repaired battle damage, sickness was rampant, provisions were inadequate, and there was fungus in the water coupled with insufficient levels of grog...and numerous other sailing maladies married to bad weather that slowed our arrival."

Will stayed quiet and listened intently, trying not to appear too eager or fascinated with the story. He casually glanced at Elizabeth and determined she was still asleep. Unfazed, Dunsbury proceeded with the telling of his tale.

"We were compelled to sail south after reaching the shores of French Acadia. The *Firefly* was the only vessel that made the crossing. All the others were forced to turn back to England. We made port once we were offshore of British-held colonial territory. Repairs were slow and impermanent. We were forced back to port time and again, unable to free ourselves from the numerous malfunctions that hampered our ability to carry out our mission. The captain's name was Rostrum—Philius Rostrum—who carried little favor amongst the officers and crew. He was not a particularly good sailor, in my estimation. He made mistakes that could not be disguised...even to the lowest able seaman. We would sail for weeks at a time and never come across another vessel, friendly or otherwise. Rostrum had an uncanny knack for not being where he was most needed or useful. He was fat, pompous, disagreeable, and ignorant to the needs of those he commanded. As the weeks of inactivity turned into months, the crew, bored, sick, and without guarantee of pay, began to get rebellious. There was even talk of mutiny among the officers."

"*Did* the crew mutiny?" Will asked.

"Nay. Rostrum realized that the lack of action was turning all hands against him. He must have sensed the grumblings amongst his naval officers, as he turned to me one day inquiring about where my marine's loyalties lay, as well as my own loyalty toward him. It was clear that Rostrum was becoming more and more dependent on my men to protect him against any mutinous activity from the crew. As elite soldiers, our sense of duty and honor holds us to a higher standard than the average sailor impressed into service for the Crown. Duty demanded we remain steadfast to the captain."

"Were thy Royal Marines forced to act in protection of Rostrum?"

"Nay. Direct and potentially violent confrontation was avoided. One fine and sunny day, Captain Rostrum stood tall on the quarterdeck and made a grand speech to the entire crew. He blatantly and foolishly announced he was going to exceed his orders and sail into the Caribbean to hunt down and engage Spanish warships or capture rich, cargo-laden Spanish galleons. The goal was to fill our hold with captured riches that would support the war effort, ingratiate Rostrum with the Crown, placate the crew, and make our mission a success with a swift return to England. He even decreed that the crew would have equal shares in whatever wealth was brought on board. This was complete disregard for naval policy and made him sound more like a rogue freebooter than a captain in the Royal Navy. The tactic—unorthodox as it was—proved effective. The crew cheered, morale was boosted, and the mutinous scuttlebutt was suppressed."

"Wast thou successful in thine endeavors from that point forward?"

Dunsbury coughed lightly and winced before continuing. "The *Firefly* journeyed into Caribbean waters without incident, though it took much longer than expected due to poor navigational orders from our captain. By then, it was well into the year 1714. Things looked promising at the start, as we were able to capture a few small Spanish cargo vessels carrying sugar, spices, tobacco, and rum. However, it wasn't long before our fortunes changed for the worse. Rostrum's knack for setting ill-advised courses again brought us into endless weeks of isolation on the high seas. The ship's problems resurfaced in force, a storm blew us far north of our intended hunting grounds, and the crew was at the breaking point. It was at this time when I assigned two fully armed marines to escort the captain wherever he went aboard ship. After conferring with his first officer, Rostrum eventually announced he was going to sail south and make port at Nassau on the island of New Providence. We arrived there in March of 1715."

"And what was the outcome of that line of thought by thy Captain Rostrum?"

Dunsbury chuckled a bit—which led to a loud fit of coughing that slowly diminished with the aid of more water.

"Upon arrival at Nassau, official representatives of the governor presented Rostrum with royal dispatches from England informing him of the signed 1713 Treaty of Utrecht and the end of the War of Spanish Succession. He was then informed that he and his officers were under suspicion and scrutiny for disobeying orders and general dereliction of duty. Rostrum's new orders were to return to England posthaste, where he and his entire command crew were to face charges and a general inquiry that would potentially lead to trial, court-martial, and possible incarceration. It was then, from those very dispatches, that I learned that the Royal Marines had officially been disbanded by the Crown."

"What happened next? Is the war on our soil officially over? Have the French withdrawn for good?" Will asked.

"Firstly, Captain Rostrum and his officers—including myself— conferred. We assumed that an openly disgruntled midshipman had betrayed us all. It was widely felt that the guilty man had sent word back to England of Rostrum's failings and questionable command decisions while the *Firefly* was in colonial port. Perhaps realizing that his own neck was now in the noose, the captain went unchallenged, and we unanimously agreed that we had not disobeyed orders. We took a vote and decided on a radical course of action. We all felt that none of us would be found innocent in any trial setting, and that Rostrum would implicate us all in every poor decision he made should we try to unite and turn against him. Therefore we decided to redeem ourselves in the only way possible: We would slip away aboard the *Firefly* and resume our quest to fill our hold with riches that would ingratiate us to the new ruler of Great Britain—King George the First.

"After a day of resupplying, we left Nassau without detection or deterrent. However, word must have gotten out quickly after we were under way, as three British warships were soon in pursuit. The crew, of course, was ignorant of our plans and intentions. They also had no idea why we were being followed. But as fate would have it, Rostrum was struck with a rare navigational stroke of genius that left our pursuers far behind and out of reach. He set a course around Cuba that eventually brought us to safety in a Jamaican port. We also skirted around a large storm that our pursuers were most likely unable to avoid. This greatly aided our escape, in my opinion. And to answer the other questions thou hath posed...the war may be over on parchment prominently displayed in palaces across Europe, but I fear the French will never yield their claims on this vast wilderness, and I suspect a more brutal resistance from indigenous savages."

Will nodded somberly at the thought of unrestrained aggression forever challenging his very existence in the land he called home. He forced himself to focus back on Dunsbury's tale and tried to envision the foreign and tropical places the lieutenant had spoken of. He had little knowledge of the geography of the world and could only recall places he had once been taught about. The Caribbean was familiar to him because Cyrus had shown him old maps of that region, but he had to admit he was ignorant of most of the names of the islands that comprised it and the world powers that governed each one of them.

Dunsbury had paused, leaning heavily against the wall and breathing deeply. To Will, this hesitation seemed deliberate— almost as if it were planned to add intrigue to his tale.

"It was now late in the summer months of 1715. All throughout the docks and ports of Jamaica, word spread like a dragon's fire about a Spanish treasure fleet that had recently sunk in a storm off the coast of Florida. Ships of all shapes, sizes, and countries of origin were setting sail once word of a massive recovery effort reached the ports. Captain Rostrum felt this was an ideal opportunity to seize upon. He immediately issued orders for the *Firefly* to set sail for the southern tip of Florida. I must note that he was not interested in the dangers and labors of the recovery itself—he was thinking like a pirate. He intended to go after the ships that had already salvaged the lost hordes of gold and silver rumored to have gone down. He took his time getting to Florida, and once there, we discovered we were mostly too late. Many of the recovery ships were already gone. But then, one fateful evening, a lookout caught sight of a vessel within interception range. It sat low in the water and gave every indication that it was overloaded with treasure. Rostrum gave the order to intercept, and that was the beginning of months of untold misery in an insane pursuit of the Devil's Chariot."

"The *Repulse*?" asked Will.

"Yes, the *Repulse*. A ship of sheer wickedness crewed by murderous pirates under a black flag of death. Once she saw our flag, she skillfully fled north up the coast. The *Firefly* outgunned her, but it didn't discourage her from a fight. We traded cannon fire at distance on several occasions, both causing and incurring only minor damage. For some reason, Rostrum could never get close enough to initiate a decisive engagement."

Will sensed a subtle change in Dunsbury's demeanor whenever he made mention of the *Repulse*. It wasn't necessarily an angry or frustrated emotion he projected, but rather one of uncertainty, apprehension, and even fear. He listened further with escalating zeal.

"That ship slipped in and out of sight like some dreadful apparition," said Dunsbury. "She constantly managed to elude us—nay...*haunt* us—but Rostrum's pursuit was relentless, bordering on fanatical...even suicidal. The men became wary and superstitious, relating and blaming every little misfortune on our inability to capture and conquer that devilish ship and the perplexing scourge commanding her. We chased her up the coast, bending every sail in an all-consuming effort to catch her. But she was built for speed, even with a full load in her hold. Our larger and slower warship just couldn't overtake her. For a time, she evaded us completely and nearly escaped our pursuit entirely. She managed to slip away in an early-morning fog bank somewhere off the coast of South Carolina. Rostrum acted on instinct and ordered the *Firefly* to turn around and sail south again, assuming the *Repulse* had managed to find safe harbor in a hidden cove or the mouth of a river close to shore. We sailed back south for days and then miraculously rediscovered that accursed vessel weighing anchor in a shallow cove. As if assisted by Lucifer himself, that ship managed to raise sail and get under way before our guns came to bear. The chase resumed. We managed to get into range once or twice, and our cannons did inflict some damage, but it wasn't until we entered these cold northern waters, devoid of much-needed food, sick crewmen nearly starved and at the breaking point, where we were finally able to take advantage of the weather gage and overtake the Devil's Chariot. It is also where we met our own demise trying to outduel a ship spawned from the depths of Hell."

"I saw the battle from the highest point on this island," said Will, shaking his head. "I was astonished at what I witnessed."

"The *Firefly* was struck ablaze by rapid cannon fire. The weakened crew led by inept officers trying to conduct a pointless naval battle couldn't contain the flames. The fire reached our powder stores and blew the ship apart. I remember nothing after the explosion. I was on the quarterdeck directing my marine sharpshooters to pick off every pirate who ventured in range of our muskets and swivel guns. I felt a sharp pain and saw a blinding light...the next thing I knew, I was here."

"The morning after the battle, Elizabeth and I rowed over to Belle Island where the *Firefly* sank and the *Repulse* ran aground," Will said. "We found thee on shore and barely alive. I tended thy wound before bringing thee here. We found no other survivors, and I buried the dead at sea."

"I must thank thee for the toilsome and merciful work thou hath preformed in the service of our Lord. I owe my life to thee, good sir," said Dunsbury. "Thank thee for rescuing an honest man and a soldier. I'm sure my wife and child back in London thank thee, as well."

Will nodded and picked up the doubloon again. Silence ensued for several moments as he studied the coin.

Dunsbury could sense the workings of Will's thoughts as he became increasingly entranced by the gold resting in his palm.

"That ship is cursed, Will. Let the sea have her and the wretched cargo entombed in her rotten hold."

"She's aground and at my mercy," Will replied. "There isn't a better time to relieve her of her precious load than now. Soon the sea will rise and a tremendous storm will wrench her free and swallow her whole before scattering her remains over miles of murky, frigid ocean depths."

"What makes thou so certain?" asked Dunsbury.

"There is a reason why this island was named 'Storm,'" Will cautioned. "Ferocious gales lash at our shores and snap the tallest, strongest trees like they were little dry twigs. That ship will be permanently lost when the next one arrives. Our situation here is tenuous. We're in desperate need of fresh provisions, or we may not be able to survive the coming winter. Anything...anything aboard that ship that is of value must be recovered, or we risk losing everything we've built here. I am in great need of food, seeds, and building supplies primarily, but if she's filled only with precious metals and gems, I will recover them and find a way to use that wealth to my advantage in reviving this colony. As God is my witness, I will save this land even if I have to purchase it directly from Massachusetts Bay and King George the First himself!"

"I admire thy convictions, William Estes, though they are a bit lofty for a young man such as thyself. Even with help from that pretty young lass of thine, I doubt the two of thee could endure the rigors of such a dangerous endeavor. I doubt thou would even desire to endanger sweet Elizabeth with such grueling work."

Will was silent as he remembered nearly drowning, isolated and alone in the hold of the *Repulse*. He shuddered to think of what could happen to his beloved Elizabeth in a similar circumstance.

"Against my better inclinations, I will offer thee a business proposition," said Dunsbury. "In return for thy gracious help, and with the guarantee of necessary food and drink to speed my recovery along, I shall assist thee with thy salvage of that damnable ship. I must also insist on just a tiny percentage of the treasure aboard. I should like ten percent, which I deem fair and ample. I estimate that will buy me passage back to England after my trek down to Massachusetts. I shall also require an equitable portion of provisions for my journey. I believe that to be a reasonable price considering what's at stake. Imagine the tales I'll have to tell upon arrival in Massachusetts."

Will pondered for a moment and came to his decision.

"We have a contract, sir," he said as he shook Dunsbury's hand. "But I must warn thee, when our work is done and our agreement fulfilled, I can put thee ashore on the Neck, but the land is infested with savages, and the journey thou speak of—an overland trek south to Massachusetts—is a perilous one, and one thou certainly could not survive, even armed with numerous weapons, abundant supplies, and a soldier's determination."

"I will take that risk. I have a family waiting for me across this vast ocean, and I *will* see them again," Dunsbury stated with confidence. "Our business is concluded for now, and I am so weak, I do not believe I can remain awake a moment longer. I must sleep. I encourage thee to retire, as well. Embrace that beautiful young lady by the fire. Hold her tight and let nothing harm her. Goodnight, William Estes."

"Goodnight, Leftenant Philip Dunsbury."

Will watched as his new business partner lay down and fell asleep. He took the man's advice and snuggled next to Elizabeth by the fire—but not before putting both his knife and his musket out of Dunsbury's reach.

CHAPTER 7

The Neck

It rained during the night, bringing much-needed relief from the unusually hot and dry weather that had smothered the region of late. As the first rays of the morning sun cascaded down upon the barracks, Will awoke, rubbed the sleep from his eyes, and got to his feet. He stretched long and hard and then opened the door to let in the spreading sunlight. He scooped up a dipper of water from the replenished rain barrel and brought it to Dunsbury, who was beginning to stir.

"Help me...I cannot sit...my legs," he muttered through labored breath.

Will propped him up and brought the dipper's edge to his lips. Dunsbury drank, trying in vain to hold the cup with his own trembling hands.

"My limbs are devoid of strength yet lively with pain," he struggled to say. "I feel as weak as a newborn kit."

"Thou must eat to regain a more robust constitution," Will stated. "I will fetch thee a more potent beverage...for the moment, our food is gone."

Will procured a cupful of the salvaged rum and served it to Dunsbury.

"This is all we have left of substance for now. I shall arrange for more food to be brought posthaste," Will declared. "Perhaps the drink will help invigorate and heal thy wounded sinews."

Dunsbury willingly choked down the alcohol between drawn-out coughing fits and bouts of wheezing. His every exertion was arduous, unsteady, and seemingly exhausting. Sweat poured off his forehead, and his face turned a hectic flushed red.

"Thou art unable to be of any use in thy present state," Will told him. "Thou must rest and build up thy vigor. Elizabeth and I must leave here and assemble the necessary plans and tools for our endeavor. I cannot say how soon I will return, but rest assured, Elizabeth will rejoin thee with fresh food and water and will attend to thy needs."

Just then a soft gasp came from behind. Will turned around and saw Elizabeth standing there with her hands over her mouth.

"Good, thou art awake, my dear. We must leave the leftenant for now...and I have much to discuss with thee," he said. He turned back to Dunsbury and announced, "I will leave some water and rum by thy side and well within thy reach. Try to ration it for thy benefit and rest as much as thou art able. Elizabeth will return as soon as it is practicable."

Dunsbury nodded and slowly slid back on the mattress with shuttered eyes. Will motioned for Elizabeth to step outside. Seemingly confused and frightened, Elizabeth paced and wrung her hands out in the courtyard. Will—musket and satchel in hand—joined her a moment later.

"Have thou lost thy head?" Elizabeth snapped. "Doth thou honestly believe I will nourish and minister to that man unaccompanied and unprotected...especially now that he has been relieved of his restraints? Thy presumptions are far too lofty and ignorant, William Estes!"

"Hold thy sharpened tongue and listen to what I propose," Will interjected. "Come...let us return home. The walk will allow me ample time to inform thee of my plan."

Elizabeth sighed and disgustedly threw her hands in the air. Will led her out of the fort and secured the doors. They then took to the coastal trail that would lead them home.

"Thou art just going to leave him there, unrestrained and freely able to engage in whatever mischievous or thieving act his scheming mind can conceive?" queried Elizabeth.

"I spoke with him at length while thou slept," Will answered. "We entered into a binding contract that will be mutually agreeable and profitable for us all. However, we need his help, and fortunately for us, he needs ours."

"I don't understand."

"That ship out there is surely loaded with ineffable riches. The leftenant spoke of his service aboard the now sunken HMS *Firefly*. He was in command of a detachment of Royal Marines, and his ship was tasked with hunting down thieving pirates. The *Repulse* is indeed a pirate ship laden with Spanish treasure. Here is proof of it," Will said, again showing Elizabeth the doubloon from this pocket.

"What form of scurrilous agreement was reached?" Elizabeth asked, staring out at the sea and showing little interest in the gold coin.

"He needs us to assist in his recovery. We need him to help in the *treasure's* recovery. I cannot salvage that ship alone without seriously endangering my life. But with the help of another able-bodied man, I'm positive we can do it. In its simplest form, we help Leftenant Dunsbury recover from his wound, and he in turn helps me salvage the treasure. Once our efforts are complete, he collects but a very small percentage of the spoils for himself and then takes leave of us by journeying down to Massachusetts Bay. There he will purchase passage back to England and his family who await him...but not before he spreads the news of our resolute existence here. When the fathers in leadership of Massachusetts Bay hear of us, they will send others to repopulate and reinvigorate our lost colony. And when they arrive with all their ideas and resources, it will be *our* families who will have the wealth and power to dictate how our new colony is shaped and how it will thrive. The Neck will be like our own little kingdom, only this time we won't fail. We will have the resources necessary to put a permanent end to the threat imposed by the savages or by any wily Frenchman foolish enough to try to take what is rightfully ours."

Will spoke with confidence and enthusiasm as they trudged along the trail. It was as if new life and purpose had been injected into his very soul. Elizabeth sensed that nothing was going to halt him from pursuing his vision. However, that didn't stop her from speaking her mind.

"The man is dangerous, Will," she said bluntly. "He tried to kill thee. Hath thou conveniently forgotten that? Does the mere thought of obtaining great wealth hopelessly blind all men to the simple truths and perils that dangle so obviously before them?"

"His earlier actions were undoubtedly driven by a clouded mind brought on by his injury. He is more lucid now, and in full control of his faculties. He spoke with great clarity when describing the events that delivered him into our midst. I believe the evidence is pure and that he is who he says he is. He poses no risk—he is too infirm to inflict physical harm on either of us. He needs us. He cannot survive or get home to his family in England without our help. I would not dream of putting thee in harm's way if I were not absolutely certain. Thou must tend to him and help facilitate his recovery. Time is of the essence, and I must prepare for this salvage without delay. One violent storm could decimate that ship and scatter its contents clear across the ocean floor and forever out of our reach. We must act now. Our ability to continue on here is uncertain as winter looms. Thou knowest this. Our very survival may depend on what can be pulled from the watery hold of that ship. I see no other option, Elizabeth."

"To make a contract on the word of a stranger who tried to harm thee is both reckless and absurd. I do not agree with this course of action," said Elizabeth. "But my words will not sway thee...of that I am certain. I cannot be a hindrance to thy plans or I risk making matters worse for all of us. I see little choice but to gamble and hope that our undertakings are successful. Perhaps upon further reflection, I will more clearly realize the merits of thy plan. Perhaps it is not without value. However, I must ask...what of my mother and thy father? How do they figure into thy quest?"

"I am uncertain at this time," he said. "I have ideas, but we must determine where thy mother's emotions are leaning when we confront her."

Elizabeth stopped abruptly, forcing Will to turn and face her.

"This ugly business between the two of thee cannot go on

forever," he said firmly. "It must cease forthwith. We must face her now or put all future endeavors in jeopardy. Doth thou understand what thou must do, Elizabeth?"

Elizabeth did not answer. She simply looked down the trail and resumed walking at a grittier pace. Will fell in behind her not knowing what to expect when they reached the Eustis cabin, now just a short distance away. He quickly began to organize an idea that had been brewing in his mind. It was taking shape just as the trail came to an end and the smoke from the Eustis chimney could be seen wafting toward the heavens.

The cabin was soon in full view, and Will held his breath the moment Winnie emerged from inside. Elizabeth stood close to Will with her head slightly bent, not wanting to make eye contact with her mother. Will stood tall with his head high and a look of confidence on his face. He knew full well his involvement was key in what was about to transpire.

"Look whom the Lord hath returned to me," said Winnie with a scowl on her face and arms folded across her chest.

"The Lord didn't bring her back, Mrs. Eustis; I did, as I said I would," replied Will. "She is here and ready to make amends for whatever still festers between mother and daughter."

At that moment, the air became eerily still, and the normal sounds of the island's wildlife, nestled in the trees and scurrying on the land, suddenly went silent. It was as if all the entities of nature were focused on the Eustis cabin, eagerly watching the scene about to unfold.

"Is there something thou desire to say to me and to the Lord, who so patiently tolerates thee and thy devilish acts of defiance?" Winnie roared. "Hath thou been permitted enough time and freedom away from thy chores to rid thy soul of the demons that infest thee? Tell me why I should not lash thy bare backside with a leather strap and beat the insolence right out of thee!" With a tremble in both body and voice, Winnie commanded, "Speak and be heard, child! Defend thyself if thou art able!"

Will glanced at Elizabeth. He expected her to burst forth with a verbal tirade, laced with profanity and directed solely at her mother. In that case, he knew he would have to act quickly to intervene before the situation turned physical. However, to his great surprise and relief, what came next was nothing short of remarkable.

Elizabeth stepped forward with her head down and her hands clasped in front of her. Her posture lacked strength and confidence, and it looked as if she might drop to her knees and beg for forgiveness at any moment—and that's just what she did.

"Oh, Mother, please forgive the wretched behavior that has plagued me of late," she pleaded. "My sins are evident but not without forgiveness. I have seen the error of my ways after a time of solitary reflection. I have spoken with the Lord through hours of heartfelt prayer, and He has cast His divine light upon me. I am liberated from the wickedness that possessed me earlier and feel blessed and utterly repentant for the friction between us. I am ready to continue my resurrection in the eyes of the Lord and through thy bountiful holy tutelage."

Will watched as Elizabeth started to weep. He was captivated by her performance and amazed by her thespian talents. She had brilliantly demonstrated her uncanny ability to speak convincingly in falsehoods and display emotions completely foreign to her real feelings. Her talent for deception and manipulation was truly without comparison, and Will wondered how suited she would be to the stage if ever given the opportunity. What came next surprised him even further.

"God be praised!" said Winnie, breathing a huge sigh of relief. "My daughter has finally come back to me."

Her voice had swelled with renewed confidence as she spoke, and the trembling Will had noted earlier was now gone. All sense of trepidation had seemingly been driven from her by Elizabeth's eloquent soliloquy. The old woman now seemed much stronger-willed and poised to dictate her intentions without fear of reprisal from her daughter.

"We shall test thy sincerity, my young one. Rise up and take thyself inside. Strip off that whorish rag and dress thyself in proper attire—*after* bathing away the mud and odor, of course. Go now!" Winnie said, pointing to the door.

Elizabeth scrambled to her feet and quickly disappeared into the cabin.

"And thou, William, fetch thy father from the crop fields and return at once. It is time we all sat down to partake in the Lord's teachings."

Winnie spun on her heel and retreated back inside the cabin.

A bit stunned, but relieved about how the situation had so easily been resolved, Will found himself at a loss for words. He turned toward the fields and set out to find Cyrus.

An hour later Will, Cyrus, and Elizabeth were seated in a row facing the fire inside the Eustis cabin. In front of them, as if speaking from a grand pulpit, was Winnie. Her Bible was in hand and the words of God spouted from her lips. The sermon was lengthy and tiring, but the tiny congregation of three endured until Winnie finished by leading them in prayer. When the service was concluded, Winnie went about preparing something to eat while Will busied himself chopping firewood. After some instruction, Cyrus began to gather and stack the wood next to the cabin. Elizabeth remained inside and dutifully helped her mother with whatever tasks she was given. Will paused every few minutes to wipe his brow and peer through the open door of the cabin. Inside was a version of Elizabeth that he instantly admired. She was humble and accommodating. She listened and went out of her way to be helpful. Occasionally, a smile would creep across her face, and she would say something sweet and tender that made her mother reciprocate with a kind gesture or Godly praise. This was the pure character of Elizabeth Will truly adored and wanted to marry. He was convinced that she had many qualities that would make her a wonderful wife and mother. However, he was not blind to her use of deception and manipulation to obtain things she wanted. He wondered if he even knew the real Elizabeth at all. What was abundantly clear was that he dearly loved her and was smitten, oftentimes beyond all reason. He hoped it would not be his undoing, but found it increasingly hard to guard against. His thoughts then wandered back to a life of prosperity at the head of a revived community—a lovely wife and children at his side.

The hours slipped by as they all kept busy with chores around the Eustis home. Soon it grew dark and the cabin was illuminated by newly made candles and the glow from the fireplace. Will and Cyrus sat down at the table and were served heaps of smoked cod and a few under-grown blemished potatoes that looked very unappetizing. When Elizabeth and Winnie joined them, Winnie offered another lengthy prayer before they were allowed to eat. During the meal, Will decided to reveal his intentions.

"If I may expound for a moment, Mrs. Eustis, I'd like to have thy blessing on a bold endeavor that will greatly advance our existence here on Storm Island before the drudgery of winter is upon us."

Elizabeth's eyes grew wide upon hearing Will's words, as she feared he was about to reveal all that had transpired over the previous few days. She held her breath.

Will went on, "I wish to venture out a bit farther than normal to test a new fishing ground which I believe to be plentiful and untouched. There I hope to haul in an exceedingly ample supply of cod that should last us well into the fall."

Winnie nodded her head between bites while Cyrus happily grunted upon hearing the word *cod*, which he had learned meant food.

"Before my quest upon the sea is to begin, however, I must journey out to the Neck and scavenge for supplies that I feel are essential for success on the sea, as well as necessary for the resurrection and holy salvation of our tiny colony here."

"Thy plan sounds intriguing, Will; please continue," said Winnie.

"I endeavor to locate materials to aid in the repair and eventual expansion of our homes here on Storm. I intend to salvage every iron nail, every length of rope, every beam of useful timber, every unbroken piece of glass, and every saw, axe, maul, and mallet I can find, and bring it all back here. I also aim to locate the old church and salvage every book, Bible, and piece of Puritan symbolism I can save. It shall be my personal tribute to our Lord, who so faithfully looks down upon us from heaven."

"The Lord be praised, young William. I am delighted to hear

of such devotion to Him—and to us, as well. Thy spirit is strong and will no doubt be rewarded with success," said Winnie.

"Indeed, Mrs. Eustis," Will replied. "However, I shall need thy help, which I hope will not be disagreeable or overly burdensome to thee."

"Oh? And what doth thou require of me, young sir?"

"I must ask for assistance from Elizabeth. Strong and able am I, but in need of another pair of capable hands to assist in my efforts. I beseech thee to allow her to accompany me for a minimum of several days so that I may accomplish my goals without hindrance or delay. I assure thee, no harm will come to her, and her help will be immeasurable in my eyes and those of the Lord. In return, I simply ask that thou watch over my father and see that no harm comes to him. Thou knowest how helpful he can be when put to a menial task and shown what to do. He is of little trouble, but I dread leaving him alone for long periods without supervision. I fear his feeble mind worsens every day."

Winnie rose from the table and clutched her Bible. She paced a bit and glared at both Will and Elizabeth.

"William, you must know that I will be most enraged if I discover this quest of thine is nothing more than an excuse to gain further carnal knowledge of my daughter."

"Mother—"

"Be silent, child! Do not pretend to deny it. A mother knows when such sinful activities have besmirched her only daughter. To what extent, I dare not contemplate. And I further—"

"I believe I have made my intentions on the matter clear, Mrs. Eustis," Will interjected. "I have also made my feelings toward Elizabeth clear. I have told thee that I have never acted with sinful intent while alone in her presence. With God's blessing, perhaps someday we will be married...which is my wish...but until then, I will not disgrace her or myself by engaging in sinful activities out of wedlock."

The room went silent except for the sounds of Cyrus fidgeting at the table. Elizabeth, a look of confused disbelief on her face, said nothing, even as Will stared ardently into her eyes. It was Winnie who eventually broke the silence.

"See that thou does not, William," she said sternly. "I will take thy word and honor thine intentions by placing the safety of my daughter in thy hands. Do not make me regret my decision."

"I won't."

"And when does this quest of thine commence?"

"We'll strike out tomorrow at dawn. Is that agreeable with thee, Elizabeth?"

"I will be ready," she replied in a low voice.

"I thank thee, Mrs. Eustis, for thy trust and thy hospitality. We will not fail," said Will. "Come, Father, let us take our leave and return home."

Cyrus stood up and followed Will out the door. They made their way home and retired to their beds, and as Cyrus snored, Will lay awake devising his plan for the next day. He knew what needed to be done, but he could not be sure that success was imminent— or even attainable. A sudden sea wind whooshed through the small cracks and chinks of the cabin walls and swept across Will's face. It sent a shiver up his spine and a foreboding twinge through his stomach. It was another hour before he fell asleep.

As dawn broke the next morning, Will took Cyrus through their customary routine before leading him back to the Eustis home. The old man slumped and slowed his steps when he realized where he was going. As they approached the cabin, Will spied Elizabeth sitting outside the front door next to a small burlap sack. She stood up when they got close and opened the door for Cyrus— who turned to Will with a sullen look on his bearded face.

"I have to leave for a while, Father," Will explained. "Mrs. Eustis will take care of thee in my absence. She will treat thee well and make sure thou art not left hungry or alone. She will keep thee safe. Be a good guest...listen and do what she asks of thee."

Cyrus mumbled a few piteous and incomprehensible words in response, but it was his overall tone and uneasy gestures that truly conveyed his discontent with the idea of being placed in Winnie's care again. Will was slightly taken aback, as he was unused to Cyrus asserting any resistance to his instructions. Moreover, it had been a while since his father had so fervently tried to express himself both vocally and physically. It was not normal behavior for him, and it seemed to suggest a degree of intelligence and independence that Will had not seen in a very long time. Nevertheless, Will convinced him to go inside the cabin.

"Let's be off," said Elizabeth impatiently, picking up her sack and tugging at Will's arm.

He shifted his musket to his free arm and adjusted his satchel so that they could walk with their arms locked like a couple on a leisurely stroll. The tender gesture pleased Will, but puzzled him all the more. It was unlike Elizabeth to walk arm in arm or to hold hands—even after lovemaking. But before anything was said, Will looked at her face and discovered what the cause of her peculiar behavior might be.

"What happened?" Will asked as he examined Elizabeth's right cheek, which was slightly puffy and noticeably red.

"It's nothing," she retorted. "I do not wish to speak of it."

"Did thy mother strike thee again?"

Elizabeth clutched his arm harder and increased her pace, pulling Will along with her.

"Elizabeth, I require an answer," Will said as his anger toward Winnie strengthened inside.

"I have no answer I wish to share at this time, Will, as there are more pressing matters to attend to. I will say, however, that I have unfailingly followed thine instructions and recommendations...and sacrificed much to keep our current endeavor a secret from those who could jeopardize its success. I have sacrificed *much*," she said again with emphasis.

"What can I—"

"Nothing, Will. Hold thy tongue. Escort me back to the dragon's den and pray that he does not devour me when the young knight bids us farewell to seek his treasure."

"Thou knows that I—"

"Speak no more," she said curtly. "I am in no mood to listen. Just hear and obey this last thought: If thou ever expects to win my hand, thou shalt not speak of it to others again."

Elizabeth released his arm, swung her sack over her shoulder and trudged on ahead of him. In a haze of confusion, Will could only follow behind in silence, unable to make sense of what he had just heard. He could never completely grasp or gauge Elizabeth's true emotions or the intricate workings of her mind. Try as he would, employing all manner of his own genuine honesty and sincerity, he could never fully capture her heart or gain her absolute trust. Thus she remained cold and distant when it suited her, and gave her power that she often used to her advantage. He wondered if the day would ever come when she'd give herself fully to him and unlock all her secrets in a union of trust. But after observing Elizabeth's tense posture and quickened pace on the trail, Will shook his head ever so slightly and understood that that day was definitely not today.

Fort Hope soon came into view. They stopped at the front gate and paused before entering. Will unslung his musket, used the barrel to push open the doors, and stepped in with the gun raised. Cautiously, he scanned the courtyard with both his eyes and the musket for any threat that might be lurking there. To his relief, all was quiet.

"Thou doth not instill a great measure of confidence concerning my safety," said Elizabeth.

Will lowered the gun. "What have thee in thy sack?" he asked.

"Food mostly...and a few items to help occupy my time," she replied. "Shall we see if the dragon is awake? I'm sure he's quite hungry by now."

Will dismissed the sarcastic barb, and they walked over to the barracks. It was quiet inside. Will opened the door and looked down at Dunsbury, who was awake, and noticed that both the water and the rum had been drunk and the cups upended. Elizabeth hurried inside and set about building a fire.

"Some water and food...please...I beg thee," said Dunsbury weakly.

"Elizabeth will see to thy needs with due haste. Has thy condition improved since we last spoke?"

"Nay, the strength has not returned to my limbs, nor has the pain abated."

"I'm sure that will change with the introduction of proper food and drink. I would stay to help in thy recovery, but I must journey to the mainland and procure the necessary trappings needed for our salvage. Time is precious...I must go. I will return as soon as that task is completed."

"Godspeed, William. I look forward to our next meeting and pray I will be of sounder mind and body—and of more *use*, of course."

Will nodded and turned to Elizabeth, who had succeeded in sparking a new cooking fire to life.

"Come, my dear, let us fetch some water and converse a moment in the fresh air," he said.

Outside, they stood opposite one another over the rain barrel.

"He's of no threat. Do not fear him, but don't linger in his presence if thou art uncomfortable. Stay busy with purposeful tasks and remain in the courtyard if the barracks prove unaccommodating. The sky is empty of clouds and the threat of rain is nil. I must make my way back to the southeast shore and ready the longboat for the sail over to the Neck. If all goes well, I will return tonight, but I cannot guarantee that."

Elizabeth sighed and looked away.

"Here," he said, drawing her attention back to him, "take his knife and keep it close and hidden on thy person."

Will produced the knife from his satchel and tucked it into Elizabeth's palm.

"It will be all right. Thou hath nothing to fear. He needs us or he'll never see home again," Will said as he downed a dipper of water.

"Thou art so certain, and thou art such a blind fool," said Elizabeth in response. "I cannot believe thou hath put me in such a position of peril. He will turn on us as soon as he is able."

"Trust my instincts...nay, trust *me*, my dear one. I'd sooner face the fires of hell than let any harm come to thee. We will succeed in this endeavor and bring prosperity and purpose back to our lives. I am confident and have faith. Repay thy faith in me. I love thee."

"Go," said Elizabeth sullenly. "Go before another moment is wasted. Make good use of the day. I hope to be here and still breathing upon thy return."

With that, she scooped up more water and took it inside. She didn't look back at Will or show any interest in his departure. Feeling as if an unseen force had sucked the life out of him, Will gloomily plodded out of the fort, closed the doors, and began to question his own judgment.

Will's preoccupation with Elizabeth and her moods seemed to shorten the amount of time it took to reach the other side of the island. With swift precision and determination, he readied the longboat and shoved off. When far enough out, he hoisted the sail and set a course for the mainland. The sea was a bit unsettled, and the small vessel tossed and rolled amid the whitecaps and swells whipped up by the breeze. Will leaned heavily on the tiller, trying to keep it steady with both arms as the sail billowed out and the wind threatened to blow him off course.

Storm Island began to shrink behind him while the mainland grew larger and more vast as he approached. Anxiety gripped Will as it always did whenever he ventured away from the relative safety of the islands, but the mainland, particularly Falmouth Neck, was the most fearsome and dangerous place he had ever known. The Indian wars were still fresh in his mind even after several years without violence from the elusive natives. Frightening visions of horrific acts of brutality still plagued his thoughts whenever he dwelled upon the doomed colony and the courageous escape of a precious few families to the sanctuary of Storm.

The year was 1703, and he was only seven years old then, but in his mind's eye, he could still see the slaughter and hear the cries of the dead and dying as the natives successfully reclaimed what was originally theirs. He could still see glimpses of his father bravely fending off pillaging Indians at the last moment while his mother loaded him and what few possessions she could carry into a small fishing boat. Cyrus had leapt aboard and shoved off just before a torrent of flying arrows and hurled tomahawks came at them. That was the end of life on the Neck as the Estes family had known it, and the beginning of a harsh existence on Storm Island— an existence shared and suffered by several others including the Eustis family.

Will struggled to drive the foul recollections from his mind by concentrating exclusively on his present task. The longboat sailed into the shallows, where Will jumped out into knee-deep water and pulled the boat onto a small beach. He had used this particular landing in the past, and it was to his liking. Not only did it serve as an easy and convenient place to port, but it was also surrounded by high, thick grasses that hid the boat.

As soon as the craft was secure, Will's demeanor changed and his hunting instincts took over. Silence and intense observation dominated his every move as he prepared to enter the ravaged land sprawled out before him. With his satchel slung at his side and musket at the ready, he inched up the beach and started inland. He kept his body in a crouch, alert for any movement around him. Once he got his bearings, he moved along silently and with resolute purpose.

The Neck bore no resemblance to Will's earliest recollections. With the French as their accomplices, the Indians had torched every dwelling. Only the occasional charred foundation could be found amid the seas of tall grass and brush. As the years had passed, the native flora had reclaimed the crop fields, while the fishing boats—many of which still lay lined up and abandoned along shore—rotted away from neglect and exposure to the harsh elements. Predatory wildlife had returned to the area, freely prowling and foraging without concern for human interference. Where there were once neat dirt roads, now only remained grassy indentations in the earth; and where there were once landmarks indicating directional orientation, accompanied by clear signs of human habitation, now only remained what nature had originally wrought.

The whole area was extremely discomforting and often put knots in Will's stomach. He had scavenged and explored small areas of the Neck in the past—hoping at least to locate a stray deer

or a moose to shoot and butcher—but each time felt more trau-
matic than the last. Often, to his horror, he would stumble upon
human remains, particularly bones that had been gnawed on by
animals. These gruesome discoveries were painfully unsettling,
as they always unleashed reminders of the brutalized English
settlers—and what still might be the fate of the remaining souls
on Storm.

Over time, it had become more and more difficult to find
anything to indicate the existence of an English community on the
Neck. In years past, Will had been able to successfully scavenge
usable timber, fishing hooks and lines, pewter cups and plates,
candles, knives, saws, axes, stray nails, various lengths of rope,
and a smattering of personal items such as books, jewelry, toys,
and clothing. But now, virtually all traces of what was had been
reclaimed by nature. Despite that, Will persevered with an optimism that made him believe there was always something more to
be found—something useful. And on this particular day, he was
determined to locate and recover one essential piece of machinery that he knew would be key in relieving the *Repulse* of its prize.

Will skulked along through the trees and overgrowth in the
direction of a place he dreaded. It was a structure that had ceased
to exist long before he was even born, a place that only remained
in chilling stories told to him by his father years ago. It was called
Fort Loyal, and it was the earliest garrison on Falmouth Neck. As
a young man, Cyrus had helped build the fort in 1678 along with
several other returning colonists who had been driven out by
the carnage and destruction wrought by the earlier King Philip's
War. Fort Loyal was the center of the colony at the time and the
unfortunate victim of yet another Indian war, this time called King
William's War.

Cyrus had told Will of a military leader from the Plym-
outh Colony named Benjamin Church, who commanded a colonial force of two hundred fifty men, all of whom arrived in 1689.
These men were part of a raiding party seeking to inflict damage
on French Acadia. While in Falmouth, these men helped defend
against a massive Indian attack that threatened the small con-
tingent of English colonists. The defense was successful and the

Indians thwarted, but all was not well in Falmouth when Church and his men returned to Boston soon after.

In the spring of 1690, the Indians, with their French conspirators, returned to Falmouth in force to attack the now undefended English settlers. Those who survived the initial slaughter—including the Estes and Eustis families—took refuge for several days within the confines of Fort Loyal, now commanded by Captain Sylvanus Davis. Besieged beyond all hope, the ill-fated English had no chance except for surrender. Betrayed by the French negotiators whom they trusted would treat them with civility and mercy, the awaiting Indians pounced on the unsuspecting English with unrestrained savagery. Many were slaughtered and far fewer were taken captive. Among the prisoners were Cyrus Estes and his wife, Mildred, his friend John Eustis and his wife, Winifred.

In the dead of night amidst the chaos and confusion, a band of captives managed to slip away and head south. Led by Cyrus and John, and after several days of terrifying and exhausting travel, the wet, ragged, and nearly starved group managed to find sanctuary in the untouched English settlements in York and Wells. Soon after, several survivors including the Estes and Eustis families boarded a ship that granted them safe passage back to Salem, Massachusetts.

All that remained of Fort Loyal now was an indentation in the earth and some remnants of charred timbers hidden in the grass. It took a bit longer and was more difficult to find than usual, but Will eventually reached the site and made his way to what had been the center of the fort. Over the years, he had scavenged the site repeatedly, particularly for anything made of iron, wood, or stone. But today he was deliberately searching for something he had found in years prior but had initially failed to recover and had subsequently lost and bungled to reacquire on return trips. Today had to be different.

As he carefully poked through the tall grass, he tried to orient himself and remember exactly where he had been when he'd first made the find. It was not an easy task because so much had changed since his last visit to the site. He got down on his knees and blindly groped around, at times using his fingers to claw into the earth when an unusual bump or unnatural-looking patch of ground revealed itself. An hour passed with no success. Will sat down in a clearing and rested. He was hot, sweaty, dirty, tired, and hungry—and getting eaten alive by swarms of mosquitoes and black flies. He built a fire. Once it roared to life, he added pine brush soaked in seawater until it billowed plumes of white smoke that helped keep the insects away. He then nibbled on a potato retrieved from his satchel. He skewered it with a stick and held it over the fire in hopes of cooking it a bit and improving the taste.

After resting for a short time, he got up and collected more wood from a fallen tree. It had undoubtedly been the victim of a storm and was now an excellent source of dead and broken branches with which to feed the fire. As he impatiently picked up the branches, he noticed an odd indentation in the ground with something curious sticking out. He immediately reached for it.

"Heavy cordage," he said out loud with a degree of renewed excitement. He picked and scraped away at the dirt until more of the rope was revealed. Eventually, he uncovered enough of it to grasp and pull it with both hands. With each tug, the weighty rope punched its way through the covering layer of topsoil, and soon a substantial length was exposed. Will finally reached the point where he was unable to pull any more out of the ground. The end was stuck in the earth, anchored by something that was unwilling to budge. Will began to dig, pulling up the soil in clumps until his hands were raw. His eyes lit up when his hands touched upon something hard...and made of metal. In an instant, he knew he had miraculously found exactly what he had been looking for.

It was there...thank God it was there. Wrenched from the earth was a large iron hook attached to a wooden block of pulleys. Threaded around the pulleys was more cordage that led to another block. Will freed it all from the earth and hauled the whole apparatus into the open by the fire, where he could carefully examine it. This particular pulley assembly had three grooved wheels and was known as a ram's head. It was powerful enough to lift and handle hefty loads of shipboard cargo, including ponderous objects such as cast-iron cannons. The hook was rusty on the exterior but intact and still sturdy at the core. The wood blocks and pulleys showed only minor rot on the surface, but they, too, appeared both durable and capable. The cordage, on the other hand, showed a lot of rot and fraying, and its reliability was questionable at best. No matter. Will was certain he could scavenge plenty of rope from the *Repulse* itself.

This particular ram's head had been taken from a ship and used to help raise the palisades during the construction of Fort Loyal. Cyrus, always proud of his accomplishments in helping build the community at Falmouth Neck, never hesitated to tell detailed stories of how the settlement's structures had been conceived and constructed—and what manner of tools and instruments had been used. Proof of his tales was now in Will's hands, and, more importantly, he now possessed the vital implement he would need to successfully hoist whatever booty lay in *Repulse*'s hold.

Will gathered up his gear and smothered the fire. He now had a substantial load upon his shoulders and knew his trek back to the longboat would be cumbersome and without the caginess of movement needed to detect and avoid potential threats. He would not be able to move as silently or as swiftly as he preferred, so he simply focused on getting back to the boat as quickly as possible.

The heavy load proved more burdensome than expected. Will had to stop numerous times to rest his aching muscles and catch his breath. He soldiered on, however, and fought his way through the overgrown thickets and over the uneven terrain. His perseverance was rewarded when he reached the longboat and dumped the pulley assembly over the side and placed his satchel and musket alongside it. He was prepared to shove off when he heard a sudden rustling in the woods. Instantly, he went silent and fixed his gaze in the direction of the noise. At first he saw nothing, and then he was able to barely make out a shape of sorts, mostly obscured by the woods. Slowly, he reached for his satchel, drew out the spyglass, and peered through the lens. It was a big buck.

Will's stomach growled at the prospect of fresh venison for supper. He had eaten so much fish lately, he couldn't bear the thought of letting this opportunity pass him by. He grabbed the musket and satchel and began to stalk his prey. The buck, unaware of his movements at first, gradually began to sense the danger. His head shot upright and he momentarily froze in place. A second later, he turned and bolted deeper into the woods.

"Damn!" cursed Will, knowing he had somehow clumsily revealed himself. With no other option, he charged after the buck hoping for just one chance to squeeze off a shot. He ran as hard as he could into the woods, tripping and stumbling as he went, but all he saw was the deer's hind end...and then nothing at all.

"Bloody hell!" he cried out, his body still charged with adrenaline.

He spun around in hopes of spotting some sign that the buck was still nearby. But all remained still save the gnawing and gurgling sounds from his innards. Unwisely, Will allowed his stomach to overrule his brain, and he decided to probe further into the woods instead of retreating back to the shore.

He resumed his hunter's posture and crept along for several minutes until he entered a clearing. The place seemed unfamiliar to him, yet he knew he had traveled deeply in this direction before. He looked around and began to notice fresh tree stumps and other subtle signs of what he knew to be human activity. What he saw next paralyzed him with fear.

On the edge of the tree line, carefully placed and nearly hidden, were several Abenaki wigwams. The wood-framed structures varied slightly in appearance, as some were conical and others were dome-shaped. They were covered with sheets of birch bark, woven tule mats, and animal skins, all secured in place with taut ropes. Will counted five wigwams, and each looked large enough to house six or more. The sight was a shock, and his mind raced with terror. The wigwams appeared to be the semipermanent lodgings for a much larger village. The clearing was certainly big enough to support more spacious, reinforced longhouses that might be two hundred feet in length and capable of sheltering hundreds of Abenaki men, women, and children.

Will had never seen a native encroachment so close to the shore facing Storm Island. The Neck had been thoroughly deserted for so many years that he had thought the Abenaki would never reclaim it. He had assumed they were too weak and scattered after years of war. He'd imagined the pockets that still did exist were simply uninterested in the area or had declared it too foul and tainted for permanent resettlement. Suddenly those thoughts began to change radically.

Will finally snapped out of his trance and realized just how much danger he was in—and how critical it was that he leave the area immediately. Odd as it was, there wasn't a single Indian in sight; however, he knew that could change in the blink of an eye. He turned around and started to hastily make his way back to the longboat. He became disoriented once or twice, but soon could hear the sound of the waves lapping against the shore. He was almost there...almost safe.

He reached the tree line and saw the ocean and Storm Island off in the distance. But when he looked in the direction of the boat, he again froze with a fear more petrifying than any he had ever felt. Standing before the longboat were two Abenaki warriors. They were dressed in tan breechcloths and fringed leather leggings secured by strips of cloth. Their footwear consisted of long-tongued moccasins, and upon their heads were elaborately designed peaked hoods also made from leather. The distinctive headwear also covered their shoulders and was embellished with tufts of animal hair and feathers. Both men were armed, and Will could hear them conversing in their native Algonquian tongue as they examined the boat.

Unsure of what to do, he slipped behind a tree, but as he did, he lost his footing on a loose rock that kicked out and made a noticeable sound. Instantly, the two Indians looked up and spotted him. Will steadied himself, then turned to face his adversaries. With weapons drawn and a bloodcurdling war cry, the Indians rushed him. Still gripped with disabling fear, Will's instincts took over. Without thought, he raised the musket and cocked the hammer. He pulled the trigger, and in a blinding flash, the gun discharged and sent a ball of lead hurtling into the chest of the closest Indian. The impact threw the warrior backwards, and his tomahawk flew out of his hand as he hit the ground...silenced forever.

The other warrior charged forward, his own club held high and ready to crash down on Will's skull. Will had no chance to reload the musket for another shot, and before he could do any-thing, the Indian was on him. He used his gun to block the first blow from the club, but the powerful thrust caused him to tum-ble and fall on his back. The savage pounced and hammered at him with the primitive but deadly weapon. Will cried out and used the musket—as best he could—as a shield. When the Indian drew back for a decisive wallop, Will swung the musket's butt end and crashed it hard into the Indian's skull, sending him toppling to the side. Will was free and quickly scrambled to his feet. He grasped the musket by the barrel and prepared to wield it like a truncheon, but he was not fast enough. The savage jerked it out of his hands and flung it to the ground. With a mighty shriek and his club raised high, the Indian leapt at Will, who barely had time to pull his knife.

The combatants slammed into each other with an intensity that knocked them both to the ground. They rolled several times, trying to free up and use their weapons. The Indian lost control of his club, which fell from his grasp and far out of reach. Now with both hands free, he caught Will by the throat and held on. Will used his left hand to break the deadly grip while fumbling to position his knife for a thrust with his right. On the edge of losing consciousness, he finally got his chance. He drove the blade hard and deep into the Indian's side. The savage screamed and released his grip. Will gasped for air as the blood rushed from his head. He grabbed the knife's handle and ripped the blade free before repeatedly plunging it back into the Indian's bloody wound with every ounce of strength he could muster. As the blood gushed forth, the life force drained away from the Abenaki warrior. Soon all movement ceased, and the native lay dead.

Dizzy and disoriented, Will pulled himself up and stag-gered over to the boat. He coughed loudly and then vomited on the ground, his arms and the front of his body covered in blood. After taking a moment to compose himself with deep breaths, he waded unsteadily into the water to wash away the crimson. It was then that he noticed two birch bark canoes partially hidden just a few feet away on the shore. He pulled his knife and waded over, heaving both flimsy native vessels off the land and into deeper water. When they were out far enough, he drove his blade repeatedly into the bottom of each canoe until they both sank out of sight.

Back on shore, he recovered the musket, and upon returning to the longboat, he sat down until he felt strong enough to push off. He had never killed a man before, and the feeling did not sit well with him. It was only after several intense minutes spent recollecting what the savages had done to the former settlers of the Neck that Will was able to justify his actions and feel less remorseful. He tried to put these thoughts entirely out of his head and focus on other pressing matters and responsibilities. Feeling that precious time was slipping away from him, he eventually pushed his boat into the water and rowed away. Though he tried to put the ugliness out of his mind, he knew that other Abenaki were nearby and would eventually discover the bodies.

Why didn't I dispose of them? he mused erratically while hoisting his sail. *Now the others will become angry and more brazen. They will search for whoever was responsible—they will search for me. But perhaps they will not need to search; perhaps they know exactly where to find me...*

Will stared in the direction of Storm and again wondered if the alleged curse would still keep the Abenaki away and off the island. His thoughts then wandered back to the arrows he'd found in the mast of the *Repulse*. Perhaps they had already been on the island! Perhaps they were there now, hidden in the interior and biding their time for the right moment to strike...

Will shuddered with fear and uncertainty. The day was waning and he needed to get back. He sailed on, determined to make landfall on the rocky northwest shoreline, nearest Fort Hope. He began to worry obsessively about Elizabeth's safety. He couldn't bear to imagine Abenaki savages raiding the fort in force and what might happen once they were inside. And what of Father and Winnie? Were they in imminent danger, too? And then there were the questions surrounding Lieutenant Dunsbury. Had he made the right decision by leaving Elizabeth with this stranger? Could the man be trusted, even in his weakened state? The questions became too perplexing to ponder. Will's head began to ache, and he was sure it was not because of the recent battle. All he could think about was getting back to Storm Island as quickly as the winds would carry him. He needed answers, and he hoped to have them within the hour.

CHAPTER 8

The Elizabeth Gambit

Elizabeth's day had unfolded much differently than Will's. At first she was aloof and withdrawn, unwilling to spend any time inside the barracks. She didn't trust the man and felt apprehensive when in his presence, but she was also inexplicably fascinated by and attracted to him. The more she tried to stay away, the more she yearned to be in his company. She was outside now, strolling in the courtyard with silly notions of busying herself by making soap and candles or stitching a quilt. But it was late in the day, and she had wasted most of it eating smoked cod, sipping rum, looking at her picture books, and taking short walks down to the shore…all the while thinking about Dunsbury and little else.

She had faithfully tended to him with food and water and had made sure he was comfortable when he stretched or while he slept, but although he tried, he could not engage her in conversation or capture her full attention. While inside, she tended the fire, prepared food, drank her rum, and pretended to be busy. Her responses to his questions were terse and vague, never insinuating further interest or curiosity. And she kept her distance, never lingering too close lest he put his hands on her in a disagreeable or sinister fashion.

The sun was now starting to set, and Elizabeth hiccupped as she peered giddily into the empty cup in her hand. Wishing to refill it with the intoxicating elixir she had so quickly grown to relish, she wobbled her way back into the barracks. She headed straight for the rum cask despite the unusual lightheadedness she was experiencing. She was not entirely sure why she felt the way she did, but what she *could* distinguish was that she liked it.

"It's good, is it not?"

Elizabeth wheeled around and nearly toppled over. Dunsbury was awake and sitting up on the mattress, painfully massaging his legs. She giggled as she steadied herself.

"It gives one a warm feeling inside and melts all the world's troubles away," he said. "There is no better libation to make one feel truly carefree and alive...that is, until the next morning, of course."

Elizabeth guffawed foolishly at Dunsbury's remark. She decided to take a seat at the table in an effort to regain control of her senses and emotions, which had slightly gotten away from her.

"Well, it appears I have thine ear at last. May I now have the pleasure of a few minutes' conversation—and some more food, perchance?" he inquired.

Elizabeth ignored his request and stared at him intently.

"I must say that thou look fitting and most refined with thy figure draped in Puritan apparel. Though I admit I much prefer a simpler woman...with simple values...in a simple dress like the one I first saw upon thee," he avowed.

"Such as a peasant girl...or a whore?" Elizabeth said scornfully. "I *am* a simple woman," she retorted, "and I wear the attire suitable for a Christian in the eyes of God."

"Of course," he replied, unable to mask his doubt. "Tell me, doth thou feel comfortable in those clothes? As I've observed thy movements, I cannot help but think that such a beautiful lass would find more contentment wearing thine other dress...particularly in such warm weather."

"I hate these garments," Elizabeth admitted, slurring her words, "and I wish thy mind and mouth would not prolong the subject any further. I wear this ghastly garb to protect myself from the religious tyranny of my insane zealot of a mother."

An uneasy silence ensued as Elizabeth's partially inebriated mind tried to tame the words that came out of her mouth.

In the end, it was a losing battle: The liberal amounts of rum she had ingested clouded her judgment, and with it, all capacity for rational thought and speech. She had no idea just how vulnerable she was.

"Thou hath a mother? A father, too? Why are they not here?" asked Dunsbury.

"My father is dead and I wish my mother was buried beside him!" snapped Elizabeth. "She is the bane of my existence...and I will endure only so much before certain measures are taken."

She paused and let out a foolish giggle. The rum had a firm grip on her mind, yet her tongue remained loose.

"And what of thy friend William? Does he have kin on this island as well? I thought the two of thee were here alone."

"Will lives with his father, a feeble-minded mute incapable of accomplishing the simplest of tasks without constant help. He's a worthless hindrance...just like my mother."

"Where are they now?"

"I do not know...and I do not care," slurred Elizabeth as she drew closer to Dunsbury and imprudently put her hand on his forearm.

"Shall we both have a drink? Methinks it would do us good," he said.

"Splendid!" Elizabeth agreed. "I shall refill the cup and we shall happily imbibe together."

With that, she went to the cask and procured another measure of rum. She sipped some herself before unsteadily handing the cup over. Dunsbury took a long draught and handed what little was left back to Elizabeth. She boldly sat next to him on the mattress, her inner fire fueled by the savory grog and building in intensity.

"Ahhhh...sweet nectar," said Dunsbury. "It dulls the pain and revives the senses."

"Has thy pain dwindled, or does it still linger?"

"It lingers with less intensity...thank God. I feel the strength returning to my limbs and hope to stand under my own power quite soon. I have been hurt badly before, but fortunately the good Lord has blessed me with a wondrous ability to heal. I shall employ this ability with all possible haste, as my strength will be sorely needed if we are to be successful in our salvage endeavors. I presume Will informed thee of our contract and all it entails?"

"He did indeed," Elizabeth answered as her eyes roved up and down the lieutenant's chest examining each and every scar. She drank the rest of the rum and fingered the brim of the cup.

"Thou hath no objections? The enterprise could be quite perilous."

"I object to no action that increases the likelihood of forever abandoning this wretched island and improving my overall existence."

"Thou art not happy here?"

"How can one be happy in exile, isolated on this accursed soil where even the simplest of crops barely grow?" she responded. "Our lives are under constant threat from merciless savages who lurk just off our coast and ancient demonic spirits that infest the very core of the island. There is no one to help us. Our colony is dead and Massachusetts Bay has abandoned us. I have grown weary of this futile and meaningless existence, and I yearn for civilization, culture, and luxury beyond the confines of this dreary place."

"It is my presumption that thou art educated. I sense burgeoning intelligence in thy manner of speech," said Dunsbury. "Doth thou challenge or dispute that claim?"

"Nay; my mother is a very learned woman. She took it upon herself to instruct both William and me from a very tender age. She taught us to read and write and gave us lessons on a variety of subjects from an extensive library of books in her possession. Will's father was also keenly astute and a staunch proponent of education beyond the Bible."

Elizabeth rose and collected her favorite art book from her bundle of possessions. She brought it over to Dunsbury, saying, "This is one of Mother's many tomes."

Elizabeth opened the book on her lap, Dunsbury leaned closer, and together they silently perused the opulence and elegance portrayed on each turned page.

"Quite extraordinary," Dunsbury said. "This is the kind of life thou envision for thyself?"

"It is what I deserve," she said flatly. "And thee, sir? What doth thou seek?"

"I am a soldier...wounded in battle. At present, I simply wish to regain my former vitality, which will enable me to set my own course under my own power and authority."

"That certainly can't be all if it's treasure thou seek—"

"It is the first step," he interrupted. "I have a personal score to settle with that damned ship. The misery heaped upon me by that floating spawn from Hell hath no boundaries. It nearly took my life, and I'll have my revenge one way or t'other."

"It's nothing but an abandoned tomb of ghosts now. How doth thou intend to exact revenge on a hulk of wood and iron?"

"There are many forms of revenge, dear girl. If thou wish to know one simple thing about me, know this: I know what I want, and I know how to get what I want—and nothing ever stops me from acquiring what I desire...nothing. Woe unto any man, beast, or spirit who tries to get in my way. I *know* what I want," he repeated with emphasis, "and I always *take* what I want."

Dunsbury stared deep into Elizabeth's eyes as he rested a suggestive hand on her thigh. Elizabeth knew not how to respond. In one sense, her heart raced and she was filled with a lustful tension that nearly overwhelmed her, half drunk and vulnerable as she was. She almost responded with blind animal instinct; however, the last vestiges of sobriety, rationality, and fear within her surfaced, and she abruptly rose to her feet. She wanted him—and all the new erotic pleasures he might offer—but she also feared and mistrusted him in a way she could not explain or easily dismiss. There was something she sensed about him that was disturbing and beyond their limited encounters and conversations. Strangely, she had heard a bit of her mother in his last comments, and that unsettled and alarmed her. Even in her partially intoxicated state, her instincts told her to retreat rather than advance.

She took several steps away to be sure she was completely out of his reach. She observed that he was still very weak and clearly unable to stand on his own. Knowing that he had limitations and was vulnerable in his own right put her somewhat at ease. She masked her rebuff of his advance by returning to the cask and pouring another measure of rum. The simple ploy appeared to work, yet her yearning to tempt fate and play with fire inexorably drew her back to him. She swallowed more of the sweet liquor and slyly fingered the knife hidden under her petticoat.

"Shall we drink and parley some more?" she asked impishly, defying all discretion and standing just barely within his grasp.

"Indubitably," he leered as he took the cup and slowly put it to his lips, never taking his eyes off hers. Those emerald orbs—hypnotic.

Wind and tide were against him. The sail back from the Neck took much longer than Will had anticipated. He fought and struggled to keep on course, eventually furling and abandoning the sail in favor of the oars. His back ached under the strain of each stroke as the longboat tossed and rolled on the uneasy sea, but he knew he was making better progress as Storm grew larger and closer with each dip and pull. He labored on as the sun set, feeling some shred of relief knowing he'd arrive before nightfall.

Eventually, the northwest shore was in sight. Will secured the boat on the rock-strewn sand, hauled his gear, including the ram's head, and his very weary bones up the trail leading to Fort Hope. All appeared calm and normal with no suggestion of incursion by raging Indians. There was neither signs of movement nor distressing sounds in the air, which relieved his apprehensions.

He wheezed and coughed loudly as he entered the fort and stumbled over to the barracks. There was light inside shining through the cracks, and he could smell the smoke from the fireplace. He stopped at the rain barrel for a much-needed drink, then opened the door and went inside. He promptly relieved himself of his burdens, which hit the floor with a thud. The noise was not sufficient to rouse Dunsbury from his slumber, Will observed, but it definitely caught Elizabeth's attention as she turned from the cooking kettle over the fire and greeted him.

"Thou hath returned..." she said, stopping in mid-sentence after seeing his blood-stained clothes.

"My goodness…what happened? Art thou hurt?" she asked.

Before he could answer, Will noticed that she had changed into her common dress at some point after he had left, and that her hair was loose and disheveled. Her skin glistened with perspiration, suggesting that she had labored hard throughout the morning and afternoon while he was gone. Had it not been for the obvious absence of any work completed, coupled with the strong scent of rum in the air, he would have had no reason for suspicion. However, he began to wonder what she had been up to all day as he casually looked over at the resting Dunsbury.

"Did thou not hear me? What happened?" Elizabeth inquired again, coming over to inspect his stained attire.

An exhausted Will gingerly sat down at the table. He removed his hat and raked his fingers through his hair. The smell of the rum grew more intense the nearer Elizabeth drew to him. Not only could he smell it on her breath, it was also on her dress… and in her hair.

"I found what we need," he said in a low voice as he gestured toward the ram's head. "That should enable us to accomplish our task," he added.

Elizabeth briefly glanced over at the heavy apparatus, but quickly turned her attention back to Will.

"Perhaps a third attempt will deliver the required answer, so I ask again, what happened?"

Will hesitated a moment, thinking that a harmless untruth involving the butchering of a deer or moose would suffice and not raise alarm. However, like his body, his head was weary, and the dangerous reality of the situation was too important to ignore. The truth was easier, and it was all his torpid mind could muster.

"I was attacked by two Abenaki warriors on the mainland," he said, his head lowered. "I…I…killed them both. I am not injured… this is not my blood."

"My God in heaven!" Elizabeth replied with great fear in her eyes. "Were there others? Are they going to come for us?"

Though he knew a full revelation would only intensify her worries and add more obstacles to an already tenuous situation, he felt it best to tell her everything.

"I saw several wigwams clustered in a peculiar location that had been recently cleared. I did not spy any other Indians, but cannot in good faith discount the possibility of numerous additional natives lurking in the area. To the best of my knowledge, my murderous act was not observed, so our presence may still remain unknown."

"That last sentiment rings hollow and does not offer any comfort, in my opinion, Will," said Elizabeth. "Neither thou nor I have laid eyes upon a savage since those horrible days leading up to our exile here. Knowing of their existence is terrifying enough, but to have actually seen and killed two of them...I shudder to imagine what horrible fate is in store for us now. We must leave this place immediately," she proclaimed with more certainty than Will had ever observed from her during prior discussions on the matter.

"We remain loyal to the plan, Elizabeth," said Will firmly, stealing a look at Dunsbury. "If all goes as I foresee it, by the time our business is done, throngs of colonists will pour into this vast land of ours bringing industry, community, and security back into our lives. And with that, the scourge of the native savages will be driven out forever. And who will lead this brave new colony? It will be *us*, Elizabeth, with our newfound wealth, and we will guide our fellow countrymen into a bold new future of promise and prosperity."

"How can that occur if the savages do not adhere to our schedule?" Elizabeth snapped. "What happens if they decide to combine all their forces and attack this island with impunity? We will be slaughtered and our ashes spread to the wind!"

"This island has protected us for many years," Will said calmly. "There has never been any evidence to suggest the savages have entered our domain. Thou know the legends of Storm as well as I do. They are partly the reason our predecessors chose this place. The Abenaki are fearful of Storm, and they will not rouse the wrath of their dead buried here. We should thank the demons and spirits alleged to haunt the island's interior, for it is they who help keep us safe."

"I have neither the strength nor the patience to dispute or debate thee now; I have had a very trying day. I have made my feelings on the matter known in the past, and they have not changed," she stated coldly as she turned away from him.

Will again glanced around the barracks and then directly at Dunsbury, looking for any sign of productive labor. As before, he found nothing, and his mind immediately began to generate mistrustful and mildly enraging thoughts. Those thoughts intensified when he noticed that the sacks, boxes, and chests of the recently salvaged goods were askew.

"I would not dream of questioning thy sincerity concerning the day's toil, my dear," he offered with a hint of sarcasm, "but I would truly love to see and share in the fruits of thy activities today so that I may reward thee with glowing words of praise and generous acts of affection. Perhaps we could toast with a substantial measure of rum...that is to say, if there is a single drop left."

Caught off guard, Elizabeth paused in her stirring of the kettle. She sensed the growing annoyance, suspicion, and combativeness in Will's voice and was inclined to retaliate with an equally unpleasant verbal salvo of her own. Yet despite her feelings, she chose a different course of action: She began to cry. As the tears washed down her face, she turned back to Will.

"Thou doth not know the crippling anguish I have endured today," she sniffed. "Step outside so that we may converse in private."

In the rapidly diminishing daylight outside, Elizabeth embraced Will and pleaded, "Break this contract, and let us flee this place at once and for all eternity. I implore thee."

Will opened his mouth to speak but was immediately interrupted.

"It is not a sound plan. Thou art partnered with a scoundrel who cannot be trusted. His mouth is full of lies and his eyes full of lust and dishonorable notions. If not for his weakened state, I fear he would have had his way with me...perhaps have even killed me. At day's beginning, I was steadfast in my duties concerning his care. I gave him food and water and carefully cleaned around his wound. I did everything I could to ease his suffering and help bring vitality back to his body and soul."

Elizabeth stepped back and wiped away some of her tears. She clasped Will's hands and looked into his eyes.

"I feared him immensely upon thy departure this morning, but I gathered my courage and engaged in conversation in hopes it would improve his mood and foster some trust. At first it was constructive and encouraging, but as the day went on, he became quarrelsome and demanding. He spoke to me in a most disagreeable and ungentlemanly fashion. He spoke of carnal cravings and how he had not been with a woman for months on end. His speech was salacious and unbecoming of a soldier. It soon transformed into mild threats...and the only substance I could conjure up to tame his blathering was our newly acquired rum. He demanded more and more after each drained cup. Eventually, the elixir calmed his chatter and induced him to slumber. I confess I imbibed a small volume of the brew—perhaps beyond reasonable judgment—but I only sought to calm my own nerves. Have pity and understanding of my ordeal and its toll on me...I beg of thee."

Elizabeth again wrapped her arms around Will and nuzzled his neck. He felt the warmth in her touch, but also a subtle and uncharacteristic trembling, which he took to be genuine and sincere.

"We both have endured much today," said Will with a sigh.

"The thought of losing thee to an onslaught of savages only strengthens my resolve to leave this place," Elizabeth murmured.

"I see no alternative, Elizabeth," Will said morosely. "Death awaits us a hundred times over if we abandon this island now. That simple yet remarkable piece of machinery I nearly sacrificed my life to recover today is the key to the pirate treasure. And those riches will insure our survival—and ultimately, our revival. I cannot recover that prize without the help of another young, strong back. Without the leftenant's help, the treasure is lost. Without *our* help, he dies. We need each other, Elizabeth. Only together, through our arrangement, can we both survive and prosper."

"He is of no use to anybody or anything at this time," she scoffed. "He is as helpless as a baby."

"That will change with our succor."

"And when his strength returns...and he decides to rape and kill me whilst thou art away? That is to say, if he gets to me before the savages do...or before Mother finds out about our deception and beats me to death with her bloody Bible."

"I will never let any of that happen. May God strike me dead if I do. Have faith in me, my love. Trust me...I will be the first to run that man through at the initial sign of trouble. He shall not harm a single hair on thy head without feeling my wrath. I promise thee."

"I do not trust him, and neither should thee," Elizabeth said, firmly pushing away from Will. "I cannot dissuade thee from running thy course which is so firmly set. I simply pray we all survive it."

"We must be unified on this, Elizabeth. I cannot in good faith proceed knowing thou art not with me in both mind and body. Division and lack of conviction only brings turmoil and loss of time, which we cannot afford. God has given us a unique opportunity to breathe life and prosperity back into our world...a chance to reclaim what was brutally taken from us. It's a chance fraught with risks and danger, but still it's a chance we must pursue at all costs. I see no other path to follow."

Will took Elizabeth by the hands and pulled her back close to him. He looked her straight in the eyes, refusing to allow her to turn away from him. With the dark of night nearly upon them, Will asked in a challenging tone, "Are we united in this quest, my love?"

Through tear-swollen eyes emerged a hard and fast gaze that swiftly erased all hints of vulnerability from Elizabeth's face. Her thinking was rapid and methodical, her answer unswervingly decisive.

"Now and forever," she replied almost hypnotically. "God be with us and protect us in this inestimable gamble," she added with conviction.

"Good," he responded, trying to gauge her candor. "We will triumph, as God is my witness, and speak of this no more. Now, what is the condition of the leftenant, physically?"

Elizabeth stepped away from Will and answered, "The use of his arms has returned to him, and he requires little help to sit up, but his legs remain dormant thus preventing him from walking. He is still confined to the mattress. It's difficult to guess when that will change. Today he took liberal amounts of food and drink. I anticipate his strength should return fully in a short time, and we still have ample stocks of smoked fish here to feed him. It should last for several days, if necessary."

"Good. Early tomorrow I will journey back to the *Repulse* with the ram's head. I shall work in the rigging to assemble a sturdy hoist in preparation for our salvage efforts. For now, I need some food and rest."

"Not before thy body and clothes are cleansed of those horrible stains and odors," Elizabeth insisted. "Strip whilst I fetch the washbasin, soap, and water."

An hour later, Will found himself wrapped in the bearskin blanket as his freshly laundered shirt and breeches hung near the fire to dry. His stomach was happy and full after a plentiful supper of smoked cod. Elizabeth had finally succumbed to her partial inebriation and fallen asleep by the fire. Will looked over at Dunsbury with a mixture of emotions ranging from benevolence to outright fury. Even if he didn't trust the man, he knew he had to. In that moment, he silently adopted a compromise policy of both vigilance and tempered reliance concerning his business partner. After much reflection, and after reaching the point where he could stave off exhaustion no longer, Will covered Elizabeth with the blanket and crawled in beside her. The last thing he saw was his musket propped against the wall where he'd put it—well out of Dunsbury's reach.

Will opened his eyes the next morning to find Dunsbury already awake. He stood up, dressed himself, and went over to the lieutenant.

"I would appreciate thine assistance," said Dunsbury, indicating he needed to relieve himself. With much effort, Will got the injured man to his feet.

"Stop," said Dunsbury, taking a deep breath. "Just one moment before we proceed." He wrapped his arms around Will's shoulders, putting nearly all his weight on him for support. His legs were like rubber and tingled as the blood rushed down to his feet. He still couldn't walk.

"One step at a time," said Will as he practically dragged the man out the door.

When their business outside was completed, Will got Dunsbury back inside and sat him up on the mattress.

"Here is thy shirt."

Will tossed the garment onto Dunsbury's lap and watched as he put it on without tremendous effort or discomfort. This simple act led Will to conclude that the lieutenant was indeed a quick healer. The color had come back to his face, and his intense sweatiness had noticeably subsided. Barring his apparent inability to walk or move about without support, Will estimated that it would be but a short time until his help could be counted on.

"How doth thou feel this morning?" Will asked warily.

"The pain around my wound has diminished, and the burning upon my brow has gone missing—to my delight. However, my legs do not readily respond and my brain still spins at the slightest exertion. Fear not, though, for my strength and focus shall return quickly."

"Thine appetite is hearty...a good sign."

"Yes, the food and water has done me good."

"That is not all that has done thee good," said Will, casually glancing back at both the rum cask and the still sleeping Elizabeth.

Dunsbury looked up and said nothing, yet he sensed Will's tension, especially after Will rose up and collected his musket.

"Today," Will announced, "the early-morning tide is to my advantage, and I shall board the Devil's Chariot. Yesterday, I obtained this ram's head, which I intend to secure among the ship's rigging. Once it is in place, I am confident we can use it to haul the treasure out of the hold."

Elizabeth stirred and got to her feet, and both men's attention was temporarily drawn to her.

"Thou hath left me in good hands, young William. I rest easy knowing Elizabeth is here to care for me. I am confident thou will be successful today, and I will eagerly await thy report."

Will paused for a moment, then looked at Elizabeth, who stood silent on the other side of the room.

"Elizabeth will accompany me today," Will said deliberately.

"I require her assistance with the tasks I've set forth. While I ready the boat, Elizabeth will provide thee with ample food and water... left at thy bedside and within easy reach. Thy body needs sufficient rest, and a day of undisturbed solitude should do thee good. Agreed?"

"Yes...of course...I should fare quite well on my own," replied Dunsbury. "Fear not, and godspeed," he added.

Will gave Elizabeth a nod and began to gather up his satchel, his gun, and the ram's head. Elizabeth rationed out more of the cod and put it on a plate near Dunsbury. She did the same with several cups of water from the rain barrel. She exchanged no words with the lieutenant and promptly retreated outside to the courtyard when her duties were complete.

Down by the shore, Will loaded up the longboat with everything he thought he might need. Aside from the usual necessities kept in his satchel, he packed a bundle with extra food, candles, rope, a lantern, and tools. He secured everything on board, unfurled the sail, and waited for Elizabeth to arrive. While he waited, his mind spun endlessly, trying to determine if his last-minute insistence on Elizabeth's accompanying him was because he sincerely wanted to protect her...or because he really didn't trust her.

CHAPTER 9

The Hunt Commences

Elizabeth eased down the unforgiving trail in her bare feet, making sure to avoid sharp stones, loose gravel, and exposed roots that could potentially cause injury. Reaching the shore, she climbed into the longboat and scampered to the stern without saying a word. Will paused a moment as if he expected her to say something—anything—but after observing her fixated gaze into the water as she draped her arms over the tiller, he simply shook his head in bewilderment and rammed his shoulder into the bow. The vessel slid off the beach and into the sea. Will jumped in and took up the oars.

Once far enough from shore, Will shipped the oars and stood up to hoist the sail. Soon the wind picked up, and the longboat was gliding along under natural power. Will tied off the last rope and looked back at Elizabeth.

"The tide will be receding by the time we reach the ship. We need to swap positions now if I'm to effectively handle the boat," he said. Elizabeth looked up at him and immediately relinquished her spot in the stern. Will sat down at the tiller and began to steer the familiar course toward Belle Island. Elizabeth seated herself amidships facing him. Their eyes met.

"Why did thou insist upon my company this day?" she asked.

"I have surrendered to the fact that I am not comfortable leaving thee alone in the leftenant's presence. After thy description of his behavior while I was away, I feel it best that thou remain by my side for the duration of our contract. Thy eternal safety and well-being are of the utmost importance. And it occurs to me that I shall most likely need thy assistance in today's endeavors."

Will was unsure of his last statement, but felt it was necessary for reasons even he did not fully understand.

"And what of the leftenant's injuries and need for looking after?"

"His body appears to be healing at a faster rate than I had anticipated. I believe him to be past the point of needing continuous care. Today will be the test. Upon our return to Fort Hope, we will bear witness to just how incapacitated he really is. In the meantime, I will keep thee safe...and with me."

Elizabeth looked away from Will for a moment, then turned back to him and said, "It pleases me to know that thou finally acknowledge the danger lurking under thy very nose. I need not remind thee yet again of what I have been so outspoken and clear about since the very discovery of that man."

"Understood, my dear," Will retorted, keeping his seafaring gaze fixed on the watery course he had set.

Elizabeth observed as Will's attention became increasingly drawn to the sky. His eyes methodically surveyed the horizon and seemed particularly attracted to several jagged, low-hanging cloud banks. For a few minutes, she quietly tried to understand Will's focus on the heavens, and then she tried to imagine what thoughts might be running through his mind. But she quickly grew bored and lazily leaned backwards, closed her eyes, and became concerned with little else but the rising sun and the way it warmed her face.

Driven by a healthy wind funneled between the islands, the longboat plowed forward through the channel until the wreck of the *Repulse* gradually emerged into full view. The morning fog—which routinely draped the vessel in a natural cloak—was absent, and the ship was entirely exposed from stem to stern, making it appear less ominous and more accessible. At a certain distance, it even gave the illusion that it was still seaworthy and just quietly biding time at anchor.

After a slight jolt of the small craft, Elizabeth opened her eyes and sat up. She looked back and saw Will shortening sail and working the tiller in a more concentrated fashion. The long-boat began to sweep back and forth in a tight pattern—a nautical maneuver Elizabeth had witnessed previously whenever Will had his nets over the side and was trolling over a large school of fish. Without questioning him directly, she was finally able to establish *what* he was doing but not necessarily *why*. He was now clearly employing a slower, more indirect, and most decidedly overcautious approach toward the *Repulse*. *It would make sense if the fog was thick and his visibility impaired*, she thought, *but there is not a single obstruction to our primary course—for as far as the eye can see. What game is afoot?* She could stand it no longer.

"What is the matter?"

"I do not care for how the wind is shifting so unpredictably," Will answered, never taking his eyes off the horizon. "It is most erratic, and the sail, when full, is not agreeable to such random and misdirected gusts. I have made the proper adjustments so that we do not lose control and slam into the side of the ship and cause more damage to it and ourselves."

Will finally lowered his gaze to meet Elizabeth's. He looked at her earnestly until she offered a simple nod in reply and then looked away. Whether his answer was sufficient for her did not matter. He was not about to reveal the true reason for his course of action. He pretended to struggle with the tiller to add merit to the lie he had just told. In reality, his guarded advance toward the *Repulse* was initiated so that he might have advance warning of any potential threats that could be dangerous to the foolish and unsuspecting. Most specifically, his eyes swept back and forth in search of birch bark canoes beached along the shore, or any sign or sound of two-legged movement.

As the longboat drew closer, Will couldn't prevent the perspicuous images of enraged native savages from flooding his every thought. His recent battle with the two Abenaki warriors on the Neck replayed over and over in his mind until his hands began to shudder. He also couldn't help but recall the mysterious arrows stuck in the ship's mainmast, the uncertainty about where they had originated, and how and when they had gotten there. He had always lived with a degree of fear—it was an ordinary part of life on Storm Island—but never had it manifested itself into something so potent and foreboding that it literally rendered him unable to think clearly or act unhindered. He contemplated turning back. But after one final visual inspection of Belle Island's shoreline, the immediate surrounding waters, and the deck of the *Repulse* itself, and after detecting no sign of danger, Will smothered his fears and summoned up the courage to set a direct course toward the ship and what he was convinced would be the key to a new and better life. He took a deep breath, and a moment later he brought the longboat alongside the *Repulse* in exactly the same spot he had used to board the disabled vessel before. He dropped the sail and tied up to the ship.

"Here," he said to Elizabeth with an outstretched arm, "let me help thee."

She stood up and took his hand.

"I shall climb up onto the deck," he stated while they looked at the tangled rigging dangling over the side. "Once on board, I'll lower down a secure line. We'll use it to fasten off the gear and hoist it up. After all is secure, tie a line around thy waist and I will pull thee aboard."

Elizabeth, unsure of the plan, looked around a bit confusedly, then back at Will before nodding.

"I shall be but a moment," he said, slinging his musket and satchel over his shoulder. He grasped the damaged rigging and began to pull himself up. Once on the deck, he crouched and hurriedly scanned all directions. Spying no immediate threat, he quickly discovered a suitable length of loose rope, which he did not hesitate to put to use. He lowered it down to the waiting Elizabeth.

"Tie off the ram's head," he instructed. "Place the bundle of goods in my fishing net, then draw up the corners and slip the iron hook through the webbing. I will attempt to haul the entire load up with one mighty heave."

Elizabeth acknowledged his request with a nod and set about securing the gear in the order Will had specified. As she worked, he waited nervously, glancing over his shoulder every few seconds for any signs of trouble. He couldn't shake the apprehension swelling within him and tried to stave it off by forcing himself to focus on the task at hand. The sudden and pleasant sound of Elizabeth's voice granted his worrying brain the reprieve it badly needed.

"The bundle is secure and the knots are tight," she called. "Haul away!"

Bracing his left foot against the gunnel, Will spit on his hands and clutched the rope. With a massive tug, he gauged the weight of the load and determined it was within his hoisting capabilities. The netted supplies started to rise as he hauled on the rope, and soon the awkward bundle was within sight of the deck. One final and mighty yank heaved the load aboard. Will let out a huge breath and gasped for air to relieve the strain on his back and chest. He smiled at the gear now safely on deck, but knew his job wasn't finished yet.

"Here...take this line and tie it around thy waist," Will said after undoing the rope and tossing it down to Elizabeth.

Once she was secure and ready, he braced himself again and steadily began to pull. To his joy and relief, Elizabeth proved lighter than the netted bundle on the deck, and he took extra care to lift her with as much grace as his tired muscles would allow.

"Give me thy hand," Will said when she got within reach. His right hand came off the rope and grabbed her outstretched arm. With one last steady tug, he pulled her aboard, and they crumpled together onto the deck to rest. After a minute, Elizabeth stood up and began to take in her mysterious new surroundings.

Will slowly got up and watched as Elizabeth began to timidly wander about the deck. She leisurely twirled around trying to take it all in. As her reticence melted away, the speed with which she began to explore and examine every little shipboard detail increased. Even Will found himself in awe again as the vessel—with all its secrets and ties to a world largely unknown to him—came to represent a portal into a revitalized existence for their tiny colony. To Elizabeth, simply being able to walk on and touch something she had seen almost exclusively in books made her feel alive and full of hope. It was as if the images in those volumes had miraculously come to life. She longed to see with her eyes and hold in her hands everything with ties to true civilization—anything that did not originate from the prison of Storm Island or the ravaged settlement on the Neck.

Will lingered about and began to organize his gear while Elizabeth happily dashed around the deck, seemingly oblivious to the ship's battle damage and the life-threatening hazards it presented. She tiptoed in her bare feet through the charred wood, broken glass, and twisted metal fragments with a grace and precision that Will could not explain but merely marveled at. Soon her hunger for more alluring evidence of the world she yearned to be a part of became more than the upper deck could satisfy. Will joined her near the front of the ship.

"Take me belowdecks," she said enthusiastically. "I want to see more."

"With all due haste," he replied with a nod. "I will take thee below to better illustrate our goal and the challenge at hand. Be warned, however: I cannot guarantee thou will not lay eyes upon sights that prove unsettling."

Elizabeth nodded and motioned for Will to take the lead. They made their way from the bow to the quarterdeck, pausing only briefly at the mainmast. Will cleverly masked his concern and total astonishment at what he saw—the native arrows were gone! With a casual glance around the base of the mast that went largely unnoticed by Elizabeth, Will confirmed his greatest fear. It was unlikely that any natural occurrence had dislodged and swept the arrows overboard. Most assuredly something—or someone—had removed and reclaimed their property. The evidence appeared indisputable, and a sharp bolt of fear seared Will's gut. He briefly thought about retrieving his musket, but decided against it for fear of alerting Elizabeth and instilling panic. There was still no sign of danger, and a voice in his head reasoned it was best to proceed with the plan. He continued on belowdecks with Elizabeth in tow.

"Stay close," he warned. "It's dark and there are many hazards lying about that could cause injury with a sudden shift in wind or surge in tide. Take my hand."

Skillfully, Will retraced the path he had taken during his earlier exploration and took care to watch for any new surprises. Elizabeth's excitement diminished noticeably in the tight and dank spaces—especially where the sunlight did not penetrate— and she clutched Will's hand more aggressively, pulling him ever closer to her. It was as if she was beginning to absorb the true eeri- ness and potential danger of her surroundings.

"Come this way," Will said. "The captain's quarters are just ahead."

They entered the Great Cabin and felt a refreshing gust of sea air wash across their faces. The shot-out windows and cavernous holes in the stern were a comforting and welcome sight for Eliz- abeth, who relished both the breeze and the light that the dam- age allowed in. She released Will's hand and began to poke around, picking up and examining anything that caught her eye and kindled her interest. She went from one thing to the next, eventually set- tling on the damaged violin and bow. The instrument was far too ruined to ever play a pleasant tune again, but that did not stop her from cradling the remnants under her chin and drawing the bow across the two remaining strings in hopes of producing her own imaginary symphony. Unfortunately, the only sound was that of the instrument itself as it crumbled to pieces and clattered to the floor.

"Remain here a moment," Will said, taking advantage of Eliz- abeth's preoccupation with her new surroundings. He added, "I must check the flooded lower deck to be sure it's safe to proceed."

As if she had not heard a word, Elizabeth said, "Look here, Will. Perhaps this case holds something of interest."

From under a pile of charred wood and broken glass, Eliza- beth pulled out a long, slender, dark wooden case. Will set upright a small overturned table and gestured for Elizabeth to set the case upon it. They looked at it and then at each other.

"Open it," Will said.

Elizabeth undid the latches and opened the cover, reveal- ing a truly tremendous find. Inside and lying opposite one another were two pristine and ornate flintlock pistols nestled on a bed of soft red satin. Will reached in and carefully retrieved one for closer examination.

"They were destined for Spain, I would wager," he said. "The inscriptions on the side appear to be in Spanish. A gift for royalty perhaps? There is a date as well...1715...and the metal plating on the side...that's gold accented with small gemstones—diamonds I believe!"

Elizabeth picked up and examined the second pistol, a great smile beaming across her face as her fingers slid up and down the barrel. Instantly, she became entranced with the treasure in her hands and longed to find similar items of value.

Will placed his gun back in the case and motioned for Elizabeth to do the same with hers. She complied and carefully closed the cover.

"This could be the first of many valuable finds," Will said. "Who knows what unbelievable wealth lies just a few feet down from where we are standing? We must not delay any further. Stay here, and I will return posthaste."

Elizabeth resumed her foraging of the Great Cabin's contents while Will made his way down into the flooded lower regions of the ship. Again he found himself in knee-deep water, slogging toward the hatch that led down into the dark, flooded hold. As he got to the edge, he was reminded of his earlier experience involving the three floating dead bodies. He looked around, but to his surprise, like the arrows topside, the bodies were also missing. A chill prickled down his spine and sent a surge of fear through his heart. There was no doubt left in his mind now: At some earlier point, the savages had boarded and searched the ship.

But why would they have taken the bodies? he mused. *What purpose would that serve, and what advantage would they gain by such action? And just how emboldened have they now become? And are they still lurking nearby?*

Just then, Will wheeled around in terror and fell down into the water as something touched him from behind. Scrambling to assume a defensive posture, he hurriedly swiped water from his face and looked up.

"It's only me," a friendly voice said. "I did not mean to give thee such a fright."

Now soaked to the bone, Will got to his feet and said irritably, "I told thee to wait in the Great Cabin."

"I grew restless and... This water...it is...it is very cold," she stuttered.

Will could see the bottom of her dress floating in the frosty seawater.

"We should not remain here in the shadows for long," he said more calmly. "The sun does not breach this deck enough to raise the water temperature. Soon we'll both feel the bone-numbing effect the ocean brings upon lingering fools. But before we depart, I must show thee this open hatch."

Will pointed downward as Elizabeth's eyes faithfully followed his finger. She peered through the opening into the dark and tenebrous depths below with both trepidation and curiosity.

"This is the primary access point into the ship's main hold. We must properly position our hoisting gear so that it goes easily through the hatch opening above and drops freely to where it can be manually attached to whatever lies submerged beneath us. Once the hoisting apparatus is ready and threaded through the hatch openings, I shall swim down deep and secure the goods with the hook and net. Standing right here on the edge will be my assistant holding a rope tied around my waist. At any sign of trouble, I will tug three times on the line to indicate distress. The assistant will then pull me up to safety."

"The leftenant is to be thy assistant, I presume?" Elizabeth asked.

"That is my plan," Will answered. "Come now, let us get topside before thy bare toes turn blue and snap like icicles. I must devise a proper hoisting system before we do anything further."

"Perhaps we should devise a plan to obtain some nourishment first, Will. I am quite famished, and I assume thou art as well."

"Without question. For the moment, let us adjourn in favor of some much-needed food and warmth."

An hour passed as the two sat on deck drying off in the sun and eating small rations of cod. Will refused to sit idle and took the opportunity to rethread the ram's head with new cordage scavenged from the damaged rigging. With that chore accomplished, Will looked up at the mainmast, then at the sky. It was a calm and rather hot day, but despite the agreeable weather, Elizabeth couldn't help but notice the worried expression on Will's face every time he stared off into the horizon. She had seen the look before and was aware of the dozens of potential unpleasantries it foretold...yet she offered neither comment nor question in its regard. Instead she chose to rise up, swallow the last bit of her food, and pose a different query to Will.

"How doth thou propose to attack this formidable task?" she asked, glancing around.

"We'll use this pivoting cargo boom that's connected to the mainmast," Will replied, pointing upwards and also rising to his feet. "I'll secure the ram's head assembly to the boom and then swing it over the hold. We'll lower down the hook and lines with my attached fish net. Only we won't be catching any fish—this time, I hope we'll be netting something far more valuable."

Elizabeth stared up at the boom and then back at Will. "It looks damaged at the base...probably from the battle. Art thou confident it is secure and able to perform its duty?"

"Nay," he answered. "But I shall climb up the damaged shrouds and shore up the boom with my topmaul and nails...and any sturdy scraps of loose planking available to use as braces. Once the repairs are complete, we will test the boom's strength and haul up a single coffer of goods. It shall be our day's reward!"

With that, Will gathered his tools and some rusty wrought-iron nails from the bundle of gear and placed them in his satchel. He then collected several suitable lengths of battle-damaged planking that could be used as bracing. Using the ship's shrouds as a rope ladder, he climbed up until he reached the base of the damaged boom.

"Elizabeth!" he shouted to capture her attention. "Stay close and keep thine eyes open and alert to any danger that might elude my awareness. Watch for movement and listen for irregular sounds. Beckon to me if you see or hear anything unusual."

Elizabeth signaled her understanding and Will got to work.

The boom was in worse shape than he had hoped. A cannon blast had taken a fist-size chunk out of a key section, causing a noticeable sag under the strain of its own weight. The damaged part was barely within Will's reach, and he struggled to repair it, constantly stopping for fear of losing his balance and plunging head first onto the deck below. Nevertheless, he persevered, using all his ingenuity to keep his body stable while holding the pieces of deck planking in place. Pounding in the nails was a painstakingly awkward process. It was slow going, and Will had to pause every so often to climb back down and retrieve a dropped piece of planking, some disobliging nails, or, on more than one occasion, his topmaul.

He rested every few minutes to wipe away the sweat pouring off his brow and to look down at the sea and over at Belle Island. He had a unique vantage point and was keen on not letting the opportunity go to waste. He enjoyed the magnificent view the ship's heights afforded, and he especially liked watching the slow rolling ocean and the swaying of the small island's saplings in the mild ocean breeze. It gave him comfort and security for a reason he could not readily explain but also did not question. Ultimately, however, his attention was drawn back up to the sky, which made him scowl and resume his repairs at a speedier pace.

As the day went on, Will's acute focus on his dangerous repair work caused him to lose track of Elizabeth and her general whereabouts. Though requested to stay nearby and keep a watchful eye out for any sign of trouble, Elizabeth had paid no heed to her obligations and had taken it upon herself to engage in activities that more suited her fancy. At first she casually roamed the upper deck, fascinated by the many battle implements strewn about. She ran her fingers down the barrels of the deck cannons while quietly imagining the destruction they wrought when discharged. Then she playfully rolled several loose cannonballs down an exposed scupper line, gleefully watching the heavy lead orbs splash into the sea. Afterwards, she picked up a discarded sword with a broken hilt and a twisted blade, swinging it about as if she were a soldier or a pirate herself. And when she was certain Will wasn't looking, she crept back down belowdecks to indulge her whims even further in the discovery of more unusual—or valuable—items. She was crafty, though, and always cunningly reappeared just below the mainmast whenever the sound of Will's topmaul went silent—as if she had been there the whole time and not neglected her duties.

The day continued to slip by, and Will was not pleased with the exhausting amounts of time it had taken to complete his task. But with one final effort, he crawled out onto the newly reinforced boom with the ram's head dangling from a line around his waist. He hugged the horizontal structure with both his arms and legs tightly wrapped around it, and inched his way farther and farther out. His heart beat wildly with every little creak and crack from the wood just below him, but he kept going, determined to finish what he had started and had worked so hard to accomplish this day. Elizabeth watched intently from below, but dared not utter a word. Finally, Will reached the end and slowly sat up, his legs now straddling the boom. He pulled the rope around his waist until the first block of pulleys was within reach. He successfully secured it by inserting a small hook on the top of the block through an iron loop bolted into the boom's tip. When it was in place, he secured and uncoiled the hoisting lines until they dangled down to the deck. He then used them to climb back down himself before tying them off around the mainmast.

"It's done," said Elizabeth with excitement. "Doth thou think it will work?"

Will reached up and grabbed the large hoisting hook attached to the bottom block and pulled it down just a few feet above the deck. He checked the tension and stepped onto it with all his weight. The boom showed no sign of failing—an encouraging sight, but not a true test of its strength.

"We shall see," Will replied. "I shall attach the net to the hook before lowering it down. The weight of the cargo below will be the true measure of our hoisting assembly's overall resilience. It is not just the boom's strength that is in question. The blocks, the pulleys, and the cordage they are threaded with are all suspect. Any one of those components could fail and lead to disaster."

"To be sure," said Elizabeth with a mischievous smile. "But I think this is a moment of triumph that needs to be celebrated, and I intend to do just that."

As soon as the words slipped off her lips, her arms crossed

over her body and pulled her dress off. Instantly, the sight of her naked form—as was normally the case—made Will forget everything else. His heart began to thump and his breathing became more rapid. He desired her, and at that moment he wanted to plunder her body more than he wanted to plunder the ship. He reached out to embrace her.

"It is so hot this day...and thou must catch *me* before all other considerations," she said with a giggle before darting off and diving over the side into the cold sea below.

A bit stupefied, Will raced over to the gunwale and watched with relief as Elizabeth's head breached the surface—the mischievous smile still on her face as she winked up at him and lazily treaded water. He began to undress with thoughts of jumping in and joining her, but he thought better of the impulsive notion, and for once mastered his sexual drives with practical logic.

"We have much more to do, my love," he shouted down to her. "As much as I desire to join thee in a wet and refreshing frolic, we must finish our work and be off before nightfall is upon us. The most challenging and dangerous chapter of today's undertakings are still before us, and I shall need thy direct assistance if we are to succeed."

Elizabeth responded by swimming about with as much of her body exposed as possible in hopes of enticing Will to bend to her lustful inclinations. He fought back his natural urges by conjuring up discouraging thoughts about wasted time and energy-draining toil, both problems Elizabeth had just needlessly created. Surprisingly, the more he looked at her, the less aroused and the more vexed he became. He kept his growing anger in check, however, and made sure not to lash out with a verbal tirade that would ignite a quarrel resulting in nothing but ill feelings and more wasted time. He waited patiently, as he knew she would become uncomfortable and eventually tire in the cold water, and it wasn't long before her aquatic prancing ceased, replaced by a more sedate attitude accompanied by a dour expression.

As he watched her, Will had an idea. He went back to the cargo boom and grabbed the rope attached to the pivot point. He pulled hard, and with great difficultly managed to swivel the boom outboard so that the hook dangled over the water close to the hull and also near Elizabeth. He lowered it down until it was just above the waterline.

"I regret to mention this now, my love, but I have spied sharks in this stretch of water during past fishing excursions. Perhaps it's best thou clasp the hook and come back aboard? Such a short time has passed, yet I find myself missing my dearest one tremendously. Please come back to me."

Elizabeth responded with a sarcastic leer and shook her head. She reluctantly swam over to the hook and placed both feet on it while using the rope to pull herself into a standing position. Once she was stable, Will grabbed the hoisting line and began to pull, slowly lifting Elizabeth out of the water. Will was pleasantly surprised at how well the ram's head eased the weight of the load, and he now fully realized how essential the machinery truly was if he hoped to successfully hoist anything out of the ship's hold. Nervously, he fretted over his repair efforts with every back-straining heave. He prayed the whole assembly wouldn't collapse and kill his beloved. The very thought made him pull for all he was worth.

"Grab onto the side while I tie off the rope," he said as soon as Elizabeth's head appeared over the gunnel. "Let me help thee," he added, rushing over to pull her aboard. He slipped and fell backwards onto the deck with Elizabeth tumbling on top of him with a terse little shriek. When they got to their feet, Will wrapped his arms around his quivering lover, holding her close and offering intimate warmth. He looked into her eyes and said, "Thou art the loveliest thing this fisherman has ever caught. God has truly blessed me. I do love thee." He moved in to kiss her, but was abruptly stopped.

"My dress," she said.

Will slowly stepped back and pointed to the ragged garment still lying in a heap on the deck. He said nothing and tried to conceal the puzzlement on his face.

Elizabeth quickly used the dress to towel the chilly seawater from her body before slipping it back on. She then turned to Will and proclaimed rather stonily, "Thou said there was more to be accomplished before our departure. We must make haste. Agree?"

Unsure of his own emotions and at a loss for words, Will simply nodded and gestured for Elizabeth to help him swing the boom back inboard and over the deck hatch opening. Will was pleased with the boom's integrity and confident that it could do the job, but his thoughts meandered back to Elizabeth, wondering what was going through her mind and why his simple act of affection had been so firmly rebuffed.

This is how she acts when she doesn't get her way or must submit to authority...no matter how sensible or trivial the request, he thought. *This is her method of rebelling and preying upon my feelings. It is but an impulse...not reflective of her true nature. I mustn't let it irk me. We're in love. She does love me...doesn't she? My God... what goes on in that skull of hers?*

Will collected his fishing net and removed his hat and his boots. "I'm going below. When I say so, lower the hook down to me."

Elizabeth took the rope and nodded her compliance.

Will soon found himself back in the cold water, which was now clearly above his knees. He found the temperature very displeasing, but it did have one positive effect: The icy chill quickly drove all the passion from his mind and body. Nowhere was the effect more profoundly felt—physically—than in his breeches.

The tide is rising, he thought. He looked up at Elizabeth and said, "Lower the hook now...and slowly."

Amid the loud squeaking of the cordage rolling over the pulleys, Will watched as the hook steadily sank down within his reach. He threaded it through the net's webbing in a way that would keep it tight and secure but would also employ maximum lift.

"Resume lowering, Elizabeth," Will shouted topside, adding, "Do not stop until the hook rests on the bottom."

Slowly the hook and net disappeared into the cold black water. A minute later, Elizabeth shouted, "It is done."

"Tie off the rope and come hither," replied Will.

As Elizabeth made her way down to him, Will produced an appropriate length of rope he had procured earlier and had stored in the Great Cabin. He tied one end tightly around his waist and handed the other to Elizabeth when she reached his side.

Will took a nervous breath, hesitating to speak as he stared down into the abyss. Finally, he summoned the courage to proceed with the final part of the day's plan. He looked squarely into Elizabeth's eyes.

"I'm going to swim into the hold now," he said, his voice not exactly brimming with confidence. "I'll follow the hoisting line down to the net and then pull it over to where the cargo is located. With luck, I shall entangle a wooden box or chest, swim back up to this deck, and together we will go topside and attempt to haul it up."

"What am I to do with this rope?" Elizabeth asked.

"It is cold, dark, and very easy to lose thy sense of direction in that devilish pool below. This rope is to act as a safety line and also to guide my orientation. Keep it taut, but allow me all the slack my movements dictate. Should I give any indication of distress, pull me back to safety. Doth thou understand?"

"I understand," she replied. "Now go before the icy water saps all our vigor."

With reluctance and foolish courage astride a mountain of uncertainty, Will plunged into the void. Elizabeth gradually let the safety rope out as Will followed the hoisting line down, eventually disappearing into the darkness. Sporadic air bubbles at the surface were the only indications of life below.

Will followed the line until he reached the bottom. Blindly, he groped about until his hands found the hook and net resting on a pile of debris. He grasped the heavier hook and tugged it toward the stern—where he remembered previously discovering what he thought felt like stacked boxes or sea chests. With one hand firmly holding the hook and net, and suspended horizontally in the water, he used his free hand to feel along the bottom of the hold until...

That's it, he thought as his fingers finally prodded the box-like mass. He madly groped to find an edge or a sharp corner—anything he could snag with the net. Applying tremendous force that nearly caused him to lose consciousness, Will barely dislodged a very heavy box from the stack. It moved just enough so that he could catch the exposed corner of it with the net and drape the rest over it. He was unsure how secure it was, but he was rapidly running out of time. He began to feel confused, and his strength as well as the air in his lungs was diminishing in a watery cloud of blackness. His head started to spin and his only recourse was to swim out of the depths of the ship's belly. He reached out for the hoisting line intent on using it to guide him back to the opening. But as he probed the chilly darkness, his whirling brain made him tumble further away from the line and into a realm of oxygen-deprived disorientation. He began to panic again, just as he had before. He swam in the direction he thought was up, but thumped into something hard that sent him tumbling back down through the depths. He lashed out with one final thrust, not knowing where he was or what direction he was going...then his breath was gone, and everything went black.

And then, as if the hand of God itself reached down from the heavens to pluck his nearly lifeless soul from the watery pits of Hell, a light emerged through all the darkness and a tremendous surge of air brought life back into Will's body. A thunderous gasp escaped his lungs, followed by a barrage of coughing. His arms wildly flailed about and his eyes tried to focus and make sense of where he was and what was happening.

"Be still...I've got thee...Will...steady thyself!"

As the water drained from his ears, the words became more coherent, and he slowly regained his senses. At first he felt like a baby being held tightly in his mother's arms, but as his eyes focused, he saw Elizabeth and realized that it was her protective embrace giving him comfort and support. She patted his back to ease the coughing and help expel the remaining seawater from his lungs.

"Settle thyself. Thou art safe now," reassured Elizabeth.

"What happened?" Will choked out in response.

"Perhaps thou should tell me," Elizabeth answered. "The safety line jumped about erratically and then just seemed to go limp. I surmised there was a problem and decided to bring thee back up. It proved a daunting task, I might add."

"I lost my way down there," Will said. "I got turned about and could not recover. I felt nothing but frigidness, heard nothing but silence, and saw only an unending expanse of darkness. I was surely on the brink of death...I would have died down there if not for thee. Thank God for thy precious body and soul, which I could not live without," he said, giving her a weak but passionate hug.

"We must get thee topside before we both freeze down here," Elizabeth replied as she undid the line from around Will's waist. "Come, I shall help thee."

She aided Will to his feet, keeping him close and supporting each step as they made their way to the upper deck. There, they crumpled into a single shivering heap.

"Hold thy body close to mine," said Elizabeth. "We will share warmth for comfort and let the sun's heat assist our recovery."

Thus intimately entwined, their trembling gradually subsided. A warm breeze and the heat from the sun's rays brought energy back to their wet and tired bodies. As his strength intensified, Will began to sense the familiar carnal urgings he had experienced earlier reignite. He pulled Elizabeth's lips to his and kissed her with undisguised desire. He was delighted and somewhat relieved that she did nothing to shun his advances, but his thoughts quickly soured when his hands began to wander and were immediately restrained when they encroached upon select areas of Elizabeth's anatomy. She pulled away from him and stood up.

"Ease thy storm, Will. Now is not the time. We have to finish what we set out to do before night is upon us," she said.

"Thou saved my life. I am eternally grateful...and was only trying to express my gratitude through—"

"I understand, Will," she interrupted. "But we have other matters requiring immediate attention. How is thy condition...physically? Have thy sinews recovered sufficiently? Shall we test thy scavenged ram's head?"

Will slowly rose to his feet and stretched his legs and back while reaching toward the sky. As he looked up, he paused, and Elizabeth again noticed the unpleasant expression return to his face.

"Has the Lord insulted thee in some fashion?" she asked. "What is the source of thy grave disgust whenever thine eyes glance at the heavens?"

Will looked up again and then back at Elizabeth. He said, "I've seen this kind of sky before...at this point in the hot season."

Elizabeth glanced up and then back at Will quizzically. The sky's characteristics looked no more peculiar to her this day than any other. She shrugged her shoulders a bit, indicating the need for more explanation.

"My extensive time on the water has made me extremely sensitive to the slightest changes in weather. When the wind blows with a curious style, or the clouds hang in an unusual fashion, or the seabirds wheel about unnaturally, it almost assuredly portends the approach of foul weather—more specifically, a storm or string of storms. I fear a powerful tempest is bearing down on us and is only a matter of days away. I can smell it...almost taste it."

"We've weathered powerful gales before," said Elizabeth.

"It is not *our* survival that concerns me, it is this ship's. Its damaged hull is fragile and dangerously exposed. One massive storm could obliterate the vessel and scatter its remains—valuable or otherwise—across miles of deep ocean waters, forever out of our reach. I've spoken of it before, but more as a warning. Now I see it as an unavoidable truth—a monstrous natural menace careening our way."

"How much time do we have?"

"A week perhaps...maybe just days."

"Thou could be mistaken. The danger may just be an illusion conjured up by a strained mind and exhausted body."

"Perhaps," Will answered doubtfully. "But I trust my senses and pay heed to what they portend."

"Well then, there isn't a moment to lose," Elizabeth said. "We must act now."

She scurried over to the hoisting rope, clutched it with both hands, and gestured for Will to join her.

"We must discover if the island's best fisherman has caught anything!" she added with exuberance.

Will put on his boots and hat, spit on his hands, and grasped the rope, motioning for Elizabeth to take up position behind him. He dreaded the possibility of pulling up nothing but a loose, dangling net, but there was nothing else he could do at such a late hour. The thought made him sick, but the time was now. Will readied the cordage and they began to heave in unison. Initially, there was tension and weight on the line indicating that the net wasn't empty—or at least was still snagged on something. The pulleys squealed under the strain until an unexpected jolt caused the rope to slip through all four of the hands clutching it. Both Will and Elizabeth were caught by surprise, lost their balance, and tumbled backwards onto the deck. There was a muffled thud below.

"Did something break?" Elizabeth asked.

Will got up and examined the boom as well as the exposed block and hoisting line. All appeared to be sound.

"I think our efforts were successful in pulling a box off the top of the pile. Let's try another heave," said Will.

Much to their relief, there was still tension and considerable weight on the line when they resumed hoisting. Again they pulled in unison, but the physical strain quickly took its toll on Elizabeth. She weakened rapidly, forcing Will to compensate for her diminishing strength and effort.

"Pull hard, Elizabeth! Use all thy vigor. It's halfway raised...I can feel it. Just a bit more and we'll have it!" Will said through gritted teeth.

Elizabeth started to bawl with pain, but she didn't give up and continued to pull for all she was worth. Will's hands and arms started to go numb, but with each squeal of the pulleys came hope and anticipation. The higher the box rose, the more the boom creaked under the strain. Will prayed that the whole apparatus wouldn't snap and come crashing down upon them. His spirits soared when the top of a wooden box began to breach the opening of the upper deck's hatch. It was drab in color and clearly visible through the netting.

"There it is!" Elizabeth cried out through her tears.

"One more good and hearty heave and we'll have it!" Will thundered.

They pulled with all their remaining strength. The box, water dripping from all sides, was finally raised into full view, leaving them awestruck with the anticipation of discovering the priceless treasures it might contain.

"Steady!" Will commanded. "Ease over to the mainmast. Keep in step with me. We've got to tie off the rope."

They struggled but managed to reach the mainmast without stumbling. Suddenly, the pain became too much for Elizabeth. She released the line with a shuddering sob and crumbled to the deck in a pool of her own sweat and teardrops. The box lurched and nearly lifted Will completely off his feet, sending a sharp bolt of pain through every muscle in his body. But before the prize could plummet back to the depths from whence it came, Will was able to wrap one coil around an iron cleat coupled to the mast. He wrestled and writhed with the heavy and unruly line as if it were a snake trying to break free and bite him. But just as it seemed his efforts would be in vain, he managed a knot that firmly secured the rope to the cleat and freed him from his pain. The second his body sensed it could relax, Will dropped to his knees and lay down on the deck, breathing heavily and waiting for the tingling sensation to return to his nearly paralyzed limbs.

Elizabeth took a breath and brought her sobbing under control. Will rubbed and stretched his worn-out arms and aching backside. Eventually, they both sat up and took a hard look at the netted box precariously suspended over the open hatch. After a quiet moment of disbelief—which was quickly followed by a grand sense of accomplishment—they fell into each other's arms.

"We did it," Will whispered.

"Nay, it was *thy* courageous actions that have rewarded us this day," she purred back at him. She kissed his cheek and took his hand as they stood up.

"The sun is sinking fast," Will said. "We must secure our prize and be off before nightfall jeopardizes our safety."

"Will," said Elizabeth, "how and when doth thou intend to confront Mother again?"

Will, startled by the question, could not come up with a response.

"Surely we cannot remain at Fort Hope forever. Eventually, she will expect us to return home. What happens when her suspicions and intolerance for deception overwhelm her patience? She will uncover our ruse and stalk us like a mad hunter. How can we preserve our secret and avoid attracting her meddlesome tendencies and unpredictable wrath? I shudder to think what she will do once she discovers we've lied to her. And what of Dunsbury? What happens if she unearths evidence of his existence?"

Will thought for a moment and said, "We have time...several more days until it will become absolutely necessary to act with regards to Winnie. We cannot fear her, yet we also cannot ignore her intrusive and volatile leanings."

Will paused again. He wiped the sweat from his forehead, adjusted his hat, and put his hands on his hips.

"I don't have an answer that solves our problem concerning thy mother," he confessed. "We must think on it more when time allows, but for now we have more pressing matters, matters that, if not attended to properly, make thy whole discussion concerning thy mother...and possibly our own future existence...moot."

Will again looked to the sky with contempt and worry. His thoughts shifted from the problem of Winnie Eustis back to the impending weather. Suddenly, time, and what lay hidden beyond the horizon, became, in his mind, a monstrous predator that needed to be outwitted, outrun...or in some miraculous fashion, slain. As the problems mounted in his distracted thoughts, an unsettling sound commanded his attention.

"Will!" shouted Elizabeth, pointing urgently to the box.

A corner of the weighty prize had punched through the fish net and was exerting added pressure on the boom. The structure made cracking sounds as the box began to sag through the failing gear.

"Quickly...we must swing the boom inboard and away from the hatch!" yelled Will.

But before either he or Elizabeth could get to the rope, the net broke open and the box plummeted straight down through the bowels of the ship, offering nothing in return but a mighty splash of seawater.

In an instant, feelings of elation and accomplishment turned to dispirited shock, disappointment, and utter despair. Both Will and Elizabeth hurried to the edge and stared down. There was no sign of the box, just a noticeable increase in water level due to the rising tide. Elizabeth broke the stunned silence.

"Doth thou think—"

"No," Will interrupted, knowing full well what her question was. "It is too late in the day. The water is too high and it will soon be dark. I have neither the strength nor the turn of mind to dare and reenter that hold under the present conditions. We must come back another day. The boom needs further bracing, and all my spare fishing nets are unsound...they have been too badly eroded by use and partial neglect. I have a bigger and stronger one at home. It should be up to the task of lifting multiple boxes without fraying under a heavy load. Besides, we both need food and rest. I think it wise that we immediately set sail back to Storm, retrieve my net from home, and then check on Leftenant Dunsbury's condition upon arrival at Hope."

Elizabeth sighed and lowered her head, but she knew Will was right. As much as she desired to see a treasure chest opened before her very eyes, she knew it was impossible under the current circumstances. She acquiesced to Will's wishes by asking, "What must be done before we depart?"

"Let us gather up and load our supplies. I do not wish to leave anything of use here for fear of losing track of it."

So they collected and bundled up everything they had arrived with, taking care in lowering it down into the longboat. The tide was much higher, so it was easier to load the small vessel. When they finished, the sun had disappeared completely below the horizon. Will gently took Elizabeth by the arms and dangled her over the side. It was but a short drop into the boat, where she landed securely and unhurt. She took her place up front amid the gear. Will then climbed down the side and took his own short leap aboard.

"The day was not without some reward," he said as he untied the line and pushed off with an oar. "Thou did find those beautiful firearms. Imagine what else awaits."

Elizabeth recovered the splendid pistol case and opened it again. She held up one of the guns and was instantly entranced with the gemstones and gold plating that adorned it. She took great delight in her new acquisition, and after having so easily seized this prize, her appetite and impatience for more precious plunder was whetted.

Will sat amidships and reluctantly took up the oars. Rowing

was the last thing his exhausted body wanted to do, but the ocean was curiously tranquil and there was a strange absence of wind. Will silently cursed the calmness and refused to ready the sail, knowing it would only hang limp and useless without a proper breeze. And with the sail furled, not only would the journey back to Storm take longer, but it was apparent to him that the current conditions on the water were yet another sign of the impending storm he'd predicted earlier. With a short sigh and a noticeable lack of enthusiasm, he dipped the oars into the sea and pulled away from the wreck.

Slowly, the gap between the two vessels widened. It was now just dark enough that Elizabeth felt the need to pull the flint from Will's musket and the fire striker from his satchel to light the candle in the lantern they had brought along. It took more than a few attempts, but she got a spark to ignite the wick and bring the lantern to life. She hung it from the mast.

"That's much—"

Before Will could finish his remark, a blood-curdling shriek echoed through the channel. Both Will and Elizabeth stiffened in terror and instinctively went silent as the sound manifested into a more drawn-out and amplified bellow. The second out-cry—far more frightening and intense than the first—resonated across the water as an indescribable howl like nothing they had heard in recent years. And though they were uncertain as to what could produce such a terrifying cry, there was one thing they both understood immediately...and dreaded.

"No animal could produce such a sound as that," Will stated as he turned to face Elizabeth in the bow.

Gazing past him, she cried out, "Look!"

Will wheeled back around and felt his stomach begin to painfully churn with fear and disbelief. Rounding the bow of the *Repulse* and heading straight for them were two Abenaki canoes, each carrying two warriors. Upon sighting the longboat, the canoes maneuvered into a direct pursuit course, with each stern warrior feverishly paddling and each bow warrior equipping their bows. Their war cries intensified and indicated just one thing— they were out for blood.

The lead canoe swiftly drew within firing range. Crippled with fear, Will watched as the warrior pulled back his bow. He fired into the sky at a high arcing angle. The arrow majestically sailed upwards and then plunged back down hard and fast with deadly accuracy. Will flinched as the arrow found its mark and stuck into the boat only inches from where he sat. It was then that his blood began to boil and his drive for self-preservation took over.

Elizabeth screamed again as Will grabbed the oars and rowed harder than he ever imagined he could. The longboat was big and heavy, and did not easily glide across the placid channel waters like the lighter and more nimble canoes. Will needed the sail to get away...but there was no wind and no time to unfurl and ready the canvas. Frantic, he tried to devise a plan of escape as the canoes gradually closed the distance and more arrows rained down on them. The beach on the southeast shore of Storm was the nearest landing, but it was still too far away. He could row until his arms fell off, but he knew the savages would overtake the longboat before he neared the shoreline. There was just one drastic option left—and he needed to act fast.

"Elizabeth...my musket...and satchel!" he shouted. "Bestir thyself if thou ever wishes to see the dawn again!"

She sprang to her feet in a panic, fumbling the gun and the bag right out of her hands. Will didn't react and kept on madly straining at the oars. Knowing that Elizabeth had never fired a gun in her life and was completely ignorant of how to load or handle the musket, he knew the next step was critical and fraught with the most risk.

"Ready thyself to swap positions! Thou must take the oars," he commanded, "and afford me enough time to fight them off."

"I can't!" she cried.

"It is our only gamble," he fired back. "We will not escape to safety unless we halt their pursuit. Be brave, my love...now!"

Will shot up and leapt to the stern. Elizabeth tossed him the musket and satchel and replaced him at the oars. Tears streamed down her panicked face as she began to row. The heavy wooden blades were an unmatched fit for her small hands and arms, and she cried out in pain with each lumbering stroke.

Working methodically, Will transferred powder, shot, and wadding into the muzzle of his gun, compacting it with the ramrod. When he began to fill the flash plan, he turned back to Elizabeth in horror.

"The flint! Where's the flint?" he demanded in desperation.

"I don't know...I must have dropped it after lighting the lamp!" she cried back at him.

Will leapt back toward the bow and began rummaging for the only substance aboard that could save their lives. Precious seconds passed, and the cries of the Indians grew louder and closer, as did the barrage of arrows. Finally, Will spied the flint resting in a pool of water. He picked it up knowing it was useless in its current state. A wave of desperation and despair crashed over him as he realized that the Abenaki were only a minute or so away from reaching a lethal range of fire—where it was all but assured they could not miss.

Just as Will's thoughts began to focus on what it would feel like to have an arrow puncture his chest or a tomahawk expose the innards of his skull, he conceived a radical idea that just might be their salvation. He grabbed the fancy pistol case and threw open the lid. He yanked out both guns and hurriedly checked each one before loading them up with what little powder and shot remained in his satchel. He prayed they would function and that his aim was sound. He leapt over Elizabeth's left arm in midstroke and cocked both pistols.

The nearest canoe was now within twenty feet with the second almost as close. Will raised the guns and pointed the one in his left hand at the raging warrior in the lead canoe, who was lining up a shot specifically for him. Just as he was about to pull the trigger, he switched targets and trained the barrel on the stern paddler. In a flash of smoke, the pistol fired and the shot struck the native in the head. The Indian fell backwards and dropped his paddle, causing the canoe to shift and wobble. The warrior up front lost his balance and his control of his bow, and the arrow flew harmlessly into the sea. He toppled over backwards and nearly capsized the dugout.

Will then took aim at the second canoe's paddler. Without

even blinking, he discharged the second pistol and watched as his target quailed in agony after being hit in the left shoulder. The after-effect was much the same. The paddle was dropped and the warrior in front was caught off balance and lost his weapon in the sea. Both canoes slewed and came to a stop. Will didn't even attempt to press his attack, although he now had a slight advantage. There wasn't enough powder to finish the job with pistol shot, and he didn't have the strength or the stomach for combat with just a knife. He dropped the guns and turned to Elizabeth.

"We need to use all our might and row together," he said, sitting down next to her. Each took an oar, and they heaved with determination. Their combined efforts proved fruitful as they began to pull away from the threat.

The southeast shore drew closer and the canoes grew more distant. Elizabeth, still awash in tears, refused to give up and kept pace and rhythm with Will's oar strokes. They were both on the brink of total exhaustion, and they were not out of danger yet. They watched in horror as the Abenakis regrouped. The wounded paddler climbed into the canoe with his dead tribesman, and the two uninjured natives took to the remaining canoe, both aggressively shrieking and paddling after the longboat. Again they began to close the distance, but it was too late...the southeast shore beckoned.

Just then an arrow slammed into the oar Elizabeth was using. She screamed in terror and ducked down, and the oar slipped away into the water. Will continued to pull, but the boat veered off course. Before he could make the necessary correction, the craft barreled into a partially submerged pile of rocks that sliced into the larboard side of the bow. The longboat slammed to a stop and began to take on water, and they were still a good thirty feet from the beach.

"Swim for it!" Will shouted.

They jumped up in unison and plunged into the cold water. Arrows rained down all around them, but they swam for all they were worth until their arms and knees finally dug into sand. With what little remaining strength they possessed, they crawled out of the surf and onto the beach. They tried to get up and run, but there was nothing left. Their muscles refused to respond, and they could flee no further. All they could do was stare back at the sea and impending death. But what they saw shocked them.

The Abenaki warriors halted their pursuit and remained an appreciable distance from Storm Island's shoreline. There appeared to be an invisible threshold they did not dare cross, and Will took notice of it. The Indians screamed their threats and frustration before launching a final salvo of arrows, and then oddly drew back in the direction of their comrades and Belle Island. Soon they were out of sight, and night descended.

Wet, cold, and weary, Will and Elizabeth mustered just enough strength to hold one another and share what little body heat remained. They lay in the sand, both close to losing consciousness. The last thing Will saw was a curious little glow suspended above the water. Then his eyes finally went dark.

CHAPTER 10

Shadows of Salem

D arkness…then the familiar soft whimpering of a loved one gently penetrated his ears. His eyes opened and his mind slowly regained awareness. Will sat up and looked at the stars with scant thoughts of whether he was alive or dead. For a moment, he didn't recall where he was or what had happened. As his head began to clear, he presumed he was home in bed, and that he had just woken prematurely, before the dawn, and that just another normal day of fishing was upon him. Then his mind began to work…and remember.

He could barely see Elizabeth through the darkness, even though she was just a few feet away. She was lying on her side curled up on the sand in a tight ball, her sobbing face buried in her knees. When she became aware of Will's awakening, she unraveled herself and crawled into his waiting arms. He held her tight and whispered encouragement to ease her anxiety and physical discomfort.

"How long was I asleep?" he asked.

"I don't know…not long…an hour maybe," she replied. "There was a moment or two when I thought death had claimed thee."

"Did thou sleep as well?"

"A little…but fear has kept me awake."

"We must get home. My cabin is closest. We will rest there for the night and journey out to Hope at dawn."

"I can't. I'm so very tired and hungry," she lamented, staring down at her hands, which were calloused and cut from the

frenzied rowing. "And what about the longboat?" she asked, pointing out to the still dimly burning lantern suspended from its mast.

Will let out a short groan, having forgotten all about the
recent fate of his fishing vessel. He got to his feet and waded into
the sea until the water reached his waist. From there, he peered
intently at the damaged craft. From what little he could see, the
boat was only partially submerged at the bow and not floating
freely. The tide was outgoing, and Will knew that the boat was
close enough to shore that it would be beached during the next
low tide; he would haul it in for repairs at that point. In the meantime, he had an idea.

He dove forward and swam out to the stricken craft. Elizabeth hobbled to her feet and then to the water's edge, keeping
her eyes on Will. He swam up to the bow and climbed aboard. He
picked the lantern off the mast and shone it toward the damaged
hull. Ironically, like the *Repulse*, the longboat had also become
impaled on a strip of jagged rocks. Fortunately, the damage was
not severe, but it would have to be dealt with at a later time. Will
sloshed about and recovered everything that could be stuffed into
his satchel, including the pistols.

"Elizabeth," he cried out, "catch!"

He flung the bag into the air and watched it sail down into
Elizabeth's arms. He then took the lantern and climbed out of the
boat. With one arm, he held it above the water while he used the
other to backstroke into the shallows. Miraculously, the glowing
candle remained lit.

Wading back ashore, Will said, "There's still a bit of smoked
cod left in my bag. Let's gather some wood and build a fire. Food...
and warmth to dry our clothes will do us both good."

Elizabeth nodded, and they started to gather dry twigs and
grass to spark a modest fire right on the sand. Will touched off
the kindling with the dying flicker of the candle and nurtured the
fragile flame until it was strong enough to consume larger pieces
of wood. Soon a hearty little blaze was burning, and Will and Elizabeth huddled around it while chewing on the remainder of the
fish. Neither said anything for quite some time. It was Elizabeth,
who, after composing herself, broke the silence.

"I remember seeing them as a little girl. I remember the horrible sights and sounds of the slaughter that ensued during their attack in 1703. I remember fleeing...my father...my mother...coming to *this* accursed place. I've tried to rid my mind of those heinous memories...but they still haunt me. And now..."

Will watched her through the flames and listened as her voice quivered and trailed off. Her face looked pale and ragged, chiseled with an expression of sheer terror. He wanted to say something comforting, and offer strength and reassurance, but he struggled to find the words. He himself was now gripped with fear and uncertain of the murky future. A bit shaken, and unable to reason clearly, words just began to stumble out of his mouth.

"We cannot...that is...it is not—"

"Be silent, Will," said Elizabeth. "There is no more mystery, only certainty. They are here, and they mean to do us permanent harm before reclaiming what was once theirs. They're probably stalking us this very moment...and now—now we're trapped. Without the longboat, we're marooned on this prison of an island. We're completely at their mercy and will be massacred without pity. All our meager possessions and every trace of our existence will be scattered to the wind. Perhaps we should deprive the natives of the pleasure of destroying our lives and just slit our own throats? It would be simpler and less terrifying than dying at the torturous hands of a savage."

Her last comment was too much, and she began to weep again. Will, understanding that he needed to offer up some plan of action in order to restore confidence and resurrect a fragment of hope on Elizabeth's behalf, finally formulated a plausible idea; and alongside it an interesting, and possibly comforting, theory.

"All is not lost, my love," he said. "We will seek shelter at my cabin tonight as planned. I will get us there if I have to slay every living creature that dares to stand in our way. I will create fresh oakum from old tarry rope and cordage I've salvaged from the Neck. Mixed with hot pitch, it will make fine caulking to repair the longboat. The damage, I trust, is not that severe...and even if some new planking is required, there is a small supply of planed timber at Hope that I can cut and shape as needed. We'll gather *everything* we require to further our plans. Nothing shall hold us back. We will salvage the treasure and reap the rewards."

"And the savages? Hath thou forgotten the deadly ordeal we just faced? What say them of thy plans and dreams of wealth and entitlement? Surely they will embrace thy lofty devices and even offer assistance," she quipped. "How can one spend one single ounce of gold when one is dead?"

"There are savages on the Neck. There might even be savages over on Belle, but there are no savages here on Storm Island!" Will thundered.

"And what makes thee so convinced?" she hollered back.

"The curse," he answered smoothly. "They are kept at distance by the curse. The legend is true. My father spoke of it years ago and it's true. The savages will not set foot on Storm Island for fear of angering the spirits of their dead. We saw evidence of it this very day. Did thou not witness the native canoes stop their pursuit once we entered Storm's waters? They could have beached their dugouts and run us down dead on shore or shot arrows into our backs at point-blank range while we struggled in the surf. Why did they stop their attack and leave before killing us? It was the curse, I tell thee...the curse of Storm saved our hides this day...and God will not allow us to fail at our mission."

"Even if that is true—and I don't believe it is—surely Belle Island, just across the channel, is now infested with savages. In God's name, even if thou *can* repair the longboat, how can thou return to the ship without being discovered and killed before one tiny speck of treasure is garnered?"

"We don't know if Belle is occupied or not," he answered. "Father always said the curse extended to Belle. The savages were in canoes. They could have paddled over directly from the Neck and—"

"Thou art blind, William Estes...and foolish with thy notions. We are doomed. Death is looking for us, and when it finds us, it will be merciless and cruel and—"

"What would thou have me do, Elizabeth?" Will snapped, his temper rising and his patience waning. "We cannot just abandon this place for reasons I am tired of repeating. Our situation grows more desperate by the minute, and I fully realize the severity of our ever-shrinking pool of options, but I have put forth the best plan I can conceive for the betterment of us all. All we can do at this time is overcome the immediate obstacle that hinders our path. First, we must get home and prepare what is needed to fix the longboat. Without *it*, we are most assuredly dead. Everything depends on making that craft seaworthy again. Doth thou at least agree on that course of action?"

"What other choice is there?" she said sullenly.

Will took her by the shoulders and looked deep into her eyes.

"Please...without thy trust, there is nothing to build a future on," he said. "Without thee at my side, I should be inclined to give up entirely and welcome death's blow."

There was a pause, and then she replied, "Perhaps I speak too freely without enough careful thought. Thine intentions are always for the best, I know. I do trust thee, Will, and again pledge my faith in thine endeavors...wherever they lead us in this world or the next."

They kissed briefly and gathered up their things. Elizabeth recovered a fresh candle from the satchel and replaced the spent one in the lantern. Will snuffed out the fire, and they began their trek back to the Estes cabin.

"Will, what about our parents?" Elizabeth asked. "What should happen if we come across them this evening? How will we explain where we've been and what we've been doing while away?"

"It's so very late, and both thy mother and my father should be sound asleep at thy mother's cabin. We should find avoiding them to be very simple at this hour of the night. To be honest, I am more anxious to discover the goings-on with Leftenant Dunsbury back at Fort Hope. I pray he hasn't been in much pain or feeling overly neglected."

They crept along cautiously, hampered by the darkness, and increasingly sensitive to any strange sound or sudden movement that could indicate danger. As the trail led them farther inland, a peculiar glow, well off the trail and coming from a fixed point deeper in the interior, drew their full attention. They halted and crouched in silence as they tried to determine exactly what they were looking at.

"That's firelight...there's nothing else it could be," Elizabeth whispered. "Where is thy curse now? I warned thee...savages...Oh Lord, have mercy on our souls."

Will, about to take Elizabeth's hand and rush off down the trail, paused as the faint sound of a woman's voice, injected with random bursts of laughter, suddenly pierced the still night air. They couldn't comprehend the words, but they recognized the inflections of civilized speech. Then, as if mindlessly heeding a siren's call, their sense of self-preservation was overwhelmed by dangerous curiosity. They grasped hands and headed straight for the light, leaving the lantern behind.

Moving with careful precision, Will led the way and Elizabeth mimicked his every footstep. The mysterious light grew larger and more distinct, and soon the unmistakable shape of a bonfire, its embers and flames racing up toward the heavens, was revealed. The bright fire, built in a large clearing, temporarily cast the nocturnal eeriness of the woods aside. For the moment, there were no voices to be heard, nor was there another human soul to be seen.

Will and Elizabeth prudently remained in the shadows, peering from the cover of a towering pine. They watched and waited for the mysterious voice to reveal itself more completely. What they saw next was almost beyond their wildest imaginings. Emerging from the darkness was a strange and haggard-looking figure. Its form was slender and unrecognizable at first, but as it swayed near the fire and directly into the light, its identity became shockingly clear.

"Mother," whispered Elizabeth, her tongue barely able to function after laying eyes upon the utterly implausible scene. Equally stunned to silence was Will. Before them, a mere twenty feet away, stood a bedraggled and repulsive version of a woman entirely devoid of anything representative of God or the Puritan faith. She swayed and mumbled in the firelight—completely naked. Her gray, stringy hair was loose and hung down over her bony shoulders nearly to her waist. She was filthy, with blotches of mud smeared over certain portions of her face and body. Outwardly, she resembled someone from a medieval time and place; inwardly, her perverse gyrations and expressions seemed driven by a demonic presence. Clearly, what now stood before Will and Elizabeth was not the pious mother and pedagogue both had known their entire lives, but something else...something rather vile, unhinged, and decidedly wicked.

As the fire raged, Winnie's unbalanced movements intensified, as did her voice. The words that roared through her lips were robust but incomprehensible. It was as if she was speaking—or attempting to speak—some ancient pagan language. She twirled about in irregular circles, oftentimes ringing the fire itself. Occasionally, she would stop and pick up a stick, which she would use to draw odd symbols in the dirt. Once a symbol was complete, she would stare up at the sky and bellow a hideous cackle. Moments later, she went silent and slumped down to the ground. It appeared as if all the evil energy she had been channeling had finally drained her very life force.

At this point, Will took Elizabeth's hand and motioned for them to make a quiet and hasty exit. He pulled her away—only to step down hard on a broken tree branch that snapped loudly under the weight of his boot. Winnie looked up abruptly in their direction. Without glancing back, Will and Elizabeth took off into the woods. They scampered back toward the main trail like two spooked squirrels. When they came upon the spot where they had left the lantern, Elizabeth grabbed it. Now, with the dim light back in hand to help guide them, they hurried back toward the Estes cabin.

"Doth thou think she saw us?" asked Elizabeth.

"Hard to tell...I do not know," Will replied, urging Elizabeth to move faster.

"What in God's holy name was she doing? Has she abandoned all sense of righteousness and taken up allegiance with the Devil? Has she—"

"Keep thy feet lively...we've got to get home before we can attempt to sort out any of this madness," Will said.

It wasn't long before they emerged from the forest and into the open meadows. It got quiet again except for their own wheezing breaths. Once the overhead canopy of the forest was behind them, the sky lit up with a display of twinkling stars that helped lead them home.

They burst into the cabin with relief, only to be faced with another unsettling surprise. Elizabeth slowly closed the door and backed up against it with her hands covering her mouth. Will held the lantern up high and set about picking up and lighting random candles that had been scattered on the floor. Once the room was illuminated, he and Elizabeth stared in astonishment and mounting fear.

The room had been ransacked and torn apart. All of Will and Cyrus's possessions lay about on the floor either damaged or in disarray. The table, chairs, and both beds were upended, and all their food was gone. After the initial shock passed, Will repositioned the furniture while Elizabeth built a fire. When both tasks were complete, they sat down at the table in the midst of the mess.

"My father...we must find him," Will said, trying to get to his feet again. "He could be in trouble or—"

He collapsed back down in his seat. He could not fight the overwhelming fatigue any longer. Elizabeth was no better off. Nothing, not even the terror of the unknown, could compel them to any action but sleep. With his last ounce of strength, Will barricaded the door and extinguished all the light in the cabin save that which came from the fireplace. He staggered over and tumbled onto his bed. Elizabeth joined him, and they instantly fell asleep in each other's arms.

The first light of morning arrived without incident. Will and Elizabeth woke to find their immediate surroundings unchanged, with no signs of a threatening incursion. All was quiet except for the normal sounds of the tide and the chirping of the early-morning birds. Will chased the lethargy from his mind and body by going outside and investigating the cabin's grounds for evidence of who or what was responsible for the damage. He found nothing. He then turned his attention to the net and tarry ropes stored behind the cabin; fortunately, they were present and untouched. He collected them and brought them inside, where Elizabeth had begun straightening up.

"Did thou uncover anything?" she asked wearily. "Any sign of the savages?"

"Nay," was all he said as he dropped the net and rope onto the floor.

"This is what we need...thank God it was still here," he said. "We must hurry now and get to thy cabin. I pray Father is there and unharmed. We'll bring him along with us and care for him at Hope, thus forever freeing him from thy mother's evil influence. If we're facing imminent attack from any native force, our best chances lie within the defenses of the fort."

"I cannot go back home, Will. I cannot stand to confront her... ever again," said Elizabeth. There was a pause and then she continued with, "Mother has gone completely mad. After all her talk of Salem and the evils of witchery...now she has become one. She has succumbed to her own demons and betrayed God, to say nothing of the emotional and physical torture she has inflicted upon me for many a year now. This place has driven her mad...and if we are not careful, we will suffer the same fate."

After witnessing the previous night's unholy ritual, Will could not dispute what she had said—in fact, that unfortunate episode only confirmed what he had suspected about Winnie Eustis for quite some time—but he was unknowing of how to handle such a situation. He could not conceive of simply apprehending the deranged old woman and burning her at the stake, nor could he just suddenly invoke Puritan law and hold a trial to address her outrageous actions. He had neither the time nor the knowledge of such proceedings. He simply did not know what to do.

"I will stand by thee, William Estes, and follow thy lead, as I am convinced thou hath our best interests at heart, but I will not be part of any plan that includes my mother, now or in the future. From this moment on, she will fend for herself and live her despicable life without me. I desire to be with *thee*...and no one else. Never again will she decide what course I shall follow...so help me God."

As they embraced, Will told her, "We shall discuss the matter further when it becomes more pressing. Thy mother must now be viewed as a threat and treated accordingly."

"Then we must—"

"Nay...it's in God's hands now. And if the Lord chooses not to act on the matter, then we will leave it to man once new law, order, and civilization is brought back to this region. And if they choose the gallows, so be it...but her demise will be by their lawful hand and not ours. In the meantime, we will shun her and build a new life without her influence. I can't imagine God punishing us for that."

"So be it," Elizabeth replied.

"Come now. Let's be off and on guard. If the unknown wickedness that struck this home is still lingering nearby, it is my desire to meet that threat within more defensible confines. Let us find my father and make haste to Hope."

Before leaving, Will pawed through his scattered possessions littering the cabin floor in search of his remaining supply of musket powder and shot. His quest was futile however, as he quickly discovered there was no trace of the munitions anywhere.

Food, powder, and shot, that's what they wanted—and that's what they took, Will thought. *They are indeed an intelligent adversary.* Apparently, curses and currents were not keeping the Abenaki off Storm Island; there was just too much evidence to suggest or even hope otherwise.

Will sighed and motioned for Elizabeth to follow him as they took to the trail leading back to Fort Hope. But he stopped dead as a new and horrifying thought entered his head. *The crop fields,* his mind echoed. He spun around and headed for the gardens on the edge of the grassy meadows, Elizabeth at his heels. Moments later, the reason for Will's abrupt diversion from the path became all too real. What had been cloaked in darkness the previous evening was now bathed in broad daylight—and revealing a new morass of uncertainty and danger.

Before them lay a pilfered and destroyed patch of land that bore little resemblance to the farmed crop fields they relied on for food. Will walked up and down the obliterated rows of previously tended soil to discover that every harvestable vegetable was now gone, and that what remained of the topsoil would need extensive work if anything was to be replanted. But at the moment, there was nothing that could be done. Will and Elizabeth looked at each other forlornly, unable to find words to express their dismay. So they did the only thing they *could* do and turned back to the trail.

Neither said anything along the winding path. They simply moved as quietly and as swiftly as they could, feeling like hunted prey. It wasn't long before they reached the point in their journey they both had been dreading. Neither felt they could handle another unpleasant surprise. Regardless, they stopped, looked at one another warily, and proceeded until the Eustis cabin came into full view. They crouched in the tall, concealing grasses and carefully observed the house.

"No smoke," Will whispered, pointing to the chimney. "I do not hear anything, either."

"Nor do I," she whispered back. "No sounds of activity from within."

"Stay here. I shall investigate...and pray I'm not walking into an ambush," he replied.

Will stood up and slowly approached the front entrance, watching and listening for anything out of the ordinary. Once there, he took a deep breath and flung the door open. Elizabeth watched intently, her heart beating in wild anticipation of whatever might happen next. Will stepped inside and effectively out of sight. Elizabeth rose to her feet and moved out of the grass and back onto the trail, never taking her eyes off the cabin. A few seconds painfully slid by before Will reemerged, waving Elizabeth over. She scurried to the entrance and froze in place upon laying eyes on the interior.

"My God, they've struck here, too," she said, her eyes sweeping back and forth over the floor now laden with heaps of waste—most specifically, ruined books. Tears welled up as she sifted through her scattered possessions for anything she deemed useful or cherished. One item caught her attention almost immediately.

"Look at this," she said.

On the floor, nearly shredded into unrecognizable fragments, was Winnie's prized Bible. What little remained intact fell to pieces when Will tried to pick it up.

"It's been intentionally mutilated," he said. "Many of the other books have been ruined, but this Bible looks as if it was preyed upon with deliberate furor."

Will examined the deeply slashed pages and torn-open spine with intense trepidation. He took the desecration of the Holy Scripture as much more than an act of mischievous destruction; to him it was an indisputable warning from a vengeful, determined, and very cunning adversary. The message was clear.

"Mother...thy father?" Elizabeth sniffled.

"Difficult to say," Will replied weakly. "There's no blood...no evidence of slaughter...just destruction and theft. They might not have been here. Father could be—" Will stopped, then changed direction by asking, "Is there any powder or shot in thy possession?"

"Of course not; Mother would never have allowed that in the cabin."

"Then it seems the savages intend to deprive us of all means of feeding and protecting ourselves," Will surmised. "I must assume—"

"Enough of this!" Elizabeth interrupted, peering out the door. "There's nothing here worth saving. The food is gone from the smoking racks and the rain barrel has been kicked over. Say no more and take me to the fort without delay," she added, visibly shaken and fighting back further tears.

"My father," Will muttered, choking back his own sadness as the reality of the grisly fate that had most certainly befallen Cyrus finally set in despite all his attempts to rationalize things otherwise. "He's gone...God help him—and us."

Will and Elizabeth took a few minutes to collect themselves, then Will set the rain barrel upright and they hurried back to the trail leading to Fort Hope. En route, not a second of time was wasted as they cast discretion aside and rushed noisily along. It wasn't until the walls of the fort were in view that Will forced Elizabeth to stop and assume a more defensive posture. After they caught their breath, Will silently walked the perimeter and found, to his relief, that nothing seemed to have been disturbed.

He pushed open the gate and entered the courtyard with Elizabeth close behind. Once inside, they sealed the doors with the crossbar, insuring they were locked in securely. Elizabeth dashed to the rain barrel and drank several dipperfuls of water before eventually offering one to Will, who gulped it down.

When a curious noise came from inside the barracks, Will motioned for Elizabeth to step back as he dropped the net and tarry ropes, then drew his knife. Fearing the worst, he summoned up every fiber of courage in his being, thrust open the barracks door, and stepped boldly inside. Elizabeth blindly followed him in—and let out a shriek at the sight that awaited. She and Will stood side by side in shock and amazement.

"Have no fear, it is only I," were the confident words spoken by a surprisingly upright and now apparently *mobile* Lieutenant Dunsbury. He stood by the fireplace amid several lit candles, fully dressed and appearing quite able—and imposing.

Will and Elizabeth stood in silence, not quite sure how to react or what to say.

"I was beginning to worry...I thought thou might be in trouble," Dunsbury continued. "I must confess I did fret some when thou did not return last night. I feared thy mission was a failure. However, it does me good to lay eyes upon thee now. What news from thy recent adventure?"

"I see thy condition has improved by leaps and bounds," Will said. "It appears thy vigor has been restored. Quite miraculous, I might add."

"The good Lord has blessed me with wondrous recuperative abilities. As a soldier, my body is no stranger to wounds, and in the service of the Royal Marines, my tolerance for blood and pain has been tested time and again, as one might imagine."

"How does thy body and mind feel presently? Balanced and free from pain?" Will asked.

"My head is clear and my legs are now able to support the weight I put upon them. I can walk freely without fatigue or a constant spinning in my skull. Alas, there is still a pain circulating around my wound...but nothing that shall stop me from upholding my end of our bargain," promised Dunsbury.

"Indeed," Will replied, sensing an eagerness for information and action in Dunsbury's voice. "Take a seat at the table. We have a lot to discuss and not much time to spare," he directed. "I shall return shortly. Elizabeth, please build us a fire and procure three equal measures of rum...if there is any left."

Will hurried out the door and over to the northwest corner blockhouse, where he unearthed a pear-shaped powder flask made of copper. From two small kegs—one containing powder, the other shot—he quickly filled the flask and packed it in his satchel. He then found a small leather pouch and stuffed it with shot. Back in the barracks, Elizabeth and Dunsbury sat opposite one another, staring uncomfortably in silence. The stalemate was broken when Will returned and Elizabeth got up to build the fire. Will took her place at the table.

"So, Will, were thou able to accomplish the task thou set out to conquer aboard the Devil's Chariot?" asked Dunsbury.

"With considerable difficulty and several unexpected problems," was his reply. "Tell me, Leftenant, did thou sense anything out of the ordinary while we were gone...strange voices or movements? An unidentifiable sound or cry perhaps? Something one might associate with a ghost or other unworldly entity?"

"Nay," said Dunsbury. "I neither heard nor saw anything I would term *unworldly*. All was quite peaceful in thine absence. I slept very soundly, and during my waking hours, I ate, drank, and moved about in an effort to build up strength. I believe my efforts have been fruitful."

Will went silent, closed his eyes and rubbed his head.

"What troubles thee, young William? Are we in danger? Understand that a soldier can always sense that. What happened while thou was away?"

Feeling overwhelmed by an intense wave of loss and uncertainty, Will began to explain their precarious predicament, knowing that full cooperation and trust was needed if their plan was ever to succeed—and any of them were to survive.

"We were able to board thy Devil's Chariot and successfully mount the ram's head into an effective hoisting mechanism. However, our first test failed due to an insufficient net that broke. Fortunately, I have a stronger one that should prove reliable in further attempts."

"That sounds promising."

"Indeed, but that is the only encouraging thing I can impart... unfortunately."

"Go on," replied the lieutenant.

Will sighed. "The hold is severely flooded and devoid of light even at low tide. The water is cold and cannot be tolerated for more than a few minutes. The cargo is difficult to locate in the dark and even harder to latch onto, even utilizing a net. If not for Elizabeth, I would surely have drowned during my last effort. And to make matters worse, the boom is damaged and may require further repairs before another recovery can be attempted. And at least two men are needed to haul up a large coffer or barrel," he added.

"All problems that the three of us can overcome, I am certain," said Dunsbury.

"That is not the worst of our difficulties, however," Will said.

"Oh?"

"Upon our departure from the *Repulse*, we were attacked by Abenaki savages in canoes. We fled in the longboat and managed to make it back ashore on Storm, but the boat rammed some rocks and sustained bow damage. We were forced to abandon it temporarily and flee into the woods."

"And the savages?"

"They did not immediately pursue us, as two of their warriors were either wounded or killed."

"So they did not come ashore?" Dunsbury asked. "Perhaps the curse thou spoke of—"

"That was my initial assumption," Will interrupted, "but what we came across later has left me with doubt."

Elizabeth stood up from her crouch after getting the fire going. Her eyes locked with Will's, wondering what he would divulge next. He took her gaze to be a cautionary one. He responded accordingly and motioned for her to retrieve the rum.

"We returned to our homes only to find them in shambles and our crop fields pillaged beyond any immediate usefulness. All our food is gone...and..."

Will stopped, unsure of what to say next. Elizabeth looked at him again as she poured what little remained of the rum into three wooden cups. She joined them at the table before serving the drinks.

"Elizabeth and I were not alone on this island," Will confessed. "She lived with her mother, and I with my father. When last we spoke, neither was aware of thine existence or the naval battle that brought thee here. Now both are missing and most certainly dead. It is my belief that savages have infiltrated this island, ransacked our homes, taken our food, and murdered our parents. The legend of the curse has not held them at bay—unfortunately—and I fear it is only a matter of time before they find and attack this fort in force to obliterate us and every trace of our existence."

Will drank his rum with shaking hands before offering a sarcastic chuckle and saying, "And there is a bad storm bearing down on us. It will strike within days...of that I am certain."

"Well, it seems we have a few wrinkles to contend with, my friends," said Dunsbury after a quick swig. "I do not intend to break our contract, and I hope thou doth not intend to, either. I have a wife and child in London...and I will see them both again before my time in this world is over. Since I am a soldier, let us have a war council and discuss our options right here and now. I propose we start with our immediate surroundings. How defensible and sustainable is this fort? What sorts of munitions, food, and other usable goods are stored here?"

Will reached into his satchel and pulled out the pistols recovered from the *Repulse*. He laid them on the table and said, "Our arms have increased by two. These ornate guns were salvaged from the ship's captain's quarters yesterday. We have a decent supply of powder and shot to equip them with, but other than my musket, which is currently languishing in the damaged longboat, we have no other firearms here."

Dunsbury picked up one of the pistols and examined it closely. "There must be more flintlocks on that ship. I've never known a pirate vessel that wasn't bristling with small arms—daggers, knives, and cutlasses, at the very least. All could prove useful if recovered in time. And the fort itself...supplies?"

"There is a limited supply of tools, timber, rope, fishing gear, and foodstuffs kept here. In addition, we managed to salvage some usable goods from the sea after the *Firefly* was sunk—small amounts of tea, salt, sugar, a bottle of wine—consumables of that nature," answered Will.

"I propose a thorough inventory of the premises be conducted. It is important we know what we have and where we have it," said Dunsbury. "Perhaps that is a task best suited for our lovely Elizabeth?"

The two men looked at her with raised eyebrows. She glanced at each of them before turning her head to the pile of salvaged boxes, chests, and barrels stacked up in the corner.

"With thy blessing, I shall endeavor to thoroughly inventory all items deemed essential for survival and defense," she stated rather formally. "It shouldn't take long," she added with a sarcastic twist.

"Very well," said Will. "Our agreement—nay, our very existence—is completely untenable without use of my longboat. Without it we cannot salvage the *Repulse*, we cannot fish for food, we cannot escape this island should it be overrun by the Abenaki. Our very lives depend on the repair of that small craft."

"What doth thou suggest?" asked Dunsbury.

"If thou art able enough, I propose thou accompany me to the southeast shore. Armed with tarry rope and scraps of timber, we shall make oakum and repair the boat. That is the task upon which all others depend, and we should set out as soon as possible. While we are away, Elizabeth can remain here in safety and tend to her responsibilities."

"Jolly good. As a boy in London, I helped many a sailor repair small boats along the Thames. I am skilled at both creating and using oakum. I know I can be of useful assistance," said Dunsbury.

"Good," Will nodded. Then said, "Time is not our friend. We must make preparations and set out posthaste. If our work is successful, we should be able to make it back here before nightfall."

"And what of the savages, Will?" Elizabeth interjected. "What happens when they discover this fort and commence their inevitable assault? What am I to do if neither of thee returns before the sun sets?"

"It is a risk we must endure. *Everything* depends on making my boat seaworthy again. We have no other options," Will said. He then picked up one of the pistols and handed it to Dunsbury. The second gun he kept for himself and proceeded to load it. When he was done, he handed the powder and shot to the lieutenant.

"We will act as hunters and ferret out any native presence lurking in the wooded interior," said Will. "I only hope the bravery of a simple fisherman can match that of a Royal Marine," he added.

"I have no doubt it will," Dunsbury replied. "Are there any swords in thy possession? In battle, I should like to know that I have a weapon that doesn't need reloading."

"Nay," Will answered. "There are no swords here...but the *Repulse*..."

"Yes indeed!" Dunsbury trumpeted. "There will be all manner of blades, rapiers, and cutlasses aboard that damned ship!"

"If thou art able to get to them," Elizabeth sneered.

A moment of silence ensued before a visibly annoyed Will turned to Elizabeth and said, "Perhaps there is some food to be had. We all should have something to eat...now."

Elizabeth said nothing, stood up abruptly, and defiantly poured herself the last bit of rum from the cask. She drank it quickly and deliberately, pausing to make her point before serving up any food.

"There is hardly anything left," she said, uncovering the cod. "Perhaps the leftenant's appetite demanded more than the ample rations we left for him," she added.

"I'm sure whatever *is* left will be sufficient. Perhaps some treacle and sugar will complement the fish and help satiate our hunger," Will suggested.

Elizabeth did not reply. She simply carved what was left of the cod into three equal portions and served them with the sweeteners Will had mentioned.

When the meal was finished, he stood up and said, "The tides should be in our favor. We must not hesitate or risk having the longboat swept out to sea."

"We shall waste no more time, then," said Dunsbury. He stood up slowly and steadied himself. "I am in need of a good walk," he said, tucking the pistol in his belt. As Will checked his satchel and slung it over his shoulder, Dunsbury said to Elizabeth, "I must thank thee for laundering my shirt. Perhaps upon our return, I may beseech thee to stitch up the bullet hole?" The soldier opened his coat and pointed to the damaged area of the garment.

"I should think that would not be too difficult a task," Elizabeth responded. "More thanks should be bestowed upon William for stitching up thy flesh, however."

"Quite right. I do owe thee a tremendous debt of gratitude, sir," he said, lightly patting Will on the back. "I shall never forget thy kindness...no matter where our future paths lead."

"William," said Elizabeth, "please escort me down to the shore. I should like to collect some wood before thy departure, and I require thine assistance."

She stepped out the door, and Will followed her to the front gate, where they removed the crossbar and exited the fort. Once outside, they scrambled down the path to the rocky beach. Puzzled by her choice of locations, Will remarked, "There is no—"

"Hush and listen to what I have to say," said Elizabeth.

"I have no time for another argument railing against our course of action," Will retorted.

"Listen to me!" she exclaimed. "That man is not who he says he is. I can sense his masquerade with every fiber in my being, William Estes."

"What nonsense is this?" said Will.

"Did thou not notice his soldier's coat?"

"What of it?"

"It is decidedly too small for his large frame. It simply does not fit him. I find it odd that a Royal Marine in service to the Crown would be issued a uniform coat that did not fit."

"He was on a long and arduous journey. Perhaps his original coat was lost or stolen. Theft can be rampant aboard ship and even in port. Unexpected occurrences and all manner of depravities happen frequently to sailors at sea...even aboard a disciplined naval vessel."

"To the ordinary seaman, perhaps, but to an officer?" she asked sarcastically.

"There are many reasons that could account for his coat not fitting, Elizabeth."

"Though I certainly am not well schooled on the formal appearance of soldierly English uniforms, what I have seen in books and heard in stories simply does not match what confronts us now. Consider: He claims to be a leftenant, but that red coat of his seems far too plain to be worn by an officer. There are no frills, no fancy lace, and no clever embroidery that would indicate a man of position or power."

"I don't...his story..."

"And there is one clue that has completely eluded thee," she stated.

Will stood still, crossed his arms, and waited for her revelation.

"There is no bullet hole in the coat. I examined it while he slept.

Will looked away from her with a puzzled expression on his face, trying to accurately recall the moment when they'd first discovered the injured lieutenant.

Elizabeth went on, "He was wearing the coat when we found him, Will. He was shot and bleeding. How could there be a bloody hole in his shirt underneath and no hole in the coat covering it?"

"His coat may have been open when he was hit," Will reasoned. "And why does this whole coat business matter anyway? He's here...we have a contract...and we need his help just as much as he needs ours."

"I don't trust him, Will, and neither should thee. His rapid recovery vexes me. It forces me to wonder just how serious his wound really was."

"Thou cannot deny the severity of his injury nor his extremely weakened condition upon discovery. He is a man—nay, a *soldier*— of fortitude and resolve. What doth thou know of injuries inflicted by sword or flintlock? Art thou a physician?"

"No, but thou art not a physician, either, William Estes," she snapped coldly. "Doth thou not remember the knife held to thy throat? Art thou inclined to just dismiss the peculiarities surrounding his coat? Art thou genuinely satisfied with his—"

"Stop!" Will commanded. "No more! He needs us and we need him. There are no other considerations at this time...if we desire to live. I cannot—*we* cannot—go it alone. There is just too much to contend with without his help."

Stony silence grew between them.

Finally, Elizabeth warned, "Keep thy guard up, William, for thy sake and for mine. Do not turn thy back on this stranger from the sea, or risk the dagger he may plunge into it. A woman can sense such danger—danger that blinds men and puts them in peril. Thou hath asked me to trust thy judgment in the past. Now it is my turn to request the same of thee."

Will sighed, as deep down he could understand her point, but he could not afford to alter his course of action. He nodded his tacit agreement, then motioned for her to pick up some driftwood to carry back to the fort. He did the same, and they lumbered back up the trail.

They dropped their loads into one pile at the center of the courtyard. Dunsbury emerged from the barracks a bit wobbly, but determined to stamp vitality back into his weakened legs. Will went into the blockhouse and retrieved a large sack that he filled with a wooden canteen, some nails, and several small lengths of timber.

"Here," he said, handing it over to Dunsbury. "Put the tarry ropes and net in this, and fill up the canteen from the rain barrel. Art thou able enough to carry this load without much difficulty?"

"Of course," he replied. "Lead the way."

After taking a moment to get organized, the two men stepped outside the fort. Will turned around to Elizabeth and said, "Shut the doors and secure the crossbar as soon as we are under way. Do not open the gate until thou hears my voice again. Understood?"

Elizabeth nodded affirmatively and said, "Be safe, my love."

At these words, Will looked up from his gear with a little smile on his face that dissolved instantly when he noticed Elizabeth's fixated gaze—on Dunsbury.

She slowly turned her eyes back to Will, then quickly retreated inside the fort. Will watched and listened as the doors closed and the sound of the crossbar locked into place.

"She carries great pain," said Dunsbury, "but she is strong-willed and determined to press on, that is obvious. Before we depart, allow me to express how deeply sorry I am about thy parents and their unfortunate demise. If there is any justice in the world, there will be vengeance on those that perpetrated such a heinous act."

"That justice may be found this very day. Follow me," Will replied with a scowl. He glanced in the direction of the coastal trail, but then headed out behind the fort, into the dense woods and toward the island's interior, where there was no clear path.

The two men prowled along like a pair of foraging foxes. Each step was fluid and calculated to make as little noise as possible. They kept their bodies in a crouch-like posture, with Will stopping frequently to listen and search for signs of unnatural activity. He found nothing, and all remained quiet. As their journey progressed, he realized they were approaching the site where Winnie Eustis had performed her bizarre ritual the night before. Something compelled him to bypass the area entirely, and he took a longer, less accommodating route to the southeast shore.

After a few more stops to allow Dunsbury some rest, Will eventually brought them out of the interior and back to the shoreline. Following the rugged coast for only a short distance, they reached the southeast shore's beach. To Will's delight and relief, the longboat still hung on the rocks, its stern bobbing in the shallow water. To his further delight, the lost oar Elizabeth had dropped into the surf had washed ashore allowing him to retrieve it with little effort. Dunsbury put down the sack and got out the canteen. He took a drink and offered it to Will.

"Stay here," said Will. "I'll wade out and dislodge it from the rocks."

He stripped off his boots, gun, and satchel and hiked up his breeches. The tide was low and the water was only slightly above his knees. The first thing he did was retrieve his musket, the second oar, and the watery bundle of tools and other supplies. *Thank the Lord they are still here*, he thought. He waded back onto the beach and laid everything out in the sun to dry. Returning to the boat, he latched onto the side of the craft and tried to wrench it free. His first attempts were unsuccessful and discouraging. Not wishing to cause any additional damage, he tried a gentler rocking approach that also proved ineffective. He lowered his head and put his hands on his hips while he tried to figure out what to do.

"Reach down and lift up on thy side of the boat," said Dunsbury, who had waded in without Will's noticing. "Then push back toward the sea, and I shall do the same on my side."

The two men reached down and grasped the bow. With a combined effort, they were able to heave the nose high enough to free it from the impaling rocks.

"Now push it back toward the sea and away from this snaggle-toothed jaw of stone," commanded Dunsbury, and seconds later, the longboat was dipping freely in the water.

Will grinned and said, "Quickly now, let's haul it ashore before it floods past a manageable level."

Together, they heaved again until the boat was pulled up onto the sand. Will climbed aboard and took down the mast. Then with another joint effort, they managed to upend the craft so that the water drained out and the hull damage was more visible and accessible.

"Not nearly as bad as I had imagined," said Will. "Some minor woodwork complemented with liberal amounts of oakum will remedy the problem nicely, I should think."

"Agreed," said Dunsbury. "Thou should build a fire whilst I begin unraveling thy tarry rope. There is not a moment to lose."

Will nodded, and the two set about their tasks. While Dunsbury began the tedious chore of undoing the rope, Will built a fire and used his knife to cut deep notches in the trunk of a young pine tree. Soon there was a sluggish, even flow of resin hemorrhaging from the cut. Will methodically collected the amber liquid in a metal cup taken from the *Repulse*. Next he turned his attention to the longboat's damaged hull. With Dunsbury's help, he properly cut, whittled, and shaped small pieces of the planed timber from Hope into usable replacement planking. With topmaul and nails, he set about repairing the boat's broken exterior.

The day grew hot and the work bogged down. Will found himself occasionally searching the sky for any signs that less threatening weather might be on the way. To his dismay, he saw nothing that would change his earlier prediction. Every cloud, burst of wind, or salty scent in the air led him to believe it was still just a matter of days before the skies would darken and a massive gale would be upon them.

As the afternoon sun beat down, both men took a cooling dip in the ocean followed by a short rest in the shade away from the fire. Dunsbury continued to unravel the rope with Will's assistance. It was a grueling job that left their fingers throbbing.

"This task was meted out as punishment aboard ship. No man ever wanted to be forced to make oakum," said Dunsbury. He paused for a moment, then asked, "How far away is the *Repulse*?'"

"Over there," Will pointed, adding, "just across the channel off Belle Island. It's around the bend a bit—one cannot see it from this beach until far enough out on the water. Then it becomes quite visible on a clear day."

"We shall see it soon enough," replied Dunsbury.

"How does thou feel about boarding that vessel...knowing the trials and tribulations thou hath suffered in battle with her?"

Dunsbury hesitated, then answered, "It shall give me great pride to stand upon her wretched decks."

"How's that?"

"I will gladly strut across and piss on her empty quarterdeck, knowing that the evil scourge that manned her has been eradicated by brave soldiers and sailors of the Crown who gave their lives to destroy the pestilence of piracy on the high seas," he said. "I will then pay homage to my fallen brethren in arms before I set about purging her rotten hold of every ill-gotten gain and item of value she acquired by murderous force. And when our task is complete, and we are safely away, I'll watch that ship burn under a personally kindled curtain of flames...and she will descend into the watery depths of Hell, forever entombing every demon and apparition that haunts her unholy innards. That, Will—that's when I'll have total contentment in knowing that I have slain the beast responsible for inflicting so much pain and suffering."

"An interesting proposition," Will remarked. "I don't mind helping eradicate the grim reminders of death and piracy, but I simply seek every advantage to help resurrect this land and take my vengeance upon the savages that have stolen so much from me—peace, prosperity, community, and my very family."

"It seems each of us has demons in need of purging," said

Dunsbury. "And we have the power to enrich our very beings and permanently quell our enemies. We shall use the *Repulse*'s treasure to help us do both."

With that, they shook hands.

"Now let us get about caulking this boat and making her seaworthy again," said Dunsbury.

A while later, Will's cup contained an adequate amount of resin. He held it over the fire until it boiled down into a sticky liquid. Dunsbury eventually finished picking and preparing the oakum. He then proceeded to pound and wedge the tarry fibers into the repaired planking seams of the longboat. Once everything was set and in place, Will poured the resin over the repaired portion to seal the seams. After that, there was nothing left to be done except wait for the resin to cool and harden.

"We should get back to Fort Hope before the sun sets," Will suggested as he covered the boat with leaves and tree branches as he had done so often in the past. "But we mustn't lower our guard lest we fall victim to a savage ambush. We should count our blessings and be thankful we encountered no sign of them on the way in this morning, but they're devious and easily move about without being seen. We must be mindful and cautious of our course back to Hope."

"I leave the navigation in thy good hands, sir," said Dunsbury, who seemed preoccupied with something in the water. "Perhaps we should harvest some of these lovely creatures and have Elizabeth serve them up for dinner," he added.

Will walked into the chilly brine and stared down upon several crawling lobsters seemingly lost in the sand—as if they wanted to but did not know *how* to return to the cold, rocky depths of their seaweed encrusted lairs far from shore.

A smile emerged on Will's face as he and Dunsbury reached in and grabbed several of the blackish-green crustaceans and stuffed them in Dunsbury's sack. Then Will re-bundled his tools along with the other gear, and slid everything under the longboat. Taking only what he deemed essential—and all that he could fit in his satchel—he loaded and readied his musket before blazing a new path back to Fort Hope.

Ignoring the obvious trail that led back to the Estes and Eustis cabins, Will retraced his steps from the route he'd employed on the way in. It was longer and more cumbersome, but safer—in his mind—for numerous reasons, some of which he kept to himself. Fortunately, Dunsbury questioned nothing and simply followed.

With the same wariness they had utilized on the trek in, they cautiously traveled back through the woods. Soon they were again close to the site where Winnie had carried out her pagan-like ritual. That fact eluded Will this time, as he pressed forward unaware, and distracted by the setting of the sun. He was instantly alert when he heard the sound of Dunsbury's voice.

"Will, come hither," he said. "Look," he added, "native sign. Could be recent."

"Indeed it could," Will replied somberly, staring down at the charred remains of Winnie's bonfire. Just then, an unfamiliar sound came from nearby. Will raised his musket and Dunsbury drew his pistol. Both went silent as they strained to hear the sound again and identify its source.

"It sounds like someone in pain," Will whispered upon hearing what he could only recognize as a low moan.

They followed the sound until they came upon an immense pine directly in their path. Realizing that whatever was causing the noise was most definitely on the other side of the tree, they looped around in a wide circle, guns at the ready. Will's emotions spiked with joy and relief, for bound on the other side of the tree was Cyrus, weakened and in pain, but alive.

"Father!" Will cried. He put down the musket and drew his knife. Cyrus moaned again as Will knelt by his side and cut away the lashings that held him prisoner to the tree.

"This man is thy father?" asked Dunsbury. "Bloody savages!" he added coldly.

"Yes, and he lives, thank the Lord."

Will pulled Cyrus to his feet, but he was too frail to stand on his own. With care and ease, Will sat his frightened father down against the tree as he and Dunsbury squatted low to face him.

"These ropes are not native made," Will said. "They're what I use to haul in my nets when fishing in deep waters."

"Perhaps they were stolen when the savages sacked thy cabin," offered Dunsbury. "They must have abducted thy father and camped here briefly. Perhaps they were alerted to our movements and fled before we were upon them. Perhaps there is hope for Mrs. Eustis, as well. She too may still be in the area...alive."

"Perhaps," Will answered with diffidence. He turned his attention back to his haggard father, whose head hung limply as if it was about to fall off his shoulders. "Father, how did thou get here? Who did this?" Will asked directly, knowing an answer would not be forthcoming.

Unable to lift his head or voice any kind of response, Cyrus just moaned with fatigue and cowered away from every movement or gesture Will made. The old man was weak, terrified, and clearly traumatized. A swelling sense of urgency and danger started to flood Will's every thought, and he felt the need to leave immediately.

"We must return to the fort without further delay. My father needs food and rest before he succumbs."

"And Mrs. Eustis?" Dunsbury asked.

"Night will soon be upon us. Time is precious and we cannot expend it in a fruitless search just now. We are in no condition to fumble around in the dark with my father in such dire condition and danger lurking all around us. We must see to his needs first... and pray we can find Winnie in the morning."

"I am in no position to disagree," replied Dunsbury as sweat poured from his head, evidence of the pain he was unsuccessfully trying to conceal.

"Help me get him to his feet," Will said.

The two men wrapped Cyrus's arms around their shoulders and lifted him from the ground. Cyrus's moans slightly intensified, and he shifted more of his weight onto his son as if to minimize contact with the strange man on his right. With their free hands, Will and Dunsbury picked up their gear, and the three stumbled along through the woods back toward Hope.

The journey to the fort was long and arduous. Cyrus was all but dead weight, and Dunsbury was noticeably withering under the added strain, no longer able to disguise his discomfort and fatigue. Will trudged forward feeling as if he had a dead elephant strapped to his back. On four separate occasions, they all fell to the hard, uneven ground, grunting with pain and exhaustion. But Will persevered with the lion's share of the load, and successfully guided his ailing companions back to Hope just as darkness enveloped the land. They staggered up to the gate and collapsed in a heap.

Will called out loudly, "Elizabeth...it is William and the leftenant. Father is with us also. Bestir thyself and open the gate without pause...we are in dire need of food and sanctuary."

A moment later, the sounds of the crossbar falling to the ground and the massive wooden doors swinging open were heard. Lantern in hand, Elizabeth emerged.

"Help my father inside while I manage the leftenant," Will said.

Elizabeth hurried over and struggled to assist the nearly lifeless Cyrus to the barracks. Will fared better with Dunsbury, pulling him and all the gear inside and securing the huge doors behind them. He then helped Dunsbury over to the barracks, stopping only once to slake his ferocious thirst at the rain barrel. Dunsbury also cupped his hands and scooped out a few gulps for himself. They entered the barracks, and Dunsbury slumped onto the nearest stool by the table.

"Let thy father have the mattress. I shall sleep on the floor from this point forward," said Dunsbury, his eyes closed and his hands gripping his side.

Will helped Elizabeth lay Cyrus down on the crude bed. She fetched some water and helped him drink it. Then, almost instantly, his eyes closed and he fell asleep. Will removed his father's boots and trousers looking for any sign of injury. He then opened his shirt, but aside from a few minor bruises and abrasions, there was no indication of harm.

"What happened to him? Where was he found?" Elizabeth asked impatiently.

"We discovered him in the woods...he was bound to a tree," Will answered as he eased down onto a stool at the table.

"Savages? Did thou encounter savages?" she asked with worried eyes as big as saucers.

"Nay," Will answered, "but they are most assuredly responsible for abducting my father and reducing him to this sad state. What puzzles me is why they didn't just kill him. Why tie him up and leave him to suffer?"

"A warning...a morbid example of what is to follow for the rest of us," Dunsbury interjected. "Torture is an effective motivator...more so than sudden murder."

"Perhaps. It does make sense," replied Will, his head turning back to Elizabeth.

"Mother?" she asked in a low voice, never taking her eyes off Will.

"No sign," he responded softly, "but we will search for her in hopes that she has not met with a more gruesome fate."

Silence ensued for several seconds as Elizabeth ambled over to the fire and stared into the empty cooking kettle suspended over it.

"Here," said Will as he retrieved the almost dead lobsters from the sack. "Prepare these. They shall be our sustenance for as long as they do not attract flies."

"They are better served as bait for cod," she responded disgustedly. "I shall fetch salty brine for the pot so it diminishes the foul taste."

Dunsbury lay on the floor attempting to ease the pain in his aggravated wound and rest his tired body. His eyes were closed, and hunger was the only thing keeping him awake.

"Were there any disturbances here today?" Will asked Elizabeth, now seated beside him at the table. "Did thou witness any sign of danger or feel threatened?"

"Nay," she answered. "All was quiet and serene. I kept myself busy working on the tasks set before me. I did worry immensely about thy safety and am relived by thy return unscathed."

"Thou need never worry about my whereabouts. I shall never abandon my beloved," said Will, noticing new evidence of work and organization in the barracks. It was apparent that Elizabeth had, in fact, stayed busy throughout the day.

"Was thou able to salvage and repair the longboat?" she asked timidly, unsure if she wanted to hear the answer, yet knowing her life depended on it.

"Yes."

Elizabeth let out a sigh of relief. She leaned over and hugged Will before asking for details.

"Is the boat sound? Will it sail without foundering?"

"Time will tell of its seaworthiness. All I can offer is that it was brought ashore, and the damage was skillfully addressed with scraps of fresh planking, oakum, and hot resin. The leftenant was most helpful. If not for him and his experience, our situation would be extremely grim. Many thanks, good sir," he added with a glance at Dunsbury. The lieutenant acknowledged with a short salute, not bothering to speak or open his eyes. Will said to Elizabeth, "If the conditions are right and all appears sound, we will test it on the water tomorrow."

"Let us pray thine efforts were fruitful. In the meantime, let us punish our stomachs with this abominable catch from the bottom of the sea."

Will helped Dunsbury to his feet and the three of them sat at the table cracking open the bright-red shells and devouring the meat therein. They ate heartily, and no one complained about what was served or how it was prepared. What meat remained was covered in cloth and put away for later use. There was no rum left to help ease the tension, so they sat quietly at the table staring into the dying fire.

Finally, Will asked Dunsbury how he was feeling.

The lieutenant looked up and said, "The pain has settled, but my weariness seems to know no boundaries this evening. I shall no doubt rejoice in a good night's rest."

"Tomorrow?"

"Tomorrow I will be strong enough to assist thee again. Thou hath my word."

"Good," Will replied. "Then we shall set out at dawn and test the longboat's repair. If it holds, we shall venture over to the *Repulse* and assault that treasure hold with due haste and without mercy. With any luck, we can recover the bulk of the riches in a solid day's work. Perhaps...perhaps even claim it all."

"Yes...and in the days following, we will divide it up accordingly. The moment I'm able enough to undertake my long journey,

I will gather my spoils and supplies and await thy transport to the mainland...and eventually, home to England," said Dunsbury.

"And what of our supplies here, dear Elizabeth?" asked Will. "Please share with us the rewards of thy day's work."

"The news is unsettling at best," she said with lowered eyes. "Our food, save for the lobster remains and the recovered items from the ship, is gone. What was left of the smoked cod went afoul and had to be disposed of. We have limited treacle, sugar, tea, and salt, and one bottle of wine. Alas, the rum is all gone...and with our crop fields destroyed, we have no vegetables. The rest of the useful supplies include limited amounts of gunpowder and lead shot stored in both blockhouses, Will's tools, nails, some lumber, candles, twine, several burlap sacks, and various amounts of coiled fishing line, ropes, and hooks. Everything else is of little significance—some books, writing implements, ink, and other useless personal items of fancy."

"An unhealthy situation at best," said Will. "If we're forced to barricade ourselves here in defense of native attack, without free access to hunt or fish, grim—grim indeed. I shudder at the thought of a lengthy siege."

"Let us hope it doesn't come to that," said Dunsbury. "Perhaps thou should consider abandoning this place...perhaps thou should come with me at the proper time."

Elizabeth's head shot up and she looked beseechingly at Will but said nothing. He in turn looked over at his sleeping father then back at Dunsbury.

"I will not abandon my home...ever. I will breathe new life into this land with my dying breath if need be. That's simply the way it is. The Estes name will thrive in this region for generations to come—I swear it!"

With that, Will angrily got up from the table and stood facing the fireplace. Elizabeth's head drooped, and her face scowled with disappointment. Dunsbury simply slumped back, closed his eyes, and crossed his arms in anticipation of sleep. During the next several minutes of silence, ugly thoughts of their unpleasant situation and of each other swirled in their heads. No one was prepared for what happened next.

A bloodcurdling screech pierced the stillness, and all three snapped to attention. They remained motionless and listened intently until the sound came again with more ferocity. Dunsbury struggled to his feet and picked up his pistol as Will retrieved his musket and satchel. He went to the door and glanced back at Dunsbury, who indicated he was able enough to follow him out to investigate.

They burst outside into the courtyard and immediately caught sight of light above the wall of the fort that faced the ocean. Will ran to the northwest blockhouse and climbed up the inner ladder and onto the ledge. He looked out over the palisades and down toward the cliff. Near its edge, a massive bonfire with bright orange and red flames hungrily licked up toward the sky. Then an anomalous figure emerged from the shadows and let loose another indescribable shriek. Seeing it as the opening war cry signaling an assault, Will expected a swarm of Abenaki warriors to burst out of the woods and attack the fort from every direction.

"Who is that?" asked Dunsbury, hobbling up to Will's side.

"In the name of all that is holy!" exclaimed Elizabeth, who had also rushed up the ladder and onto the ledge. "*Mother!*"

Stepping into full view and illuminated by the massive fire behind her was the unmistakable silhouette of Winnie Eustis. She looked incensed and frightfully deranged. She was dressed in her normal Puritan garb, but it was muddied and tattered, hanging loosely and exposing several parts of her body. Her hair was a dangling, unkempt mess with no bonnet to conceal it, and there was a glowing wickedness in her eyes. She looked up and pointed a bony finger at Will. Then she started to shriek again.

"William Estes!" she bellowed. "Release my daughter from thy reprehensible and salacious influence, and I shall rid her from all sin once and for all! She has abandoned God and now must answer to a darker power...a power that now surges deep within me. Send her out, and witness her blood boil!"

"What sordid business is this?" said Dunsbury. "What's she going on about? Who is that witch, and why does she threaten us so?" He turned to Elizabeth and asked, "*Is* that thy mother?"

They looked on in horror as Winnie danced around the flames, contorting her body in unnatural and vulgar positions. She threw her hands into the air and chanted nonsensical and disturbingly wicked-sounding prattlings that could only be construed as the language of the Devil. Then, with a mighty cackle, she thrust her hands toward the flames, instantly causing them to roar higher and explode with a sharp crack. The spectacle made her audience recoil in fright.

"What evil armament of sorcery does this witch possess?" asked Dunsbury as he raised his pistol. "Is she bent on destroying us? Damned if I'll allow her evil intentions to do me harm. I'll put a ball in her head before—"

"She's no sorceress," interrupted Will, pressing Dunsbury to lower his gun. "She's gone quite mad, however, and she's obviously obtained some gunpowder...from where I do not know," he said, looking with suspicion at Elizabeth.

"Return Cyrus Estes to my charge!" Winnie further barked. "I have concocted a potion that will cure his idiocy and set his caged mind free. The condemned sisters of Salem have spoken to me in my dreams and shown me the method of their magic. Mourn their untimely loss and have no pity on those who denounced them. They will all suffer a gruesome fate at the hands of my vengeance. I shall unleash an unrelenting plague of death and destruction upon Salem, and they will all pay for their sins!"

Winnie again danced around wildly, stopping only to laugh and point straight up at Elizabeth, who remained mostly stationary and silent during her mother's performance.

"And William...William Estes, I shall flay the skin off thy hide before removing the very manhood from thy lustful loins. Thy seed will never contaminate another person or beast again!"

With that, Winnie produced a knife that she brandished without restraint. Her rantings intensified with further invocations of Salem's turbulent past and her dark desires to embrace and resurrect them rather than preach condemnation.

"She has lost all her senses, Will," said Elizabeth. "She's become the very thing she has moralized against for as long as memory serves. This place and all its evils and depravities have poisoned her very soul. God cannot help her...and neither can we. I will look upon her no more."

Elizabeth turned her back and lowered her head. She buried her face in her hands and tried to block out all the ghastly sounds assaulting her ears. Will remained silent and motionless, unsure of what to do next.

The situation grew more ominous when Winnie reached into the fire and pulled out a flaming branch that she wielded like a torch. Slowly advancing toward the gate as if she intended to set the doors aflame, the critical decision about what action to take was finally made—but not by Will.

Winnie's advance came to an abrupt halt following a sharp crack from Dunsbury's pistol. The ball failed to connect with any part of her anatomy, but the shot was close enough to get her undivided attention.

"Begone, witch, or get a bullet in thy brain!" he yelled, still pointing the barrel of his pistol at her. Will, reacting without thought, aimed his musket and fired his own warning shot. A patch of earth kicked up in front of Winnie, forcing her to step back. Then, with a mighty wail, she hurled the torch over the cliff and ran off into the darkness.

"Should we hunt her down?" Dunsbury asked after a moment of reflection.

"No, she poses little threat, and we are in no condition," Will answered. "We'll deal with the consequences of her actions, should that be necessary, in the morning light."

Will peered at Elizabeth, who appeared downtrodden but offered up no words.

"Both of thee should return to the barracks. Settle in and get some sleep. Tend to my father and see that he is resting well," Will said.

"And thou?" asked Dunsbury.

"I shall remain here on post and guard against any further surprises from unwanted visitors," Will said, reaching for more powder and shot to reload his musket. "Go now. We have much to do when the sun rises on the morrow."

With that, Dunsbury nodded and started back down the ladder. Elizabeth looked at Will mournfully, hesitant to leave.

"I shall be fine," he said. "Do not despair. I will check on thee frequently before retiring permanently for the night."

"Very well," she replied meekly.

Will watched as they walked across the courtyard and back into the barracks. As the door closed, he returned his attention to the raging bonfire. He watched for movement and propped his musket atop the palisades, searching for the ideal range and field of fire. Many thoughts entered his spinning head—most of them patently unpleasant.

CHAPTER 11

Tides of Turbulence

Will opened his eyes to a startling sight. Below him was nothing but air and a twenty-foot drop to the ground. At first he thought he was just dreaming, but then he realized he was indeed awake and in a very precarious position. It took a few heart-thumping seconds to comprehend that he wasn't lying on his bed at home or curled up on the barracks floor. He was still on the ledge of the fort's wall, high above the courtyard, his head dizzily dangling over the side. In fact, his entire body was lying right on the edge. Any move might send him plummeting to the ground. He drew his head back onto the ledge and gently tried to move his left arm—but it was pinned under his body and completely numb. His left leg was not much better off. Cautiously, he raised his right arm and let it fall behind him. This allowed him to gently roll onto his back and away from the edge. Once out of danger, he rested for a minute to allow the blood flow back into his numbed extremities. Lying still, he stared up at the early-morning sky, which was leaden with gray clouds and no sign of the sun. The foreboding sight made his stomach twinge.

When he finally stood up and looked down across the courtyard, he spied his father gulping water from the rain barrel. Curiously, there was no one else to be seen and no sign of activity that he could detect from inside the barracks. But as he made his way down, he began to hear muffled voices from within. Then suddenly, all went quiet again.

"Father," Will said as he approached Cyrus. The old man looked up and smiled at his son. Will gave him a hug and couldn't resist questioning him further even though he knew it was useless.

"What happened, Father? Who placed thee into bondage out in the woods? Where was Mrs. Eustis? Our cabin...who—" Cyrus just stared back with a blank expression, forcing Will to cease asking questions; no answers would be forthcoming. Finally, Will raised his fingers to his mouth and made a chewing gesture with his jaw. This simple act of basic communication triggered an immediate response from Cyrus, who grunted and smacked his lips. Will smiled and motioned for his father to enter the barracks—but the old man would not move.

"Come, Father, let us get thee something to eat," Will said as he grasped his father's hand and tried to pull him toward the door. Again the old man resisted, this time physically. "Enough of this nonsense," Will said, his patience wearing thin. "The food is inside. Come now," he ordered as he tried again to move his father to the door. Cyrus broke Will's grip with a surprising strength and defiance Will was not accustomed to. Cyrus shook his head stubbornly and sat down on the ground. He became even more resolute after Will mentioned Elizabeth. Immediately, Will recognized this peculiar behavior as similar to what he had witnessed days earlier when he'd first left his father in Winnie's care. He wanted to observe the behavior further, but there was no time to spare. He went to the door and tried to push it open. Surprisingly it would not budge. He pushed harder, and still the door would not open. After one last shove, he called out to those inside. The door finally swung open and Will entered. Standing in the corner adjusting her dress and pulling back her tousled hair was Elizabeth. On the mattress, with his eyes closed and his head turned away, lay a bootless Dunsbury.

"I'm sorry; that scrap of firewood got caught under the door. I must have dropped it and not realized..."

Will picked up the small chunk of wood, and his curiosity was aroused when he noticed that one end looked as if it had been hastily whittled down to form a wedge. He dropped it and stared at Elizabeth, who rushed into his arms and held him tight.

"I was so frightened last night...I barely slept. I worried about thee incessantly. Did Mother return?" she asked.

"No sign," said Will. "I remember seeing the fire burn down to hot embers...then my memory becomes hazy. I must have fallen asleep. Why is the leftenant on the mattress and my father outside?" he asked brusquely.

"Cyrus woke not long ago and went out on his own accord. I assume he wanted water and to relieve himself," she answered. "The leftenant's wound did not agree with the floor. It was my suggestion he take the mattress after thy father went out."

"Fix him what's left of the lobster and spare him some treacle as well. Bring it outside, if thou please—he is uncomfortable in here."

"As thou wish," she answered with a hint of disdain.

Elizabeth fixed a plate and brought it out to Cyrus. Will watched through the door as the old man backed away from her, thus forcing her to leave the plate on the ground. As she walked back inside, Cyrus cautiously took the food and began to eat.

"Shall we parley for a bit before we get under way?"

Will turned and saw that Dunsbury was now sitting up and appeared quite alert as he pulled his boots on.

"I feel that's wise," Will agreed. "Let us sit a moment. I do have several matters to discuss."

The two men sat down at the table while Elizabeth served them cups of water and what little remained of the treacle. Will spoke first.

"After witnessing last night's bizarre activities, I think it is safe to conclude that thy mother is lost to us," Will said, addressing Elizabeth directly. "I feel she is of little immediate threat, however, and will expire naturally within a very short time...a result of her lunacy and inability to survive without adequate shelter or assistance. Therefore, I submit that we simply exclude her from all present plans and future endeavors, thus allowing nature to take its course and rid this land of her wickedness. Thy thoughts?"

"I have no mother; she is already dead to me. I will not endorse any action that allows her to continue her cruel and sinful activities, which are a blatant affront to God. She has sold her soul to Satan, and I have no misgivings concerning her total banishment from our lives...But what if she returns and again becomes violent in our presence? What are we to do if she threatens our lives...acting with the power of the Devil?"

"We will then deal with her swiftly and accordingly—as God would have us do," Will said quietly.

"And the savage threat?" Dunsbury asked.

"I have new thoughts concerning that," said Will. "I have changed my earlier thinking based on recent events and discoveries. I have determined that the Abenaki have indeed *not* pierced the shores of Storm Island. Of this I am now certain. The island legend is true: The curse of Storm has kept them away. We are safe here...as we always have been."

"And what hast directed thy thinking to such a reckless conclusion?" Elizabeth demanded. "Perhaps my mother is not the only person on this island to have suffered a bout of madness."

"Our parents are still alive," Will shot back. "Neither was found slaughtered by savage tomahawk or arrow. My father was bound to a tree with ropes originally in our possession, not native crafted bindings. The leftenant and I found no sign of savage encroachment in the island interior or along the southeast shore during our travels yesterday."

"But the fire remains we encountered near where thy father was discovered—" Dunsbury started to say.

"Made by Winnie the previous night," said Will. "Elizabeth and I saw her there while returning from the wreck."

"Art thou forgetting our pillaged homes and the destruction of the crop fields?" Elizabeth asked.

"Crimes committed by thy mother herself. She abducted my father and tied him to that tree with intentions of performing her witchcraft on him during that queer ritual we witnessed. I can only guess when she ransacked both our homes...no doubt the result of demonic influence. Savages would have burned both cabins to the ground and simply stolen our crops. They would never have desecrated the soil that precious food grew in—land they wish to reclaim. Their fury is with us and our possessions, not the soil they say is theirs. Both heinous acts are the work of a woman gone mad under the spell of unholy powers."

"I have doubts," said Elizabeth. "Thy thinking is filled with foolish conjecture and blind optimism."

"Use thine own senses, dear Elizabeth. Remember when we fled the wreck and barely made it ashore with our lives?" asked Will. "Thou saw them in their canoes...and though they were enraged and quite able, they did not come ashore and finish us off. They did not pass the threshold but turned away. The curse is real, if only in their beliefs. Here, we are safe. It is our island sanctuary."

Elizabeth shook her head in doubt and defiance.

"Thou art sure of thyself and instilled with a boldness I admire, William Estes," said Dunsbury. "Are we to proceed with our plan this day?"

"We are indeed," he answered. "The skies grow more angry by the hour, and I fear the impending storm may arrive much sooner than expected. We must pray that the longboat repairs have taken and make haste for the *Repulse* before she is swept away...forever leaving us as paupers. Elizabeth, please remain behind and forage the shore for any kind of edible shellfish, seaweed, and kelp. Lobsters, crabs, and mussels are plentiful. Though unappetizing, they are nourishing and desperately needed. Take my father with thee. If properly shown what to do, he can help."

"And the savages—"

"There are no savages," Will said impatiently. "There is no threat. Just...just do as I ask, my love."

Elizabeth turned away in angry silence, leaving Will and the lieutenant to collect their gear for the journey. Gathering everything they could carry, the two men set out, but not before Will gave his father a reassuring hug and motioned for him to go back into the barracks to help Elizabeth. Again he was reluctant, but eventually complied. A moment later, Will and Dunsbury exited the fort and were again cutting a path through the woods toward the southeast shore.

Despite Will's bold proclamation, they proceeded cautiously and remained on alert. Though both believed there was no danger, their movements indicated a much different bent of mind. Will tried to calm the conflict in his head and travel along as if it were just another ordinary trek, but his instincts wouldn't allow it.

The day grew cooler and was eerily calm. Eventually, they reached the shoreline and followed it until the longboat was in sight. Upon reaching the boat, Will looked up and studied the sky. It was cloudy and dark, making it seem much later in the day than it actually was. He listened hard and, in his mind, could almost hear the crack of approaching thunder hundreds of miles away. The sea was flat calm, and there was no sign of life wheeling about in the sky or scurrying around on the shore. In fact, the only company the two men had were swarms of mosquitoes buzzing about in search of warm blood. The insects were an annoying incentive to get out on the water fast.

"Let's see how that repair looks," said Will.

They gently flipped the boat over and loaded it up after Will erected the mast. With extra care, they shoved it into the placid waters just far enough to see if the hull was indeed sound. Will leaned over the side and watched for any water seeping in. To his delight, the boat remained dry.

"Methinks she will hold," he said with relief. "We simply must not add any undue stress to the repaired portion of the hull," he added. "We will have to stow as much weight as possible *away* from that area."

"That may be difficult," Dunsbury chuckled. "Gold is very heavy—especially in large quantities."

Will smiled at the joke, and the two climbed aboard. Will took up the oars and began rowing while Dunsbury remained in the stern to man the tiller. Neither made mention of danger, but they often caught each other looking out over the water for any sign of approaching canoes. As the shoreline of Storm grew farther away, Will broke the silence.

"Is thy constitution a match for the day's toil, Leftenant?"

"I am still hounded by brief stints of pain and fatigue, but *this* day I feel more robust than any other since being under thy care."

"Good," said Will between strokes. "Our task will require a healthy amount of strength and courage."

"I possess an abundance of both," said Dunsbury. "A Royal Marine is never found lacking in those soldierly attributes."

"Then we shall *both* be up to the task," said Will with an extra powerful and confident pull on the oars. "Tell me, what are the primary duties of a marine such as thyself? Aboard ship...and otherwise, of course."

"Guard and sentry duties, mainly," answered Dunsbury. "Royal Marines help enforce discipline and naval regulations aboard ship. We stand guard when punishment is meted out on orders from the ship's captain. When in a friendly port, we perform security duties and maintain order by ensuring that wayward sailors do not get drunk and decide to desert their ship. We also serve as garrisons in captured fortresses until formally relieved by infantry troops."

"And what of the military role in battle aboard ship?" Will asked.

"We act as sharpshooters and gunners when engaging a hostile vessel at close range. That was, in fact, my last duty aboard the *Firefly*, as thou art aware. Royal Marines also serve as boarding parties to seize ships by force and assist in sailing them back to friendly harbors once under control. Alas, that mission was left unfulfilled where the Devil's Chariot is concerned. However, I intend to have the last word on that matter."

"Did thou ever fight on land?"

"Of course. Every marine's duty is to fight in land battles alongside regular infantry when the situation demands."

"Well, let us pray that that particular duty will not be called for any time soon," replied Will.

The longboat eventually rounded the point jutting out from Storm that kept the *Repulse* hidden from view. Will rowed steadily with his back to the bow, relying on Dunsbury to be his eyes and to keep the boat on course. But suddenly Dunsbury stiffened and looked uneasy as his gaze became fixed in one direction. Will glanced over his shoulder and saw that the *Repulse* was now in full view. He rowed on, wondering how his companion would react once he was nearer to and eventually on board the ghostly ship. He felt the need to say something, but prudently decided against it. Surely the horrors of the bloody naval battle, coupled with the loss of so much and so many, already weighed heavily on the lieutenant's mind.

Will edged the boat alongside the damaged rigging. The tide was low but not low enough for his liking. It became yet another worrisome factor that needed to be considered and kept track of. Will tied off the boat and looked over at Dunsbury still seated at the tiller.

"This is the easiest way aboard," he said. "I'll climb up and lower down the ram's head. Gather up everything in the net and attach it to the hook. Once I hoist it aboard, climb up and join me."

"It shall be done," said Dunsbury as he began to spread out the net and place the gear at the center of it.

Will climbed up the rigging and leapt onto the top deck. He drew his pistol from the satchel and cocked the hammer. He pointed it in all directions, carefully looking and listening for signs of trouble.

"William," Dunsbury shouted up, "I'm ready! Send down the hook."

Will put away the gun then went over to the boom and swung it overboard. He undid the rope and lowered the ram's head. Dunsbury cinched up the corners of the net and attached them to the hook.

"Haul away!" he called out.

Will pulled up the gear and swung the boom inboard. Dunsbury quickly climbed up and boarded the ship that was responsible for so much of his recent misery.

"I claim this 'vessel of the damned,' this Devil's Chariot, in the name of the king—His Majesty, George the First."

For a moment, Will found himself taken aback, unsure of exactly what Dunsbury's proclamation meant.

The lieutenant, sensing Will's confusion, calmly said, "A ceremonial gesture only, young William. Our contract is still in force."

Immediately, Dunsbury began to survey his surroundings. He patrolled the deck, examining the wreckage and ruin strewn about. He discovered two intact cutlasses and put them aside but within easy reach. He then proceeded aft and promptly disappeared belowdecks. Will, slightly puzzled by Dunsbury's actions, eventually followed him below, bringing along a lighted lantern.

As expected, the lower decks were darker than usual due to the cloudy skies. Will crept along, checking each nook and accessible compartment for the now stray marine. He caught up with him in the Great Cabin, his coat tucked under his arm and a red silk sling draped across his chest and cradling his pistol—with room for many more. Upon first sight of the stylish sling, Will wondered how it had escaped Elizabeth's notice.

Without saying a word, Dunsbury slid by and exited the captain's quarters. He now moved about with determination and without caution, despite the numerous hazards the derelict vessel posed. Will didn't question it and assumed all seamen possessed an innate knowledge of various ship types. He eventually followed Dunsbury down to the flooded lower deck, where they stood together over the open hatch.

"Down there, I assume?" Dunsbury asked.

"Yes," Will answered. "I shall lower the hook and net down to this level with enough slack to reach the bottom of the hold. I will then tie a separate line around my waist and give it to thee. Then I shall swim down and guide the net over a chest, wooden box, or barrel and swim back up. At that point, the two of us will return topside and haul up the goods. Should I founder in the murky water, use this line to pull me back to safety."

"Understood," said Dunsbury. "And the boom and hoist thou hath rigged? Is it sound?"

Will hesitated before confessing, "It could do with a bit of shoring up, but that will take time—time I fear we do not have as I look to the skies."

"We will make do, then," said Dunsbury. "Let us begin before another moment is wasted," he added. He hesitated, looked at Will, and said, "But first let us acquire some insurance before we make our rich withdrawal. Follow me."

Back on the main deck, Dunsbury led Will to a bronze swivel gun mounted on a post on the quarterdeck.

"This should provide a most powerful response to any threat of force from the savages," Dunsbury said, gently patting the potent and portable weapon. "It shall add iron to the glove should any attack against the fort be attempted. Let this be the first treasure we officially take into possession this day."

Grasping both sides of the muzzle and the breech, they lifted the gun until the pintle was extracted from the stanchion. The small cannon was not nearly as heavy as Will had imagined, and they easily carried it over to the boom.

"There...open that box and display its innards," Dunsbury said, pointing to the wooden case nearest the gun mount. Will pulled off the cover. "Aye, now there's a comforting sight," Dunsbury said with a smile.

"What are those?" Will asked as he gazed down upon several curious-looking cylinders of metal.

"Ammunition—hailshot, to be precise," answered Dunsbury. "Tin canisters filled with musket balls and dipped in a beautiful beeswax lacquer to prevent weathering. Attached to the end is a lovely measured powder charge. It's much better than settling for ordinary langrage and sloppy handfuls of powder. The swivel is a favorite among pirates. It makes one musket feel like a hundred. It's very destructive and deadly when used against infantry assaults...or in the employ of pirates. It's a tremendously effective tool of intimidation when seizing but not wanting to sink a rich merchant vessel. For our purposes, however, we shall utilize it only as a tool of defense and self-preservation."

They placed the gun and ammunition into the net and lowered it down to the longboat using the hoisting boom. Dunsbury scrambled down to secure the plunder while Will swung the boom over the hatch and lowered the net into the dark reaches of the hold.

"Something puzzles me, William," said Dunsbury when he was back on the deck. "Such carnage and destruction wrought upon this wretched ship, yet I see no bodies, no bloody pirate scum lying about with blown-off legs or headless torsos."

"Those same thoughts entered my mind when I first climbed aboard," Will replied. "I have no ready explanation save one. It is my belief that savages, prior to my arrival, boarded this vessel. I discovered evidence of it sticking out of the mainmast. I have little doubt they finished off the wounded and any able man incapable of defending himself. They must have taken the bodies—the reason...of that I am decidedly unsure. However, I did witness three bodies floating in the water on the flooded lower deck, but they, too, were gone during my next exploration. I, of course, did bury many a lost soul at sea, and it certainly would not surprise me to learn that among the slain soldiers laid to rest in watery graves were corpses of dead pirates."

"Perhaps," said Dunsbury thoughtfully. "In my travels," he added, "aboard the many vessels to which I've been assigned, we frequently visited foreign lands and encountered savage tribes that practiced cannibalism."

"The Abenaki have shown little mercy toward our people, but I have never known them to engage in such an unholy act as cannibalism," said Will. "A macabre gesture of warning perhaps?"

"It is irrelevant. I do not intend to be around long enough to find out," said Dunsbury with a dismissive shake of his head. "Let us go about our business so that we may leave this vile ship once and for all."

"Agreed," said Will, noting that the skies now appeared unsettled and the sea was beginning to churn to life.

Again they headed to the flooded lower deck with Dunsbury leading the way, a glowing lantern in his hand. Will removed his boots and hat and stuffed them into a dry nook near the hatch. He stepped down into the knee-deep water, retrieved the safety line, and tied it securely around his waist before placing the free end in Dunsbury's hand. He then looked down into the cold, dark water, a sense of dread slowly overpowering the initial surge of anticipation.

"Godspeed," said Dunsbury. "I shall pull thee directly to safety at the slightest hint of danger or distress," he assured Will as he hung the lantern on a nearby post.

With that, Will nodded and plunged in, successfully pushing aside the specter of cowardice before it could rear its ugly head. Dunsbury let out slack from the safety line as the black water swallowed Will up. Using his memory for navigation, he followed the hoisting line until his fingers became entwined with the fishing net. Instinct took over as he moved automatically toward the prized stack of sea chests, wooden boxes, casks, and barrels.

Almost immediately, his hands found the square corners of a box that had become dislodged from the stack. He groped around some more and surmised that some natural force had shifted the pile of goods so that they were no longer tightly stacked upon one another, but now lay more loosely askew in random positions. This was extremely fortunate—it would now be easier to get the net around or partially under an individual object without having to lift it.

Quickly, as his breath began to give out, Will pushed the box over onto the net and fumbled around until the corners were cinched up. He reached for the hoisting line, intending to follow it back up to the surface, but a powerful flow of water pushed him away and further toward the stern of the wreck. Again, as in his earlier dives, he began to tumble through the hold and become disoriented. His strength faded and his mind grew dizzy. He tried to swim up but felt pinned by an aquatic force determined to keep him under. Finally, left with only one option, he madly tugged on his safety line. Thankfully, it took only a few seconds for Dunsbury to pull him back to the surface.

"Breathe, boy! Breathe!" Dunsbury commanded as he pounded on Will's back and hunched him over to force the water out of his lungs. With a mighty choking cough, Will managed to suck air back into his body while simultaneously expelling the seawater.

"Easy...sit on the edge and rest a minute," said Dunsbury as he undid Will's safety rope.

Will continued to cough and shiver as he slowly regained his senses and bearings.

"Topside...help me topside," Will stammered.

Dunsbury got him on his feet and helped him stumble back up to the quarterdeck.

"Sit; I shall return in a moment," said Dunsbury.

Will wrapped his arms around himself to help stem the shivering and silence his chattering teeth. He looked out over the unsettled channel—now pregnant with rising swells—with a sense of foreboding urgency. He silently cursed the lack of sun.

"Here, wrap this about thee," Dunsbury said as he handed Will a blanket.

"We mustn't delay," Will replied, slowly getting to his feet. "We have to haul up—"

"We will, but rest a moment," Dunsbury interrupted. "Wait; I have another idea. One that should do us both good on this gloomy day."

Dunsbury disappeared below again. A moment later, he reappeared carrying a small black iron cooking kettle that was cracked near the base. He placed it on the deck and filled it with scraps and large splinters of damaged planking. Then, using Will's fire striker, some flint from a damaged pistol, and pieces of shredded rope, he ignited a small blaze. The two of them huddled around it, grateful for the instant warmth it provided.

"I got one box secured in the net," Will announced over the increasing noise of the wind. "But this approaching storm has generated a troublesome current below. It presents us with a new problem. I...I...don't know if I can handle another dive. I've been in that hole three times now, and each time I've nearly drowned. Clearly, this abominable ship won't give up her riches without a substantial sacrifice."

"Then I shall be the one who dives next," replied Dunsbury.

"Art thou able enough?"

"I feel as strong as I once did, and I have always been an excellent swimmer. I shall dive next and relieve thee from the burden. The fire shall protect and invigorate us, and we shall tend to it and keep it hot between each dive. Now, if thou art ready, let us test the resilience of this hoist."

They went over to the boom and grasped the line.

"Together now," Dunsbury instructed.

They heaved in unison as the pulleys squealed and the boom creaked. The power of two men made the load rise much faster, and soon they could hear the net breach the lower deck. The sound of water cascading off the load was music to Will's ears, and he pulled harder and faster with growing anticipation.

"There it is!" exclaimed Dunsbury as the wooden box rose out of the top hatch and dangled precariously in the net. "I've got the rope secure. Swing the boom over and I'll set it down on the deck. Hurry now!"

Will grabbed the rope fastened to the boom and pulled it away from the hatch. Dunsbury gingerly released the main line until the box came to rest on the deck. Will untangled the net and strained to lift the box off it.

"God...that is heavy," he said, stepping away to retrieve his topmaul.

"No," said Dunsbury. "Do not open it."

Will shot him a quizzical look and said, "Surely thou must know—"

"We should load directly into the boat," Dunsbury said. "Time is not our ally. If we stop to inspect and marvel at whatever riches we uncover, we will become entranced and filled with avarice. That will waste time and further endanger our ability to recover more—nay, it will endanger our very lives."

Will glanced at the skies and immediately understood. He slackened the main line and swung the boom over the longboat.

"I can raise the prize myself," said Dunsbury. "Climb down to the boat and guide the load into place."

Will complied and they worked together until the first sealed wooden box was in place aboard the longboat. Will climbed back aboard the *Repulse* and observed the lieutenant already removing his boots, his pistol, and the silk sling. They repositioned the boom and lowered the hook back down into the hold. Then they went below again after a brief respite by the fire. Will recovered his own boots and hat, putting them both back on.

"Damn this frigid water," scoffed Dunsbury. "Tie the line around my waist."

"Follow the hoisting line down to the bottom and feel around to thy left. Just a few feet away will be the prize. Be mindful of the current and signal if thou feel in peril," said Will.

Dunsbury nodded and took a deep breath. In seconds, he was underwater and out of sight. Will watched the bubbles as they surfaced and let out slack on the rope as needed. After two minutes had elapsed, he started to worry and began passively pulling on the safety line. He knelt down and peered as far and as deep into the black hold as he could, but saw no sign of life. Even the bubbles had ceased. But before he could get to his feet and yank the line, Dunsbury shockingly thrust himself up and out of the hold. Will helped him sit up on the edge.

"Art thou all right?" Will asked.

"Quite well, quite well indeed," Dunsbury replied, breathing heavily. "Come, let us get topside." he added.

They returned to the top deck and began heaving on the second load, which proved heavier than the first. Will grew increasingly uneasy with every pull as the strain on the damaged boom intensified with unnerving creaks and cracks. But soon the second load was in sight, and this time there were two netted prizes—a large locked sea chest and a cask.

"More rum, no doubt," said Dunsbury as he eyed the cask with glee. As before, he held the suspended load in place while Will swung the boom over the longboat. The load was then carefully lowered, positioned, and secured aboard the small craft. Will climbed back aboard and immediately sought refuge under his soggy blanket near the fire, which he revitalized with more scraps of wood and rope. Dunsbury joined him, looking stronger and more resilient than ever, and Will began to admire the man's apparent fortitude and wondered if he himself could match it. He was weary, though. The cold wetness had sapped his strength, and he didn't want to leave the fire. He was unwilling to move until Dunsbury was ready—which proved to be sooner than he had hoped.

"We must keep going," the lieutenant said. "I counted at least seven more chests and hogshead barrels down there. With concentrated effort, we can have it all recovered and be on our way before sunset."

Will shook his head and hauled himself up. He felt ashamed; he was the younger, uninjured half of the duo, yet the wounded marine was clearly stronger and more resourceful. Dunsbury carried on with the drive and discipline of a trained soldier that Will secretly envied and wished to emulate. His conscience got the better of him, and they resumed their salvage work with Dunsbury as the diver and Will in support.

Each load took a toll on them. Neither wanted to show it, but they were exhausted and rapidly reaching the point where they could not continue. The weather grew more ominous as the day wore on, and the wreck was beginning to sway with the rising tide and the strong winds. Thunder cracked in the distance, and scattered raindrops began to plop onto the deck. Pieces were being hauled up one at a time now, as the boom's collapse seemed imminent. Additionally, longer periods of time were spent near the fire because recovery between dives took longer and longer. Both men were cold, wet, tired, and hungry—but there was one more piece as yet untouched.

Will looked over the side and counted nine pieces of salvaged cargo now stacked in the longboat. Two wooden boxes, four locked sea chests, one cask, and two hogshead barrels were the fruit of the day's labor.

"Should we make sail and be on our way?" Will asked as he joined Dunsbury by the dying fire.

"Nay, there is one last chest below. It is larger and heavier than those already recovered. We'd be fools if we left it here," said Dunsbury between coughs.

Not wanting to press on any further, Will began to question the lieutenant.

"Don't we have enough? Shouldn't we be prudent and leave this wreck once and for all?"

"The chest could contain a fortune. There isn't any time left. If we leave it, we may never have another chance to recover it."

"The boom...it won't hold the added weight," argued Will. "Can we even get a net around it?"

"We won't need the net. There's a heavy metal handle on the top. We can use the hook and haul it up that way. Come, we have to do this now," Dunsbury insisted as he stood up, removed the fishing net, and lowered the hook down into the hold.

A bolt of lightning streaked across the sky, and taking that as a truly worrisome sign, they hurried belowdecks. The ship's interior was now almost completely dark except for the pathetic light from the lantern on the lower deck. It was difficult to see much of anything, and it was only getting worse.

"Give me the safety line," demanded Will.

"What?" asked Dunsbury.

"I'm going down. Thou hath shouldered the brunt of today's labors, and though thou doth not show it, thou art too weak for another bout below water. I will lead this last plunge into Hell."

Will took the safety rope and tied it around his waist, which was now even with the waterline thanks to the approaching storm that was amplifying the rising tide. Without thought or fear, he dived in and headed straight for the bottom. It took no time to find the block and protruding hook. He grabbed onto it and groped around for the chest Dunsbury had mentioned. At first he felt nothing but the emptiness of the wreck's hull, but then, as a misdirected fish or two grazed his head, his fingers found the corner of the prize.

This is it, he thought. As before, a surge of water knocked him back toward the stern, but he managed to hold onto the hook, which helped steady him and acted as its own lifeline. He located the chest again and guided the hook through the handle. This time, without hesitation, he used the hoisting line as a guide and successfully made his way back to the surface just as his breath was about to give out. Dunsbury pulled him up, and the two staggered back to the top deck and immediately over to the fire.

"It's hooked," Will gasped, lying prone on the deck and coughing loudly.

"Good...but a moment's respite is sorely needed at this time," Dunsbury said as he added more scraps to the fire. Then he, too, collapsed on his back to rest.

Will's eyes flew open and he bolted upright as multiple bolts of lightning coupled with deafening cracks of thunder roused him from sleep. He did not know if he had been unconscious for minutes or hours, but he instantly looked about for Dunsbury, who was getting to his feet and heading for the boom.

"Come now, Will!" he shouted over the howling wind. "This is it!"

Will got up and saw that the storm was nearly upon them. At any time, the skies would open and release a deluge of rain and wind strong enough to wash them clear off the deck and into the sea. The skies were black, and it was nearly as dark as night. Will hurried over to the boom and grabbed the hoisting rope. Signaling he was ready, they once again heaved in unison. The strain on this final haul was more than either of them had anticipated. The boom cracked and creaked constantly, and the pulleys squealed in protest with every turn. The two men pulled with all their remaining strength, and it seemed like an eternity before the chest breached the inner hatch and was freed from its watery tomb. However, they were only halfway there, as they still needed to raise it to the top deck.

"Pull! Pull until thy liver and lungs explode!" yelled Dunsbury. "Earn thy salt!"

With one mighty heave after another, the massive chest finally came into view.

"Heave!" Dunsbury hollered again.

And suddenly, half of it was through, then finally all of it was suspended over the top hatch.

"Quick, swing it over the longboat," ordered Dunsbury.

"I can't let go of the main line," said Will. "Thou cannot hold it thyself. I must tie it off first."

"No!" fired back Dunsbury. "The boom is giving way. Swing it over now or we lose it forever!"

Will let go of the line and grabbed the rope attached to the boom. Dunsbury was nearly lifted off his feet but managed to keep the main line steady.

"Hurry!" he shouted, his grip weakening and the chest slipping away.

Will pulled on the rope and painfully swung the boom over the deck. Just then, there was a mighty snap as the hoist finally gave way and came crashing down as the men dove for cover. Dunsbury narrowly escaped the falling debris and got up unscathed, as did Will. They were relieved to see the prized chest resting on the deck just two feet away from the top hatch.

"We'll tie a rope on it and lower it down by hand," Dunsbury said.

"Let's be quick about it," Will replied, his heart racing.

The two went to work, and with tremendous effort lifted the heavy chest with the help of the metal handles on either end. They secured ropes to each handle and wrestled it over the side. Finding one last burst of strength, they painstakingly lowered it into the longboat before once again collapsing onto the deck to catch their breath and relieve their aching muscles.

"Let's get out of here," said Dunsbury several minutes later.

Will put on his boots, hat, and satchel and collected his musket. He bundled up his tools and tossed them down into the boat. Dunsbury gathered his silk sling, pistol, and coat—which he didn't put on, but decided to carry with both arms. Then they both took a moment to warm themselves by the fire one last time. At that moment, true terror was viciously unleashed upon them.

Screams, shrieks, and chilling howls suddenly swept over the deck and sent fear ripping down their backbones. They looked at one another and then raced to the larboard bow facing the shore of Belle Island. They stared in disbelief. There, lined up along the water's edge, stood at least thirty Abenaki warriors. Behind them was a huge bonfire. The distance between the shore and the wreck was enough to deter the angry natives from attempting to swim over and climb aboard the stricken vessel, but Will quickly realized that they were well within arrow range. To make matters worse, the angry bowmen were going over to the fire and setting the shafts ablaze.

"To the boat!" yelled Dunsbury.

They ran to the other side facing the channel just as flaming arrows began to land on the top deck.

"Look!" hollered Will as he pointed to the sea below. Dunsbury gaped at the churning channel waters and saw dozens of Abenaki canoes approaching from all directions. The *Repulse* was effectively surrounded.

"There's no way we can sail or fight our way through them!" Will cried. "The boat's overloaded and sitting too low in the water.

Even if we could get to it and raise sail, we'd never outrun them. The boat would capsize with us scrambling to defend it. We'd lose the treasure forever at the bottom of the channel—not to mention our very lives."

"We'll have to fight them!" replied Dunsbury vehemently. He put down his coat, thus revealing what he had been hiding under it. It was a blunderbuss with a short flared barrel, and a dragon pistol. "Get thy musket and pistol ready. It's time thou experienced how a Royal Marine fights," he said, hastily donning the red coat. "To the swivels!"

Dodging arrows left and right, Dunsbury manned the one larboard bow swivel gun that still had an undamaged ammunition box next to it.

"Light the hemp at the tip of that linstock and bring it here," he ordered, pointing to a long staff lying on the deck. Will grabbed it and used the embers of the fire to light the slow-burning hemp at the tip.

Dunsbury loaded the muzzle of the swivel gun with canister shot and took aim at the largest cluster of shrieking bowmen on Belle's shoreline. He adjusted the pitch of the small cannon using the monkey tail–shaped tiller, then snatched the linstock from Will's hands and touched off the gun by joining the burning end of the staff to the weapon's vent. The gun fired with a powerful boom that scattered dozens of lead balls into the unsuspecting natives. Several toppled backwards, crying out in agony and soon forever silenced. The survivors of the initial blast quickly dispersed, but kept launching flaming arrows high into the air and onto the ship's deck.

"Take thy musket and point it at the threat from the sea!" commanded Dunsbury as he rammed another load of canister shot down the muzzle of the swivel gun. Will hurried over to the other side of the deck and took aim at the closest canoe. He fired. Missing badly, his trembling hands fumbled to retrieve more powder and shot from his satchel.

Another deadly blast cracked from Dunsbury's swivel cannon, spraying hot lead into the dwindling ranks of the Abenaki on shore. The brutally effective weapon forced them to fall back to the protection of the thick woods to their rear, where they remained mostly out of sight.

Will finally reloaded his musket and took aim again. This time he found his mark, felling a warrior and forcing his canoe to capsize. However, an avalanche of dread swiftly overwhelmed the brief moment of euphoria he initially felt. The dozens of approaching canoes drew closer and were only seconds away from boarding the wreck. Will knew he couldn't load his gun fast enough to eliminate them all. He would have to fight hand to hand and risk being bludgeoned and cleaved to death by Abenaki tomahawks.

The fire on the deck began to spread, adding another lethal hazard to the already perilous situation. Will froze as he peered through the flames threatening to cut him off from Dunsbury. Rife with fear, his mind suddenly went blank and he was unable to act even when he heard the sounds of several warriors climbing up the damaged rigging. He slowly turned his head and watched in terror as four natives wielding tomahawks climbed over the gunnel. As soon as their feet hit the deck, they let loose a vicious war cry and were poised to strike a lethal blow with one swift thrust.

Paralyzed with fear, Will dropped his musket.

"Duck!" yelled Dunsbury.

Instinctively, Will's legs went out from under him as the swivel gun's muzzle swung around and pointed in his direction. A second later, the gun fired, releasing another torrent of canister shot that tore through all four native warriors, killing them instantly.

"Get to thy feet and repel all boarders!" Dunsbury commanded after abandoning his swivel. He quickly rearmed with the blunderbuss and one of the two cutlasses he'd found earlier. The other, he tossed through the wind-driven flames. Miraculously, Will caught the cutlass by the hilt while simultaneously drawing his pistol. Dunsbury leapt over the burning deck and joined Will by the gunnel. He aimed his weapon and fired at a group of warriors attempting to climb up the rigging. Several fell backwards into the roiling sea, turning the water a bloody red. With the blunderbuss now empty, Dunsbury let it fall overboard into the longboat.

"Regroup astern!" he shouted at Will as the fire began to envelop the bow.

Together, they struggled back to the quarterdeck only to be taken by surprise by several warriors who had managed to get aboard undetected. Will raised his pistol and fired at an Abenaki lunging toward him. The Indian fell dead at his feet just as another one charged. Will raised his cutlass to parry the chopping blow of the tomahawk intended for his skull. He then drove his boot into the gut of his attacker, pushing him backwards and off balance. They thrust and slashed at one another, each trying to gain the advantage. When the warrior screamed out a deafening cry, Will tripped and fell backwards. But before the tomahawk could deliver the final blow, a shot rang out from Dunsbury's flintlock and ripped through the warrior's chest, killing him on the spot.

But no sooner had the lieutenant saved Will's life than his own fell into jeopardy.

"William," he called out while fending off two warriors with just his cutlass, "strike with thy sword!"

Will sprang up and slashed at one of the attackers, promptly drawing him away from the lieutenant. Dunsbury dodged a hammering blow from the now lone warrior facing him, and responded with an incising stroke of his own that effectively sliced off the native's right hand. The stricken man cried out in pain, helplessly exposing himself to Dunsbury's sword, which was immediately driven into his midsection. He then pulled the bloody blade free and drove it into the back of the other savage attacking Will. The two then turned and faced the sole remaining warrior, forcing him overboard after a series of slashing attacks wrenched the tomahawk from his hand and wounded both arms.

"Powder and shot...while we have time," said Dunsbury as he pointed to Will's satchel. They hurriedly reloaded and cocked their Spanish flintlocks. "We have to make our exit or risk being scorched alive," he added as the burning wreck started to shudder and break apart.

Another thunderous boom was followed by multiple bolts of lightning that lit up the angry sky. The wreck rocked heavily as the sea swells intensified and almost knocked both men off their feet. The blaze had spread to the mainmast, and fiery debris showered the deck. Will and Dunsbury eyed the starboard midsection

where the longboat was docked. Only a narrow corridor free of flames remained, and there was no guarantee the treasure-laden craft was still afloat.

"Should we go over the side and swim to Belle—make our final stand there?" Will asked.

"Never! We shall not surrender our gains or our lives so easily!" shouted Dunsbury.

With that, he secured the bloody cutlass in his belt and drew the dragon from his sling. In one hand he held the smaller Spanish pistol, in the other the bigger, fatter dragon. Determined to keep the treasure, whatever the cost, Dunsbury hurried to the point of embarkation amidships before it became completely enveloped in flames. Will hustled behind him. They looked over the side and were relieved to see the longboat still attached and intact. A deluge of driving rain began to pour down from the heavens, and it was only a matter of time before the full fury of the gale would be squarely upon them.

The weather, daunting and dangerous as it was, provided an opportunity for the beleaguered pair. The Abenaki warriors on the water had used their canoes to form a perimeter around the starboard side of the wreck to prevent escape via the sea. However, the rapidly decaying weather had made conditions in the channel extremely rough, causing many canoes to break formation and some to flee for smoother water or risk foundering.

"Climb down," said Dunsbury with pistols ready. "I'll cover thy descent."

Will scrambled over the side and into the boat as two Abenaki arrows slammed into the hull just above his head. Dunsbury fired a single shot before slinging his pistols and climbing down himself. Once aboard, he drew his cutlass and slashed the line connecting the two vessels. Instantly, the longboat was caught up in a swell and pushed away.

"Make sail," ordered Dunsbury as burning debris crashed down on the spot where they had stood just seconds earlier.

Will, fearing his sail would be ripped to shreds and the longboat sunk, reached for the oars.

"No!" hollered Dunsbury. "Risk the sail, or we'll never make it back. Hand me thy pistol."

Will complied and hoisted the canvas. It immediately caught the wind and billowed out, causing the boat to lurch forward and take on some water. Will fell back onto the tiller, trying to ease the strain and keep the craft from capsizing. He pointed the boat toward what he perceived as calmer water along Storm Island's southeast shore, but soon began to doubt whether they'd even make it across the channel. The boat was dangerously overloaded, even for ideal conditions.

Dunsbury blasted away with his three shots, saving the most potent weapon—the dragon—for last. Only two canoes remained in their path, and the scattered blast of lead that erupted from the blunderbuss effectively cleared the way. The remaining canoes fell into the longboat's wake and soon became scattered and tossed as the weather forced the savages to withdraw and seek shelter. Their birch bark canoes simply could not tame or cope with the harsh wind whipping up the stormy waters.

"Course is clear," said Dunsbury. "Get us ashore."

Will looked behind him and watched as the *Repulse* continued to burn and break apart. Waves rolling in from the open ocean began to pound what remained of the hull, and then, as if moved by the hand of God, the ship broke loose from its rocky impalement. Will and Dunsbury watched in astonishment as, for a brief moment, the *Repulse* eerily appeared to be sailing out to sea under its own power. The image was spellbinding, as the vessel refused to succumb—first to the British Navy and now to the elements.

Defiant to the bitter end, the *Repulse* eventually rolled over and was swept under the waves, the light from the fires on deck extinguished forever.

When a powerful swell hit the bow of the longboat, it nearly swamped the craft for good. Will and Dunsbury madly bailed out as much water as their cupped hands could scoop, but it became increasingly futile. Slowly, the boat sank deeper until the gunnels were nearly submerged. Dunsbury wrestled with the load, shifting what he could to keep the boat balanced while Will manhandled the tiller and sail, both being pummeled by the wind. The longboat plowed heavily forward as Will prayed the sail would not be torn to shreds before the wind carried them to shore.

The darkness, intensified by the storm, made navigation more difficult, but without consulting Dunsbury, Will decided to forego the southeast shore—which was closer—and make a run for the northwest beach directly facing Fort Hope. The course would take longer and expose them to more hazardous weather conditions, but it was the only logical choice for offloading and securing the treasure on solid ground and under shelter. He had no intention of leaving it on the beach and having it swept out to sea or buried in the sand. He wanted it on land and protected by the four walls of Fort Hope—even if it meant risking his own life.

With each passing moment, the gale seemed to strengthen. The wind dug deep into the canvas until it seemed the bent mast itself would snap in two. Under tremendous strain, the sturdy boat plunged ahead and approached the northwest shore. Will put up his arm to shield his face from the pelting rain and continuous blasts of wind, while Dunsbury continued to bail and do everything in his power to prevent the boat from foundering and losing the treasure forever. His efforts were clearly in vain as the water continued to rise and the boat began to slip under the waves. Then the sail gave way and ripped apart into flapping rags and tatters.

Just as all seemed hopeless, and with death hovering just above them ready to strike, the northwest shore was finally within reach. Will strained at the tiller to beach the longboat in the most advantageous location. As they neared the spot, a huge wave crashed over the stern and helped push the boat ashore, knocking both Will and Dunsbury into the water. They were swept under momentarily and surfaced as the pounding surf shoved them into the shallows and onto the beach. Getting to their feet, they saw the longboat, its keel dug into the sand, listing heavily to the side. Waves continued to break over it, threatening to smash the stricken craft to splinters while sending several sea chests overboard.

"Quickly—we must get the cargo ashore before this unholy whirlwind insists on a hefty ransom in exchange for our lives!" hollered Dunsbury.

They tried to pull the boat farther onto the beach, but were completely unable to budge the weighty craft. Instead, they began

taking the sea chests, boxes, and barrels off one by one and hauling them out of reach of the crashing waves. Piece after excruciat-
ing piece was offloaded or pulled out of the surf until only the largest chest remained. They tried to lift it, but were far too weak to do
so. Another wave broke over the boat, filling it entirely with seawater and debris. Will could hardly summon the strength to lift
his drenched head, but something caught his eye and he looked
up. Through the darkness shone a solitary light that appeared to
be moving down the cliff trail toward the beach.

Elizabeth! Will thought and hoped. With every bit of strength
his voice and lungs could muster, he cried out, "Elizabeth!"

Dunsbury mimicked the call, and they watched as the light
grew closer. It was indeed Elizabeth, brandishing a solitary lantern, with Cyrus in tow.

"My God!" she cried upon seeing the sad state of both men.

"Elizabeth...Father...come hither and help before all is lost,"
pleaded Will. He directed them to the boat. "Help us lift this chest
out and ashore. All four of us need to work together."

Another wave crashed over them as they each took a corner.

"Lift together...now!" commanded Will.

With a mighty heave, the largest prize salvaged from the
shipwreck was lifted over the gunnel and dropped onto the sands
of Storm Island.

"We must get this up the cliff and into Hope," said Will.

Amazingly, Cyrus showed the most enthusiasm and resolve
as they struggled and lumbered up the cliff trail until they were
again on flat ground. After stopping to catch their breath, they
hauled the chest through the open gate of the fort to its final location—inside the northwest corner blockhouse.

"Come, there is more to recover," said Will. "We must hurry
before the full brunt of the storm is upon us."

They returned to the beach, where Will paired up with his
father and Dunsbury with Elizabeth. Both teams fought the rain and
wind to painstakingly lug the remaining goods up to the fort. The last
items recovered were the swivel gun and the box of canister shot. As
for the longboat, there was nothing that could be done. Will hoped it
would still be wedged into the sand and intact when next he saw it.

With the last of the salvaged goods sheltered in the block-house, Elizabeth closed the gate and secured the doors with the crossbar. She and Cyrus then helped Will and Dunsbury into the barracks, where both immediately collapsed and fell unconscious. Soaking wet, tired, hungry, and afraid, Elizabeth was speechless as she stared down at the two helpless souls. Unsure if they were alive or dead now, she crumpled down by the fire and began to weep. Cyrus kept his distance and crawled up in the far corner near the mattress. He let out a small grunt and never took his eyes off Dunsbury as he curled up into a wet ball with his knees pressed into his chest on the dirt floor.

Elizabeth's attention turned to the storm and the pounding the island was now suffering. Thunder and lightning filled the sky as the rain continued to fall and the wind refused to relent. She covered her ears and closed her eyes tight as the tears continued to stream silently down her face. Morbid images haunted her thoughts, and she wondered if any of them would survive to see the dawn.

CHAPTER 12

The Aftermath

For three days and three nights the mighty gale ravaged Storm Island and the surrounding region with remorseless ferocity. Besieged as they were by the weather, the beleaguered foursome could not venture far from the shelter of the barracks. Only the need for firewood, and water from the overflowing rain barrel, forced Elizabeth outside to momentarily brave the tempest.

They survived on bits of shellfish and raw seaweed, heavily salted and served with brewed tea and sugar. At the moment his head cleared and his body regained enough strength to function normally, Will was the first to approach the door, yearning to be the principal witness to the havoc wrought by the weather. The storm's fury had reached its zenith the previous night. Now it was morning and the winds and rain were gone. The skies were free of storm clouds and lightning, and the booming sounds of thunder were heard no more. Elizabeth and Cyrus were eager to see the sun again, while Dunsbury moved about sluggishly, still hampered by his wound, the lack of food, and overexertion.

Everyone stared at Will as he reached for the latch and opened the door. Bathed by a warm ray of sunshine, he immediately looked skyward at the clear blue heavens, happy that they had survived unharmed. His contentment was short-lived, however, as his gaze lowered and took in the destruction in the courtyard. He stepped outside and was soon followed by everyone else.

They looked around in dismay. Littering the courtyard were dismembered tree limbs, piles of tangled brush, and great pools of standing water. The walls of the fort remained upright but appeared severely weakened by the barrage of wind and soaking rain. Portions of the barracks roof were damaged, as was the roof on the southeast blockhouse. Everywhere they looked, something lay askew or appeared damaged.

"The whole world is just plain bent," said Will, shaking his head.

"Will," said Dunsbury, "the boat?"

All four of them wound through the twisted mess and cleared debris from the front entrance doors so they could be opened. Outside the wall, conditions were no better than those in the courtyard, but they found their way to the edge of the cliff and looked down at the beach.

"There she is," Will pointed. "Thank the Lord she wasn't swept out to sea."

He led the way down the sloping path with the others close behind. On the beach, the longboat was on its side, draped in seaweed and partially buried in the sand at the bow. The hull was visibly scarred, and the removable mast was dislodged, but beyond that, the sturdy craft had survived and looked remarkably sound.

"I shall exhume and repair this boat where needed—at once," Will said. "The Lord has spared us this vital instrument of our livelihood...nay, our very existence. A miracle...no less. We should all commit to a rapid clearing and reorganization of the fort—"

"William," Dunsbury interrupted. "I appreciate thine industrious and prudent sentiments, but hath thou forgotten something? Surely a few brief moments can be afforded to reveal and savor the fruits of thy efforts and sacrifices suffered but a few days ago?"

Will paused as his mind shifted from grinding pragmatist to eager visionary. He looked up and smiled, as new life seemed to flow back into his haggard soul.

"By all means," he agreed. "Let us discover what riches now rest in our possession."

Back inside the walls of the fort, they were dismayed to discover a large tree limb blocking access to the northwest blockhouse.

"After all our toil and hardship thus far, our path continues to be fraught with hindrances," Will lamented.

"Even with her demise," said Dunsbury, "the Devil's Chariot will not give up her pickings so easily. I told thee she was a demon ship."

"I shall not be dissuaded," replied Will.

"Nor I," said Dunsbury.

The two men grappled with the broad limb, which was partially impaled in the earth. They wrenched it free and pushed it aside to gain entrance to the mysterious chests and barrels awaiting them.

"Elizabeth, fetch the stools from the barracks and set them up in a clear, dry spot. We shall haul out the goods and look upon them in the bright sunlight," said Will.

"Nay," said Dunsbury. "Let us bring the entire table out into the sun. We shall then feast our eyes upon mountains of pirate treasure!"

"It shall be done!" said Elizabeth eagerly. "Mr. Estes, come forth and assist me," she added. "Cyrus...Cyrus? Cyrus!" she bellowed, demanding his attention and response.

The old man reluctantly looked at her and then at his son.

"Go with her, Father," he said, making long and deliberate gestures signaling what he wanted him to do.

Cyrus relented and followed Elizabeth into the barracks. They emerged a minute later carrying the table, which they set up near the center of the courtyard.

Will picked up one of the two boxes and carried it over to the table, and Dunsbury did the same with the second box. They placed the boxes side by side on the table. Will retrieved the top-maul from his bundle of tools and went to work on the lid of the first box, which was nailed shut. With little effort, it was pried open and tossed aside, and everyone peered down at the contents.

"What are those?" Elizabeth asked.

"I'm not sure," said Will in response. He looked over at his father, who stood scratching his head.

"Grenades," said Dunsbury in a disappointed tone.

"*What* are they?" Will and Elizabeth asked, in near-perfect unison.

"Grenades," again said Dunsbury. "Iron balls loaded with gunpowder and ignited by a cloth fuse threaded through this wooden plug," he said, pointing to the object. "Ideal for creating confusion and terror in battle, but nothing of a valuable nature."

Elizabeth looked away in disgust and disappointment while Cyrus looked on in puzzlement at the curious black balls.

"That may not be entirely true," Will said, looking squarely at Dunsbury—who immediately understood his meaning.

"Yes, they may serve some useful purpose..." he said quietly as he gazed up toward the pointed palisades.

"The next box, Will," Elizabeth insisted impatiently as she shoved it closer to him.

As before, he pried off the lid with the topmaul then looked down and away again in disappointment.

"Bar shot," said Dunsbury this time. "Used in cannons to rip apart sails and rigging. Pirates love this manner of load because it allows them to disable a ship's means of propulsion without destroying it entirely."

Dunsbury turned away, visibly struggling to contain his ire.

"The cask, William," he said, "bring that here. It had better be overflowing with rum and not fungus-infested fluid of some other kind. I don't mind saying that I shall be quite annoyed if, when this day is over, I find out that I risked my life to procure ship's armaments and diseased water."

Will carried the cask to the table and turned the spigot at the base. He released a tiny amount of liquid onto his fingers, brought them to his nostrils, and then to his lips. He smiled.

"Rum indeed," he declared. "Cups all around."

Elizabeth brought the wooden cups from the barracks and they all ardently imbibed the delicious alcohol. Cyrus hiccupped happily after swallowing his cupful of the amber-colored elixir and indicated that he wanted more. Elizabeth drank vigorously, but Dunsbury refrained and began to grow impatient again. He got up and rolled both large barrels over next to the table. He stood them up, grabbed the topmaul, and smashed open their lids.

"Damnation!" he shouted upon viewing their contents.

Will and Elizabeth looked inside and then at each other. One barrel was filled with dried tobacco leaves, and the other contained an assortment of dry spices.

"Prized commodities on the open market in London, but quite useless here," griped Dunsbury.

"The chests...bring forth the chests," he said with growing exasperation.

"Yes, bring them hither at once," chimed in Elizabeth.

Will stumbled back over to the blockhouse. Dunsbury joined him, and together they carried over the first of the four heavy sea chests. The prize was fortified with a large padlock in the front that Will smashed away at with the topmaul. After a few formidable blows, the lock fractured and fell off. Will held his breath as he slowly opened the lid while the others looked on.

"Aye, now fancy that," said Dunsbury.

Elizabeth gasped, and Will reached down and grabbed the first item he saw. He held it up high in the sunlight and then looked to Dunsbury with a renewed sense of satisfaction.

"Spanish silver...pieces-of-eight coinage to be precise," Dunsbury said. "Straight from the wellspring of mines in the mountains of Charcas."

The chest was overflowing with the irregular-shaped metal currency. All four, including a seemingly bewildered Cyrus, scooped up handfuls of the clipped coins—embossed with the cross of Spain and the royal coat of arms—and playfully let them slide through their fingers and jangle onto the table.

"The closest thing to global currency thou will ever find," said Dunsbury. "I shall most certainly allocate the deepest portion of my ten percent share to these silver coins. They will be the most useful to barter with once back in civilization." As an afterthought, he added, "Each weighs approximately eight Spanish *reales*."

"On to the next chest!" applauded Elizabeth.

Will and Dunsbury lugged the remaining four chests over to the table, saving the largest one for last. The old wooden stand creaked under the weight, threatening to buckle and collapse entirely. However, the table's cries went largely unnoticed amidst the growing avarice of the group standing over it. Will concentrated on opening the next padlocked chest, hammering away until the lock broke free.

With as much awe and breathlessness as before, the lid was raised, and the group was delighted by another spectacular hoard of silver—only this time, the precious gray metal was in bar form. Though all were excited, none would be content until they laid eyes upon what manner of riches the next coffer might contain.

Will whacked away at the lock of the third chest. It proved harder to break, but he eventually got the better of it. As he swung open the lid, his eyes bulged until he thought they would pop out of his skull. Instinctively, he reached into his pocket and pulled out the golden doubloon he had first discovered days earlier in the hold of the *Repulse*. He held it over the chest, which contained a bounty of similar coins, all shining brilliantly in the sun.

The gold was entrancing to the point where no one dared move or say a word for fear of waking from a perfect dream. But once the initial captivation faded, the group happily plunged into the glimmering trove, tossing the lustrous coins about as if they were mere amusing baubles.

"Quickly, the next one, the next one!" Elizabeth cried.

Will, feeling the strength of Hercules, smashed open the lock on the fourth chest with one mighty blow. Inside was yet another glowing golden treasure. Melted and molded into portable chunks of various size and shape, knife-scored ingots of gold half-filled the chest and commanded everyone's full attention. Each piece was closely examined and admired while held up in the sun.

"I've seen this before," commented Dunsbury as he ran his fingers over the knife marks in the gold lump in his hand. "Once looted and safely in their possession, pirate quartermasters often tested the gold to determine if it was pure and not just a worthless hunk of iron enrobed in a thin golden coating. Such a dismal finding could turn deadly among a hostile crew impatiently expecting their hard-earned share."

A moment of silence ensued before Will and Elizabeth simultaneously broke out into frivolous laughter. The mere sight of the grand fortune that now spread across the worthless table beneath it filled them with a giddiness neither had ever experienced. The feeling impelled Elizabeth to lay siege to the rum cask, and once again the precious liquid flowed freely into her waiting cup. The others quickly joined her as they continued to marvel at the new-found riches.

"Huzzah!" cheered Dunsbury as they toasted their success.

So preoccupied were they with the celebration, they absent-mindedly overlooked the final unopened chest and its—as of yet—unknown contents. It was the gold exclusively that kept everyone spellbound; the way it glistened in the sun with a hypnotic, lustrous radiance was surely unlike anything else in the world. One could not help but admire it and long for it, and once in possession of it, one could not help but feel entitled to all the happiness and luxuries the world had to offer. Neither Will nor Elizabeth had ever seen or even imagined such a cache of riches, but despite their inclinations to celebrate all day, it was Will who first came back to his senses and realized there was much work to be done and many preparations to be made.

"Father, come hither," he said.

Will began picking up debris and lugging it to a central location in the courtyard. Once his demonstration was over, Cyrus copied his son's actions and set about clearing up the mess the storm had produced.

"Elizabeth, please build a fire out here in the open. We'll safely burn as much of the smaller debris as we can and chop up the rest for firewood."

"I shall make it so," she answered. "I shall also set about casting some new candles that are sorely needed...perhaps do some laundry and stitching as well."

"Leftenant, shall we attend to the longboat?" asked Will.

"Indeed we should," he answered.

Soon everyone was temporarily freed from the spell cast by the treasure and occupied with more useful activities. Will and Dunsbury tended to the longboat, freeing it from the sand, draining out the excess water and debris, and testing its seaworthiness. To their pleasant surprise, the battered craft had weathered the storm admirably and floated atop the calm waters with no signs of foundering. The previous hull mending was still intact, and only minor work was needed on the fitting for the mast. That point was ignored, however, as the sail was ripped to shreds and beyond repair.

"Doth thou possess spare canvas?" Dunsbury asked.

"No," answered Will. "But we still have the oars and a seaworthy craft. It's more than enough to get thee over to the Neck and on thy way south. Come, help me pull her up onto the beach properly."

"I should need but a few days to rebuild my strength, gather my supplies, and claim my portion of the treasure before I leave," said Dunsbury.

"The savages?" inquired Will.

On their way back to the fort, they discussed the growing threat from the Indians. It was decided that the swivel gun would be mounted over the entrance, and that other defensive preparations would be made in the event of another attack. Try as he might, Will was unable to convince Dunsbury that the island's curse would protect them by keeping the natives away. The two disagreed on that point, but agreed to recognize and enforce the notion for Elizabeth's sake.

While Will and the lieutenant were gone, Elizabeth had worked outside casting new candles while Cyrus cleared away and burned much of the debris. Upon their return, Will and Dunsbury sat at the table to talk some more. The lieutenant's attention became focused on Cyrus and the tasks he was doing so willingly.

"He's quite the industrious sort," Dunsbury remarked. "For someone his age and suffering from a lack of mental prowess, he seems to carry on quite well...physically, that is."

"He was once a great man," said Will. "He was the leader of our community. Years ago, he possessed both strength of mind and muscle. He was an educated man and a pious one, as well. He only wanted the best for everyone and was determined to overcome all obstacles to make this community thrive. He never withered in the face of adversity and always believed in the common good of people. He was most disagreeably reduced to his present state by a blow to the head during a fall."

"An example to be proud of nonetheless," replied Dunsbury.

"Yes, indeed," said Will before pausing and stating, "I desire to see his dream fulfilled. He deserves that much."

"He understands instructions? Is he able to carry out tasks on his own?"

"Mostly. His mind is a void, however," answered Will, adding, "yet his body does not reflect his age nor his mental privations. Though thin and frail in appearance, he is remarkably resilient and shows no desire to simply laze about. He is excellent at mimicking the actions demonstrated to him. Once he understands how to perform a task, he will work to complete it with little or no distraction. I believe he associates work with food and recognizes that the accomplishment of the former often results in the reward of the latter. One could say that food is his gold."

"Would thou consider him a threat to himself or others under unusual circumstances?" asked Dunsbury thoughtfully. "Would he be able to fight or defend himself? Can he load and fire a pistol or successfully wield a sword?"

"He is harmless and very trusting of others. I do not believe he would injure a fly by his own hand…though I must admit he has acted a bit peculiarly toward others of late—a result of the mistreatment by Winnie Eustis, no doubt."

Will paused a moment before concluding, "Through God's grand plan, my father is what he is. I can neither dispute nor change that fact. As long as there is breath in my lungs, I will provide him with as much care and protection as he requires…until the day comes when he is no longer among us."

"Very noble of thee, young William. Now may I suggest we find a proper vantage point atop those palisades to mount our newly acquired primary weapon of defense," said Dunsbury, indicating the swivel gun lying on the ground in the blockhouse.

"I shall need my axe and saw."

The day progressed with Elizabeth burning storm debris on the large fire in the courtyard. She embraced this laborious duty because it allowed her to sneak over to the table and pour herself liberal amounts of rum without drawing much attention. Meanwhile, realizing that food was now a major priority, Will took Cyrus down to the shore, where they boarded the longboat. Armed with a new net and fresh hooks and lines, they rowed out into deeper waters to catch more cod. Dunsbury remained on the fort's ledge to finish mounting the swivel gun.

Keeping the fort in clear view, Will cast his net and set his lines. It wasn't long before they were on the fish, and a little over an hour later, a modest catch littered the bow of the boat. Will hauled in his gear and began the short row back to the fort, keeping a watchful eye on the surrounding waters. His attention was soon drawn back to Cyrus, who seemed a bit on edge. The closer they got to shore, the more fidgety he became. Will looked into the old man's eyes and sensed that he desperately yearned to tell him something, yet his thoughts could not bridge the damaged pathways between his injured mind and his voice. Something was apparently amiss though, and Will couldn't put his finger on it. Though historically a waste of time, he shipped the oars and looked straight at his father. He asked what troubled him and how he could help. Most times, like a child, Cyrus did not comprehend or simply ignored what was being asked of him. But now his gaze was more focused, and for the first time in a very long time, he appeared to understand what was being said to him and wanted to deliver a clear response. Unfortunately, as usual, the words did not come, and Will was forced to simply row on.

The boat was beached, and the catch, still flopping in the net, was brought ashore and up to the fort. There was no sign of Elizabeth or Dunsbury in the courtyard. For a brief second, remembering her distrustful inclinations toward the man, Will regretted his unwitting decision to leave her alone with him, even if only for a short time.

He saved my life twice on that wretched wreck, Will thought. *He's been nothing but helpful and offered friendship to us. He has lived up to his end of the bargain and risked his own life to help better ours...and he'll be gone soon. I have no reason to distrust him. He is my friend.*

Just then the barracks door opened and Elizabeth and Dunsbury emerged. Will started to speak but was abruptly cut off.

"Ah, I see thou hath brought supper," said Elizabeth cheerily.

"Aye," said Will. "Perhaps Father can assist thee in thy preparations?"

"Yes, of course," she said. "Cyrus, bring the fish inside so that we may clean and cook them," Elizabeth said, gesturing for him to follow her.

Will nodded his head and motioned for Cyrus to carry the fish inside the barracks. With noticeable reluctance, the old man complied. Will then looked to the lieutenant.

"Come see our new armaments," Dunsbury said.

Will followed him up onto the ledge and inspected the newly mounted swivel gun. He grabbed the monkey tail and traversed the weapon back and forth. He noticed that the blunderbuss was propped up nearby, and next to it were the salvaged boxes of grenades and canister and bar shot.

"How much powder and shot is stored here?" Dunsbury asked.

"We have a limited amount," Will answered. "It never seemed that way before, as there was only the need for my musket, but now, with these weapons, I fear our supply is woefully lacking."

"Show me."

They climbed down to the lower level of the blockhouse. Stored in the corner under a layer of burlap sacks were two small kegs. Will removed the lids on both. The first was half filled with loose musket shot, and the second contained an even lesser amount of powder.

"We should keep this where it's handy and load the swivel and blunderbuss immediately," said Dunsbury. "In fact, we should account for all weapons and position them accordingly—excluding those kept on our persons, of course."

"My musket is gone," said Will. "All I have is this Spanish pistol."

"And I the other," replied Dunsbury as he pulled back his coat to reveal the sling. Will spied the pistol, but also noticed the dragon tucked away nicely, as well. He wanted to inquire more about the hefty little hand cannon and the blunderbuss, but decided against it for the time being.

For the next two hours, Will and Dunsbury worked to transform Hope into more of an offensive threat and a decidedly stronger defensive fortification. The swivel and blunderbuss were loaded, the parts of the walls most impacted by the storm were shored up, standing water was drained, and supplies were shifted to places where they would be most needed and most effective. Both men now kept a cutlass from the *Repulse* at their side.

As dusk approached, and the dying sun began to cast brilliant, fiery colors on the few scattered clouds, Elizabeth emerged from the barracks with a pot full of cooked fish. She was pursued by Cyrus, who was eager to eat and wasted no time taking a seat at the table.

"It seems like such a pleasant and cool evening. After being imprisoned by the weather for so long, I thought we could eat out of doors and enjoy the sunset," said Elizabeth.

"A splendid idea," replied Will. "But first we must make some room," he chuckled, gazing upon the table still covered with treasure.

Will and Dunsbury carefully loaded up the chests and stacked them on the ground. Elizabeth placed the kettle on the table and returned to the barracks to gather plates, cutlery, and lanterns. She then set the table, and just as they were all about to take their seats, Will said, "Look, there's still one chest yet to be opened."

"Lord in heaven, how did we overlook that?" asked Dunsbury.

Will picked up his topmaul and prepared to attack the lock, but was abruptly stopped by Elizabeth's voice.

"Will!" she cried out. "Let us savor our meal and this beautiful evening first. Then, after our stomachs are content, let us reward ourselves with whatever spoils that lovely chest contains... agreed?"

"Whatever thine exquisite heart desires," he said with a grin.

Everyone sat down, and after Elizabeth offered a brief blessing, the rum was poured and they all ate heartily.

Halfway through the meal, Will looked at Dunsbury and said, "I haven't thanked thee for saving my life while aboard that pirated wreck. I owe thee a large debt of gratitude, good sir."

Dunsbury shook Will's hand and poured himself more rum.

"What happened out there...besides the weather?" Elizabeth

cringed. "Did thou run afoul of the savages? Thou returned so battered and lifeless, I feared thou both would be dead when next we saw the sun."

Dunsbury remained silent, feeling it was Will's place to offer her an explanation. Sensing this as well, Will spoke up.

"There are savages encamped on Belle," he said. "We were ensnared in their trap once our salvage was complete. We were surrounded and fell under attack as we made preparations to depart. They shot flaming arrows onto the deck from Belle's shore, and several warriors boarded the *Repulse* from the sea. We had to fight them hand to hand."

Elizabeth's eyes grew wide and a worried expression appeared on her face.

Will took another bite of food and then continued his tale.

"If not for the soldierly skills of the leftenant here, the usefulness of superior weapons, and the weather itself, we would never have been able to escape alive...to say nothing of recovering the treasure. I suppose God had something to do with it, as well."

"So that's why the leftenant has mounted that gun," said Elizabeth. "That's why such a grand effort has been made to strengthen the fort's defenses. And that's why swords and pistols hang from thy belts—thou fear another savage assault...on *this* island."

"They will not attack us here because—"

"Enough of this curse nonsense!" Elizabeth fired back. "Thou would not take such precautions if thou felt an attack was not imminent!"

"We are safe on this island, now and forever," said Will firmly. "The savages will never step foot on this soil. We've witnessed evidence of this time and again, Elizabeth. I will not get into another argument with thee on this matter. Defensive precautions are only—"

"I wish to hear no more," she said as she stood up and turned away from the table.

"Perhaps both of thee should reconsider leaving," said Dunsbury. "The four of us could slip away—"

"Never!" bellowed Will. "I will not abandon my home! Not now and not ever! This community will be reborn, so help me God."

Elizabeth turned back to the table with a nasty scowl etched on her face. She reached over and grabbed the topmaul just out of Will's reach. She raised it high in front of him, and with no warning, she swung it with such ferocity that Will ducked for fear she would crack open his skull. Instead, the hammer came crashing down on the lock of the large sea chest just behind him. Elizabeth struck the lock repeatedly until it fell apart. Cyrus and Dunsbury pushed away from the table, shocked by Elizabeth's actions. She threw open the lid and then stood stock-still with the topmaul dangling from her hand.

Will crept back onto his feet while Dunsbury picked up a lantern and held it close to the sea chest. Cyrus came around, and all four stared in stunned silence at what now lay revealed before them.

This particular chest—like the others—contained an astonishing fortune. However, *unlike* the others, its riches were more captivating and extraordinary than the silver and gold previously unveiled. Bars and coins of the most sought-after metals known were truly remarkable finds, but what now lay before them were riches worthy of European royalty.

Glimmering in the candlelight and what remained of the dying sun were piles of emeralds, rubies, sapphires, and diamonds of various shapes and sizes. Many of these precious gems were set in elaborate gold rings, bracelets, earrings, pendants, and necklaces. Chains, crosses, candelabra, goblets, a small scepter, and even a jeweled chalice, all forged and finely crafted from pure gold, occupied the simple wooden sea chest. Small figurines of exotic creatures meticulously carved from pure creamy white ivory and light bluish-green jade were interspersed among the more prominent jewels and gemstones. A heavily jeweled golden tiara, fit for a queen, immediately caught Elizabeth's eye. She untangled the ornate piece from several strings of pearls before placing it atop her head with a beaming smile. The amount of jewelry was staggering, and for all any of them knew, the chest and its contents could have been destined for the personal jewelry collection of Spain's Queen Elisabeth Farnese. For the moment, however, the only royalty was the newly self-anointed Queen Elizabeth Eustis.

She dove into the chest with childlike abandon, gleefully scooping up small mounds of precious stones, draping golden chains and diamond necklaces over her bosom, and jamming every finger with as many rings as she could fit on. She laughed and twirled about as if she was Cleopatra...and the world was hers for the taking. Will and Dunsbury watched with delight, while even Cyrus found her playfulness amusing at first. After watching her for a few minutes, the old man's attention was drawn back to the jeweled treasure, and he soon became enthralled with several distinct pieces. Will had observed his father throughout and joined him beside the sea chest. He then looked back at Elizabeth.

"Thou remember...yes...I see it in thine eyes, Father. Thou remember Mother and how she strutted across her imaginary stage in front of the fire with her nose held high and we as her audience. The 'Queen of Storm' character and all her comedic adventures...I was so very young, but I remember—and so doth thou," said Will. "And the way she described her princely robes of silk and the endless array of jewelry she pretended to be wearing. The styles...her detailed descriptions...so vivid and seemingly so real, almost as if she had painted a picture. It is as if her props have been magically conjured and now lie before us as a heavenly reminder of how wonderful she was. Oh, how she loved to entertain us!" he reminisced. "I doubt Shakespeare could have penned a better play or directed a better performance than what she happily presented on those dark and cold winter nights."

The old man slowly closed his eyes and let his head droop before a faint smile emerged on his heavily bearded face. Will patted his father on the shoulder and said, "We shall choose and set aside prized pieces of jewelry that will remain in our possession forever—a beloved and eternal reminder of my dear departed mother."

With that, Will retrieved a very small sack from the blockhouse, and he and his father filled it with select jewels and gemstones that they found most appealing. Small gold chains, a few rings, some pearl necklaces, a variety of colored gemstones, and even a number of gold doubloons were added to the sack until it bulged and weighed heavily in the palm of Will's hand. He held it up high and then handed it to Cyrus, who happily cradled it like a baby.

"Drink!" called out Dunsbury. "Let us drink, be merry, and celebrate this magnificent find!"

As darkness enveloped the land, the fire in the courtyard burned high and bright. Once again, the rum flowed freely, and the four happy souls imbibed to excess. They ate what little they had, drank with intemperance, and danced about merrily. Elizabeth leapt onto the table and tossed handfuls of gemstones and gold coins into the air, joyously watching them shower the others as they rained back down to earth. Dunsbury broke into song, warbling every sea tune his inebriated mind could remember. He brandished his sword and fired his pistol into the air. Will and Elizabeth laughed and danced around the fire while Cyrus drank and milled about with a foolish grin on his face.

The celebration progressed unimpeded for hours as the young threesome whooped, hollered, and frolicked about under a spell of alcohol-induced foolishness. Will eventually sat down on the hard earth amid scattered batches of treasure and watched through hazy eyes as the flames from the fire shot up toward the stars. Soon his eyes began to close and the buzzing in his brain lulled him toward sleep. But before his head hit the ground and his eyes shut for good, he caught a fuzzy glimpse of Elizabeth laughing and staggering with open arms in Dunsbury's direction... then all went dark.

The sound of the waves washing against the shore and the whooshing of the wind in the treetops were the first sensations that registered in Will's throbbing head. His eyes flickered open, settling to a painful squint as he discovered it was now daytime. Slowly, he sat up and realized he had fallen dead asleep exactly where he last remembered sitting down. His father was still peacefully asleep on the ground near the smoldering ashes of the fire, so Will moved about softly, hoping not to disturb him. As he looked around, he became more and more disgusted at the signs of his reckless behavior the prior evening. Now, everywhere he gazed there were riches strewn over the muddy soil and needing to be found and gathered before they were lost forever. He shook his head as he determined that the entire courtyard would have to be painstakingly scoured to ensure that every ounce of treasure was recovered.

He walked over to the blockhouse and collected the burlap sacks. He brought them to the table and laid them out. Just then, his father stirred at the sound of the barracks door being opened, and Will looked up to see Dunsbury stepping outside. His left hand cradled the bowl of a long-stemmed clay pipe while his right tugged and adjusted the bottom of his shirt as if it had just been put on. He brought the pipe to his lips and took several long and satisfying puffs while stretching his lower back and staring up at the sky. A second or two later, Elizabeth emerged, her hands busily running through her tousled hair, the jeweled tiara precariously still entangled therein. Cyrus stood up and stretched, then looking around sleepily. Will, still feeling the effects of last night's carousing, stared at Dunsbury until the lieutenant's attention was fully captured.

"How is thy head?" he asked.

"Thumping like a drum during roll call," Dunsbury answered. "But the pipe helps calm me down and dull the ache. Tobacco's good. I helped myself to some last night," he added, pointing to the barrel.

"We should tidy up this mess before all is lost," Will said in reference to the scattered treasure. "We'll collect thy deserved portion first—ten percent, correct?"

"That was the contract," answered Dunsbury. "I have calculated what that amounts to, established by what was displayed as a whole last night. I know precisely what my share should be."

"Good," said Will as he tossed Dunsbury a sack. "Use this to harvest thy stake in the prize, and we shall endeavor to recover the rest posthaste."

Everyone began to scoop up and bag the dispersed trove, including Cyrus, who worked the most diligently after Will demonstrated what he wanted him to do. In time, they were satisfied they had gotten it all, and the sacks—excluding Dunsbury's—were neatly secured back in the sea chests, and the chests were returned to the blockhouse. Will looked over Dunsbury's portion, which consisted mainly of silver and gold coins.

"Sufficient—and fair?" he asked.

"Aye," said Dunsbury tersely. He then began to pace about, turning his attention elsewhere.

Will rubbed his aching head. As he watched Dunsbury linger about the courtyard, he began to wonder if the man was truly satisfied with his share of the prize. His movements and subtle posturing suggested a looming problem of some sort, but the nature of it was a mystery. Then thoughts of Dunsbury demanding additional compensation—by threat of violence or other means—began to flood Will's mind. Unsure if his worries were legitimate or just unfounded delusions conjured by a brain still recovering from inebriation, Will decided that rest and recovery should be the main orders of business for the moment. He slumped onto a soft patch of earth and pulled his hat over his face. Dunsbury and Elizabeth retreated to more comfortable surroundings in the shade and fell asleep. Cyrus simply sat down and stared at the sky as if he were a child picking out shapes in the clouds. Everything became silent and peaceful.

Startled by the shriek of a gull, Will's eyes popped open. He bolted upright and took a moment to let his head clear. Looking at the sky, he realized it was very late in the afternoon and the sun was setting.

"Asleep all day," he grumbled.

Getting to his feet, he walked over to the blockhouse where Cyrus was sitting and admiring the open sea chests and sacks of riches. The old man placed his hand on the jewels—his favorite part of the treasure—and beamed a great smile. Will patted his shoulder and then turned his attention to the barracks, as neither Elizabeth nor Dunsbury could be seen anywhere in the courtyard. He started slowly toward the building, then quickened his pace with growing urgency. He stopped at the door, paused briefly, then quietly opened it. He peered inside and found Dunsbury unconscious on the floor, an empty cup next to him. Over on the mattress was Elizabeth. She, too, was unconscious and appeared to be sleeping off the effects of severe drunkenness. The rum cask was tipped over in the corner, and it was apparent that both Elizabeth and Dunsbury had imbibed to excess throughout the day.

Will sighed and closed the door. He glanced up at the colorful sunset sky and then at his father again. In his mind he repeated, *I will use this treasure to ensure thy dreams of this community are realized and fulfilled.* He walked back over to the old man and sat down next to him, putting his arm around his shoulder. He looked at the treasure and reached down to touch it, holding up a handful of doubloons that seemed to radiate a beam of gold toward the orange and red sky. They watched the remains of the sun disappear, and with it, the brightly illuminated heavens. As the clouds turned gray again, the two men looked at each another and smiled, each with pleasant thoughts of Mildred Estes in his head.

Will awoke the next day on the mattress next to Elizabeth. He had positioned himself between her and Dunsbury, who remained unconscious on the floor, but was now fidgeting in his sleep and snoring loudly. Will stirred first, making no effort to be quiet. He went outside and found Cyrus happily asleep in the blockhouse next to the closed-up sea chests. He gently woke him, and they moved the table back into the barracks. An hour later, the others were up and about, as well.

"Leftenant, I propose we embark on one last critical excursion in preparation for thine eventual departure," Will said as they sat together at the table in the bright morning sunlight, Dunsbury smoking another clay pipe.

"What did thou have in mind?"

"Let us journey to the other side of the island this day," said Will. "I shall guide thee to the highest ground and give direction that will aid thy trek on the mainland. Perhaps we can forage in the woods and find some food for thee, as well."

"An excellent idea," said Dunsbury.

"Elizabeth," Will called out, "stay in the fort today and keep my father alongside thee at all times. In our absence, will thou prepare a bundle of supplies for the leftenant? Perhaps some candles, a blanket, and other items that can be spared for his journey?"

"Yes, of course...a bevy of belongings for one and all," she answered in the sarcastic manner Will had, regrettably, become used to of late.

However, this time he sensed there was something more to the caustic response, and her overall behavior. There was a cold uneasiness surrounding her. It was apparent in her gait and mannerisms, both of which seemed out of sorts. Reluctantly, Will's thoughts and focus shifted back to Dunsbury...and their drunkenness in the barracks.

"Elizabeth," said Will as he walked up to her. "Does something vex thee?"

She didn't answer. Instead she glanced at Dunsbury—who had wandered over to the blockhouse and now had his back to them—and then back at Will. Though her face showed a hardened expression of strength, her eyes revealed a potent distress that seemed all too telling of her true emotional state. Will raised his hand to caress her cheek, but she immediately stepped back out of his reach. She looked over at Dunsbury again and then back at Will, saying nothing and then scurrying off, pushing Cyrus aside as she went. Will's head began to fill with thoughts and images of such a repugnant nature that he shuddered in disbelief and forced himself to concentrate on more pressing matters.

"Shall we make haste?"

Dunsbury turned around upon hearing Will's question from across the courtyard. He continued to puff on his pipe as he approached.

"Aye, and let us arm ourselves appropriately before our departure," he said in a low voice.

The two men gathered their swords and pistols. Will slung his satchel over his shoulder while Dunsbury put on his coat, tucking his pistol and the heavier dragon into the sling underneath. After drinking liberal amounts of water from the rain barrel and replenishing the wooden canteen, they made their way to the gate. Elizabeth joined them there as Cyrus wandered into the blockhouse, still fascinated with the treasure chests.

"Food is needed," said Elizabeth frostily and directly at Will, keeping him between herself and Dunsbury.

"We shall do our best to procure something upon our return," he said. "Our absence shall not be a lengthy one, and our reappearance should precede the setting of the sun. Stay here and do as I have asked. Also, make this day an industrious one. My father will assist thee in thine endeavors. Look after him with all the care and grace thy noble soul possesses. Now, let's be off, Leftenant."

They removed the crossbar and opened the doors. They took a few paces outside and froze in place like statues. Elizabeth stepped out behind them, releasing a gasp before covering her mouth with trembling hands. Dunsbury looked about and turned to Will.

"It appears the witch still remains in our midst," he said.

"Lord in heaven, what evil is upon us?" a somber Will responded.

The three slowly fanned out, taking in the extraordinary sights before them. On the ground were several scorched spots indicating that small fires had recently burned there. Interspersed among the blackened areas were strange symbols drawn out in the dirt. Spirals, spiked arrows, squares, triangles, and perverted eye-shaped ovals, in no discernable pattern, made up the bulk of the images firmly etched into the soil. More disturbing than the symbols themselves was the presence of several small dead birds. They were whole and not mutilated, which made Will wonder how they had been caught and killed.

"This is a warning of dire things to come," Elizabeth said shakily. "I have seen this before, and it does not bode well for us."

"Where hath thou seen this, and what precisely does it portend?" asked Will.

"Come with me," she answered, leading them back into the

fort and up onto the perimeter ledge facing the ocean. "Look," she said as she pointed downward.

Will and Dunsbury peered down and quickly recognized a larger and more menacing shape and structure to the devilish site.

"That's a pentagram," Elizabeth explained. "A symbol of evil. Mother never shirked an opportunity to strike fear into the heart of my very being with cautionary revelations of Salem...and the trials of those accused of witchcraft. She...she was eerily fascinated by it all." As she spoke, her face drained to a gray pallor, and her body started to shudder.

"The fires were lit at each point of the star," she continued. "The symbols therein represent worship and obedience to Satan. The dead birds...a sacrifice...and a warning. When I was younger, Mother showed me paintings of such images in her books and preached to me about the evils practiced by the condemned women of Salem."

"The birds—what kind of warning do they represent?" asked Will.

"I don't know precisely," said Elizabeth. "Mother always said that witches were most active at night, and whenever they held their fiery rituals and drew symbols like these for all to see, it...it meant that mayhem was afoot and that good people were likely to die. Those birds were somehow lured into her domain and poisoned by some foul brew of her creation."

"That could mean she intends the exact same fate for us," said Dunsbury. "Remember her threats when last we encountered her? They were very direct."

"I had hoped it would not come to this," Will muttered. "God forgive me, but I thought the storm would have expedited her riddance and swept her off this island for good."

"Obviously, it did nothing of the sort," Elizabeth retorted. "Will," she said more directly, "we must take action and deal with this problem. She could poison our water...set the walls ablaze... gain entry and murder us in our sleep—or...she could abduct thy father again and perform all forms of demonic witchery upon his helpless mind before forcing his untimely demise. Thou must—"

"Murder thy mother? Is that what I am—a murderer of my

own people?" Will barked.

"She is not a Christian—not anymore. She has become an agent of Satan...and remember, thou hath..."

"What? Thou hath *what*, Elizabeth? Killed before? Are those the words hanging from thy tongue?"

"She must be dealt with," she said tearfully but with an icy tone Will had never heard from her before. "She'll kill us all. Heed what I say."

With those chilling words of warning, Elizabeth climbed down from the ledge, ran across the courtyard, and disappeared into the barracks.

Will looked at Dunsbury, who said nothing, and they climbed down together.

Cyrus, still preoccupied with the treasure, looked up momentarily as Will motioned for him to follow. The three men walked to the gate, where Will picked up the crossbar and demonstrated how he wanted his father to secure the doors after they left.

"Should thou go and talk further with her...in private?" Dunsbury asked before they closed the doors.

"Nay, it would do no good. In fact, there is little I can say that wouldn't upset her further. Best to let her be and ponder the consequences of her deadly intentions."

"And the threat from this witch? It *is* real, thou understand."

Will looked directly into Dunsbury's eyes and stated, "I will not hunt down and slaughter that old woman, no matter what threat she poses. Her lunacy and lack of resources will cause her to expire naturally, and in God's good time. I will not have a Christian death on my head, no matter how much wickedness she exudes."

"That is thy choice, of course. However, I must warn thee that I do not hold those same sentiments. I walk upon a different path in those regards. I always do what a *man* must do...and perhaps someday thou shalt, as well."

A moment of tense silence followed as the two stood nearly toe to toe and eye to eye.

"So be it," said Will. He turned and started to walk away.

Dunsbury made sure that Cyrus secured the doors and fell in behind his younger companion.

This time Will did not lead Dunsbury into the woods behind the fort, but took the well-trodden shoreline trail facing the mainland. Though only one had been mentioned, there were several reasons Will desired to venture out from the safety of Fort Hope's walls. For the moment, he kept them to himself.

They plodded along at a sluggish pace. The going was difficult because the trail was littered with heavy debris. Broken limbs, slippery leaves and gravel, heavily eroded soil, and even towering trees uprooted by mighty gusts posed formidable obstacles and were grim reminders of the storm's wrath. They moved along with care, silently astounded by the damage. Will constantly caught himself looking out onto the water, nervously checking for any sign of danger from the Abenaki. For now, all seemed calm. In time, he and Dunsbury emerged into the clearing where the Eustis cabin stood.

"Is this thy home?" inquired Dunsbury.

"Nay, this is Elizabeth's home, and I'm pleased to see it still standing. My fear was that it was destroyed in the storm. Thank God it remains intact."

"Why hath thou brought me here?"

"It is on the way to our final destination, as is my home," said Will. "But curiosity is the main reason. I wish to find out if any threatening entities, natural or otherwise, have taken root here."

"The witch?"

Will looked at Dunsbury and said nothing. He then approached the cabin with his pistol drawn, and Dunsbury fell in step behind him. They entered cautiously, and Will was relieved to find the house dark and empty. He stuffed the pistol back into his satchel.

Inside, the ruination appeared unchanged from the time he'd last cast eyes upon it. Of most interest to him were the fireplace and cooking kettle. Will closely examined both before concluding that neither had been recently used. Puddles of water all around the hearth helped confirm that conclusion. As he puttered about, Dunsbury watched quietly and occasionally picked a book or other item up off the floor to look at.

"I see no indication of her presence," Will commented. "Perhaps she's sheltered somewhere deep within the island's interior."

"If I were a gambling man, I would wager we could find her near where thy father was bound," said Dunsbury. He added, "I know what thou said back at the fort, but now that Elizabeth is not with us, is it thine intention to hunt down and dispose of this witch before she causes harm to thee, thy father, or the one thou loves so fervently?"

Will lowered his head and did not answer.

"We could swiftly put an end to her wickedness," said Dunsbury, "and Elizabeth would be none the wiser. The evil would be eliminated, and thou could sleep soundly knowing Elizabeth was safe. Eventually, thou could profess the witch died naturally, absolving thyself of any crime thou felt thou hath committed. Who would know the truth? Who could possibly prosecute thee? Nobody. Thou art lord and king of this island realm."

Will was uneasy with Dunsbury's tone, which he thought was slightly arrogant and reckless. He stood by his original decision.

"No, it will not be done that way," he said as he exited the cabin.

"I truly do not understand thee, William," Dunsbury said as he followed him out. "Elizabeth has all but told thee to destroy that cursed woman."

"The matter is not for Elizabeth to decide; the matter is in God's hands, and I will not anger him by committing the sin of murder against one of his disciples...troubled though she is."

"Thy words ring hollow, William. They are ignorant and bathed in a brittle self-righteousness that will shatter when put to the test. I pray I will have left this place for good when that time arrives."

"The point of thy departure is rapidly approaching," Will snapped, and they eyed each other aggressively for a moment before Will backed off.

"My apologies," he said. "I hath saved thy life once while thou hath saved mine twice. Thy help of late has been immeasurable...

and I am grateful for what thou hath done for both myself and Elizabeth. Thou art key in the future resurrection of this community...whether thou realize it not."

"I am a soldier, William, and used to hard and sometimes brutal decisions that must be made for the greater good of others. I will defer to thy judgment on the matter, but will not hesitate to indulge my own inclinations if put to the test."

"Fair enough. Now let us move on so that we may address other and more pressing matters."

Will continued down the ravaged trail with Dunsbury close behind. Their next stop was the Estes cabin. Upon arrival, Will's heart sank at the bleak sight before them—the depressing spectacle of a cabin now crushed and utterly destroyed by two massive toppled pines.

"What hath God wrought?" Will said, turning his eyes to the heavens.

"Thy home?" asked Dunsbury.

"It was," Will responded, his breath and body both deflated.

There was nothing left except a barely recognizable heap of timber buried under the mass of two uprooted pines and all the debris brought down with them. Will started to weave his way through the tangled limbs and branches, but was soon forced to surrender his efforts. The cabin was far too decimated, and its salvageable contents—what few remained—were much too firmly entombed to be recovered without a great deal of time-consuming labor.

"Let's move on," Will said. "There's nothing to be done here... at least not now. Imagine if either my father or I had been inside when this happened. God's will...God's good will."

They continued onward through the ruined crop fields and meadows where the open spaces provided easier going. Occasionally, Will paused and casually looked toward the ocean. When they finally entered the woods and connected with the trail that led to the southern end of Storm, Dunsbury noticed he was being led uphill. As the trail gradually became steeper, the trek became more taxing for his still healing body. He was about to stop and assault Will with a tirade of questions and quibbles just as they reached the crest and stood tall on the island's highest ground. They took a moment to catch their breath and take in the view of the ocean. Will dug into his satchel and retrieved his spyglass. He extended the lens and peered out over the water in all directions before fixing his gaze on the southwestern shore of Belle Island.

"She's gone...I detect no sign of her. The sea must have swallowed her up—what was left of her, that is," said Will.

"The Devil's Chariot?"

"Yes...I sight no flotsam, no indication that she was ever wrecked...or ever even existed—wiped clean from these very waters. There must be fragments of her scattered for miles across the ocean floor."

"So much the better. Let us hope she never returns to haunt these waters in the form of a ghost ship. Such phantom vessels are known to terrorize the sea lanes, wreaking havoc among mortal mariners who mysteriously disappear, never to see port again."

"Have thine eyes ever fallen upon a vessel of such description?" Will asked.

"Aye," said Dunsbury. "Many a time have I crewed a boat that has crossed wakes with a ship of the damned. I have even boarded such a vessel—which appeared one night out of the fog off the western coast of Africa. We rowed over to find the ship deserted, with no signs of struggle and nothing out of sorts except for the eerie absence of its crew. Everything aboard seemed to have this mysterious glow about it, and the decks oozed blood before the chilling shrieks of ghostly demons filled our ears...and then...then the specters appeared!"

Dunsbury's face went stone cold, and he glared at Will with deep, piercing eyes. Will was taken aback, almost afraid to say or do anything. Morbid, if not naïve curiosity finally got the better of him, and he reluctantly asked, "What happened next?"

After a slight pause, a smirk began to creep across Dunsbury's face. Before Will could react, Dunsbury said, "We all sat down to a ghoulish game of cards, got stinking drunk, and sang every seafaring ditty we could recall before merrily departing with arm-loads of glowing goods!"

Dunsbury chuckled, and Will looked away in disgust; he'd been taken in by the man's dramatic telling of a less than clever yarn. Embarrassed, he turned his attention toward the Neck as his spyglass swept back and forth across the shoreline.

Dunsbury curbed his snickering and began to ask, "How—"

"I shall deposit thee and thy possessions on the mainland just due south of that rocky point," Will interrupted. "From there, thou should be able to commence thy journey with few impediments."

Dunsbury took the spyglass and trained it on the location Will had indicated. After a moment of reflection he commented, "The place thou hath selected appears distant and not easily acces-sible by boat. Why not choose a spot with a more accommodating beach...and one not so far from the assumed point of departure?"

Will hesitated, then gave his answer.

"During my last journey to the mainland, I had a deadly encounter with the savages. I discovered a settlement in a loca-tion that had been devoid of activity for as long as I can remember. Their coastal encroachment on the mainland has only increased in recent times. The spot I have chosen is well south of the settle-ment. Even so, successfully evading them will prove challenging... and potentially could be fatal. They have become emboldened beyond all predictable measures, and the way they ambushed us while aboard the *Repulse* demonstrates their resolve for total extermination."

Dunsbury turned and pointed the spyglass back toward Belle Island.

"It seems that their infestation of thy neighboring island has not lessened, either. Apparently, the storm was unsuccessful at dislodging them. Look."

Will took the spyglass and surveyed the shores of Belle. He saw no signs of movement or Abenaki warriors in the open, but as he looked skyward just above the island's thick tree line, he spot-ted several plumes of smoke rising above the interior.

Dunsbury said, "That little island is the perfect launch-ing point for a massed invasion of Storm. I would wager they are ferrying warriors and supplies over from the mainland at night. There are probably multiple hidden encampments strategically located throughout the interior. When they feel their numbers are strong enough, they will attack and overrun this island, butchering all who oppose them."

"The curse of this island will shield and protect us," Will averred.

"Doth thou honestly believe that drivel to be true?" Dunsbury scolded. "They're coming—the only question remaining is *when*. The sooner thou come to terms with this impending threat—"

"I...I...there is..."

The words fumbled out of Will's tongue-tied mouth, and he eventually went silent. His mind groped for any rational explanation that could support his belief, but the evidence against him was mounting. He dropped his head, and his body started to shudder.

"Thou art clinging to every shredded tatter of hope, no matter how ludicrous, that thou believe will enable thee to remain in this remote land, William. This fantastical bit of lore, appealing as it is, will not keep the savages off this island, and the walls of the fort will not stand against the ensuing onslaught. And despite the improved armaments we procured, a simple fisherman, a feeble-minded man, and a woman cannot weather the wave of horror about to be unleashed upon them."

Will looked squarely at the lieutenant—who instantly knew what he was thinking.

"No, I shall not be a part of this madness. I have no desire to fall victim to the degenerate actions of a deranged old woman, nor be slaughtered by hordes of marauding savages. What I do have is a family. And though my chances of seeing them again are slim, I will not gamble my life away in a senseless battle with absolutely no chance of victory. I wish to leave this place as soon as possible. I have fulfilled my end of the contract, and I wish for thee to do the same."

Will angrily turned away from Dunsbury and stared out at the ocean. His rational mind knew the man was right, but something deep within his soul, something powerful—bordering on uncontrollable—prevented him from altering his course or surrendering his vision for the future, no matter the cost.

"Abandon this senseless dream of thine, William. It will be thy undoing."

Will kept his back turned and remained silent.

"At least spare Elizabeth's life. Release her from this cruel environment. Let her accompany me on my journey back to civilization, where she will be safe."

Will wheeled around and went nose to nose with Dunsbury. His eyes burned deep into Dunsbury's with a blinding rage that failed to notice the soldier's hand grasp the hilt of his cutlass.

Through clenched teeth, Will said, "Let us travel back down into the interior and forage for some food. If nothing is to be found, we will try the eastern shoreline before returning to the fort. On the morrow, I will take the longboat and fish for however long is necessary to bring in adequate stock. From the point of my return, when the sun next rises, I shall row thee to the Neck and thy *solitary* journey will commence. To that I say, godspeed, Leftenant Philip Dunsbury."

With that, Will brushed past the soldier and headed down the hill without looking back.

Dunsbury released his grip on his sword and followed in total silence.

CHAPTER 13

Fraught with Peril

The sun had long since sunk below the horizon when they arrived at Hope's gate. What sliver of daylight endured was fading, and it was only a matter of minutes before darkness fell. A small leather pouch tucked away in Will's satchel contained the only edible spoils recovered from the day's foraging. Small handfuls of blueberries and unappetizing acorns were the pitiful results of their lackluster effort.

Will and Dunsbury had spent the day largely in silence, staying off the main trails and cutting a path through the interior woods before reaching the rear wall of the fort. Each seemed preoccupied with his own personal thoughts, and neither desired to discuss what was on their minds. At the front entrance, Will called out to Elizabeth to open the gate, but heard no reply. To his surprise, upon placing his hands on the doors, he was shocked to find them unsecured. They swung open with ease to reveal an empty courtyard and no indication of light or smoke coming from the barracks. The sight was unnerving, and Will's attention turned immediately to discovering the whereabouts of Elizabeth and his father.

He headed straight for the barracks, only to find them dark and empty with no fire burning. Dunsbury glanced over at the blockhouse. The treasure chests were all in place and appeared undisturbed. Moments later, Will emerged from the barracks doorway brandishing a single lantern.

"There's nobody here," he stated. "We should conduct a thorough search of the shore immediately. She would not just wander off with night rapidly approaching and danger stirring about offshore."

"Doth thou still believe in curses?" Dunsbury asked with sneer.

A chill ran down Will's back at Dunsbury's indelicate inference of the possibility that his father and his lover had become victims of a native abduction. He didn't reply and simply rushed past the lieutenant and back outside the gates to the edge of the cliff.

Dunsbury joined him, and said in the same derisive tone, "Perhaps Elizabeth has been *unwillingly* reunited with her mother... and thy father *forcefully* bound to the same tree from whence he was previously discovered."

"Look there!" cried Will, pointing the lantern down the cliff trail.

"I see nothing," Dunsbury said flatly.

"There," Will repeated as a shadowy figure took shape halfway up the path. "It's Father!"

Both men scrambled down to retrieve the old man and discover the reason for his errant wanderings. Will cast the light upon him and noticed that Cyrus appeared disheveled and out of breath, but unharmed. As he and Dunsbury helped him back up to level ground, they couldn't help but detect a most disagreeable odor about his body.

"Father...where is Elizabeth? Why did thou wander off unattended? What—"

"The girl, where is she?" Dunsbury chimed in.

"Bring him some water," Will demanded. "He's still wheezing for breath."

"We're wasting time," said Dunsbury. "Just escort him inside and let us commence our search for Elizabeth before another moment is wasted. There is nothing he can tell us."

Frustrated and unsure of what he should do, Will turned away—and his eyes locked onto a dim orb of light slowly growing larger and apparently moving toward them along the western shoreline trail. Dunsbury and Cyrus turned to look as well, and in a few minutes, Elizabeth joined them.

"Where did thou run off to? I told thee to stay in the fort," Will chided. "Why did thou disobey me? State thy reason."

"Do not presume to order me about," Elizabeth retorted. "It is none of thy concern."

Dunsbury, wanting no part in the impending eruption of words between the two, grabbed Cyrus by the elbow and said, "Come, old man. Let us adjourn from this meeting of the minds."

At first Cyrus resisted, not wanting to follow the lieutenant's lead, but a quick nod from his son convinced him to go with Dunsbury to the barracks. Once the two were out of sight, Will again confronted his lover.

"What goes on in thy head, Elizabeth?" he said, grabbing her arm. "Why must thou be so displeasing and defiant of late? How could thou just let Father roam freely and unsupervised? Thou knowest he requires a task to occupy him whenever left unattended."

"A moment of neglect and thou consider him ill used...yet thou never thinks *me* ill used or inconvenienced, I'll be bound. I grow weary of his incessant needs and constant soiling," she barked, jerking her arm free. "He is worse than a child! I shall not launder his ragged and foul clothing nor bathe his filth-covered hide any longer!"

"Is that why thou wandered off...alone?"

"The stench was vile—beyond description. I felt faint and nauseous while in his presence. And his constant lingering...I...I needed time and solitude for myself."

She turned away from him and placed her lantern on the ground before sitting down. Will did the same, sensing that something else was troubling her.

"Has he hurt or run afoul of thee?"

"Thy father?"

"No...the leftenant," Will said.

Elizabeth turned to him without reply, a bewildered expression on her face.

"Thou hath not been thyself for quite some time. Despite all that has transpired recently—and I realize thou hath endured a lot—I see a change in thee that I cannot readily identify...I just know it is not usual and certainly not agreeable."

Her head drooped and her eyes slowly closed.

Will went on, "We have not been together for what seems like an eternity. I miss thy feminine warmth and touch. I can only assume—"

Suddenly, Elizabeth's head shot up and her eyes opened wide. She glared at him and interjected, "Always thine own needs, thine own physical desires—so typical."

The remark caught him off guard, and he dared not reply for fear of infuriating her further. His mind went to work searching for any word or phrase that would offer comfort, but nothing seemed right, and he remained stoic.

"Famished...I am so famished, Will," she said in an unexpected twist of the subject. "I see thou hath not brought back any food from today's forage. I smell neither cleaned fish nor dressed fowl upon thy person."

Boldly, he touched her chin and looked deep into her eyes, desperately trying to unlock the true source of the anger and pain hidden behind them. A moment of silence followed before her face softened and a tear ran down her cheek. And then she whispered, "Take me away from all of this...this place. I say again, do not trust that man thou hath so ignorantly befriended. I implore thee. He will be thy undoing."

Will put his arm around Elizabeth and pulled her close.

"Everything will be better in time, my love. Patience is essential to our survival...and to the *rebirth* of this community."

She looked away again, trying to hide her ongoing dissatisfaction with his lofty dream.

"Thou shalt not suffer the pangs of hunger much longer. Tomorrow I will drain the ocean of its bounty; we shall stuff ourselves with endless quantities of freshly smoked cod and whatever delicacy the sea offers up to my long line. And after our feast, upon the next rising of the sun, I shall fulfill my contract and rid us of Leftenant Dunsbury by depositing him on the Neck. His journey south to civilization will be successful, and word will spread of our existence, bringing more of our compatriots here to help rebuild. And with our newfound wealth, *we* will dictate how our kingdom will rise and flourish. It can all be ours, Elizabeth. This island...all its surrounding neighbors...the Neck—all of it can be ours to parcel out as we please now that we possess the riches to back our ambition."

"So sure of thyself and thy rosy future," she said in a low voice.

After a short sigh, Will replied, "Come, let us retire to the safety of the fort."

Helping Elizabeth to her feet, and without warning, he leaned in and kissed her. For a second, she appeared taken aback, which surprised and disappointed him, but not as much as the taste of the rum on her lips.

Back in the barracks, they discovered Dunsbury seated at the table. He had built a fire and lit several candles to bring light and warmth to the damp chamber. He sat there waiting patiently, trying not to react to Cyrus's lack of cleanliness. Will looked around glumly as it became apparent that Elizabeth had not accomplished a single task he had asked of her while he and Dunsbury were away. He made no disparaging remark, though, and motioned for Cyrus to step outside.

"I will cleanse both his body and his clothing before the evening is through," Will told the others with a prolonged sigh.

He emptied his pouch of blueberries and nuts and put them on a plate in the center of the table. Dunsbury nibbled away at the wild fruit while Elizabeth collected the acorns and put them into a pot of water to boil over the fire.

Will gathered the washtub and what remained of the soap, then went outside to fill the basin with water from the rain barrel. He built a fire in the courtyard and gradually set about cleaning up his father.

Hours later, all were asleep, with Will the last to drift off. In his slumber, his weary mind was alive with vivid dreams of happier times. But at one point, he dreamt he was awakened by the muddled sounds of a man and a woman arguing. He strained to see through the darkness, and to hear the words of the two distant voices, but his eyes saw nobody and his ears could only capture fading echoes...then nothing at all. The next thing he knew, he was gently kissing Elizabeth goodbye as she slept beside him and listening to Dunsbury snore on the mattress. He quietly gathered his gear and slipped outside well before dawn.

He found Cyrus already awake and wandering near the blockhouse. Wanting to relieve Elizabeth of this burden, Will had decided to have his father accompany him during the day's fishing. As they approached the longboat, Will thought it looked out of place for some reason. After quick inspection, he determined that nothing was damaged or missing and dismissed all suspicion after giving Cyrus a stern glance. As they shoved off, numbing thoughts of whether he should have bound Dunsbury in his sleep entered his mind.

The day was cloudy and darker than usual, and fears of another approaching storm began to roil Will's stomach. Atop the unsettled sea, the longboat gently tossed and rolled as Will wrestled with his unruly lines. Cyrus proved eager to row, and Will did not deny him the opportunity. They stayed close to shore on the western side of Storm, facing the mainland. Will knew that the richer fishing grounds were farther out to sea off the eastern coastline of Belle Island, but subconsciously he feared a deadly native encounter, and his mind couldn't shake the thought of a massive Abenaki force secretly swelling in ranks on the smaller islet. He tried to sweep the unpleasant notion from his head with every jerk and tug on his nets, but something sinister kept it at the forefront of his mind.

Hours passed with little success. The lines remained limp and the nets came up nearly empty. The few fish that were landed were small and unappealing to both the eye and the grumbling stomach. To make matters more difficult, Will constantly found himself having to stop Cyrus from rowing toward the shore near the Estes cabin. The old man would scull and point excitedly at the familiar location, which Will simply interpreted as his father's longing to return to their cabin—unaware, of course, of its demolished state.

In an effort to find more fish and distract his father, Will motioned for Cyrus to row toward the southernmost point of

Storm. From there, they would venture out a bit farther in hopes of happening upon a large school of cod to fill their nets. The old man pulled hard at the oars as a chilling breeze swept over the boat. Will watched as the towering southern hill slowly came into view. It drew his eyes upward and cocked his head back into an uncomfortable position as he marveled at the remarkable sight seldom seen from the water. Slowly his head dipped back down, and then his eyes caught a glimpse of something foundering in the surf directly below the island's most defining feature.

"Father!" he called out. When Cyrus turned around, Will gestured and pointed until the old man understood that he wanted him to sweep into shore at a specific point.

Will secured all lines and nets before jumping to the bow. He pulled out his spyglass to get a better view, and after a moment of intense observation, a look of fear and disbelief ripped across his face. Gently, the lens was lowered the closer they got, and Will eventually turned away and sat down just seconds before the boat dug into sand. Reluctantly, he hopped out and heaved the craft up onto the very thin strip of beach flanked by submerged rocks. Cyrus stood up, unaware of the problem but eagerly wanting to get back on land. As he stepped onto the shore, he looked over to where Will now stood and let out a fainthearted yelp before scrambling back aboard the longboat and huddling in a cowardly posture.

Hands on his hips, Will glanced at his father and then stared down at the grisly sight now washed up at his feet. He knelt down and examined the snowy-white figure covered in crabs that now lay before him—the corpse of Winnie Eustis.

The old woman had not expired by starvation, lack of shelter, or from an unfortunate accident. It was for certain that she had been murdered, as there was a large laceration down the right side of her face, slicing through the neck all the way to the base of her chest. The cut was so deep in certain areas that Will could actually see bone through the serrated flesh. Her hair was ragged, and what few tatters of clothing remained partially affixed to her body were beginning to wash away with the tide. The stench was gruesome and turned Will's stomach. He felt sick, and his only recourse was to turn away and vomit. Then he sat in the sand with his hands over his face, trying to decide what to do.

After a long period of reflection, he made up his mind. He stood over the body and offered a brief prayer of hope and salvation. Then he loaded the corpse onto the boat, which caused Cyrus to whimper and cower with his hands covering his face. Will took up the oars and rowed out a short distance where he knew the water was deep and unthreatened by the swirling currents. He picked up the remains of the menacing witch, cast her overboard, and watched as the body floated off before dipping down into the depths below.

"Lord in heaven," Will prayed, "put this troubled woman to rest and do not allow her wicked spirit to return and poison these plentiful waters or haunt our island home for all eternity. In the Lord's name I pray; amen."

And as if God was sending him a foreboding response, the skies turned darker and the sea began to churn. The day was slipping by fast, and Will knew it would be a long hard row back to Hope. He went astern to settle his father, then sat amidships to take up the oars. He wanted to curse the absence of his sail but wisely refrained. At this point, he knew it wasn't worth the risk of offending God with such a trifling gripe. He put his back into the oars and headed for the northwest shores of Storm.

A thousand thoughts whirled through his mind as the longboat cut through the water. At first Will could only consider how and when the natives had gotten their hands on the old woman, and where exactly they had put ashore on Storm. But the more he thought about it, the more he realized that the mortal wound more resembled the clean strike from a honed sword than a crude blow from a native's tomahawk. Both would cause instant death, but each left very different marks, in Will's view. The whereabouts and condition of Dunsbury's seized cutlass soon rose to the forefront of his mind.

A gentle rain started to fall just before they arrived at the northwest shore. Will and Cyrus gathered their meager catch and ambled up the cliff trail. It was dark now, and the going was slow. Will banged on the doors of the gate and called out for them to be unlocked and opened. There was no reply and no sign of activity. He pounded more heavily and raised his voice, shouting for Elizabeth. Again...nothing. Then, after several more minutes elapsed, Will heard the crossbar fall to the ground. He pushed the doors open and laid eyes upon Dunsbury wielding a glowing lantern.

"Where is Elizabeth?" Will asked.

Dunsbury appeared wobbly. He wavered a bit and then said, "Inside...where else would she be?"

His tone wasn't steady and his words weren't sharp. He let out a rather uncouth belch as the three of them headed for the barracks. It was clear to Will that the lieutenant was at least partially intoxicated. As the door opened, he pushed past him.

"Elizabeth!" he called out.

In the corner, from within the deep shadows behind the mattress, Elizabeth appeared. She crept into the light and glanced at Dunsbury before sending a long and troubled stare toward Will. He immediately sensed that something was wrong, and without saying a word, examined her face for any indication that she had been struck. Aside from her cheeks appearing a bit flushed, there was no sign of abuse that he could see.

"Is all well?" he asked.

"As well as can be," was her ambivalent response. She tugged at the sides and shoulders of her dress and ran her fingers through her hair. She then stepped forward, counted the small number of fish, and in a brusque manner remarked, "If this is all thou could reap from the nearby waters—the bountiful sea that thou promised to drain—I fear we shall not be able to stave off hunger for very much longer, Will. Failure is becoming all to commonplace with thee."

Will was at a loss for words. Elizabeth's scornful tone and erratic temperament had again succeeded in catching him off guard. After a few tense seconds passed, he replied, "I regret I was not able to provide in a more ample fashion. The conditions on the water and aboard the boat were not ideal, nor were the locations I chose to place the nets. I fully—"

"The longboat is sound and still seaworthy...is it not?" said Dunsbury from his seat at the table.

"Aye, indeed it is. My craft will no doubt deliver thee to the mainland, on the morrow, and without *failure*," Will said pointedly.

"That it will," the lieutenant replied through a rum-soaked breath. He then stood up and helped himself to another cup. Will noticed that the cask had been brought inside and placed in a corner. He was certain it now contained significantly less than before.

Elizabeth snatched the fish away from Cyrus, produced a knife and bucket, and began cleaning the catch by the fire. Her back was turned to the three men, as she remained silent and indignant. Will, thinking back on the earlier events of the day, thought it best not to mention the gruesome discovery of her slain mother. He surmised that such revelations would only fuel further discontent and fear in an environment already fraught with tension and peril. He helped his father to a seat at the table then sat down himself. His eyes wandered in Dunsbury's direction. He checked to see if he was armed, and was particularly interested in the physical condition of his cutlass. Unfortunately, whatever arms *were* on his person were concealed under his coat.

An hour passed before the fish was ready. All four ate quietly, reluctant to say a word, as if each had a great secret they were hiding from the others. The overall mood was irritable, and even intriguing thoughts of the treasure—which lingered in the back of everyone's mind—failed to relieve the growing tension in the room.

In an effort to relieve the mounting pressure, Will said, "Perhaps some rum would help wash the cod from my palate and soothe my dry gullet. Elizabeth, would thou be so kind as to pour me a large measure?"

She looked at him and then at the cask in the corner.

"Pour *thyself* a drink if thou so desire. It has become too crowded in here for my taste," she snapped. And with that, she wrapped the bearskin blanket around her shoulders and went to the door.

"Where art thou off to? It is dark and raining outside. Tell me—"

"I wish to be alone!"

Elizabeth stormed outside, banging the door behind her. Will abruptly stood up and nearly charged after her, but after taking a hard step toward the door, he stopped and turned to Dunsbury.

"What hast thou done to inflame her disposition so?" he demanded.

"I beg thy pardon?" Dunsbury responded with displeasure.

Will paused, waiting for enough courage to surface before roaring his next remark. It came, and, ignoring all previous business arrangements, decorum, and overall good will fostered with the man who had saved his life on at least two occasions, he said, "If I come to learn that thou hath treated Elizabeth in an ungentlemanly fashion, or caused her to suffer physical injury, I shalt—"

"Thou shalt *what*, boy?" hollered Dunsbury as he leapt from his seat, kicked the stool away, and stood toe to toe with Will.

The sudden burst of hostility put Cyrus into a panic. Clearly rattled, he scrambled to his feet and cried out before rushing out the door. Will had seen his father react in such a way during similar scenes, and his first inclination was to run after the old man to calm him down; however, he had a bigger problem to contend with first.

Frightened and confused by the looming threat now staring squarely into his eyes, Will made no sudden moves, bravely standing his ground against the taller, heavier soldier. Will was unarmed and vulnerable, naked courage his only weapon and sole line of defense. Adrenaline coursed through his veins as his eyes glimpsed the position of Dunsbury's right hand—hidden under his coat at belt level and undoubtedly resting on a weapon. Fueled by nothing more than raw nerve and the need to protect Elizabeth, Will brazenly said, "Dawn...we leave at dawn. Once thou art ashore on the Neck, our contract is terminated."

Dunsbury continued to glare and stand like a rock before Will. After a tense few seconds of silence, he snickered and looked down at Will's boots as if he expected to see a puddle of piss between two trembling legs—but it was not the case. He backed off, righted the stool, and sat down—after helping himself to more rum.

"I am not through dealing with thee or with our arrangement...yet," seethed Dunsbury. He pulled his pistol out from under his coat and pointed it at Will. "Sit," he commanded.

Slowly, Will stepped toward the table and sat down across from Dunsbury. To his surprise, the man lowered the gun and placed it in the center of the table, at equal distance from both his own and Will's reach.

"Now, let's parley like gentlemen—like men of business—shall we? I feel that recent developments and unexpected failures necessitate amending our contract."

"My father—"

"He'll be fine. Elizabeth will see to him, I'm sure. Now...our business at hand."

Will took a breath, dreading what might be coming.

Outside in the rain, Elizabeth had sulked and taken refuge in the blockhouse alongside the treasure. Preoccupied with her own desires and interests, she was oblivious to Cyrus, who had scampered unseen through the darkness, across the courtyard and out the main gate. Under the soft glow of a few candles, Elizabeth cuddled in her blanket, keeping it snug around her body as she knelt in front of what had become her most cherished source of joy.

Before her was the large chest of gems and jewelry. Like the blissful, intoxicating effects of the rum, the jewels made Elizabeth feel like a queen, lifting her spirits to new levels of delight and making her pine for a giant mirror so that she could admire her reflection draped from head to toe in sparkling, priceless adornments. The gold and silver, spectacular as they were, were insignificant compared to the endless array of colorful jewels that entranced her. For the moment, nothing else in the world existed except the prize directly within her grasp. She brought a candle in close and almost cracked a smile as she eased the lid open. As the dim light shone down into the chest, Elizabeth's eyes widened and the hint of a smile disappeared. She gasped, and a wave of terror swept over her, leaving her speechless and frozen in place—except for her head, which whipped back around toward the barracks.

"Do not think me a fool," fumed Dunsbury from across the table.

"Speak plainly," Will responded. "What is it thou demand? Thou art a soldier...art thou also a swindler? We agreed on a contract—"

"That remains woefully unfulfilled."

"Perhaps thou should elaborate on that rather tenuous point, Leftenant."

Will could sense the mood in the room taking a turn for the worse. He did not know Dunsbury's specific thoughts and motives, but resigned himself to the fact that the cost of doing business with the man would be substantially higher than he'd originally bargained for. Will eyed the gun on the table and began to wonder why he had been so careless as to leave his own pistol and cutlass by the door—well out of reach.

"Provisions, to begin with. It was agreed that I would be given all the necessary supplies and foodstuffs I could carry before my departure. I find both to be inadequate and in short supply," said Dunsbury.

"Food has not been easy to come by of late, but if thou insist on depriving us—"

"And the savage threat on the mainland...swelling beyond control," Dunsbury pointed out. "How can thou insure my safety when put ashore? So much time has been wasted. It is only a matter of days—perhaps hours—before this fort is destroyed and this entire island overrun."

"I have scouted the best—"

"Inadequate and—"

"I am speaking! Do not interrupt me—"

"I should never have—"

"What? Saved my life? Remember who it was who brought thee back from certain death..."

They bickered back and forth, interrupting and talking over each other. The argument became quite heated, with Will finding no solid, rational, or logical basis in any of Dunsbury's complaints. He had experienced and suffered through all of their recent threats, hardships, and privations, but his reasoning wasn't sound, and he went on hammering blindly, searching for fault in the most inane and accusatory fashion. Predictably, it wasn't long before the crux of his grievances reared its ugly head.

"And I shall also put forth that my portion of the treasure is far below what was originally allocated," said Dunsbury.

"I see," said Will coldly. "Now we have reached the true heart of the matter and the very source of thine indignant behavior. Ten percent was the amount agreed upon."

"Aye, ten percent of the treasure's total value, not ten percent of the physical prize itself. I estimate I am owed another sizable chunk—which I will demand strictly in gold."

"Thou collected thy share personally and agreed it was sufficient at the time!" Will shouted with a finger pointed at Dunsbury. "And now thou demand more? Not one additional coin or gemstone will be included in thy share! To Hell with thine intolerable greed, sir!"

Dunsbury let loose a sinister little chuckle before saying, "I regret to find thee so resolute in thy short-sighted thinking, Will. I pegged thee a smarter chap than that."

They glared at each other as a moment of silence hung between them. Will was frightened but stood his ground, offering no sign of weakness. He knew not what to expect next, but understood that he was dealing with a trained killer.

"I'm taking what is rightfully mine...and maybe a few precious items that aren't," said the lieutenant, the words oozing from his mouth with a sly grin. "I just might leave here with that adorable lass thou swoon over like a smitten fool...and show her what a real man can do—whether she wants to learn or not. What say thee to that?"

Will didn't reply, but again eyed the gun on the table.

"Thou desire to put a ball through my head? The gun is right there. I am unarmed. Take it and prove to me—"

Will exploded from his seat and lurched toward the weapon. But before he could grab it, Dunsbury snagged his hand in a powerful grip and pulled Will toward him so that their faces were mere inches apart.

"So pathetic and yet so typical," Dunsbury quipped.

Will struggled to free himself, but collapsed onto his knees in agony as Dunsbury's crushing grip threatened to break his hand.

"That treasure is mine—I'm taking everything," said Dunsbury as he picked up the pistol and pointed it directly at Will's head. "I could kill thee right here and now, but that would deprive me of the pleasure of imagining what those savages are going to do to thee and this place after my departure...Then again..."

Dunsbury cocked the hammer back and sneered with delight as he applied pressure to the trigger.

"Goodbye, William Estes."

Just then, the door burst open and Elizabeth rushed in. She gasped at the scene before her.

"Elizabeth! Run!" Will screamed, turning his head toward her.

A second later, all fell dark and silent. Will never saw the swing of the pistol butt before it crashed into the side of his skull.

Darkness...and then a brilliant light gave way to a clear image of a ship hurtling across an endless expanse of ocean at Godlike speed. On the forecastle stood a young man rooted to the deck watching the waves batter the hull with unnatural force. The skies darkened, and the howling winds lifted the ghostly vessel off the tumultuous waters and into a roiling tempest of lightning and fire. Amid the hellish flames, the man felt himself being lifted high off the deck... and then seeing the ship crash down onto rocks below that looked like the ragged jaws of a demon's head.

The man's body was then hurled down onto solid ground. He rose to his feet and found himself atop a high peak looking down upon a boiling blue-green sea. All around him, he could hear the cries of a woman in distress, but saw no one. The cries grew more frantic, and the man called out in a desperate attempt to locate the source of the piteous sounds. Suddenly, his attention was drawn upward, as the voice now seemed to emanate from the blackened skies above. A face began to materialize amid the swirling clouds and streaks of lightning. The man stared intently as the face of a beautiful but sobbing young woman became clear. He stretched his arms in her direction, attempting to save her from her torment.

And just when he felt he could reach out and touch her, the image began to change into something much different and more horrific. The young woman's face transformed into that of a witch-like hag. The unholy visage let loose a most unsettling wail that forced the young man to drop to his knees in terror. The face then transformed again into a giant skull that shrieked through a blinding, all-enveloping flame...and then all went dark again.

Will let out a gasp as his eyes snapped open and his ears caught the sound of a gentle sob. His head throbbed, and he could feel blood dripping down his temple from the spot where he felt the most pain. Desperate to determine where he was, his eyes tried to focus on anything familiar in the poorly lit environment. Gradually, they settled on a recognizable doorway, and he immediately ascertained—based on his last recollection—that he was still in the barracks. Realizing that he was lying on the floor on his side, he tried to move his arms...but couldn't. Next he tried to move his legs...but found they, too, were immobile. Still hazy and feeling like a trapped animal, he began to struggle and thrash about.

"Stop, Will."

The sound of Elizabeth's voice instantly stilled him.

She said, "We're bound together from our shoulders to our feet. Neither of us can move...we're trapped here."

In fact, Will soon realized, he and Elizabeth were tied up back to back on the floor with his own fishing lines. The bindings were so tight in places that he could barely feel his extremities due to the lack of circulation. He wriggled a bit more but stopped when Elizabeth started to sob again.

"I told thee not to trust him," she said between sniffles. "Thou would not hear me or heed what I said. Now look at us. Look upon our dismal fate. Greed and a fool's naïveté have blinded thee, William Estes. Thou hath doomed both of us."

Elizabeth resumed her crying, leaving Will bereft of any words of comfort. But rather than dwell on how they had gotten into this deadly predicament, Will decided he needed to find

out what had happened after Dunsbury had rendered him unconscious. Two candles lighted the room, but there was also some
daylight creeping in through the cracks in the walls. Will wondered just how much time had passed. He also pondered whether
Dunsbury was still on the island and where Cyrus might be. Only
Elizabeth could answer any of these questions, and only with her
help could he find a way to free them both.

"Elizabeth," he said firmly. "Calm thyself and think clearly—
our very survival may depend upon it. Where is the leftenant
now? Tell me what happened after thou entered the barracks and
witnessed the confrontation."

"After thou dropped to the floor, I screamed," she said after
taking a moment to compose herself. "He grabbed me and forced
me to the ground. I thought...I thought he was going to..." Her
voice trailed off and she began to weep again.

"Did he—"

"No," she interrupted. "But he wanted to. God only knows
what stopped him. Will...he's threatened me with violence and
rape from the first moment he awoke from his injuries."

Elizabeth's voice grew fearful and quivered with each breath.
She was emotionally unhinged...beyond anything Will had witnessed in the past. Little by little, he began to piece together and
understand the source of her persistent odd behavior.

"Has he—"

Again, anticipating and not wanting to hear Will's question,
Elizabeth cut him off and launched into a painful revelation.

"He's wanted me ever since he could stand under his own
power," she said. "I suppose it's mostly my fault. God forgive me
for saying this, Will, but I found him attractive and fascinating...
and my heart went out to him when he was brought into our care.
I found myself filled with lustful thoughts while alone in his presence...and perhaps my physical inclinations were acted upon too
strongly at a time when I should have been more reserved. I am
so sorry."

A bit stunned, Will asked with trepidation, "Did thou have
relations of a carnal nature with him?"

"No," she wept. "I restrained myself from that indulgence.

I knew my feelings were wrong and wicked. I could not do that to thee. I...I am in love with thee, William Estes, and I beg thy forgiveness."

At that moment, Will's heart flooded with a surge of loving emotion and contentment unlike anything he had ever felt. To hear Elizabeth formally declare her love for him was the most personally gratifying thing that had happened in his life. Despite their ominous situation, all he desired for the moment was to sing out with joy. Unfortunately, his bliss was swept aside and overcome by anger as Elizabeth continued with additional and troubling disclosures.

"When I rebuffed the leftenant's advances, he struck me on my legs and backside. He threatened me in the most horrible ways, Will. He said that if I ever revealed anything to thee, he would kill us all. His plan was to use us to get well enough that the two of thee could recover the treasure. For a time, he wanted thee to think he was more seriously injured than he actually was. That gave him more time to scheme and learn about our strengths and weaknesses...and how to put them to his advantage, I would surmise. If not for his own weakness—his overt lust for me—he might have completely fooled everyone before slaying us in our sleep and making off with the treasure. But I discovered what he really was much sooner. I tried to tell thee...in so many ways...but that treasure clouded thy mind and absorbed all thy rational thought."

"Undeniably...for that I am truly sorry. Nothing is more important to me than my precious Elizabeth. And for a while, blind greed made me forget that," said Will. "I swear on everything I hold dear and holy, nothing like that will happen again. May God strike me dead if I ever grow so unwitting as to allow anything to endanger thee or ever come between us."

"It's the treasure, Will. That was and always has been the key. That's what has kept us alive. In the beginning, it was the recovery, and now..."

"Surely he's absconded with *it* and my longboat."

"No," said Elizabeth after a long pause. "The treasure is gone!"

"What? Gone? What does thou mean, *gone?*"

"Last night I went outside to calm myself and gather thoughts on how to alert thee of Dunsbury's true intentions once and for all. I went to the blockhouse to escape the rain. I took a moment to look upon the treasure, but when I opened the first chest, it was completely barren of all its contents. I then opened all the remaining ones and discovered that they were empty as well. The treasure is gone. I looked all around the courtyard for any clue as to what had happened or evidence of its whereabouts, but found nothing. Thinking the leftenant must have somehow removed and hidden it, my thoughts then turned to thee. I panicked, thinking he was now going to kill us all. That's when I raced into the barracks and saw him preparing to shoot thee."

"Why didn't he kill us both then and there, I wonder?" said Will.

"It's the treasure, Will. He doesn't have it. It's gone. After he struck thee and bound us both, he ran out to the blockhouse. Moments later, he returned in a violent rage demanding to know what happened to it. He put a knife to my throat and threatened to gouge the very life out of me if I didn't tell him where it was."

"And what did thou tell him?"

"What could I tell him? I don't know where it is or what happened to it. I pleaded for my life for nearly an hour before he was convinced I knew nothing of its disappearance. He then turned all his anger toward thee. He yelled and screamed at thee, accusing thee of being a thief and stealing the treasure. Only thy lack of consciousness saved thee from his torturous tirade. He thinks thou hid the treasure, and so he ran off in search of it and thy father, who he deems is an accomplice. I fear that when he returns, he will have thy father in custody. He will then use him and me as pawns to forcibly extract from thee all information concerning the whereabouts of the riches. I shudder to think what he will do before he kills both thy father and me." She began to cry again.

"I don't have the treasure, Elizabeth," Will stated. "I have neither moved nor hidden it. I am just as befuddled about its mysterious disappearance as thou art."

"But if thou did not move it, who or what did? Oh, William, please, for both our sakes, be truthful with me now. Tell me where it is. It may save our lives."

"I swear, Elizabeth, I do not have it, nor do I have any clue to its whereabouts. On my word, I had nothing to do with this dastardly business. My sole intention this day was to give Dunsbury his share and get him out of our lives as quickly as the Lord would allow it."

"Who then?" Elizabeth cried out. "Where is it? Who could have taken it? Thy feeble-minded father...my mother? Who?"

"It's unlikely my father would have carried out such a strange theft without explicit instruction from me. Furthermore, to singlehandedly carry away such a large and heavy cache would be beyond his capabilities."

"Nevertheless, he is now missing," Elizabeth snapped. "And my mother? Could she have gained access while we slept and committed the theft?"

"No," Will said.

"And why art thou so sure?"

"Her mental and physical limitations notwithstanding, I *know* she didn't do it."

"Why so certain, Will?"

"Because she's dead, Elizabeth."

"What? How?"

"Thy mother was slain. I dragged her lifeless body from the ocean yesterday. She appeared to have been dead for some time. Her body was not fresh in any way. There was a significant slash to her neck and chest...one most likely caused by a cutlass."

"The leftenant?"

"Quite probably. The wounds and the state of her body rendered little evidence of an attack by the savages. I laid her to rest at sea."

There was a silence. During that brief moment, Will wondered if Elizabeth felt even one shred of remorse for her mother's fate. His question was answered—indirectly.

"Then who? Who made off with the treasure?" she again asked sharply.

With reluctance, Will answered with, "The Abenaki are the only reasonable culprits. Only they have the numbers and the necessary resources to carry out the theft swiftly and completely undetected."

"The savages have been here? In this very fort?"

"I cannot deny it any further. The evidence is too great to suggest otherwise," he said grimly.

"What purpose would it serve the Abenaki to take the treasure? It can neither feed them nor keep them warm. Why would they even want it?"

"They know we value it. They are preying on our greed, knowing it will be our undoing. By taking the treasure, they can draw us out from behind these walls. They can then force a confrontation on grounds of their choosing, or simply lure us out into a deadly trap. They've got us on the very precipice of annihilation, and they know it. Our weapons are limited and we are vastly outnumbered...I thought the curse would protect us. What a fool I've become."

Silence ensued again as they pondered their unfortunate situation—specifically what would happen if they were unable to free and arm themselves before Dunsbury's eventual return. Will again struggled to find any loose or weakened part of the lines that bound them both, but his efforts went unrewarded, and fatigue eventually forced him to abandon his fruitless exertions. Once he settled down again, Elizabeth spoke.

"Will..."

"Yes, Elizabeth."

"I'm pregnant."

CHAPTER 14

Truth and Betrayal

There were no words at first. The magnitude of what he had just heard was so overwhelming that no clear emotion of joy or sorrow could be expressed. Will felt stunned and unable to disentangle his tongue, which now felt just as tightly bound as his limbs. He tried to blurt something out but was silenced by the sound of Elizabeth's weeping.

"I did not mean to burden thy thoughts...but I felt thou should know...in case..."

She couldn't finish her sentence and began crying more heavily. Will finally regained his power of speech and clumsily spoke up.

"Thou art positive?"

"Of course," she answered through her tears. "Thy seed has penetrated and been firmly implanted. All indications of such are clearly evident."

"Then I am the happiest man—"

"Enough of that," she snapped. "What good does useless sentiment do us now? We're trapped with death lurking around the corner. Thy child will never see the light of day."

"We will find a way out of this—I swear it," Will fired back.

"And if we do? What then, Will? Despite thy dreams of grandeur, this is no environment fit to raise a child. We've barely been able to survive ourselves. Now the treasure is gone...Dunsbury has threatened murder...there are savages in our midst and no way to bring help here. We cannot endure any longer. If by God's grace we get out of these ropes and are able to flee, we must escape this island and make our way back to civilization without delay."

Will said nothing.

"Always the stubborn one," she said with a disgusted sigh. "Heed what I say, Will, for once. As thou said to me, let me now say to thee: Thy life—nay, *our* lives—may depend on it."

An hour passed with neither speaking to the other. Elizabeth lay passive while Will continued to struggle in a vain attempt to free them. Suddenly, the faint rumblings of someone opening the front gate were heard. Their hearts began to thump as the sound of approaching footsteps rapidly increased in intensity. A second later, the barracks door burst open and a bucket of cold seawater was dumped on them. Sputtering and shaking, Will looked up, and standing before him in the daylight was Dunsbury.

"Where is it?" the lieutenant hollered. "Where did thou hide it?"

He drew his cutlass.

"I will heat this sword until the blade glows red and then slowly fillet the skin off thy body until the location is revealed, or death is painfully visited upon thee."

Dunsbury waved the tip of the sword close to Will's eyes.

"Speak up!" he demanded.

"I don't have the treasure!" Will shouted back. "I did not try to abscond with it. What purpose would that serve me? I am a man of my word and would have honored our contract—"

"Bloody horseshit!" Dunsbury roared. "Perhaps thou need a more aggressive form of motivation!"

With a mighty and reckless slash, Dunsbury sliced asunder the single rope that bound Will and Elizabeth together, though both were still heavily tied. Dunsbury pulled Elizabeth roughly to her feet and stuck the sword's blade under her chin. Terrified, she simply closed her eyes and sobbed. Will looked up at her and saw for the first time several marks and bruises on her face. It was now very clear to him that she had fallen victim to Dunsbury's brutality.

"Thou filthy swine!" said Will. "I will break free from these bloody ropes and tear thy throat out with my bare hands!"

"No," said Dunsbury, "but I will surely do the very same to this lovely young lass if thou does not disclose the whereabouts of that treasure within the next ten seconds!"

And he started to count back from ten.

"The treasure is not in my possession," said Will. "A million times over—I do not have it. The savages! It is the savages. They're lurking about—thou knowest it to be true. Only they could have moved such a weighty haul undetected. They are using it as bait to draw us out and commence our slaughter. They are not dumb brutes. There is logic and purpose to their actions."

"He speaks the truth!" cried out Elizabeth just as Dunsbury's count reached two. "He knows not what happened to the riches, and neither do I."

Dunsbury pressed the blade more firmly against Elizabeth's throat. And just as she began to feel the sensation of her skin being sliced open, he released his grip and threw her back down to the floor. He let out a frustrated roar and said, "The answer lies with thine idiot father. When I find him, perhaps I can persuade the fool to reveal all that thou keep hidden from me, William. And if I can't, I'll bring him back here and unleash an unholy flood of torture on the two individuals thou hold most dear. I will slice them up with devilish precision, ignoring their screams for mercy. Perhaps then, thou will tell me what I demand to know. Think about that, William, while thou still hath some time. But I warn thee, do not put me to task, for I will show no mercy nor give any quarter."

With that, Dunsbury slid the cutlass into his belt revealing both Spanish flintlocks and the dragon pistol tucked away in the red silk sling. Will's satchel was also firmly secured about Dunsbury's shoulder. He turned toward the door and then stopped. Turning back slowly, he cast a lecherous gaze upon Elizabeth. He reached into the satchel and pulled out Will's knife with agonizingly slow and malicious precision.

"Perhaps what I most require is some womanly companionship to help alleviate any sudden physical urges I may experience during the hunt. A man's ardor can grow quite intense in a very short time. It's good to know that I have a woman to help soothe and satisfy my every passion...before it becomes all-consuming, perhaps even deadly. Wouldn't thou agree, Elizabeth?"

Horrified, she screamed as Dunsbury hauled her onto her feet and slashed away all her bindings save the single rope that bound her hands behind her back. She continued to cry out in terror as the crazed man shoved her outside and watched her tumble hard onto the ground, her face awash in tears.

"Bastard!" shouted Will. "I will tear thee to shreds if one hair is—"

Will's impassioned threat went unfinished as the wind was knocked out of him by a booted kick to his gut. Dunsbury spat on him and then pulled his face close.

"Just imagine where I am and what I'm doing to her every second we're away," Dunsbury whispered with odious and evil resolve. "I'll gut thy father, William, but that will be the least of what I will do to that sweet little flower of thine. Hearken to and heed these sentiments. I want to know where that treasure is, boy. Thou best tell me upon my return. If not, be prepared to meet the Devil himself."

Then, without another moment's hesitation, he bolted out of the barracks, slamming the door behind him. The last thing Will heard before losing consciousness again was a muffled cry from his beloved...then nothing at all.

For the next several hours, Will slipped in and out of awareness. Physically weakened by the blows inflicted upon him, by hunger, thirst, and the loss of circulation caused by the tight ropes around his body, there was little he could do but lament the fates of Elizabeth and his father. Thoughts of what they might be enduring at any given moment tormented him with indescribable visions that sickened his stomach and made him shudder. Consciousness amplified his physical pain, while unconsciousness produced horrid dreams. Either way, he suffered.

I wish I had never laid eyes upon that accursed ship, he thought. *I wish I were totally oblivious to its existence, blissfully unaware that all the evil and misery it spawned would be swept out to sea with the next storm. It could have been that simple...all of us could have been spared. God help me...God save us all.*

Gradually, the sun set and Will was encased in darkness. He realized that Dunsbury would be returning soon and that the fate of his loved ones would hinge on the answers he gave upon renewed interrogation. His mind feverishly went to work trying to develop a plan that would remedy the situation and save them all from Dunsbury's murderous wrath. He didn't have much time.

To his dismay, it wasn't long before he heard Elizabeth's cries fill the air. The gate was opened and Will's heart raced at the thought of what horrors were about to confront him. The barracks door was thrust open, and Elizabeth was pushed inside, followed by Dunsbury carrying a lantern.

She crumpled to the floor in tears, her body appearing battered and bloodied, her dress torn in several places. Neither her hands nor any other part of her body were bound, but it was apparent she no longer possessed the strength or the will to resist him. She lay there like a broken woman. Will tried to lash out at Dunsbury, but his mind could not put the vengeful words in order, and his body could not escape the tight bonds that restrained it. All he could do was gaze at Elizabeth and grieve for her sad condition as his eyes welled up with tears and his heart filled with despair. But despite his misery, he did notice one encouraging detail: Cyrus was not with them.

God, let him have safely eluded his hunter and found comfort and respite in wherever he may be hidden, Will prayed.

Dunsbury said nothing at first and then noisily banged around the room before building a fire. Thereafter, he drew his knife and wasted no time cutting the ropes off of Will, leaving only those that bound his hands behind him. He pulled him up off the floor and shoved him down onto a stool at the table. Will's throbbing head mercifully began to clear as the rest of his body welcomed the revivifying flow of blood. Dunsbury then slipped a rope around Will's neck and tied it tight. The loose end, he tied to a protruding hook in the wall. The end result was a crude noose that Will immediately realized would strangle him if he struggled or tried to stand up.

Dunsbury heaved a huge dramatic sigh. "I grow weary of asking this, so it will be the last time: Where did thou hide the treasure?"

Will looked at him with a blank expression.

The lieutenant's head turned toward Elizabeth, then back toward Will.

"So...nothing to say, boy? Then we will proceed the hard way. We'll begin with a *pleasurable* prick, and end with a *painful* one," he seethed as he drew his knife and rammed the blade into the dirt floor just inches from Elizabeth.

Erupting in fury, Dunsbury grabbed her by the hips and forced her onto all fours. She screamed in panic and said, "No... not again! I can't bear anymore!" as Dunsbury began to unbutton his pants.

Will looked on in horror and desperately tried to act, but there was nothing he could do. Finally, before the lieutenant could begin his ungodly defilement of the helpless Elizabeth, Will blurted out, "Enough! Yes! I have the treasure! My father and I hid the sacks while thou slept during the night prior to our last scouting excursion. The act was meant to provide insurance and leverage should thou turn on us and fail to honor thy contract. My father is no threat. He is alone out there...most assuredly just hiding in fear. He will do nothing until I find him and console him—unaccompanied. Spare Elizabeth from any further injury; she knew nothing of this sordid business!"

"Where?" Dunsbury roared, with no indication of stopping his assault.

"We rowed it over to the southwestern shore of the island. It was unloaded and buried in soft, tilled ground—in our crop fields. We placed it on the far southern fringe near the large rock pile that serves as its marker. It's all there."

"Rubbish," scoffed Dunsbury. "Not enough time for two to complete such a task. Nothing but a pitiful lie in an attempt to save thine own skin."

"My father—" Will quickly replied, "that evening when we returned from scouting the island and searching for the witch— remember finding my father walking up from the shore all disheveled? He was off finishing the job in our absence."

Dunsbury paused for a moment to reflect, and Will took advantage of his distraction.

"I can take thee to the exact spot. My father—"

"Is harmless, I was told...wouldn't harm a mosquito...or was it a fly, William? He will be easy to hunt down and dispose of in time," boasted Dunsbury. "Thou art a liar, William Estes," he accused while securing his breeches.

After Dunsbury moved away from her, Elizabeth crawled into a corner and sat with her arms around her shins and her knees pressed up hard against her chest. She continued to weep softly.

"However, tomorrow thou will take us to the spot in question and show me exactly where the treasure lies. And if thou art proven a liar, and the treasure is nowhere to be found, well, I don't wish to say what will happen at that point...not in front of the lady, that is."

"Please, the treasure is thine, all of it. Just leave us in peace, for that is all I humbly beseech of thee."

Dunsbury began to chuckle, and soon burst out into a fit of loud laughter. He walked over to the rum cask and poured himself a drink before casting his eyes on Elizabeth and pulling her to her feet. Then, with a mighty shove, she was toppled back to the ground in front of Will. Slowly, she raised her head and mournfully locked eyes with Will.

"I'm so sorry," he whispered. "I'd give my life if it would spare thine and bring thee a world of comfort and happiness."

After a moment's silence, she softly replied, "Well, in that case, thy wish will be granted, William."

Suddenly, the tears evaporated from Elizabeth's face. She rose up until she stood fully erect before him, brimming with confidence and showing no sign of weakness or physical injury. The woeful expression on her face vanished and became a devilish sneer that made Will feel as though he had just been struck by lightning.

Unable to speak, Will watched helplessly as Dunsbury pulled Elizabeth into his arms and kissed her long and hard. She leapt up and briefly wrapped her legs around him before slowly easing them back down onto the floor. Dunsbury placed the cup of rum in her hand and poured a fresh one for himself. They drank and snickered while a single tear ran down Will's cheek. The noose would not allow him to turn away, so he closed his eyes tight, not wanting to believe what he was seeing. His head started to spin and he felt he might faint again at any moment from sheer emotional pain. It was all so overwhelming, and he could not readily comprehend what was happening or why.

He eventually opened his eyes to find Elizabeth kneeling down before him, but everything he held pure and dear about her was obliterated forever within the span of a few seconds. All he saw now—as he looked at her ruddy and bruised face—was a lie cloaked in betrayal and lurking behind a venomous sneer.

"How could...? Why?" was all he could manage.

"Always the optimist...the naïve fool blind to the real dangers of a harsh and cruel world," she said. "My life has been nothing but hardship and pain with no advantage ever granted me by my family, this *appalling* land, or even God himself! Opportunity is the driving force in life, Will, not optimism! One must seek out and seize every opportunity that presents itself—no matter the consequences. Dreams are for fools—fools like thee. I do not want this life, this place, or any part of thy senseless vision for the future, reckless, unwise, and completely unachievable as it is. And most important, I do not want *thee* in my life—now or ever."

Her cold words struck hard and deep, leaving Will dispirited and soundly defeated. It was at that moment when he felt his whole world had just been torn to shreds and blazed into ashes by the fiery tongue of the Devil. To his further dismay, Elizabeth was not finished.

"I am a chancer, Will. Opportunity has graciously fallen into my life, and I will seize and embrace it with every fiber in my being. And woe betide anyone who tries to deprive me of that."

She stood up and again suggestively embraced Dunsbury, smothering his face with lusty kisses. The two then bellowed a sadistic laugh and greedily imbibed what remained of the rum. Will could do nothing but look away and try to ignore the twisted sounds of their abhorrent glee. But what happened next went beyond pure torture for him.

Dunsbury lifted Elizabeth off her feet and carried her over to the mattress. With one swift stroke, her dress was off and her busy hands were at his belt. Will forced his eyes shut and tried to turn his head away without strangling himself. What followed was an assault on his auditory senses that was more unbearable than any blowing gale, Abenaki war cry, or even his late mother's final breath.

The gloomy barracks was filled with the licentious moans of aggressive carnal activity. It was Elizabeth's groans that trampled upon and stung Will's heart the most. The sounds of pleasure she emitted were far louder and more extended than any he could remember from his own intimate times with her. Earlier, and against his will, he had envisioned how Elizabeth might sound while being raped by Philip Dunsbury. The cries of anguish that had played over and over in his head had fueled his anger and desire to escape their imprisonment at the hands of the betraying lieutenant; however, those imagined outbursts of protest and pain were nothing akin to the moans of ecstasy he was now being subjected to.

After what seemed like an hour, the final throes of Will's suffering ended with the distinct and decisive sounds of the two lovers' sexual climax. Some light kissing was heard next, followed by the sounds of their getting dressed. Reluctantly, Will opened his eyes.

"Break open that bottle of wine, Elizabeth," said Dunsbury. "I'm still feeling saucy...and my thirst for alcohol—and other sources of pleasure—has grown most unquenchable."

Elizabeth shot Will a mocking glance as she walked past and started to rummage through one of the sea chests originally salvaged from the *Firefly*. She uncorked the wine and poured two glasses, keeping one for herself and setting the other on the table in front of Dunsbury who had helped himself to a seat beside Will. He took a swig and then addressed his captive.

"We went through those crop fields and meadows on our way back here the other day, and I don't remember noticing any large rock pile, boy. Could thou be mistaken or deliberately misleading me?" he said as he scraped under his fingernails with Will's knife.

"It exists," said Elizabeth from the shadows. "It's not tied directly to any of the main paths that cut through the fields, but it is easily found if one knows where to look—as do I." She continued with, "He is correct that it lies on the southern fringe—and it is a place both he and his father would logically hide something. They have taken it there, I have little doubt. Originally, Cyrus was going to build a rock wall from those stones, but then he fell on his head and turned idiot—right, William?"

Will glared back at her, resentful of her deliberate cruelty toward his infirm father. Wishing to reply with an equally unkind remark, he thought better of it and held his tongue.

"I can guide thee to it," Elizabeth told Dunsbury, "that is if William, here, becomes troublesome or uncooperative. In fact, I see no reason to risk his meddlesome involvement any further. Let us do away with him here and now. We have the information we need, and his enfeebled father poses no risk to anything. Cyrus is helpless and no doubt just idling the time away by soiling his pants under some pine tree right now. As thou said, he will be easy to dispose of."

"Thou immoral and indisputable whore!" Will exclaimed.

"Kill him," said Elizabeth. "Spill his guts open right here and now," she said as she probed Dunsbury's eyes with not the faintest hint of remorse or mercy.

"Oh no, my dear," he quipped back to her. "He will prove most useful in our quest tomorrow, for it shall not be *me* digging any hole or loading the booty. It shall be our mule here that relieves us of those grating tasks."

The two grinned at each other before Dunsbury added, "And when the hole is dug, and our vessel laden with riches, we shall reward our worn-out mule by laying him to rest—most permanently—in the very pit he has so graciously quarried. And whether he dies by ball or by blade…well…"

Another sinister chuckle erupted from the pair as they

proceeded to drain the wine bottle and lick the remains of the sweet treacle from its little jug.

Will glared at Dunsbury until he captured his attention. With a raspy voice, he said, "Thou art a disgrace, Leftenant Dunsbury, not only to the Royal Marines, but to all those who serve to protect and defend the Crown. How can thou call thyself a soldier— nay, an *officer?*"

"Ha!" exclaimed Dunsbury, and burst into a fit of hilarity that was immediately joined by jocund giggles from Elizabeth.

"Tell him, Ripper," said she between chortles. "Why not just tell the fool? What harm could it do now? Go ahead!"

"My bloody name is not Philip Dunsbury, and I sure as bloody Hell am not an officer in armed service of England." Will gawped in astonishment as the man Elizabeth had just referred to as "Ripper" added, "I'm called Rogers McGee, but am more widely known by the moniker 'Ripper.' That ship—the Devil's Chariot, more commonly referred to as the *Repulse*—that vessel was under my command. *I* am her captain. All that she was and all that remains belong to me! And death shall visit upon anyone who challenges my assertion!"

Will tried hard to comprehend what he had just heard. And though he felt it prudent to remain silent, fragmented questions— which he was unable to contain—began to pour from his parched throat.

"How...? The *Firefly*...? Why this treachery? I saved thy wretched—"

"Because the world, and everything in it that I desire, is mine! That booty thou so graciously helped salvage is but a fraction of the vast fortune that awaits me."

"But the ship is gone...there's nothing left. How—?"

"Thou desire that I tell the full tale?" he asked with a rhetorical bite in his tone. "Very well," he added after pause. "Considering thou will never have the opportunity to retell it, listen closely. I was a sailor, yes; of course, I am a man intimate with the sea. Years ago, I was a privateer aboard an armed English ship owned and officered by individuals who held a legal government commission—a letter of marque—and who were authorized to capture and plunder enemy merchant shipping in time of war. A most honorable calling and service to my country, and one I was most suited for. But after the War of Spanish Succession, the Queen's merchant fleet, of which I was a part and in line for a captaincy, was largely dissolved, and I was turned out on the wharf along-side many other disgruntled seamen. It was then that I spat on the throne of England and my life took a darker turn. I found passage across the Atlantic to the colonies, ending up in North Carolina, where I sought out more enriching opportunities. After falling victim to numerous cheats, liars, and thieves, I worked my way south to the port city of Charleston in South Carolina. One night in late summer of 1715, I was drinking in a tavern and heard whispers about a Spanish treasure fleet that had fallen victim to a massive storm and sunk off the southern coast of Florida. Later, I found myself huddled in a dark nook with a drunken salty old sea dog who wouldn't rest his jaws about the greatest cache of riches any man could ever clap eyes upon, and how he intended to acquire it."

McGee took another drink. His bloodshot eyes glazed over and his mouth let out a conniving titter as he recalled that night in Charleston. He motioned for Elizabeth to refill his glass before continuing his story.

"He called himself Nelson Pope, a bedraggled old bloke, soaked in ale and smelling as if he hadn't had a bath in years. He was the cap'n of a battered, rat-infested brigantine named the *Flora Gale*. It was rotten to the gunnels, just like him. He appeared little more than a loud braggart, but his story intrigued me enough to stay and listen to his eventual proposition. The scurvy bastard claimed he knew the quickest sea route to, and the exact location of, the Spanish salvage camp that had been established to recover the booty. All he needed was to finish assembling an able and loyal crew. Myself and twelve other men were recruited that very night with the understanding that we would be able to plunder without mercy or restraint—and for the first time in my life, I called myself a rogue...nay, in fact, a *pirate*."

The man's distinct and refined English accent no longer carried on his voice. The façade of the soldierly—and fictitious—Lieutenant Philip Dunsbury had been effectively lifted and replaced with the true identity of the brutal pirate Rogers "Ripper" McGee. In that moment, Will finally began to understand what he was up against. The pieces were falling into place as the answers to his questions slowly came into focus. He was wary and frightened of what further revelations would ultimately be disclosed, but deep down, he yearned to hear more—and more is precisely what he got.

"Before our last drinks were poured, a pair of drunken louts drew their daggers and confronted me and my new associate. Well, before they were able to express their grievance with us, I hurled myself upon them and slit their throats with one of the very blades used to threaten us. That was where I earned the name 'Ripper'—a most suitable moniker, says I," he laughed.

McGee drew in close to Will and made a slow slashing motion with his finger across his throat. He sneered at him again before sitting back more comfortably.

"We boarded the *Flora Gale* that night and set sail two days later. Cap'n Pope was so impressed by my abilities and my past as a successful privateer that he effectively made me his quartermaster after a near unanimous vote by the crew. It took just a few days to reach our destination. After a hasty plan was concocted, we formed several raiding parties and assaulted the Spanish salvage camp. Much to our dismay, however, it was later estimated that over half of the prized booty had already been recovered and was on its way to Spanish-controlled ports. We plundered what we could and killed many of the Spaniards, but our own losses were high and we risked losing everything if we pressed the attack longer than originally planned for. Bloodied and battered, we withdrew and sought refuge in New Providence. While in port, Cap'n Pope and I began to argue about our future course of action. He threatened me, so I took it upon myself to relieve him of his command. I slashed his throat in his sleep and made myself the new captain of the *Flora Gale*. Once we refitted, and the threat of mutiny from the crew was dispelled, my orders were to immediately get under way and resume our search for booty under the black flag of piracy."

McGee paused again like a seasoned thespian looking to add tension and intrigue to his performance. Will did his best to keep his guard up, allowing his eyes to wander only when he chose to observe Elizabeth's subtle movements, somehow trying to figure how they might work to his advantage in an escape attempt. It was not to be, however.

"After two weeks at sea in the Bahamian waters, we intercepted a British slaver. Its course suggested it was heading back to England. We wasted no time overtaking her and dispatching her crew without pity," said McGee. "The fools," he added between swigs. "No matter. I probably would have slaughtered them all even if they had surrendered."

Will shuddered as he wondered if he was in the presence of just an extraordinarily hardened killer, or the Devil himself.

"After her cargo of rum, tobacco, cotton, and sugar was discovered, I decided my new galley was a better ship than my older, leaky brigantine. I ordered half my crew to sail the *Flora Gale* back to New Providence while the other half remained with me aboard the *new* vessel—a ship named the *Repulse*."

Will's head dipped, as he finally understood how McGee had come into possession of the mysterious vessel that had caused him so much agony and nearly taken his life on several occasions. *The Devil's Chariot, indeed*, he thought. *No name could be more appropriate or ironic.*

McGee coughed loudly before summoning Elizabeth to his side. He pointed to his shoulders, which she began massaging, all the while casting cruel and indelicate glances at Will.

"After a successful rendezvous with the *Flora Gale* back in New Providence, my men set about refitting the *Repulse* to better serve our piratical purposes. We razeed the ship by clearing the top deck of unnecessary structures. We then removed the slave barricade in the hold, and finally, we brought additional cannon and weaponry aboard. The result was a faster and more intimidating vessel."

"So, exactly how did thine exploits come to bring thee to this remote part of the world?" Will asked, his blurred mind and beleaguered body laboring to stay alert.

"I demanded my rightful share of all the treasure, raw mate-rials, and manufactured goods the Atlantic slave trade so richly produced. My aim was to disrupt, steal, and plunder every ves-sel foolish enough to sail the Middle Passage and cross my ship's wake. And I decided to start with the third and final leg of the tri-angular trade route. I wanted booty destined for Europe from the Americas; I had no interest in dealing with independently con-trolled ships from the Royal African Company crammed with rot-ting slaves bound for Caribbean island plantations. I wanted gold, silver, gemstones, and any other item of value that would allow me to build my own palatial estate on some tropical isle where I could live out my remaining years in luxury and be lord and mas-ter of all I surveyed."

"Oh, yes," Elizabeth breathed with her eyes closed and her tongue slowly wetting her lips. She continued to knead McGee's shoulders in a slow, seductive rhythm.

"My immediate pursuit," McGee continued, "was to harass and attack the Spanish treasure fleet recovery effort still in oper-ation. But instead of attacking the camps on land, I went after the loaded galleons already en route to Spain. And through my extraordinary seamanship and experience as a privateer, we were able to hunt down and loot no less than nine galleons. We pil-laged and plundered without mercy, killing all who showed even the slightest resistance—but I always left a few alive to spread the word of what lay in store for others who tried to elude or best me. After taking our final prize, the *Repulse* became so overloaded with booty that we had to transfer a sizeable portion of it to the *Flora Gale*. Satisfied, and in need of fresh provisions, I ordered a return to New Providence. By then it was early into the present year, 1716."

McGee's mood began to shift noticeably after pausing at that particular juncture. Something began to irritate him, and it became harder for him to continue singing the praises of his felo-nious high-seas adventures. The sudden change in attitude made Will fret about the direction the pirate's tale might now take.

"Upon our return to New Providence, I learned that my rep-utation and word of my notorious achievements had spread well

beyond the Bahamas. Despite that, a far darker problem manifested itself. While at sea, my crew and I were ignorant of the
hostile actions being taken by numerous European governments
against piracy—most noticeably England. While both my ships
were at anchor off Nassau, a British warship snuck into the harbor and tried to force a blockade of the *Flora Gale*. I ordered both
ships to set sail immediately, but the idiot I left in command of
the *Flora Gale* decided to fire on the British frigate even though
he was clearly outgunned and overmatched. Within minutes, that
warship sent the shabby old brigantine straight to the bottom
and turned her attention to the *Repulse*. My only recourse—and
escape—was to flee northward."

McGee stopped abruptly and pounded his fist hard on the
table, causing Elizabeth to jump backwards and away from him.
Will kept his head up and resisted the urge to react, fearing the
rope around his neck might silence him forever.

"The *Repulse* was modified for speed, but she was so overladen with boodle that we couldn't outrun the larger and slower
frigate. However, we kept our course following the wind and the
swift northerly current. On two occasions, we were forced to
engage the frigate in battle after we fell into range of each other's guns. She inflicted some damage to our stern, but she could
never maneuver into position to hit us broadside. And we fired
several stern shots that damaged her bow. Our first engagement
was inconsequential, but the second was far bloodier. Her cap'n
was not without extraordinary skill, I must admit. Somehow, he
managed to lob some well-placed shot onto our decks, killing
many of my men, setting small fires, and shredding vital sail. But
we returned his greeting with one of our own, and were able to
dispatch several of his forward gun crews."

"So brave...so very brave and cunning, my captain," said Elizabeth as she resumed the shoulder rubbing.

"Relentless...that damned frigate was relentless in her pursuit. The cap'n...he most assuredly knew the likes of who he was
up against, says I. But I got 'im. I finally had a short run of luck
and was able to slip away in a fog bank off the coast of South Carolina. When the weather cleared, we anchored off an island not far

from the mainland. I ordered my crew ashore in search of food, to gather natural supplies, and to carry out the most important task of all—to unload and bury my treasure."

A confused Will looked at McGee for further explanation, but was fearful to speak out lest it enrage him. The ruthless pirate captain, however, was all too willing to proceed with his story.

"My ship needed repairs, and more importantly, I needed to lighten her load to regain the speed advantage should that damned British frigate find us again. For nearly two days, my men labored at emptying the hold and shoring up damage to the hull. What little food was foraged was immediately brought on board. We got nearly half the treasure unloaded and hidden on the island—and then...then out of nowhere, that scourge of a ship reappeared! He found me! God only knows how he managed the daunting task, but he found me. We had just enough time to get everyone aboard and weigh anchor before the first cannon blasts ripped over our stern. He had me...or at least he *thought* he had me. Once our sails were unfurled, they harnessed the wind and took us away with gainful speed. Perched on the quarterdeck, I looked through my lens and for the first time caught a glimpse of that bloody warship's official designation—HMS *Firefly*."

More and more, things were starting to make sense. Will thought back to the sordid lies spun from McGee's original story... back when he was pretending to be an officer—and a victim—of the *Firefly*. Still, there were a few remaining pieces of the puzzle missing, and Will was anxious to have them all put into their proper place.

"He was tenacious and handled his vessel masterfully...without panic, that one," said McGee. "I would have liked to have faced that Royal Navy captain alone, just his sword against mine. But as fate would have it, we would never meet. We continued to parry and joust at each other as I held my northerly course, hugging the coastline. Our lightened load sped us along, but it wasn't enough so we could break away entirely. We also suffered from a crack in the hull that required near constant bailing and couldn't be repaired while under way. The days dragged on, and the men began to suffer from illness and lack of food and water. The mood aboard changed dramatically for the worse. We couldn't make port, so those most weakened began dying. And every time the *Firefly* managed to temporarily wiggle into firing range, they unleashed a heavy barrage that killed or wounded more of my already diminished crew. Then...finally...as we approached these northern waters, those well enough to revolt began to mutiny against those still loyal to me."

McGee took another drink, and in a callous tone decreed, "Those who dared show disloyalty by raising their swords against me were dealt with...and the decks stained with fresh flowing crimson served as a warning to the others."

Elizabeth giggled at McGee's macabre declaration in a way Will could only perceive as somewhat deranged. He watched as she sauntered over to tend the fire before sifting through the salvaged goods from the *Firefly*—again. This time, though, Will noticed that she was clearly separating out items she desired and discarding the ones that didn't hold her fancy or could easily be deemed useless. What she liked, she began to pack up, and it was no mystery to Will that she was preparing for her final departure.

"That bloody bastard chased me down...night battle...crew in mutiny," McGee stuttered, now showing the effects of his drunkenness. "We drifted in too near to shore after my helmsman was mortally wounded. The enemy captain saw his opportunity and sailed up close to get his broadside and put his sharpshooters in musket range. Our only chance was to fight it out—even the mutineers understood that. What remained of the ravaged ranks of my crew united and took to the guns in a final effort to destroy that bloody frigate. Thou saw what happened to the *Firefly* from thy perch atop this island's towering hill that night—and let no man dare say I was not victorious!"

"Thy crew...thine own injury...the uniform...Belle Island?" Will squeaked out.

Elizabeth snickered again at Will's feeble and disjointed inquiry.

"Thou should have listened to me," she told him glibly. Turning to McGee, she said, "Tell him, my beautiful captain—tell him everything. The story sets my loins afire."

"So be it," McGee responded. "I watched the final exchange of cannon fire that destroyed the frigate's mainmast and set her powder stores ablaze. Her fate was sealed at that point, and I knew we had triumphed...but at what cost? What remained of my emaciated crew mostly lay dead. My ship was irrevocably damaged, and moments later we were aground, forever wrecked on those bloody rocks and my treasure underwater! In my blind rage, I drew my sword and strapped upon my person every stray pistol in sight. I then hunted the decks in search of any man still alive, mutineer or otherwise. I madly preyed upon every abject soul I encountered, spilling the guts of the wounded, and executing the able-bodied by pistol fire—and tossing many of the dead overboard. I swept the upper decks with my sword and then ventured below to find the cowards hidden in the shadows. A few were revealed and summarily shot to death. But in my fury, after discovering the flooded hold and finding no reasonable way of recovering my riches, I got careless and failed to notice the one scurvy bastard who eluded detection and managed to put a ball in my side. He was the last of the *Repulse*'s crewmen—a mutineer—to remain aboard and still alive...well, alive until he felt the sting of my cutlass across his throat."

Will flinched at the sharp slicing motion McGee made using *him* as the condemned victim.

"I recall staggering back to my quarters...feeling unsteady as the pain in my side intensified. I struggled to get back to the top deck and then collapsed, my upper body hanging over the stern gunnel. The next thing I remembered was being in the water. I swam away from the burning flotsam and managed to make it to Belle's shore. I crumpled onto the beach, dizzy and in agony. It was then that I saw a drowned Royal Marine washed up on the sand next to me. I thought only of self-preservation and worried that there could be other surviving Royal Navy officers or crew ashore who would like nothing better than to take me alive so that they could see me hanged, tarred, and strung up in a gibbet from the Tower of London. I took the dead Marine's red coat and put it on before using my last bit of strength to stumble off the beach and out of sight. The next thing I remembered was being here."

"The tales thou spun of the Royal Navy officers...the Marines... Rostrum...thine own assumed identity...Dunsbury—nothing but fiction," said Will, his thoughts rambling.

"Thou art so naïve and so blind, William Estes," Elizabeth interjected. "If only thou were the least bit crafty or suspicious, perhaps thou would not be on the precipice of death at this very hour. Perhaps the treasure would be in thy sole possession...perhaps I would still be at thy side and in thy bed."

"And what doth thou mean by that?" roared McGee.

"Nothing, my love," Elizabeth slurred, unaware of her own level of drunkenness and how it was affecting her actions. "My heart belongs solely to thee and the grand future that awaits us and us alone."

McGee swallowed the last measure of wine directly from the bottle before smashing it into the fireplace.

"Make thyself useful, thou bloody bitch! Warm the mattress and spread thy legs. I demand to be pleasured one last time this evening. We leave at dawn. Thou best be prepared."

The brutal pirate staggered over to the mattress and almost instantly fell asleep upon impact, the sound of his snores filling the room.

Will looked at Elizabeth, and she stepped toward him.

"I loved thee," he said, his voice raspy and dry. "I did everything to provide for thee and make thee safe...my life was dedicated to thy happiness and well-being. Without the love we once shared, I no longer wish to carry forward in this life."

"Thou hath failed as a provider, as a lover, and as a man," she stated in the most austere manner. "I will no longer stay here in purgatory and rot with thee. I have finally discovered a *real* man, one of purpose and adventure—and one who will furnish us both the lives we so richly deserve."

She turned away coldly and pulled off her raggedy dress until her naked body was all that remained aglow in the dim light. So powerful were her feminine influences that even now, despite the pangs of anger and betrayal that hung heavy in Will's heart, the sight of her undraped form sent shivers of arousal through his body, briefly causing his mind to madly yearn for some manner of reconciliation—no matter how absurd.

"And what of the fate of our baby, Elizabeth? How can thou bring an innocent and fatherless child into a life of such avarice, corruption, and lawlessness under the sword of that murderous scoundrel?"

"It shall not be any of thy concern," she scoffed. "And as for thy previous statement, Will, thy wish will soon be granted."

With that, Elizabeth snuffed out all the candles until only the low light from the fire remained. She then disappeared into the shadows, joining McGee on the mattress.

Will closed his eyes and channeled all his energy toward his aching head in a desperate search for any idea or plan that would save his life...and time was slipping away fast.

CHAPTER 15

The Breach

His eyes squinted open when the sunlight hit his face. It took a moment for his mind to fully realize where he was and what was happening, but when the sight of McGee filled the barracks doorway, and the pain of the rope around his abraded neck became all-consuming, the sheer horror of his situation returned in force, crowding his every thought. Will expelled a painful cough, then looked up at his captor.

McGee drew his knife and approached Will as if he intended to slit his throat right then and there. Instead, he grabbed the rope around his neck and cut it loose. Will immediately fell forward, tumbling onto the floor. McGee grabbed him by the ropes still binding his hands behind his back and wrenched him up.

"On thy feet," he commanded. "Outside—now."

Will staggered out the door. His first inclination was to make a run for the gate, praying that Elizabeth had been careless and left it ajar. But his hopes were dashed when he spotted the crossbar firmly in place. And even if the doors had been wide open, with a clear path through them to the waiting longboat, he quickly realized that his legs were simply too wobbly and weak to carry him to freedom. He decided on another, less risky action, and limped over to the rain barrel, lowering his head into the cool water and drinking up as much as he could.

"Get thy ragged hide away from there!" shouted McGee after a hard kick sent Will hurtling to the ground. "Elizabeth, show thyself."

From behind the barracks, Elizabeth emerged. She coughed loudly and turned away to vomit.

"Too much to drink...again," scolded McGee.

"Yes...too much," was her meek reply.

Will looked up and noticed that she was cradling her belly, showing no desire to move her arms from their protective posture.

"I should teach thee a lesson and beat the senselessness out of thy skull, woman," McGee said roughly. "We have much to do and thou best be up to the task. It's time to put the mule to work."

From his sling, McGee handed Elizabeth one of the Spanish flintlocks. He cocked it for her and said, "I need a moment in solitude to firm up our course. I shall consult one of my charts to verify the proper coastal sea routes to follow. Have the mule load up our craft. Watch him closely and do not fail me."

McGee then went back over to Will and cut the ropes binding his hands. He got to his feet and massaged his wrists, his palms a deep purplish color.

"Start hauling those goods down to the longboat, and don't think of making any trouble," ordered McGee.

Will glanced at the blockhouse and spotted what remained of the burlap sacks. They were filled with what Will assumed was every meager supply in their possession from fishing gear to tools, powder, shot, foodstuffs, and other goods salvaged from the *Firefly*.

"Go, make thyself useful with the little time left in thy life," said Elizabeth, pointing the flintlock at him.

Will shot her an ugly look before opening the gate and slinging a heavy sack over his shoulder. He lugged it down the cliff to the longboat with Elizabeth close behind. He repeated the process three more times until the last sack was loaded.

"Where are the mast and oars?" he asked.

Elizabeth said nothing.

Will said, "Understand that if too much is brought aboard now, there won't be enough room for the treasure. And if all is loaded, the boat will be so overladen it will succumb to the weight and founder with the first rough sea."

"My brilliant captain has already taken that into account,

William," said Elizabeth. "The boat will be balanced, and we shall hug the coastline where the water is more shallow and calmer." After a short pause she added, "Of course, it is of no concern to thee, for thou shalt be long gone before then."

Will climbed out of the boat, tripping and falling onto the beach.

"Get up!" ordered Elizabeth.

Will slowly stood up, hoping Elizabeth could not see the rusty iron nail he had pulled out of the sand and concealed in his palm.

"Get aboard and let's be off!" boomed McGee from atop the cliff. Across his shoulders was the mast and tucked under his free arm was a large cloth bundle.

McGee steadily made his way down the steep trail. He dropped everything onto the sand and began to undo the bundle. Inside were the oars, the blunderbuss, and what appeared to be navigational charts on parchment. Will wondered if they were charts mapping the area in and around Storm—or the Neck itself—and if McGee had smuggled them back from the *Repulse* with some of his other belongings.

"Go up to the bow and sit low with the cargo," McGee ordered Will. "Elizabeth, climb aboard and keep that pistol trained on him. If he moves or tries to jump overboard, wound him...with extreme malice."

Will stepped aboard and made his way to the bow. He sat down among the sacks so that only his head and shoulders were visible from Elizabeth's seat amidships. It was then that Will took out his nail and gently began to scrape at the oakum repair to the hull. He gazed at the horizon with an indifferent expression, using only his sense of touch to chip away at the crude caulking. To his relief, and as he had hoped, Elizabeth looked away, becoming easily distracted by McGee's doings.

The pirate captain erected and secured the mast, then loaded up the oars. But what Will found most curious and intriguing was the cloth bundle on the sand that McGee went back for. And instead of just picking it up, he began to unfold it until it took on an entirely different form—a form that soon became unmistakable.

A new sail, Will thought. *But how...and where?* He looked at it more closely while keeping the disinterested expression on his face. *It isn't sturdy canvas...the material is thinner and more flimsy... like a bedsheet.* Then it hit him. *Bedding from the Eustis cabin! Elizabeth has cut and sewn bedsheets to fashion a new sail!*

Soon it was properly mounted and McGee shoved them off. The new sail was raised and their course was plotted for Storm's southwestern shoreline. They moved slowly across the still waters, feeling the heat and humidity steadily rise with hardly any ocean breeze to combat it. McGee manned the tiller in the stern while Elizabeth guarded Will from amidships. All was quiet for a while, which forced Will to curtail—and occasionally stop—his picking for fear of being heard. Eventually, he decided to use the only weapon at his disposal—his voice.

"From thine own mattress, Elizabeth?" he asked in reference to the sail. "Or thy mother's? I don't ever recall seeing such fine bedding at thy cabin. And where did thee find the time to shape and sew such a princely—"

"Enough of thy drivel," she snapped, wagging the gun at him.

Just then, Will felt a good chunk of oakum loosen from his diligent picking and scratching, but he knew he had to continue to work at it, as time was not on his side. He needed to scrape harder and faster, which meant more noise and a greater chance of being discovered. Understanding the risk, he also knew he had to further antagonize Elizabeth in hopes of enticing her into a loud and extended verbal tirade. He sprang into action.

"Tell me, Elizabeth, did thy mother give thee permission to take her sheets and do with them as thou pleased? Or did thou instruct thy captain to murder her first and then steal them? If she were still alive, I would wager thou would receive a well-deserved 'motherly' wallop to thy hide...not to mention a good Bible-filled tongue-lashing for even conceiving such an ungodly act."

Pausing, he added, "Or perhaps not...now that I think on it, she wasn't exactly spreading the word of God when last in our midst. I wonder how her style of preaching has changed now that her murdered spirit serves the Devil—much like her daughter..."

Nothing further had to be said. His pointed words, combined

with the heat, pushed Elizabeth past the breaking point. She lurched at him, nearly discharging the pistol in the process.

"Sit down, woman!" yelled McGee, his hands glued to the tiller. "I want him with breath in his lungs and strength in his back! I want him alive—until the treasure is ours or until I says otherwise."

Elizabeth pulled back, but not before swiping Will's face with a hard slap.

"Hold thy tongue or I'll cut it out!" she snarled. "Thou speak of the Devil? This pistol would conjure him with one tug at the trigger, thereby opening the portal that would suck thee down to Hell at once! And thy fate will be much more painful and gruesome than that of my wicked mother. Of that I assure thee, William Estes."

Will, sensing he had ensnared Elizabeth, went in for the kill.

"Ha! It would take much more than an idle threat from a sniveling little whore to seal my fate," he stated with uncharacteristic insolence, wary of exactly how far he could push before she reacted with deadly force.

She fired back with, "Thou presumptuous louse! How dare thee assume what I am or am not capable of? I could drown thee with stories of my past doings that would turn thy face white with terror."

Her rage intensified as she again stood up and pointed the pistol right at Will's heart. He was certain she was still ignorant of what he was doing behind his back, but he needed her to keep her distance. Seeing the flames in her eyes as the sweat dripped off her furled brow, he knew she was far from finished, and he welcomed the impending verbal onslaught. It was precisely what he wanted.

"Thou presume to know me and thou presume to understand me...how I act and what I think. *Nothing*, William Estes! Thou knowest *nothing* of me or my true nature! The workings of my mind and the consequences of my actions are well-guarded secrets...secrets easily kept from inane fools like thy father and thyself."

Her next sentiment dripped out of her mouth like blood from a wolf's after a fresh kill.

"I could unleash unimaginable horrors of an unspeakable

nature upon thee," she seethed. "And thou speak of my wretched mother and the Devil? Let me impart a tale of both. And maybe— just maybe—thou might finally get a taste of the real woman thou claim to know so well."

She looked back at McGee, who met her devious gaze with an equal one of his own. When he nodded slightly at her, she turned back to Will with an insidious grin on her face.

"It was my idea to recover the sheets and fashion a new sail for our journey back to Salem," she said. "I led the captain back home after thy father and thou set out to fish the other morning. Upon our arrival, we gathered up the sheets—but not before soiling them with our sweat...and other more *pleasurable* fluids."

She snickered a bit before adding, "It seemed like *hours* had passed before we were finished...something I had never experienced before."

Will ignored the salacious remark, realizing that her only intention at that moment was to humiliate him. He was determined not to lower himself to her level.

"Having been pleasured in numerous and unimaginable ways, I was so relaxed and content that Captain McGee let me swoon in delight right where I lay while he explored thy cabin. A short time later, I awoke to the hideous sight of my mother's face just inches from mine. She grabbed me by the throat and squeezed so hard that everything went black. The next thing I remembered, I awoke to find myself in the same spot where we first discovered her many nights ago...in the throes of that same demonic ritual. I was bound to a tree near a large bonfire. My mother was writhing about chanting that my time had come, and that I was finally to be cleansed of all my ills before meeting my new master. She danced around the flames and drew fiendish symbols in the dirt using the tip of her knife. She then held the blade to the fire until it began to glow, then pointed it toward me. I spat at the witch as she approached, the knife now lifted to eye level."

Elizabeth closed her eyes and tilted her head back toward the sky. She drew in a breath and continued with, "My eyes, Will. She endeavored to gouge out my eyes and then rip open my throat before reaching down my gullet to tear my heart from my chest. In that moment, I recalled a story of the old Salem trials that she had preached at night to me on many occasions. She was attempting to recreate precisely that which she had warned would happen the day I ran afoul of God."

"Apparently she was not successful with her theatrical effort," Will said wryly, adding, "because here thou stand, while foundering in a watery grave are the remains of thy mother. Please do regale me of the no doubt astonishing tale leading up to thy harrowing escape."

"Perhaps I should stick a blade in thine own orb first," she replied with venom on her tongue.

Will refused to flinch. He glared up at her as he continued his clandestine assault on the oakum.

"A real *man* came to my rescue. A heroic leader and man among men...not a simple boy-fisherman," she said derisively. "Just before she engaged in her sadistic act, a shot rang out and the witch dropped her knife. The hag then fled. A few seconds later, Captain McGee appeared, wielding his mighty sword...and with one hard, clean stroke, he slashed my ropes and set me free. I felt such immense passion and fury coursing through my very being that I snatched away the brave captain's cutlass and ran off in pursuit of my mother."

"Before long, we caught up to the miserable crone," McGee piped up. "She had managed to trap herself atop the high peak to the south. And like a cornered rat, she hissed and clawed at us, speaking in unintelligible tongues. At that point, I pulled my dragon and—"

"I pushed it away and charged the witch, my sword held high!" Elizabeth interrupted with a wild gesture. "And with one powerful slash..."

Elizabeth went silent as a cold and pitiless smile crept across her face. She looked directly back at Will and proclaimed, "So thou understand with divine clarity, it was *I* who determined the ultimate fate of Winifred Eustis, *I* who rid this place of her evil witchery, and *I* who will not allow anything or anybody to stand in the way of my destiny. And soon that will include thine own worthless soul, William."

"Thine own mother," Will murmured in sheer amazement. Such an act of brutality would have been expected from the vile McGee, but not from an educated young lady...not from Elizabeth.

"Do not pass sentence on me," she declared, "for I am not the only one in this boat to have taken a life."

"I have never murdered a Christian...one of my own people," replied Will.

"She was not a Christian!" screamed Elizabeth. "She was a deranged old hag consumed by the powers of Satan, and I just sped her along her preordained path—straight to the fiery depths of Purgatory—a place thou will become intimately acquainted with in due time...after thou hath done our bidding."

Elizabeth glanced back at McGee, who met her glance with an approving nod. She turned back to Will and sat down, keeping the pistol on him.

At that moment, instead of being consumed by a sense of impending doom, Will instead felt a surge of hope. His fingertips detected a delightful sensation, one so simple and so pure, and yet so promising: moisture. He dropped his head, trying to look despondent, but in truth, he was just anxious to see the result of his labor. To his great satisfaction and relief, he had scraped away just enough oakum to allow the seawater to slowly seep in. He gambled that in time, the mounting pressure on the original repair would cause it to fail, making the craft unseaworthy. Unsure of the wisdom of this action, he nevertheless was satisfied he had done something that could potentially save—or, at the very least, extend—his life. The timing was just right. The southern hill was now in full view, and it would only be a matter of minutes before the longboat made landfall.

Once they were ashore, McGee furled the sail and threw a shovel at Will's feet.

"Pick it up," he commanded, brandishing the blunderbuss. "Lead us to the exact spot and start digging. If the booty isn't found in a reasonable amount of time, then I hope that pain is something thou enjoy."

"Go, Will," said Elizabeth, adding, "and do not try to be clever, for I know this area just as well as thee."

Slowly, Will picked up the shovel and led the way up and off the rocky beach. They hiked to the wooded trail that led to the open meadow and the adjacent crop fields. After a short walk, Elizabeth confirmed they were going in the right direction, and the rock pile Will had spoken of soon came into sight.

"There," pointed Elizabeth. "This is it."

They halted and McGee asked Will, "Is this the spot? The *exact* spot?"

He responded with a sullen nod, the sweat streaming off his chin with the rising heat of the day.

McGee dropped to one knee to more closely examine the ground. It did appear that the topsoil had been recently disturbed, and the area in question was large enough to support the claim that something was buried there. Satisfied, McGee stood up and pointed the blunderbuss at Will.

"Start digging, and be quick about it," he ordered.

Elizabeth sat down to rest and lounge in the sun while McGee kept a close eye on Will and the immediate surroundings. He was unconcerned with the idea that Cyrus posed a threat, but he was intent on not being taken by surprise should the old man show himself.

Will stripped off his shirt and plunged the crude shovel hard into the ground. Thoughts of his father's whereabouts were foremost in his mind with every load of dirt turned over. He labored hard at his task, but held back just enough to afford himself more time in which to formulate a plan. When an opportunity presented itself, Will seized it.

He stuck the shovel into the hole he had created and then collapsed on it, making sure to put all his weight on the handle. There was a crack muffled only by the sound of Will's heavy breathing. "Water," he pleaded. "I can't continue without a drink… I…I feel muddled…as if I could drop at any moment."

McGee's volatile anger and impatience about recovering the treasure was apparent—he wanted to stop at nothing to find and recapture the buried riches. But just as he was about to let loose a torrent of threats at gunpoint, he was forced to stop and recognize his own vulnerability to the day's harsh conditions. As he raised his weapon, his head started to spin under the siege of the sweltering sun. He looked to Elizabeth.

"Retrieve the canteen from the boat and bring it here posthaste."

"Canteen?" she replied.

"The water, woman! Fetch the water from the boat so that I may slake this insatiable thirst."

Elizabeth's face went blank.

"I told thee to pack up all the spirits for our journey," McGee said.

"The rum and the wine were gone...previously consumed in full...so there was nothing left to bring," said Elizabeth.

"What about the water?" McGee asked, his temper rising. "Surely thou must have had enough sense to load ample water stores aboard the boat before our departure this morning?"

"I...I thought we would—"

"Goddamn thee, woman!" McGee shouted as the back of his hand crashed into the side of her face and sent her tumbling to the ground. "It could be *days* before we sail far enough south to safely avoid the savages, make landfall, and find a source of fresh water! How could thy brain be so foolish and fallible?"

Elizabeth started to cry as she rubbed the spot where McGee had struck her. She looked up and apologized to him over and over until he could stand it no more.

"Keep digging!" he hollered at Will. But before he could turn his rage back toward Elizabeth, he heard another, louder crack after the shovel stabbed into the soil.

"I should gut thee where thou stand, thou useless clod!" McGee screamed as he wrenched the shovel from Will's hands. The wooden shaft was broken just above the blade.

"There are at least two more shovels back at the fort," Elizabeth offered. "We could sail back, retrieve both, and fill the empty rum cask with fresh water before our return."

McGee stood and thought for a moment.

"With two shovels," Elizabeth added, "one of us could help dig and recover the treasure with due haste. We can't remain here and wilt away; we must take action."

"*I* will make the bloody decisions, wench," McGee snarled.

"How much deeper is it?" he asked Will.

"Not much, but deep enough to require a shovel," Will choked, his parched throat swollen and painful.

"Back to the boat," McGee growled with his gun raised.

They staggered back to the shore and discovered that the rising tide had shifted the position of the longboat. It was now parallel to the beach and just minutes away from floating off. Will grinned slightly at the sight of the bow resting low in the water.

McGee stepped into the calm surf, grabbed the side of the boat, and angrily began tossing the sacks of supplies onto the beach until the craft was empty. When the last sack had gone over the side, he saw that a significant amount of water had pooled in the bottom of the bow. He reached down and felt the loose fibers around the repaired portion of the hull, then quickly tossed the blunderbuss aside and drew his knife. He grabbed Will and held the blade close to his throat.

"Wait!" Elizabeth called out. "We don't have the treasure yet! He's still more useful to us alive. We can walk back to the fort and retrieve the shovels and water. He will lug them back here for us."

"How much tarry rope and cordage remains at the fort?" asked McGee as he pressed the knife's edge to the flesh of Will's throat.

"Enough to fortify the original repair," Will answered. "Block-house supply...I can show thee exactly where."

McGee slowly pulled the knife away and picked up the blunderbuss. With a huge heave, he dragged the longboat firmly onto shore.

"Back to the fort," he said. "Time is slipping away and so is my patience."

"I suggest we avoid the shoreline trail," huffed Elizabeth. "We should cut through the center woods. It may take a little longer, but there will be ample shade to rest in if needed...I would do anything to get out of this blazing sun."

"So be it...lead the way. I shall bring up the rear and keep young William in line," said McGee.

Elizabeth led them through the decimated fields and into the woods. Their progress was slow, their energy thoroughly sapped by the sun, and the shade they so gratefully sought was unable to relieve their thirst. To compound their difficulties, Elizabeth found herself stopping on several occasions to survey the massive storm damage, which now made the familiar wooded surroundings mostly unrecognizable to her.

"Damned heat," muttered McGee. "This place is hotter than the blazes of Hell today. Woman, art thou confident we are on the speediest route back?"

Will knew the answer, but wisely said nothing. From the corner of his eye he could see Elizabeth glancing at him, almost as if she expected him to speak up. Instead, he remained silent, forcing her to answer with an abrupt lie.

"Yes, we just need to work our way around this rough patch of downed trees to where the ground is more even," she pointed. "Then we'll be better off."

In truth, she was leading them in long sweeping curves, nearly doubling the amount of time it would usually take to get back to Hope. During their trek, Will constantly looked for opportunities to gain the advantage and flee, but the pirate captain was wary of his movements and never but a few feet away with weapons at the ready.

It was late in the afternoon when they finally reached the gates of Hope. Elizabeth's dress was so saturated with sweat that it clung to her body as if she had just worn it for a swim in the ocean. McGee forced Will to open the gate, and they staggered across the courtyard to the rain barrel. Elizabeth dunked her head, greedily cupping her hands to scoop up the life-giving liquid. McGee took his turn at the barrel after tying Will's hands behind his back again and forcing him to sit on the ground.

"Watch him," McGee told Elizabeth as he walked wearily to the blockhouse in search of the shovels and what remained of the tarry ropes.

Elizabeth watched him go, then scooped up a dipperful of water and put it to Will's lips. He drank down every drop. Much to his surprise, she repeated the gesture before going into the barracks. Will coughed as he struggled to get the ropes off...to no avail.

McGee reappeared from the blockhouse carrying the ropes and shovels. At the same time, Elizabeth emerged from the barracks with an empty rum cask that she proceeded to fill with water. McGee threw down the shovels and ropes, keeping one lashing that he used to tie Will's feet. He then secured it to the rope that bound Will's hands, thereby making it impossible for him to stand up. When finished, he grabbed Elizabeth by the arm.

"Come with me," he said, taking another gulp of water and then pulling her inside the barracks.

Two hours later, it began to get dark. It was no mystery to Will what McGee and Elizabeth had been doing in the meantime—the familiar sounds of carnal activity, mixed with bouts of loud snoring, were easily heard—but what wasn't clear was McGee's next course of action. Even he had to be aware that it would be fruitless to try and return to the southwestern shore and effect repairs to the longboat at night. Will lay still and simply waited for the inevitable confrontation that would reveal the answer.

Another hour passed. Will looked to the barracks door when he heard it open. Standing there, wearing nothing but his breeches, was McGee. He held a lantern in one hand while he smoked a clay pipe in the other. He peered around, stretched his back, and then walked over to Will.

Kneeling down beside him, he hissed, "Dawn...we leave at dawn tomorrow. When we return to that rock pile, thou will dig up my treasure at once. And when that task is complete, thou will set about making fresh oakum and procuring hot pitch to mend the longboat. These tasks will be done with all haste and without fail. If any one of my demands is not met in a timely fashion, I will waste not an instant in ending thy life in a most prolonged and agonizing way. And if thine own life means nothing to thee, then I will keep thee alive, hunt down thy father, and subject him to the most barbaric acts of torture my diseased mind can conjure. And be assured, thou will be present to witness every grim detail."

McGee rose and walked away. Halfway to the barracks, he stopped and turned back to Will. He looked at him and said, "Do not cross me and do not try to best my hand through deception... for I can do far worse than slay thee if every scrap of that booty is not found and recovered."

He paused and then said, "Know, too, that I've had many a wench under my sway, William. Seduction is a talent of mine. Getting them to say and do what I desire is easy...their minds being so weak and impressionable."

McGee's face suddenly turned quite serious and grim.

"Whatever feeling, good or otherwise, thou possess for young Elizabeth at this moment, be assured that there is no point at which I will stop nor measure I will not take to regain those riches."

He stopped again and stated more coldly, "Perhaps thou would desire nothing more than to see that young lass gutted and dismembered. Maybe now that would give thee tremendous gratification. But somehow my gut tells me that thine inner fire still burns for her, despite recent revelations. I find bitches like thine Elizabeth in every port—even in the most remote and inhospitable places...like this Godforsaken land. And know that when I tire of one, I find it quite easy to find another. There are always more to swive and seduce, William...well...for some of us, that is."

McGee walked back to Will and again knelt down next to his ear. He whispered, "If the sight of thy father's guts being spilled doesn't suitably motivate thee, then perhaps exposing *Elizabeth's* innards would." He stood back up and declared, "Do not test me, boy. I will have that treasure, no matter the final cost."

McGee's chilling words sent Will's mind into a frenzy as the man finally disappeared into the barracks. Will had somehow managed to acquire what he needed most—more time—but to what end would it bring him? As long as he remained a prisoner, he was finished. Whether he gave up the treasure or not, Will was certain McGee would execute him the moment his patience ran out, or when his confidence reached the point where he knew that his "mule" was no longer needed. As for Cyrus, even if he did manage to stay hidden and elude McGee, how long could he last on his own? If the dreaded pirate didn't seal his fate, the lack of food, water, and shelter most assuredly would. And then there was Elizabeth. How was he going to deal with her? For the moment, he put that question out of his head. He had to escape; there was no other option...but how?

Will struggled in the darkness, trying to find a way to free himself. He rolled around in search of a sharp stone or any type of protrusion in the ground that he could rub against to cut the ropes. Finally, after rocking onto his back, he felt the edge of something jab him between the shoulder blades. It was most definitely a stone, and it was situated at an angle where its edge stuck out of the ground just enough to be useful. Will squirmed around until he positioned the single rope binding his hands to his feet against the stone. He then wiggled back and forth creating as much friction as possible. After several minutes of intense rubbing, the rope had frayed enough that Will could break it by extending his legs. With a mighty effort, the line snapped.

Will stretched out his legs and straightened his body, relieving the pain his contorted position had wrought. He now had a greater range of motion, but his hands were still bound behind his back and his feet were also tied at the ankles. With another great effort, he positioned his fettered wrists over the stone and started to rub. But the ropes binding his hands were thicker and tighter, and the awkwardness of his task, compounded by the position he had to do it in, made for a long and hard struggle. He prayed he would be able to cut through before his captors greeted the dawn.

Will worked with diligence and determination. Gradually, he could feel the ropes weakening, and he began to feel that he might free himself sooner than originally anticipated. But just as a small smile emerged on his face, an unsettling sound from the distance streaked into his ears and sent a shock down his spine. He immediately stopped rubbing and did nothing but listen. The sound intensified, but, far more troubling, it multiplied, seeming to come from several directions. Soon ghostly howls, shrieks, and bellows carried through the still night air and over the water like eerie harbingers of doom. They were not the hauntingly isolated and distant cries that had occasionally roused him from sleep at night, but rather something much more terrifying—and deadly.

"Lord in heaven," he mumbled. "Could it be?"

The cries grew louder, and Will turned his attention to the barracks door when he heard it being flung open. There stood McGee, fully dressed, holding a lantern in one hand and the dragon in the other. He ignored Will as if he didn't exist, ran over to the northwest blockhouse, and wasted not a second in climbing up onto the ledge and peering into the darkness over the water.

The surly pirate, a battle-hardened fiend and murderer, a man who had witnessed and orchestrated more acts of brutality, depravity, and suffering than any human had a right to experience and live to talk about, groped to find words to describe the scene unfolding before him.

"Bloody hell!" he muttered with wide eyes and a gaping jaw.

The water, for as far as the eye could see, was aglow with a seeming army of Abenaki warriors wielding torches and paddling toward shore. McGee, out of sheer astonishment, began to count the approaching canoes, stopping only when the number got so high he lost track. As far as he could tell, each canoe held two warriors, with one paddling and the other lighting the way. The northwest sea approaches directly facing the fort were clogged with canoes, and McGee assumed that the channel between Storm and Belle to the southeast was just as congested. Belle Island was no doubt the staging point. A direct frontal assault on the fort was obvious, but McGee wondered if in fact Storm would be besieged from all directions. Suddenly, the time for thought vanished as the first canoes made landfall and flaming arrows began to arc their way toward Hope's walls.

"Elizabeth!" hollered McGee. "Bring all arms hither!"

The barracks door burst open again, and a panicked Elizabeth rushed out, her arms loaded with Will's satchel, the blunderbuss, and one of the two cutlasses. In the darkness, she raced to the blockhouse not realizing she had dropped the sword just a few feet away from Will.

Up in the blockhouse, McGee sprang to life at the swivel gun. He loaded from the box of salvaged canister shot, and then used the lantern to light a thick piece of hemp he attached to a twig to make a crude linstock. The small cannon fired its first blast just as several flaming arrows rained down into the courtyard. Elizabeth joined McGee on the ledge and screamed when she saw the large number of warriors now storming up the cliff trail while others on the shore piled their torches into bonfires to light the tips of their arrows.

"My God, a night attack," Will said aloud as the war cries of the charging natives intensified on all sides.

In minutes, the darkness of night was pushed aside as fiery arrows slammed down into the fort and the bonfires illuminated the shore.

Will rubbed and thrashed against the stone until he thought he would cut his hands off, but no matter how hard he struggled, he wasn't making any appreciable progress. When a burning arrow plunged into the ground just inches from his backside, he seized the opportunity and thrust his wrists toward the flame. The ropes caught fire. He endured the pain as best he could, but just as the smell of his own burning flesh hit his nostrils, the ropes snapped free and he quickly smothered his singed hands in the dirt. Still unable to stand, he crawled over to the cutlass and went to work on his bound feet, his task frequently disrupted as he squirmed and crawled to take cover from the unrelenting barrage of flaming arrows.

Another blast from the swivel gun was immediately followed by the crack of dual pistol fire. McGee screamed a raging stream of obscenities as he reached down into the box of grenades. He struggled to light the first fuse, but finally brought the weapon to life and flung it out into the mad throng of natives. The cries of unsuspecting warriors on the cliff trail were unmercifully silenced by the modern weaponry that many had never faced before. McGee exploded with a maniacal howl and a deadly salvo of more grenades. Dozens of warriors were blown off their feet, forcing the majority left standing to withdraw back down the trail to safety.

"Reload these like I showed thee earlier," said McGee as he

handed Elizabeth the two Spanish flintlocks and pointed to the loose powder and shot kegs. He then turned his attention back to the swivel gun, reloading it from the depleted supply of canister shot. Waiting for the right moment, he touched off the cannon and again howled with delight as the deadly spray of hot lead tore through the ranks of the determined Abenaki. He lobbed additional grenades down the cliff trail, watching as they exploded, maiming all who ventured within range.

"Here," said Elizabeth, handing one flintlock back to McGee while using the confusion of the moment to keep the other for herself.

McGee, madly relishing the carnage he had created, had neglected to properly ration his ammunition. Though the enemy was in disarray and their numbers substantially reduced by the hail of fire rained down upon them, the battle was far from over. It was only a matter of time before the numerous Abenaki warriors would overwhelm the superior but very limited weaponry pitted against them.

McGee crouched on the ledge and clawed at the remaining handfuls of powder at the bottom of the first keg. He hastily replenished the flask in Will's satchel and then loaded it with the remaining musket balls from the second keg. Then he picked up the now empty barrels and hurled them over the wall and down the cliff. Looking down at the boxes, he spied one remaining grenade and one final load of canister shot.

At the foot of the cliff path, the Abenaki were regrouping, and their numbers began to swell again with the continuous flow of canoes streaming ashore. Apart from the main gathering, several warriors had made it up the cliff undetected and began to encircle the fort.

"It is time to take leave of this place," said McGee as he watched a fresh wave of warriors storm up the cliff trail firing arrows, hurling tomahawks, and grabbing torches to set the walls ablaze.

"How do we escape?" pleaded Elizabeth. "The main gate is the only way out."

"We'll climb down the outside of the wall with ropes," said McGee, adding, "and make our descent from the southeast corner blockhouse, which is furthest away from the attacking savages. We'll flee into the woods and find our way back to the longboat using the darkness as cover."

Suddenly, amid the distracting cries and shrieks just outside the main gate, the southeast corner wall of Fort Hope burst into flame. Arrows continued to fall onto the ledge and into the courtyard, and McGee looked on in horror as an endless armada of canoes lit up the sea with their torches.

"Get thee to the barracks and bring rope! There is a coil that I stashed under the mattress! Bring it here posthaste," he ordered, cramming the last load of canister shot into the swivel gun. He fired without mercy into the largest group of warriors he could target, gleefully watching as nine were cut down in the blast. Then, in a blind rage, he picked up the blunderbuss and fired it at another cluster of Indians setting fire to the main gate. Several dropped, but it was no use. There was no stopping them.

Elizabeth rushed off and down the blockhouse ladder. She scurried across the courtyard in a panicked dash for the barracks. But before she reached the door...

"Elizabeth!" hollered Will from the shadows, now free and brandishing the cutlass.

"Rogers!" Elizabeth shrieked as she drew her pistol and pointed it at Will.

McGee turned around and saw what was happening.

"Shoot!" he roared.

Will glowered at her and at the gun aimed at his chest. The stark realization that she might ruthlessly murder him in cold blood ripped through his terrified mind, but what weighed *more* heavily was his own inability to move or attempt to defend himself. Was it just the fear of death staring him in the face, or was it something deeper? He gripped the sword until he felt the hilt would snap in two.

A shot rang out. The ball whizzed past Will's ear, and he flinched and turned away. But when he regained his composure and turned back to face Elizabeth, he watched her step back and trip. Her gun slipped out of her hands and discharged, sending the ball harmlessly into the air. She scrambled back to her feet and ran behind the barracks. But before Will could give chase, a voice bellowed from above. He turned toward the front of the fort and saw McGee's silhouette high on the ledge, bright flames licking up the wall behind him. If ever Will had envisioned what Hell might look like, this was it. And now, glaring down upon him, was the Devil himself.

"Prepare to meet thy bloody maker, boy!" McGee declared, the fiery words blazing off his tongue. "I aim to slice open thy belly and hang thee with thine own slimy guts! But first, let me express my gratitude for all thou hath done for me during my time on this putrid island. Here...a gift!"

Sparks appeared in McGee's right hand, and he drew it back far behind his head, and from it he hurled the last grenade. It flew clear across the courtyard and landed a few feet from its intended target. Will leapt away and watched as the ball rolled to the back wall near the entrance of the now burning blockhouse. A second later, it exploded with such force that it blew a hole in the base of the fortification. Will whirled around and saw Elizabeth run from behind the barracks, dive onto the ground, and disappear through the opening. But just as he made his own run for it, Abenaki war cries from the other side halted his attempted escape. Their shrieks sounded like a pack of wolves that had just made a kill.

"Defend thyself if thou art able!" bellowed McGee. "And prepare to draw thy last breath!"

Will wheeled around and watched in amazement as the raving pirate drew his sword and leapt off the ledge. He plummeted to the ground twenty feet below, landing in a crouched position and somersaulting forward. Will was certain McGee couldn't manage such a reckless stunt without severe injury, but he was astonished when the pirate rose easily to his feet and lifted his sword high. Then, with an ear-piercing shriek, he charged straight at Will, intent on ending his life with one brutal blow.

The two swords collided with a mighty clang that sent Will reeling. McGee hammered, slashed, and swung his blade with deadly skill and precision that Will simply could not match. He tripped, stumbled, and retreated with each amateurish parry with McGee's cutlass. He struggled to stay on balance and could only manage a few offensive thrusts that McGee staved off with little difficulty.

"How does it feel?" McGee asked. "How does it feel to be so close to death, boy?"

With that, McGee slashed at Will's right shoulder. Will was unable to block it in time, and the blade cut through his shirt and into his flesh. He hollered in pain and blindly lunged forward. McGee parried the sword and hit Will with a slash that grazed the side of his left leg. Again, Will screamed—and McGee relished in the torture he was inflicting.

At that point, Will's strength was waning and he was growing dizzy. McGee was toying with him now, taking sadistic delight in his slow demise. All around them, the fort was in flames. The Abenaki had set fire to all sides and were wildly shrieking and dancing about in celebration. They kept their distance from the burning pyre, waiting for the moment when the structure would collapse and allow them access to finish off any survivors. There wasn't any time left, and both Will and McGee knew it.

In desperation, Will burst toward McGee in a screaming rage. He swung his sword like a club, hoping to land at least one injurious blow. He managed to force McGee backwards and close to the blazing rear blockhouse, but his sword failed to connect, and his attack was quickly thwarted with a kick to his gut that sent him to the ground in a crumpled heap of pain. His sword fell out of his hand, and he lay there staring up at the disturbing image of McGee's face framed by flames.

"I would thoroughly enjoy slicing up thine innards and feeding them to thee, William, but as fate would have it, time is not allied with me at this particular moment," McGee frothed. He dug the tip of his sword into Will's belly, but before he ran him through, he pulled it away and drew the dragon pistol. Cocking the hammer, he said bluntly, "Goodbye, thou wretched dog. I must now take my leave of this place and claim my prize."

Just then, a mighty *crack!* thundered through the air. Will looked up and quickly rolled away as a smoldering timber came crashing down on top of McGee, pinning his legs to the ground. He cried out in pain as Will staggered to his feet and picked up his sword. Holding it high, he glared down at the scoundrel with unrestrained rage.

"Touch not my treasure!" McGee roared as blood spewed from his mouth.

Will prepared to deal the final death blow, but hesitated.

"What's the matter, boy? No bloody stomach? Let *me*, then!"

The dragon was still in McGee's hand. He managed to point it, but before he could squeeze the trigger, Will swung his cutlass with as much force as he could muster. McGee screamed in agony as the blow severed his right hand clean off. Then, without warning, Will brought the bloody blade to his throat.

"Thou took everything from me...and now I will leave thee to the indescribable death which thou so richly deserve!" Will seethed. "I hope the savages will tear thee asunder—and give new meaning to thy wretched moniker. Farewell, *Ripper!*"

McGee roared out in anger, unable to free himself. Will wrenched free his satchel from the pirate captain's shoulder and put it over his own. He picked up the dragon, belted the cutlass, and threw the severed hand at the brigand's face. Then he staggered over to the hole and crawled through just as the flames began to envelop it.

Outside the blazing fort, Will crawled on his belly into the woods. He heard the cries of the Abenaki all around him, but those close enough to spot him were distracted, their heads angled high as they watched the rising flames consume the crumbling fortifications. As he groped along the ground, his hand touched upon a damp piece of fabric. Curious, he held it up in the light and discovered that it was a shred of Elizabeth's dress...coated in blood. Horrified, he dropped the bloody rag and immediately looked for a place to conceal himself.

CHAPTER 16

Fire and Flight

In the dark shadows of the woods, Will pulled himself up, hid behind a tree, and watched the Indians celebrate in the bright firelight. A moment later, the south wall of Fort Hope collapsed entirely, and the Abenaki warriors whooped with delight as they rushed in. Will's heart sank and he could look no more. He was losing strength from his wounds, and he could think of nothing but the need to flee—and quickly. He started back through the woods in the direction of the southwestern shore, praying that the longboat was still intact on the beach.

The journey through the darkness was the most treacherous trek Will had ever undertaken. His wounds bled, and the loss of blood blurred his mind and dulled his senses to the dangers lurking all around him. He had no light to travel by and had to navigate primarily from memory. The recent storm had wrought havoc with the forest and created challenging obstacles that would have been hard to overcome even in daylight. But the most difficult and frightening threat was the unknown Abenaki presence itself. He had no way of knowing how far they had penetrated, or even where they might have concentrated their reserve forces. Fortunately, the further he moved to the south, the harder it was to hear the boisterous shrieks of the victorious natives. But staying on guard was essential, and Will paid extra heed to every unnatural sound he heard in his immediate vicinity. The last thing he could afford was to run into an ambush, as it would most assuredly cost him his life.

He stumbled forward, falling multiple times. He knew he wouldn't make it if he carried on without any light, so he decided to strike out toward the western shoreline trail where the traveling would be smoother and the illumination from the stars and the moon would guide him along. He headed west using his ears and his nose to lead him. The sound of the waves lapping against the shore and the scent of the salty sea air were enough to keep him moving in the right direction, and in a short time, he emerged from under the forest canopy. A sea of stars unfurled above him, and the moon was bright enough to help light the way down the trail. Now able to move more freely, he continued on.

He came upon the Eustis cabin first, but did not linger except to gulp down some water that had pooled in a discarded bucket. He quickly moved on as the sounds of the Abenaki cries began to build again in the distance. Fearing that the conquest of Fort Hope was only the first of their goals, Will pondered the notion that they might now be moving in his direction, looking to overrun the entire island. His only thought was to keep moving.

As the decimated Estes cabin came into view, Will began to quietly call out for his father. If Cyrus was still alive, and cagey enough to remain hidden from those who would do him harm, Will knew this was where he had to be.

"Father," he said. "Father, show thyself...it's Will."

After several minutes of searching in vain, he began to think the worst. Either his father had been murdered, or he had simply met his demise from lack of food, water, and a necessary caretaker. Will's head sank and his mind began to spin again. His stomach churned and roiled, forcing him to drop to one knee and vomit. His wounds began to burn like fire, and he could now feel blood beginning to pool in one boot.

"God...please spare me this torture," he prayed aloud. "Either take me now or show me the light to salvation."

Then, at the point he felt most like giving in to death, a curious glow shone from between the massive pines that had toppled the cabin. Slowly, Will's head came up, and out from between the downed trees came Cyrus holding a lantern. Will labored to stand, but got back to his feet and stumbled over to hug his father. The old man embraced him and then led him into a little makeshift shelter he had built among the ruins.

"Look at what thou hath accomplished," Will said as he viewed the veiled shelter of small branches and brush that offered both protection from the elements and an effective place to hide. "I knew thou would be here. This is where thou find the most comfort through even the darkest moments of adversity. Home...this is home, and no matter what fate we suffer, this will *always* be our home."

Cyrus looked pale and hungry, but his eyes gleamed at the sight of his son. He was definitely glad to see him, but Will sensed that Cyrus was more pleased that he was alone.

"Come, Father, we haven't much time. We must leave here at once," Will said as he pulled Cyrus out into the clear, the cries of the approaching Abenaki steadily increasing. But to his surprise, the old man resisted. He tugged at Will, held up the lantern, and pointed off in the direction of a huge mass of twisted limbs, broken trees, and brush.

"No," said Will, "this way."

Cyrus grunted and seemed determined to lead Will over to the mangled mess. Finally, Will relented...and then it dawned on him what his father was so insistent about.

"Mother's gravesite...but it's unreachable, destroyed under that twisted mass of debris. We'll say a prayer for her later; there's nothing else we—"

Cyrus interrupted with more animated tugging and pointing. And just when Will had had enough...

"Q-Q-Q-ueen...S-S-S-torm," Cyrus stuttered. Will looked at him in amazement, stunned by his effort to speak.

"Q-Q-Q-ueen," he repeated as he again pointed to the gravesite. "S-S-S-torm," he added shortly thereafter.

Will's head throbbed with pain, but after a moment's thought, he finally figured out what his father was trying to say.

"Queen of Storm," Will replied. "Yes...Mother's character. I understand, Father. That was Mother's character that she performed for us. I remember and so doth thou. But we have no time to reminisce. We cannot remain here any longer...we must go *now*."

Will snatched up the lantern and pointed to the north.

"Savages. Hear them, Father? Savages are coming. We must depart."

The sounds of the Abenaki finally caught Cyrus's attention, and even *he* understood the danger. He resisted no further, and Will motioned for him to follow as he started off in the direction of the open meadows.

Greatly aided by the light of the lantern, Will and Cyrus crossed the meadow with little effort. They constantly checked their rear, as not only were the *sounds* of the Abenaki obvious, but also the *sights*. Flickers of ominous firelight could be seen in the woods behind them, indicating that the natives were scouring the area with torches.

"Press forth with all haste, Father," said an exhausted Will. "Our liberation is nearly at hand."

Moments later, they staggered into the crop fields. Will headed straight for the southwestern shore, aiming only to reach the longboat and praying that it would stay afloat just long enough to get them over to the Neck and away from immediate danger. He thought nothing of the treasure as he approached the rock pile. Then, through the darkness, Will heard a peculiar sound that stopped him in his tracks. He held the lantern toward the spot in front of the stones where he had been forced to dig earlier. His eyes opened wide and his heart pounded at what he saw there.

"Elizabeth!" he hollered.

She was down on her knees madly digging in the soil with nothing but her bare hands, which were now blackened and bloodied. Upon sighting Will, she scrambled to her feet and fled down the trail toward the shore. Will drew the dragon, but before he could race after her, he heard an ear-splitting howl from behind. He turned and saw an Abenaki warrior charging at him. And before he could react, the warrior knocked him down and jumped on top of him. The pistol fell out of Will's grasp as he used both his hands to hold back the tomahawk the savage was try-ing to club him with. They hollered and screamed as they rolled and struggled on the ground. Will's sword came loose, as did his satchel. He was now defenseless and on the verge of losing consciousness. Then, incredibly, Cyrus rushed over to the skirmish and picked up the sword. Without hesitation, he jammed it into the side of the savage, who dropped his weapon, cried out in pain, and rolled off of Will. Realizing what had happened, and now free, Will crawled over to the dragon, aimed and shot the warrior dead.

"Father!" Will cried out.

Cyrus hurried over to Will and helped him to his feet. Will didn't know how much more punishment he could take before succumbing, but now the resolve to live swelled uncontrollably inside of him...and after looking at his father, and witnessing what he had just done to save his life, he felt more determined than ever to survive.

Cyrus picked up the lantern.

"Hurry," Will said as he reclaimed his weapons and gear. He reached inside his satchel and pulled out more shot and powder, which he poured down the dragon's muzzle. He paused and fiddled with the weapon until he was satisfied it was ready. He cocked the hammer back and pointed down the trail toward the longboat. But first, Will had Cyrus shine the lantern into the hole in front the rock pile. To his amazement, it was empty.

On the beach, Elizabeth wrenched and pulled at the longboat, which was firmly stuck in the sand. She managed to pull the bow into the water, but could not move quickly enough to the stern for one final shove before she again heard, "Elizabeth!"

She jumped into the boat and turned around. Facing her was Cyrus holding the lantern up high, and beside him was Will pointing the dragon right at her head. He looked down into the craft and saw nothing, not even the sacks of supplies, which still lay on the beach.

"Where is it?" Will demanded.

"Thank God thou art here and still alive," Elizabeth gushed. "I thought for sure that monster had killed thee."

She opened her arms and smiled, as if she wanted to rush up to him and smother his face with kisses.

"Where is it?" he repeated in a harsher tone.

"I don't have it. I hadn't the time or the tools to dig it up," she responded. "What does that matter now, dear William? Let us get aboard and sail away to safety. We can return and claim our prize later."

"Yesterday, thou spoke most ill of me...and bragged about thy murderous exploits—not to mention the longing thou expressed to terminate my life. What in this world of ours makes thou think I would do any less than blow thy head off after what I've seen and what both thou and that vile rogue have forced me, my father, and even my very home to endure?"

"It was McGee who slaughtered my mother, Will! Not me," Elizabeth protested. "I am incapable of inflicting such cruelty and violence. Thou did not see it, and thou never knew it, but that scoundrel had me under his evil sway from the first moment he regained awareness at Fort Hope. He was never hurt as badly as he portrayed, and he threatened my life if I ever revealed his secret or his schemes. He raped and beat me, William. Look at the marks on my face!"

Will stood stone-faced and unconvinced, the heavy pistol firm in hand and trained on target.

"I tried to warn thee from the first, William," she pleaded. "'Don't trust him,' I said time and again. But thou would not listen to me. Thou became obsessed with that ship and the treasure it held. Nothing else mattered to thee. Thou were blinded by the fantastical notion of a better life—one that could simply be bought from ill-gotten gains. And look where it has brought us."

"I only thought of thee and thy happiness," he scowled. "And look how thou hath repaid me."

"I begged thee to abandon thy contract from the beginning. I told thee he was dangerous. Remember our conversation after thy return from the Neck? Remember the things I told thee, Will? Those awful things he said to me...the threats of violence and rape and how I feared being alone with him? Did thou listen? Where was thy protection then? The very next time he and I were alone, he told me he had overheard everything. He beat me and threatened to kill me if I interfered in his business again. He threatened to kill thee and thy father. He railed on about unspeakable things... grotesque things I can't even repeat."

"Why did thou not inform me of these doings aboard the *Repulse* or prior to our return to the fort?"

"I was stricken with fear," she cried. "I was afraid of what to say or do after the threats he made. He is evil, and I foolishly thought then that perhaps...perhaps the treasure, if recovered in accordance with thy contract, would hasten his departure from our lives. Then the savages...my mother...everything around us became so confused and frightening. And, I say again, thou *would not* listen to me. Thy thoughts remained firmly focused on but one thing—that treasure."

Tears began to slide down Elizabeth's face. She started to tremble, and she clutched her lower leg. Will saw that it was bleeding from a sizeable gash. He remembered the bloody scrap of her dress he had found, and oddly, he began to feel some measure of pity for her.

"The red uniform coat, Will—remember the coat and how I told thee it had no bullet hole in it even though his shirt did? Remember our private conversation down by the shore? Doth thou recall how I said the coat was too small and how I begged thee, once again, not to trust that man? I was spared a beating from that private encounter, but he did rape me again and again out of nothing but sheer suspicion that I was trying to expose and undermine him. And *still* thou would not hear me."

Elizabeth's reasoning slowly began to persuade Will to listen to her more objectively. The dragon began to dip lower and lower.

"Did thou not notice the change in my emotions toward thee, Will? I became angry and distant. It was a silent warning as well as a plea for help from that monster. It became the only way I could communicate with thee without directly arousing suspicion. And even *that* did not work. I still incurred his wrath and suffered from thy continuous ignorance and greed. The rum, Will, that was the only thing that could dull my pain."

"The time we were bound together—"

"I had secretly pledged my full allegiance to him beforehand," she interrupted. "It was a complete lie, though. I just didn't want him to hurt me anymore. Once he determined that thou had taken the treasure, he concocted this scheme to get thee to reveal its location to me. He tied us up...and I needed to find out where it was, so I pressed thee, fearing he was nearby and listening, testing my loyalty—which he was."

"And the carnal relations I had to listen to? Those disgusting threats thou made to me?"

"All a ruse to convince him of my loyalty and to keep thee alive!" she thundered. "I died a hundred deaths every time he penetrated me, Will. I admitted to thee before, and I shall admit again now, that I was initially fascinated by him and found his physical qualities attractive...an unholy feeling swept over me that I now deeply regret."

"Thy mother?"

"It was McGee who ransacked our homes and destroyed our crops while we were away. Neither my mother nor the savages had anything to do with it," said Elizabeth. "McGee nabbed and tied up thy father in the woods before conducting a vain search for my mother. He never found her and had to get back to the fort or risk being discovered. His original plan was to use them as leverage against thee—and kill them later, of course."

She went on with, "And as for that awful story I told on the longboat, it was partly fiction. He wanted me to lie for him. He derived pleasure from it for some unknown reason, or maybe it was another test of loyalty. I, of course, told him of the bedsheets and how they could be used to make a new sail. We went to my cabin that day. The rest of the twisted tale is true, but it was McGee who slayed and disposed of my mother, not I. It is true that I despised her and abhorred her wicked nature, but I could never bring myself to kill her or anybody else."

Will's head continued to spin as he thought through everything Elizabeth had said. The stress on both his mental and physical capabilities was reaching unsustainable levels, and he knew he had to force an action quickly. However, in his weakened state, he was finding it harder and harder to keep pressure on the trigger. But even more puzzling, it wasn't the lack of strength in his finger that he was concerned about. It was something else...something deep down in his heart and soul that prevented him from firing.

"Everything I said and everything I did was to protect thee, William. I pledged myself to thee and our ultimate plans for the future. Remember? At times, I was cruel and harsh, that I freely admit, but only to make that vile man think that I was staunchly aligned with him. I was constantly assaulted with decisions of life and death, Will, with little or no time to ponder...and my body always under siege."

Will started to breathe heavily and his legs began to buckle. Cyrus remained motionless and silent, still holding the lantern up high.

"Thou hath woven an intriguing web of reasoning to explain recent happenings, Elizabeth," Will's dry, winded voice rasped. "But I have grown wary of deception and lies—"

"Thou art not free of guilt in the spreading of falsehoods, Will," she said. "The treasure—thou stole and buried it and lied about its whereabouts, knowingly and deceptively implicating the savages."

"There is truth to that, I admit," said Will. "I endeavored to garner leverage in my own right, and failed miserably in the attempt."

"So we are *all* fallible, Will. And we *all* deserve forgiveness for our sins. The Lord tests us in many ways, but through it all, inside my heart and mind I always remained faithful and loyal to thee. Extend to me thy forgiveness with an understanding of the horrible acts I've had to endure."

Elizabeth began to softly weep again, as her deep, mournful eyes cried out for pity from Will's heart.

"I had many opportunities to dispatch thee, Will, but I did not. I could have shot thee in the longboat or in the courtyard...but I refrained. I could have killed thee in thy sleep or allowed McGee to do so during one of his drunken spells, but I prevented it and kept thee safe. I could have left thee to drown in the dark, frigid waters of that treasure ship's hold...but I brought thee back—I saved thy life. That conveys something...something very special from deep within my heart."

Will's exhausted mind tried to keep all his thoughts organized and sharp as both his head and his gun dipped lower. His mind and his heart now clearly opposed one another, and what the former dictated was not what the latter felt compelled to do.

"Let us flee this place and start our lives anew," said Elizabeth, cradling her belly. "We still have a chance for a long and happy existence together. We can be married and raise our child in comfort and security far away from here," she added. "Think of how wonderful it will be immersed in civilization—to visit towns and cities of culture, and to experience new things and meet new people. We will never be hungry again. The treasure...we'll come back for it and take it all with us. It shall help bring about a new and better life that we could only dream of before."

Finally, the dragon's muzzle pointed to the ground...even as the Abenaki war cries grew louder.

"I love thee, William Estes," Elizabeth declared with all the womanly passion within her. "I have loved and cherished thee for as long as I can remember. I wish to marry thee and raise a family in warm and happy surroundings. Please...let us be off before it is too late. If not for me, then for our unborn child," she pleaded.

A tear rolled down Will's cheek as the words he had longed to hear, from the very first time Elizabeth had captured his heart years earlier, finally nestled sweetly in his ears.

"I have loved thee with all the fire and passion in my very heart and soul...now and forever," Will replied.

Elizabeth beamed a huge smile and climbed out of the boat. She opened her arms wide and they embraced. They kissed long and hard as tears of both pain and happiness poured from their eyes.

Cyrus lowered the lantern and trembled at the sight before him, taking two small steps backwards.

"Climb aboard, my love," said Will as he could now see light and smell smoke from fires burning in the forest. "I must get the sacks of supplies."

Will gently turned his father toward the boat and said, "Father..."

Cyrus would not move, however.

Will grabbed the lantern and handed it to Elizabeth. She climbed aboard and hung it from the mast, then retreated back near the stern. Will set the dragon pistol down on the transom and limped over to the sacks of supplies praying he would not faint while trying to lift them. As he gripped the first bag, a voice called out.

"Where is it, Will?"

He reluctantly turned around. There, standing tall in the stern of the boat, was his beloved Elizabeth, pointing the heavy dragon squarely at him with both hands, and wearing an angry scowl on her face.

Will collapsed onto his knees and let out a pathetic chuckle as his head dropped and slowly shook from side to side.

"So, the *real* Elizabeth is now truly among us," he said as he looked back up at her. "Tell me, woman, is there even one quality about thy nature that is not patently deceitful, amoral, or sheathed in a treacherous lie?"

"Where is the treasure?" she yelled back with growing impatience.

"We both might be better served if, in fact, it was *I* who posed that question to *thee*," Will replied.

"I will not hesitate to fire, Will. Tell me where thou hid the bloody treasure!"

"Right up there, in that very hole thou so rapidly fled from upon our arrival. If it is not clearly visible to thy mendacious eyes, then I suggest thou run back up there and dig a little deeper."

"It isn't there! What did thou do with it?"

"And thou had the temerity to accuse me of being obsessed with those ungodly riches? No more questions, Elizabeth," Will said plainly. "And no more threats. I'm half dead as it is. Do me a favor and end my worthless life. Do it quickly. I have nothing to live for and have lost everything I once held dear, save my father, who shall most assuredly meet his demise soon after I am gone."

Elizabeth pointed the gun at Will and then trained it on Cyrus. Seething with anger and uncertainty, she looked behind her at the ocean and then up the trail. Will got to his feet and approached, positioning himself between her and his father.

"Why not ask the Abenaki where the treasure is? Perhaps it was they who took it, and they will be here at any moment," Will quipped.

Elizabeth looked up the trail again and heard the voices of the native warriors sounding more distinct. The Indians were now crossing the crop fields in abundant numbers.

"Load the supplies and shove me off!" Elizabeth ordered.

"No," said Will. "I will do nothing of the sort. My fate is sealed and so is thine. I refuse to be in thy shameful presence another moment. Send me on my way, Elizabeth, thou heartless, devious, Godless, gutless, disgusting whore!"

With a mighty scream of rage, Elizabeth pulled the trigger... and nothing. She clumsily cocked the hammer back again and pulled the trigger. Once again, the gun did not fire. Will drew his sword and held the tip to her throat.

"I removed the flint from the hammer's jaws. Pity thou didn't notice that," he said.

Elizabeth dropped the gun and stood still in terror. Then she reached down and tore her dress off. She stood naked before Will and pleaded, "I will give myself to thee fully and without restraint. Look upon me and remember how much pleasure I furnished thy fiery loins. Spare me...and spare the unborn child growing inside of me!"

Her last few jagged words struck straight to Will's heart. He had no use for the devilish woman exposed before him, but he struggled with the thought of murdering an innocent unborn life— and how he would have to live with that. He shuddered and the sword wobbled.

Elizabeth then looked up and saw torches just barely visible at the top of the trail.

"Can't bring thyself to do it, Will? Thou art such a fool and a coward," she said, her voice of desperation and fear now turning to intolerant rage. "My life and everything in it has been nothing but a damned curse. That rogue was the best thing that ever came into my existence. He was a *real* man...not a foolish boy like thee! He was a fighter, an adventurer, and the best lover I have known! I never wanted thee, this place, or any of thy ridiculous notions of community! God damn and condemn thee, William Estes! Strike me dead with thy sword, but take heed of these last words: A baby does grow inside of me, but I know beyond any doubt that thou art *not* the father. This child, *my* child, was born of the seed furnished by the only true *man* I have ever known—Rogers 'Ripper' McGee, privateer, pirate, and captain of the *Repulse!*"

"Then rot with him in Hell where both of thee belong!" Will roared.

Screaming, Elizabeth lunged forward in an attempt to knock the sword from Will's hand. He slapped her face with a sharp blow that sent her reeling. Then, as if powered by the fury of every fiber in his being, Will grasped his cutlass with both hands and swung it with force. The blade connected with the side of Elizabeth's neck and did not stop until it had cut clean through. Her severed head abandoned her body and plopped into the shallow water. Then the rest of her toppled onto the gunnel, gushing blood and turning the sea red. Elizabeth Eustis was no more.

Will looked toward the stars, threw down his sword, and shouted until he started to cough up blood. He then dropped to his knees and wept. Cyrus knelt beside him and put his hand on his back. Will looked up, and through the veil of his tears, he saw compassion and concern in his father's eyes. He composed himself long enough to hear, "E-E-E-vil," from his father's lips. Cyrus pointed to what remained of Elizabeth—and if that was not remarkable enough, he then pointed at Will and uttered, "G-G-Good."

Just then, fiery arrows began to pelt down onto the beach. Will turned around and saw dozens of Abenaki warriors heading down the trail straight for them.

"Get aboard," he told Cyrus, pointing to the boat.

The old man climbed in and scurried up to the bow. Will staggered over to the sacks, grabbed one, and lugged it over and into the boat. Then, summoning every bit of remaining strength in his dying body, he heaved the bloody corpse over the side and shoved the boat into the sea. Without a moment to lose, he took up the oars and rowed hard into deeper water. He watched with narrowed eyes as the natives poured down the trail and onto the beach. They ran up and down, yelling and shooting their bows until the boat was out of range or their quivers were out of arrows. Will kept rowing until he reached what he considered to be a minimum safe distance, then slumped forward at the oars.

Storm Island was ablaze and lit up the night sky. Fires were burning at Fort Hope, in the woods surrounding it, at the Eustis cabin, and in many parts of the interior. Like the joyful conquerors they were, the Abenaki sang, danced, and celebrated the vanquishment of their enemies all along the shore in the bright firelight. And not only was Storm alight, but also the visible shores of Belle. And further to the west on the mainland, numerous fires dotted the coastline of the Neck for as far as the eye could see. Eerily, it seemed as if the Abenaki had conquered the world.

Will finally managed to raise his head and look about. He commented, "They have just reclaimed what was originally taken from them. Perhaps there is an unsung honor and nobility to that end. Perhaps someday Christians and those native born of this land will live together side by side in harmony. Perhaps I will even live to see that day."

"W-W-W-ill," squeaked Cyrus from the bow, pointing his finger downward. Will looked, and in the dim lantern light he saw that his father was ankle-deep in seawater. He opened the sack and fished around until he found two pewter cups. He tossed one to Cyrus. But before he could demonstrate what he wanted him to do, the old man began to bail. Will did the same when the water crept down to his position amidships, but he tired quickly and his head started spinning again.

Will had reached the point where his injuries, his lack of nourishment, and the overall physical and emotional abuse his body had suffered were pushing him ever closer to his demise. He wanted nothing more than to fall asleep, but he feared that if he did, he would simply drift off to death. He gazed at the slowly rising water in the boat and couldn't help but sneer. The trap he had set to foil the misdeeds of others was now going to doom him.

"I failed thee, Father," he said, feeling that his end was near. "I could not bring thy vision to life. I could neither revive nor rebuild our community. I just gave it all back to the natives," he chuckled.

"I thought that treasure would change everything for the better, but it did just the opposite—it destroyed us. God damn it all!"

His meandering thoughts turned to Elizabeth.

"A truly devious soul," he muttered. "Played me the fool. Her only concerns in life involved whomever or whatever best advanced her selfish desires and motives...and she allied herself with those who gave her the greatest advantages, no matter who she betrayed, what the cost, or how many lives it destroyed. She wanted nothing of a simple, virtuous existence. She sought luxury, power, and privilege in a world she fantasized about in picture books. A corrupt, evil wench, she was...and nothing less."

Will sighed. He could feel death overtaking him, ready to snatch his unworthy soul the moment his eyes might shut. In many ways, the emotional toll on him was proving to be more lethal than the physical. Then for no apparent reason, he slid his hand into his pocket. To his surprise, he felt something. He grabbed onto it, pulled it out, and held it up in the light. It was the gold doubloon that had nearly cost him his life that first day of exploration deep within the hold of the *Repulse*. Will drew his arm back and prepared to chuck the coin into the sea.

"Q-Q-Q-ueen...S-S-S-torm," Cyrus said, pointing to the coin and then back to Storm Island.

Startled, Will at first dismissed the words, but he became intrigued by what his father was trying to express when he reached into the nook in the bow and pulled out a small leather sack. Will limped his way forward and sat down across from his father. The old man opened the sack and poured several magnificent jewels and gems into Will's hand.

"Q-Q-Q-ueen...S-S-S-torm," he said again.

Now, suddenly, things began to make sense.

"The treasure we set aside to honor Mother," Will said as he cheerfully examined the small cache.

Cyrus smiled as if he clearly understood.

"But we buried them...we buried it all. How doth thou—"

Will thought back to the hole and why Elizabeth's mad diggings hadn't uncovered anything.

"Thou moved it, didn't thee? That night McGee and I found thee coming up the cliff trail alone...the boat...thou had sailed back over and moved the treasure. But why...and where?"

Then it struck him. He thought back to when he'd first found his father hidden in the debris of their decimated home. He then remembered how much the old man had tried to draw his attention to his mother's gravesite.

"It's there, isn't it? Inside that twisted mass of mangled tree limbs and brush is the treasure! Thou wanted her to have it all!" Will laughed. "My God...Mother certainly is the 'Queen of Storm' now."

Will looked at the old man, who now had a peculiar gleam in his eye.

"I've underestimated thee, Father. Thou could see the true evil in Winnie Eustis, her foul daughter, and that rogue devil from the sea. Thou tried to warn me in thy limited ways, but I was blind... and did not understand or listen to the purest being to ever step foot on that island—my dear father. Oh, what a fool I was!"

The gleam in Cyrus's eyes was soon matched by a wide smile on his face. It was as if a whole new world of communication had just opened up between father and son. Will felt a small surge of new energy course through his body, which was amplified when Cyrus pointed off toward a dot of light on the dark horizon.

"That can only be a ship," Will said, reaching into his satchel and retrieving his spyglass. "A ship...yes...but who, and how far? Perhaps they see the fires and are sailing in to investigate. Yes, that is it...I'm sure of it."

Will motioned for Cyrus to resume bailing as the water continued to rise. He got to the mast and struggled to unfurl the sail.

"We will return to Storm Island one day, Father," he boldly declared. "Together we will reclaim that rogue's plunder and use it to build the community thou always dreamed of. It may take years of planning, and we may have to cultivate a new life in a town like Salem first, but we *will* accomplish our goal...so help me God. I owe thee nothing less."

Will readied the sail and limped back to the stern. He collapsed on the tiller and pointed the longboat in the direction of the approaching ship. Cyrus kept bailing, and Will did everything he could to remain conscious and alert. For the moment, he had regained hope and was not resigned to death.

"Lord, let it be an English vessel," he prayed aloud, adding, "with a skilled physician, a hold full of fresh food and water, and a place to lay my weary head—and a captain who does not lust for gold or murder for sport."

With one last fleeting glance, Will looked back at the burning island that had been his home for nearly his entire existence. All that he had known was now dead as a corpse, and Storm Island was its funeral pyre. But what now lay before him was not just a light on the water, but a beacon of hope—a second chance at life and redemption. It was an opportunity that William Estes was determined not to squander—not now and not ever again.

Acknowledgments

My sincere thanks to all my friends and family, long past and present, who have provided me with inspiration and support throughout all my literary endeavors.

About the Author

Christopher Morin was born, raised, and currently resides in Portland, Maine. He received a BA in Journalism from the University of Maine at Orono. He is a history enthusiast and has enjoyed creative writing ever since penning his first short story back in second grade. Along with this work of fiction, he is also the author of three additional fictitious tales titled *A Tale of Life & War*, *The Besieged*, and *The Rebel's Wrath*. He has also penned a memoir about the three family dogs he grew up with in Portland. It is titled *Three Labs a Lifetime*.